MAY   2010

DECEIVER

C. J. CHERRYH
DECEIVER

DAW BOOKS, INC.
DONALD A. WOLLHEIM, FOUNDER
375 Hudson Street, New York, NY 10014

ELIZABETH R. WOLLHEIM
SHEILA E. GILBERT
PUBLISHERS
http://www.dawbooks.com

First Printing, May 2010.

1   2   3   4   5   6   7   8   9   10

DAW TRADEMARK REGISTERED
U.S. PAT. AND TM. OFF. AND FOREIGN COUNTRIES
—MARCA REGISTRADA
HECHO EN U.S.A.

PRINTED IN THE U.S.A.

To Jane.

DECEIVER

1

It was an interesting little pile, the stack of wax-stained vellum that occupied the right side of Bren Cameron's desk, in his office, in Najida estate, on the west coast of the continent.

This stack of letters held treason. It held connivance. It held the intended fall of the whole coast.

It also held a set of interesting names.

Machigi of Taisigi clan was one of them.

Now *there* was a piece of work. A younger man, quite young for a clan lord, in fact, he had inherited the ambitions of his predecessors down on the southern coast, but he had proved himself far, far more clever—and more dangerous.

A child named Tiajo was another name. A child of fifteen—and probably not as innocent of political ambitions as her tender age indicated. Machigi had intended to marry her off, a political wedge into the west coast—and as quickly make her a widow.

Once her husband was dead, of course, her relatives would step in to help run his estate—and that estate, a Maschi clan property, held treaty rights up and down the southeast coast of the continent . . . a district long coveted by Taisigi clan.

The third name, everywhere in those papers, was the addressee and source of those papers: Baiji of Maschi clan, nephew of Lord Geigi of Kajiminda. Baiji, who was the former lord of Kajiminda, betrothed of Tiajo—and the object of Machigi's long-running plot.

Baiji, who happened, at the moment, to be locked in the basement under Bren Cameron's feet, a prisoner stripped of all titles.

Najida, Bren's estate, sat on a peninsula within Sarini Province, on the southwestern coast of the aishidi'tat, the nation-state that spanned the continent. Bren Cameron, paidhi-aiji, was interpreter and advisor to Tabini-aiji, who was ruler of the whole aishidi'tat. And in recent days, Bren himself had become the target of an assassination attempt directed from Taisigi clan.

Hence the sound of hammering, which was distantly audible. The staff was repairing damage to the garden portico from the latest of Machigi's little ventures . . . and fortifying the house against the next.

Meanwhile, up on the space station, Lord Geigi himself, the lord of Kajiminda *and* of all of Sarini Province, had enough to do running atevi affairs on the station. He had not been pleased to hear the account of his nephew's misdeeds.

Likewise Ilisidi, Tabini-aiji's grandmother, the aiji-dowager, who had happened to be Bren-paidhi's guest—along with her great-grandson Cajeiri, son of Tabini-aiji—had not been pleased with Baiji of Kajiminda *or* his promised bride, no, not in the least.

And factor in the Edi, the aboriginal people of the island of Mospheira. The Edi, uprooted by the treaty that had given that island to humans, had settled on this coast of the continent . . . and had immediately become the enemies of Taisigi clan and their whole district, further south. The Edi, lacking a lord of their own, had been represented in the aishidi'tat by the lords of Kajiminda for the last two centuries, and the Edi were up in arms about their old enemies of Taisigi clan trying to move into that lordship.

Bren Cameron's job as paidhi-aiji, interpreter, and mediator between Tabini-aiji and the two human powers—one on earth and one above the heavens—ordinarily included occasional peacemaking between atevi factions. But in this case, he was in the middle of the conflict, his erstwhile neighbor Baiji was the *object* of the conflict . . . and Taisigi clan?

Taisigi clan was not in the least interested in peace or mediation. In the whole history of the aishidi'tat, the Taisigin Marid had never been interested in peace . . . never mind their recent overtures toward Tabini-aiji. Taisigi clan and its local association, the Marid, had claimed the southwestern coast of the continent two hundred years ago, when humans had landed on the earth. They had claimed it when the aishidi'tat itself had been forming. And, denied possession of that coast, and having the Edi moved in on that land, the Taisigi and their local association had tried to break up the aishidi'tat from inside. Then they had tried to overthrow it by sceeding from it. Then they had rejoined the aishidi'tat, and most recently had tried to rule it by backing a coup in the capital—all these maneuvers without success. This last year, Tabini had come back to power in Shejidan on a surge of popular sentiment and driven the usurper out, hounding him from refuge to refuge while the Taisigin and the Marid as a whole had tried to look entirely innocent of the whole thing.

But neither had the aishidi'tat ever succeeded in bringing the Marid district under firm control. Lately, Tabini-aiji had even hesitated in kicking the Farai, another Marid clan, out of Bren-paidhi's apartment in the capital. Oh, no, the Farai were all *for* Tabini-aiji's return: they had helped him; they were a strong voice down in the Marid, and they could be negotiated with. Of course the Marid had seen the light, and really wanted peace . . . so the Farai could not be tossed out of Bren-paidhi's apartment. The apartment was theirs, after all, granted the aiji would only acknowledge they had inherited it via an obscure marriage with a fading clan fifty years ago . . .

It was, after all, all they wanted in return for their persuading the other clans of the Marid to make a lasting commitment to the aishidi'tat and finally put an end to all the rebellions . . .

This stack of incriminating letters—which the double-dealing Baiji had, oh so slyly, preserved behind a panel of his office—told quite another story about the Farai and the whole Marid.

The letters represented the proposed marriage, involving a modest marriage portion of family antiquities that weren't Baiji's to dispose of—they were Lord Geigi's—and the union of Baiji with young Tiajo and her family down in the Marid.

Fifteen. Old enough to be auctioned off, young enough that the question of an heir could be delayed a year or two. Long enough, one supposed, for the Marid to lay firm claim to the estate itself, by sheer firepower. Had the marriage actually happened, Tiajo's southern clan, one of three major clans in the five-clan Marid association, would naturally have moved some of its servants in to attend the bride. Baiji would have been dead within a year of the bride producing an heir.

And immediately on Baiji's untimely death, the grieving widow would have immediately laid claim to Kajiminda in the name of whatever offspring she had produdced. She would get the backing of the entire Marid—and the Marid would finally gain that foothold on the southwest coast that they had been plotting so long to get.

Baiji hadn't planned on that latter part—the part about him dying—but anybody of basic intelligence and any experience at all of atevi politics could see that one coming.

Anybody of common sense, too, could anticipate that, once in that position, and sitting in Kajiminda, young Tiajo's family, in Dojisigi clan, would be nudging Machigi of the Taisigi for more power and importance within the Marid.

And of course the Dojisigi family members, backing Tiajo's claim, would be sitting in Sarini Province, hiring Guild Assassins and creating their own power base on the west coast, in a bid to protect themselves within the Marid, as *their* own greatest threat. They would go after Machigi.

Machigi, of course, smarter than that, would possibly assassinate his Dojisigi cousin in the Marid, possibly simply terrify him into peace . . .

And under the guise of an intra-associational dispute within the Marid, Machigi would take control of the Dojisigi, preparatory to setting his own relatives in command of the new Dojisigi holdings on the southwest coast.

Warfare, where it regarded the Marid, was endless. If it wasn't directed outside, at the aishidi'tat, it was inside, clan against clan.

The aishidi'tat, under Tabini's newly restored regime, was too busy reconstructing itself after surviving the *last* attempt to kill it off. They would not want to involve themselves in an internal Marid quarrel, and they might think a Dojisigi-Taisigi power struggle would play itself out much more slowly, and give them time.

They didn't *have* time.

Young Baiji, not the brightest intellect on the west coast, had played for power of his own, and landed himself in very deep waters, which Baiji *still* failed to figure out. He didn't, he protested, deserve being locked up, a prisoner, in the paidhi-aiji's basement. He was innocent. He was misunderstood. He had been spying for the aiji all the while. He should be a hero to everyone. Of course he should.

Just ask him.

Baiji's unfortunate machinations had put bullet holes in the hall outside this little office. They had caused the death of one of the aiji-dowager's guard, the serious wounding of a young man from Najida village, and the complete ruin of the large front portico over at Kajiminda estate . . . not to mention the hole Bren's own estate bus had plowed through the garage gate here at Najida, to the detriment of the adjacent garden.

Forgive Baiji? The paidhi-aiji was a generous and patient man. He was, more than anything else, a man for whom policy and the aiji's welfare counted more than personal affront.

Baiji, however, had exceeded his tolerance in any reasonable consideration.

The quiet since the assault, about two days, had been welcome. Bren did not count on it lasting. Nor did his guest, the aiji-dowager.

They'd had the time, among first business, to recover this cache of papers from Lord Geigi's estate at Kajiminda.

They'd had the time, too, to patch a largish hole in Toby Cameron's boat—Bren's brother Toby had been visiting here when all hell had broken loose, and Toby had been instrumental in thwarting the Marid in a secondary attack.

So, down at the harbor at the foot of the estate, the *Brighter Days* was now calmly at anchor beside Bren's own *Jaishan*. Toby and Toby's companion, Barb, were living aboard, not that it was safer down there on the boat, but that Najida estate was running out of room in the house. It was dangerous for Toby and Barb to be down there, exposed to view whenever they went out on deck. But it was more dangerous, potentially, to put out to sea and try to head home across the straits, in the event some southern ship was lurking offshore.

It was dangerous for them to come and go up to the house for meals. But Toby and Barb had stubbornly elected to take that risk, since the perimeter seemed secure and the walk up the winding slope from the dock was now safe from snipers—so they argued.

Toby's presence on the continent, however, posed a risk in all senses, including political sensitivity, and Bren earnestly wished he could find one single twenty-four-hour window in which Toby could safely make a run home to Port Jackson, back to the human-run island of Mospheira, where there *weren't* members of the Assassins' Guild laying plans.

The grounds were under close and constant surveillance by the dowager's young men, at least, and the aiji's navy was out there somewhere—exactly where was classified. The house had reinforcements, besides: local fishermen and hunters. Najida villagers, ethnic Edi, had opted to support their local lord and his estate with their own informal armed force against the un-welcome intruders from the Marid. Edi folk were no strangers to violence or guerilla action, and their help was certainly not inconsiderable.

Add to that, the aiji's forces, Assassins' Guild from the capital at Shejidan, who had taken possession of Kajiminda grounds in support of Lord Geigi. Opposition forces had melted away from that threat—and the aiji's forces, not to mention the Edi irregulars, were busy trying to ferret at least a dozen Marid agents out of Separti Township—having already run them out of Da-laigi. The infestation had moved, and was still dangerous—but at least it was on the run.

Further south . . . no word from that operation either. But one expected none.

Bren's own bodyguard, of the Assassins' Guild, had their own opinions of their situation, and refused to let him move about even inside the house without their being constantly aware of where he was and with whom. The aiji-dowager's bodyguard, twenty members of that same Guild, counting Cenedi, who led them, was cooperating in house defense. And the aiji's eight-year-old son, Cajeiri, had just acquired two young members of that Guild to back up the two Taibeni youngsters who were his bodyguards-in-training. That was twenty-six Guild personnel under the same roof, a tough objective for their enemies. They were on round-the-clock high alert, and thus far the Taisigi *hadn't* made another try.

Servant staff, too, were encouraged to stay on the estate grounds and not to go up and down the road to Najida village; and Najida fishermen were asked to stay away from the es-tate perimeters. The less traffic that moved on Najida estate perimeters, the easier it was to track anyone who didn't belong there.

They were all wired for the slightest hint of trouble. Expect-ing it.

And a slight rap at the door drew Bren's instant sharp attention.

Household staff never waited for an acknowledgement when they knocked. Neither did his bodyguard. And indeed, the door immediately opened. It was Banichi himself . . . a looming shadow in the black uniform of his Guild. Ebon-skinned, golden-eyed, and a head and shoulders taller than a tall human, Banichi fairly well filled even an atevi-scale doorway.

And when Banichi ran errands, it wasn't about tea or the delivery of mail.

"Bren-ji." They were on intimate terms, he and all his bodyguard: he preferred it that way. "Tabini-aiji is approaching the front door."

"The *aiji*." Bren shoved back from the desk, appalled. Tabini was *supposed* to be safe in the capital. And he was *here*? On the decidedly unsafe west coast? Unannounced?

Bren got up and immediately took account of his coat—it was a simple beige and blue brocade for office work on a quiet day. The shirt cuffs—a modest amount of lace—he had carefully kept out of the ink in his writing a few notes. His fingers, however—

But it was late to make any improvement. Tabini didn't stand waiting for anybody, and safety dictated Tabini should move fast if he was moving about the region.

In very fact, Bren heard the outer door open in the instant of thinking that. Banichi turned to check, took his station at the open door, and in a moment more, his partner Jago arrived and took her place: bookends, on one side of the office door and the other, while a heavy tread in the hallway heralded a second, armed advent through that open door.

The aiji's senior bodyguard, two grim-faced men in Guild black, arrived and took *their* positions, automatic rifles in clear evidence.

Then Tabini-aiji himself, aiji of the aishidi'tat, lord of all the world except the human enclave, walked into the office. Black and red constituted the Ragi colors, the clan to which Tabini belonged . . . but Tabini wore no red today: Tabini blended with his black-clad bodyguard, right down to black lace cuffs. It was a mode of camouflage Tabini had used occasionally even in the halls of the Bujavid, since his return to the aijinate. He had used it habitually in that uneasy year he had spent on the run, and narrowly avoiding assassination.

A blond, pale-skinned human in a pale beige coat stood in quiet, domestic contrast to that dark and warlike company. His little office was now entirely overwhelmed with Guildsmen, all armed with automatic weapons, on alert and on business—not to mention Tabini's own forceful presence.

Bren made a modest bow. "Aiji-ma."

"Nand' paidhi." Tabini's tone was pleasant enough. "One rejoices to find you in good health, considering your recent trouble."

"Well, indeed, aiji-ma. And your great-grandmother and your son are both well under my roof, one is very glad to say."

"The paidhi graciously accepted my son as his guest for—was it some seven days?"

A second bow, deeper. Numerical imprecision with any ateva was implicit irony. "Aiji-ma, one can only apologize for the succession of events." A near-drowning and an assassination attempt were not the degree of care the aiji had a right to expect for his son on a holiday visit. "One has no excuse."

"My wayward son is only one of my concerns in this district."

He was remiss in his hospitality. He was utterly remiss. The aiji had arrived with the force of a thunderstorm, with considerable display of armed force, and the suddenness and implied violence had thrown his mind entirely off pace. Household staff would not be far from the door—hovering near, but too fearful to come in to the crowded office.

"Might one offer a modest tea, aiji-ma?" A round of tea was the ordinary course of any civil visit, even a visit on serious business. Tea first, and a space for quiet reflection for both parties, even in advance of knowing the reason of the call. "We could adjourn to the sitting room, should the aiji wish . . ."

"Doubtless my grandmother will drown us in tea in a moment," Tabini said, still standing, arms folded, amid his guard. "The paidhi, however, can be relied upon to tell me the truth without an agenda, so my first visit is to you. What should we know?"

The paidhi indeed knew what was going on in the district. And the paidhi's heartbeat picked up. It was a wonder the aiji couldn't hear it from across the room.

Tell the aiji his grandmother had just promised the Edi, a hitherto warlike ethnic group, a province and a seat of their own in the legislature?

Tell the aiji his grandmother had happened to involve the aiji's son and heir in her promises to the Edi, as a reaction to the Marid foray into Sarini Province . . . the Edi being the Marid's ancestral enemies?

"Aiji-ma." He could personally use a cup of tea. Anything, for a social ritual and barrier. But he had no such delay, had nothing to occupy his hands and no recourse but complete honesty. "Regarding the involvement of the Marid in the neighborhood . . . the aiji surely already knows that matter." The aiji had a large intelligence network to tell him that. "The matter of the meeting at Najida, however . . ." He drew a breath. "The aiji knows that the Edi clan staff had withdrawn its services from Kajiminda. This was in displeasure at young Baiji's dealings with the South. The proposed marriage—"

"We are aware. Continue."

"An Edi representative approached Najida covertly, advising me as their neighbor, and advising your great-grandmother as a person of revered presence, that the Edi clan was active on the aiji's behalf during the recent Troubles. The Edi claim to have kept the usurper's regime from controlling this coast. They claim to have continued this action, allied with the Gan people in the North, in the face of Kajiminda's flirtation with the South. They say that the network that protected the coast from Southern occupation during the Troubles still persists. The group that has made contact with me and with the aiji-dowager . . ."

"Who has promised them a province and a lordship! Is this astonishing news true, paidhi?"

He bowed his head. "True, aiji-ma."

"With the attendance of my minor son at the meeting!"

"That is true, aiji-ma."

Tabini glowered. It was not pleasant to be the center of that contemplation.

"Why, paidhi, did this seem to anyone a good idea?"

"One finds oneself, officially, in a difficult position with the Edi, aiji-ma. Overmuch discussion on this matter might compromise the paidhi's usefulness to the aiji in negotiations, but it does seem to the paidhi aiji that there may be advantage in considering this proposal. If one may explain—"

"We appreciate the delicacy. Continue in plain words, paidhi-aiji! And limit them!"

"The Edi's reluctance to deal with the aiji's clan persists. That has not changed. But they are finding themselves constrained by events. They claim that they supported your regime during the Troubles and will be willing to do so now—their old enemies the Marid having backed the other side. This offer has a certain urgency, in light of the Marid move against Kajiminda."

"Ha!"

"Additionally—" His allegiance should be to Tabini, wholly, unequivocally. An ateva would have trouble feeling any other thing. A human—a human was hardwired for ambivalent loyalties. It made a human particularly good at the job he did for Tabini.

But it made relationships a little chancier, and led, sometimes, to dangerous misunderstandings.

"One hopes the aiji will not doubt my man'chi to the aiji-nate and to him, personally. But the Edi request my good offices in negotiation—and they request me, as their neighbor, to maintain a certain discretion regarding their actions . . . a request with which I sense no conflict with my man'chi, aiji-ma, in regard to any—past event."

"Be careful, paidhi. Not everyone in the aishidi'tat understands your motives. And one doubts that the Edi fully appreciate the workings of your human mind."

A bow. "One is keenly aware, aiji-ma, that one is neither Edi nor Ragi. One suspects this approach on their part represents a test of some sort."

"A test, and not a maneuver for advantage?"

It was a good question. A dangerous question, worth considering. And he had. "One rather perceives it is a test, aiji-ma. And in my perception, such as it is, their secrecy in asking this meeting has in no wise involved ill intent toward the aiji or his representatives—rather a desire of the Edi to continue their actions under their own direction."

"Ha! No different than they have ever demanded!"

"But these are not the foundational days, aiji-ma. These have been troubled times up and down the coast. And the Edi have behaved civilly. Thus far—thus far, they have preserved this estate during the Troubles, and kept my staff safe . . ."

"Because their worst enemies are on the other side." Tabini unfolded his arms and took two vigorous steps to the side before looking at him askance. "One takes it you have already—under the aiji-dowager's encouragement—agreed to this arrangement?"

Bluntly put. Bren bit his lip. "Initially, and on the paidhi's best judgement, aiji-ma, yes." A deep breath. "The confidences they have given me thus far are reasonably minor, which is why I say it is a test of confidentiality. Should these confidences ever involve questionable activities—" Smuggling was only one of the local industries. Piracy was another. "Should there be criminal action—one would still feel constrained to maintain a certain discretion on their behalf, to keep the compact alive, and to keep channels of communication open, for the aiji's ultimate benefit. The point is, one cannot be totally forthcoming to you, aiji-ma, and simultaneously maintain their confidence in me. They wish me to step aside somewhat from my attachment to the aiji: evidently they wish me to mediate on their behalf."

A snort, an outright snort. "Ha! So *they* want the human! Therein lies their isolation from the mainland! *They* were the ones to come too close to your people on the island, paidhi-aiji, not we! If you look for the causes of the War of the Landing, look to the Edi, who thought they could live in two houses at once."

"We say—sit on the fence, aiji-ma. Having a foot in either of two territories."

"Descriptive."

"Humans do truly understand this behavior, aiji-ma. But my two-mindedness is a capacity that has served you. Whether the aiji chooses to grant me latitude in this case—will dictate how useful the paidhi may be as a negotiator in this matter."

"That latitude has operated profitably in the past."

When he had represented the human government on Mospheira. For the last number of years he had represented the aiji in Shejidan with a closeness that had moved further and further from representing his own species. Perhaps some atevi had begun to think he had profoundly changed in that regard. But, on the other hand, some still suspected his motives as secretly pro-human.

"It may not improve my acceptance among Ragi, aiji-ma, but yes, it could be profitable for me to do so. And my man'chi to you will not vary. It will not."

"Granted, granted," Tabini said. Which was what had made Tabini rare among atevi—an ateva willing to use a little blind faith, with adequate safeguards. "Provided you take no chances with your own safety. We are not willing to lose the paidhi-aiji. Especially to the Marid!"

Appalling thought. "One will certainly take adequate precautions."

"You are understaffed here. Woefully understaffed."

"Aiji-ma—one is compelled to rely on Edi clan irregulars for more extended security. And this does make me uneasy, since it is a security which involves the safety of the aiji-dowager and of your son, aiji-ma, for which I feel personally responsible. But one sees no choice. One cannot make this house or Kajiminda—in their eyes—a Ragi base of operations—or we lose a valuable ally, *and* the hope of alliance."

"Hence your failure to appeal for reinforcement."

Embarrassing. He bowed. "Yes, aiji-ma."

"Never mind my grandmother's obstinacy in the case. Have these Edi the force and the organization to protect this whole district?"

"One doubts they could adequately do that, aiji-ma." He saw what Tabini was aiming at. "They have been effective in holding this peninsula. One believes this is the territory they will insist on holding. Your forces, I understand, have Kajiminda Peninsula secure."

A snort. Another brisk stride. Two. "As secure as a wooded peninsula can be. You know you are making yourself a target, paidhi. And a target of more than Southern ambitions. The central clans will hear that the paidhi-aiji has abandoned neutrality in this matter: that he has affiliated with a specific district, specifically one they have never favored."

"One is aware, aiji-ma, that there may be that future difficulty."

"More than a small difficulty. And not far in the future." A pause, and a direct, calculating look. "One *would* surmise you want the Farai out of your apartment."

The Farai had camped in his capital apartment since the coup, and persisted there after Tabini's return from exile: during the Marid's new approach to dealing with the aiji's authority, they had been politically difficult to toss out on their ear. Which was *why* the paidhi had come to his west coast estate for a quiet retreat.

At which point the Marid, finding him lodged next door to their plot at Kajiminda, had promptly attempted to assassinate him.

Which was, of course, *why* he had the erstwhile lord of Kajiminda locked in his basement.

"My greatest concern in the capital, aiji-ma, would be *your* security. The return of my apartment would be a great favor to me, yes. But the Marid is up to something, I have partially exposed it, and the Farai are lodged next to *your* apartment wall: *that* situation more concerns me. This whole scheme is aimed at their gaining the coast and reopening the war. *That* makes the Farai a hazard where they are."

A grunt. A wave of the hand. "Explaining this construction of conspiracies will take preparation. One will make known the paidhi's displeasure with the South, and his current personal grievance against the Marid. That will explain certain of the paidhi's moves to public opinion."

It would go a certain way toward justifying his actions, in public opinion. If the South had attempted to assassinate the paidhi, and that event became public knowledge, the paidhi's moves against Southern ventures on the west coast achieved complete justification in the atevi way of looking at things . . . and not just for a quarrel regarding a Bujavid apartment. It was a great favor, and politically astute, that the aiji should put that information out through the aiji's own channels.

"One is very grateful, aiji-ma." He was, in fact. It lessened very major difficulties. It didn't solve them, not with the most determined of his detractors. It would, however, make reasonable people think better of him. "But I remain concerned about your grandmother and your son being in this situation with me. The aiji-dowager has been helpful, even instrumental in starting this negotiation, but if you could persuade her—"

"An earthquake could not budge my grandmother," Tabini said with a wave of his hand. "I shall at least talk to her. Where is she?"

"One believes, in her rooms, aiji-ma." A bow, a gesture toward the door. One did not dismiss the aiji of the aishidi'tat to a household servant's guidance. A lord escorted him where he wished to go, and relied on the bodyguards—his, and Tabini's, to quietly exchange information in the background. If the dowager were *not* in her rooms, his staff would quietly redirect them . . . but crowded as the house had become, it was certainly a small range of possibilities, and they were already *in* the office.

It was a short walk, out into the wood-paneled hall, with the stained-glass window at the end, darkened now by storm-shielding, down that direction to a paneled door. Banichi's single rap drew immediate attention from within. The door opened, Cenedi himself doing that office from inside. The aiji strode ahead into the dowager's personal sitting room with a loud, "Grandmother?"

Ilisidi was sitting in a comfortable wing chair by the fireplace, a notebook in her lap, the picture of anyone's kindly grandmother. Her hair was liberally salted with white, her dark face was a map of years, and she was diminutive for her kind, only human-sized. But the golden eyes had lost none of their spark and snap, and she was dressed in a brocade day-coat the collar of which sparkled with diamonds . . . the hell she hadn't gotten wind of this visit.

And considering the force of the two personalities about to engage, the paidhi-aiji decided it was time for a tactical retreat. Bren began to back toward the door.

"Stay, paidhi!" the dowager snapped. "You may be useful."

He stopped. "Aiji-ma," he murmured and, beside Banichi, Jago, the aiji's guard, and Cenedi, the chief of Ilisidi's guard, he took a place along the wall, beside a tall porcelain figurine of the recent century.

Tabini-aiji, meanwhile, settled for a casual stance by the fireplace, in which only a trace of fire burned above the embers. "Well," he said, elbow on the mantel, "honored grandmother. A new province? Or is it two? War with the Marid? When shall we declare it? Do tell me."

"We have no need to declare it," Ilisidi snapped. "*They* did. Sit down, grandson! We have a stiff neck this morning."

"We shall be reasonably brief," Tabini said, not sitting down, "since we are assured rumors of your ill health are exaggerated . . ."

"Entirely."

"So—having set in motion this interesting chain of events on the coast, will you now fly off and resume your affairs in the East? Or have you quite done with matters in this province?"

"Oh, we are not yet satisfied, grandson. *We* do not *leave* a situation to ferment for five decades!"

"You tried to push this establishment of the Edi lordship on my grandfather! *And* my father!"

"Their half-measures produced this situation!" Ilisidi snapped. "If they had listened to us in the first place, we would not *have* the difficulties that now present themselves!"

"Ah, so you *have* taken account of the difficulties . . . which are, of course, the same local difficulties that presented themselves in my grandfather's lifetime: a little smuggling, occasional piracy, and a thorough desire to see the aishidi'tat broken apart! The Edi program is not that different from the aims of the Marid!"

"Your grandfather was wrong then, he is *still* wrong, and I am right about the Edi, grandson! And if you will use good sense we shall come out of this with the arrangement we should have had fifty-three years ago."

"Ha!" Tabini gave a shove at the mantel. "This is no venue in which to debate the matter, honored grandmother. Say that *our* regime owes responsibility to *all* districts of the aishidi'tat. Say that we are determined to maintain the balance of powers within the aishidi'tat, and as usual, *you* have set a finger on the scales. You came here to see to my son, who has been reckless. But do you restrain his career? No! First you send him and the paidhi off to a meeting with Southern agents and a fool! Did you intend that? I think not! So do not pretend you are infallible!"

Ilisidi's jaw set. "*Whose* advisors made excuses for Baiji the fool when he failed to come to court this last session? *Whose* advisors, when we contacted your office regarding him *before* we thus dispatched the paidhi-aiji and my great-grandson, assured us there was *no* security problem in Kajiminda?"

It was the first Bren had known that Ilisidi had phoned the capital before sending her great-grandson on that ill-starred visit. It made him feel not quite so bad about walking into the trap himself . . . since the dowager's accesses were highest level, and outside the capital, and his were not.

Tabini retorted: "Things on this coast were under surveillance!"

"Ha!"

"And quiet, until you came here! We cannot solve every problem in the aishidi'tat in one legislative session. We have important measures coming before the hasdrawad and the tashrid!"

"While the Farai camp in a sensitive area of the Bujavid and attempt to take the whole west coast! How would the paidhi's *assassination* affect your session? One would consider that a certain embarrassment!"

"So now," Tabini retorted, "after meeting with a hostile clan on your own, you present me a new province and an unsettled condition, not just in two estates, but on the entire coast! Gods less fortunate, woman! We do not want a war with the Marid at this juncture!"

"When better? What will provoke you, if not this situation? When are your enemies to judge the aiji *will* act?"

"When he pleases. *Whenever* he pleases, woman, and do not push me." A small silence descended. One could not be sure of Ilisidi's expression, but it was probably smug. Tabini's was a scowl.

"So you singlehandedly removed Baiji's titles," Tabini said quietly.

"Do you wish to restore them?" Ilisidi asked sweetly. "You can, of course. He would not be the only fool in the legislature. He might even show up for court this year. In gratitude to you, of course."

Tabini scowled back. "The fool's distinguished uncle is on his way back from the space station." A glance toward Bren. "Lord Geigi will land in Shejidan on the fourteenth and fly directly here."

That was tomorrow. Bren had not heard. And where in hell were they going to put Geigi, with Geigi's estate swarming with Tabini's agents?

"Well," Ilisidi said. "*That* will be a pleasant visit. Another reason for us to remain. We long to see Geigi."

"Have you other adventures in mind for my son?" Tabini asked, sharp turn of subject; and not. "Or shall I take him back to his mother? His great-uncle has arrived, and is highly agitated. He is threatening to come here."

God, Bren thought. *Tatiseigi.* The old man, central clan lord of the prickliest sort and by no means an asset in negotiating with the west coast Edi, had arrived in the capital. Lord Tatiseigi, who would have been beyond upset to discover his great-nephew was not in the capital to meet him, now had to be told his great-nephew had nearly been killed while in the paidhi's care.

Upset? Oh, yes, Tatiseigi would be somewhat upset.

"You will simply have to keep Tatiseigi in the capital with you," Ilisidi said to Tabini with a casually dismissive wave. "As for the boy, we have need of him."

"Need of him!"

"It is useful," Ilisidi said, "for him to attend these events."

"It is *useful* for him to stay alive!" Tabini retorted.

"You have sent your two guards to watch over him," Ilisidi retorted. "These two *children!*"

Everybody under thirty was a child in Ilisidi's reckoning. The two children in question were twentyish and reputed, Bren's own bodyguard informed him, to be quite good in the Guild, if notoriously arrogant.

"They may at least keep up with him." Tabini struck his fist against the stonework. "If you take responsibility for my son, honored grandmother, you know what you are taking on."

"None better," Ilisidi said, and added: "At least *we* know where he is."

The aiji's own guard had lost the boy. Repeatedly. It was a remark calculated to draw fire.

It drew, at least, a furious scowl from Tabini. And Tabini's guard had to be wincing inside.

"Do not be overconfident, woman," Tabini muttered ominously. "Nobody has been faultless in overseeing this inventive child."

"The boy is remarkably prudent," Ilisidi said, "where the danger is clear to him."

"He is a year short of felicitous nine, and mostly at home in the corridors of a spaceship! A number of dangers in the world do not seem clear to him!"

"He has comprehended the ones in this locality," Ilisidi said smoothly, "even the ones emanating from the Marid, and he will now employ his cleverness in good directions. It is *useful* for the heir to form associations in this uneasy district."

"And to observe his great-grandmother meddling in affairs that do not remotely concern the East?"

"Affairs that *do* concern the East," Ilisidi shot back, "since we have in mind an excellent solution for Baiji the fool: a marriage, heirs for the Maschi that Baiji will *not* have a hand in rearing!"

"Oh, do you?"

"We do, and we shelter a hope that the intelligence and industry of his uncle's line reside somewhere in his heredity, though neither has manifested in Baiji himself. We are busy mopping up the untidiness in this province for you, grandson of mine, we are dealing with matters we shall *never* remind you are precisely those matters we argued should have been settled in your grandfather's time! And we have found excellent prospects for a settled peace in this district *while* discomfiting the highly inconvenient Marid! So we shall oh, so gladly hear your expressions of filial *gratitude* for our good offices!"

"*Gods less fortunate!* Your interference goes too far, and you have recklessly involved my son in all of it!"

"Interference, dare you say? Involved your son? *Who* lost track of my great-grandson in the halls of the Bujavid?"

"While *you* distracted the staff!"

"Oh, a far reach, that! Who allowed my great-grandson *and the paidhi-aiji* to enter a district rife with Marid plots, without advising them or apprehending the danger?"

"Yours was not doing so well in that, woman!"

"Your staff," Ilisidi said, "has been remiss!"

"So why did *you* not dissuade the paidhi-aiji from his venture to this coast, your own intelligence of course being faultless?"

"No one informed *me* of the paidhi's intentions to visit this peninsula in the first place!"

"Then where, honored grandmother, *was* the attention of your staff, since you knew full well Tatiseigi would request the paidhi-aiji to vacate *his* premises on his return to the capital? Where *else* would the paidhi go but his residence on the coast? And if you were in receipt of such remarkable intelligence regarding instability on this coast, why did you not inform *my* staff, who might have informed the paidhi's bodyguard in some timely fashion so he would not be here? Why did you not say to him, 'Nand' paidhi, do not call on the young fool next door. He is overrun with Marid agents.' No, you did not know. You had no idea, no more than we did!"

That brought a small instant of quiet.

A standstill. Bren drew very small breaths, wanting not to become involved, far less to become the centerpiece of that debate.

In point of fact, one had in the past been able to rely on the aiji's being well-informed on every district, and one would have expected his proposal to go to the coast to have met an immediate advisory of local problems. But information since Tabini's return to power was *not* wholly reliable, and there were small pockets of resentment in the aishidi'tat, where the brief accession of a Padi Valley Kadigidi to the aijinate had unsettled certain issues long dormant.

In point of fact, second, it was incumbent on *anybody* apt to be a target of assassination not to make assumptions and not to rely blindly on old associations. He had certainly assumed he was safe, when he had divided his bodyguard—Algini had been nursing a sprained left hand that day; but now Jago had stitches and Banichi had scrapes and bruises to match, thanks to his judgment. His domestic staff had hinted of difficulty, but not been forward enough and had not managed to mention that the neighboring staff had left the premises months ago. That had been the epitaph of more than one lord of the aishidi'tat: domestic staff refusing to meddle in what they considered the Guild would know; and worse, with the Edi disinclination to discuss Edi matters with outsiders.

But the ones who would take this fingerpointing most to heart were precisely their respective bodyguards, his and Tabini's, and the dowager's, who no longer had ready recourse to what had been an excellent and constant fact-gathering organization, before the coup had totally fractured the network, and that lay at the heart of the problem. They were reconstituting it as fast as they could, but speed was no asset in establishing trusted sources.

So in *two* destructions of records, one when Tabini's staff had fled the Bujavid in the face of the coup, and one when the usurper Murini's allies had attempted to cover their tracks when Tabini retook the capital, there were now distressing gaps of knowledge in some hitherto reliable places: Baiji's flirtation with the Marid was a case in point. No one would ever have expected treason in staunch Geigi's house—he certainly hadn't—but there it was. The aiji's forces had now taken possession of that estate and turned up new problems clear down in Separti Township.

The aiji-dowager, meanwhile, had not accepted the assignment of blame for bad intelligence. The cane thumped against the unoffending carpet and she levered herself to her feet, standing chest-high to her formidable grandson and scowling.

"We are perfectly settled here," Ilisidi said, "in possession now of the intelligence we need. So you may go your way and let us manage matters."

"Impossible woman!" Tabini flung up his hands and turned to leave. "I shall go reason with my son."

"You will not take him! His presence here is to his benefit— and yours!"

Tabini turned about. "I shall reason with him, I say, since reason is *one* art he is not learning from his great-grandmother!"

"Ha!" Ilisidi cried, and a wise human just stood very still, while Tabini peeled his bodyguard out of the row by the wall and headed out the door.

"Where is my son?" resounded in the hall. The staff doubtless provided Tabini a fast answer. Bren hoped so, for the honor of his house.

As it was, he had inadvertently made himself and his guard part of the scene. Getting out of the dowager's immediate area might be a good idea at the moment, but it was not that easy to accomplish.

"Are we unreasonable?" the dowager asked him, not rhetorically, turning a burning gaze on him, and either answer was treasonable.

2

"Your father is here," Jegari had reported some time past, warning enough, and a wise son who did not wish to be flown back to the capital and confined to his father's apartment with his tutor for the rest of his life had immediately taken the warning and improved his appearance.

Cajeiri had on his best brown brocade coat, and his shirt lace was crisp and immaculate. His queue was tied with the red and black Ragi colors—his father's colors, politic choice of the four, even five heraldries he could legitimately claim. His boots were polished, his fingernails were clean, and he had, after the rush of preparation, quietened his breathless hurry and achieved a serene calm even his great-grandmother would approve of.

He had, besides, accepted his father's choice of bodyguards: he had already had Jegari and Antaro, a brother and sister out of Taiben province in the Padi Valley—those two were not properly Assassins' Guild yet, and could not wear the uniform, so they looked like domestic staff, but they were his senior bodyguard. He insisted so. And his junior staff, the ones his father had just sent—Lucasi and Veijico, another brother and sister, really *were* Guild, and actually five years older. They were in their formal uniforms, black leather and silver, and looked really proper.

So he could muster a real household, and there was no laundry tossed over chair backs and no stray teacup awaiting house staff to pick it up (nand' Bren's staff never let things sit around) so the premises was immaculate, too. He was well ahead of his father's arrival when he heard the commotion of an approach outside.

His father's guard knocked once—ordinary procedure—and did not have to fling the door open themselves, since Jegari did a majordomo's job and beat the man to it. The door whisked open, Jegari bowing, and there was the bodyguard, and his father.

The guard walked in and disposed themselves on either side of the door. His own bodyguard, official and not, came to formal attention. His father walked in and stopped, looking critically about the room—which actually looked like a real household, Cajeiri thought, bowing with particular satisfaction, even a little self-assurance at his own arrangements. Father had *not* caught him at disadvantage. For infelicitous eight going on fortunate nine, he had not disgraced himself, or Great-grandmother, or nand' Bren.

"Honored Father," he said respectfully, completely collected.

"My elusive son," his father said.

Bait. Cajeiri declined it, simply bowing a second time. Arguing with his father from the outset would *not* get what he wanted, which was to stay exactly where he was, in nand' Bren's house. He did *not* to be dragged back to the capital and locked away in his rooms with his tutor. He had made mistakes, but he had remedied them. He was in good order. *Surely* his father was not going to haul him off in embarrassment.

"Your great-grandmother thinks you should stay here," his father said. "You have worried your mother, who is not pleased, not to mention you have set off your great-uncle, who has had to be restrained from coming out to the coast . . . need I say with *what* detriment to the delicate peace in this whole district?"

That *was* a threat. Uncle Tatiseigi was not inclined to be polite to anybody who was not of very high rank, *and* attached to the clans and causes he personally approved. There was a long, long list of people Uncle Tatiseigi did not approve of.

"That would not help nand' Bren or Great-grandmother, honored Father." A third, smaller bow. "We understand. We are attempting to be quiet and useful."

"By stealing a freight train and a sailboat?"

A fourth bow. "My honored father exaggerates the freight train. But we admit the sailboat. We deeply apologize for the sailboat."

His father let go an exasperated sigh and walked over to the desk and the darkened window, which was storm-shuttered because of snipers, which were still a constant possibility. Out in the hall, and faintly even in here, one could still smell new lacquer, where they had fixed bullet holes.

So it was not quite safe. His father surveyed the room—then, embarrassingly, as if he were a child, flung open the inner door and had a look in the bedroom. The bed in there was made and there was nothing out of place. He was very glad they had not just tossed stray items in there.

His father walked back again, set fists on hips and looked down at him. "The staff is keeping you in good state."

"Nand' Bren has a very good staff," he said. "And we try to be no trouble to them at all."

"Ha." His father had been arguing with Great-grandmother. He was still mad. That was clear. But he was not being unreasonable.

Then his father asked: "Do you have the *least* notion what is at stake on this coast?"

He *did* know that answer. He had listened when his elders talked, because it *was* important. "The Edi people are connected to the Gan, up the coast in the Islands and the north coast. The Edi and the Gan both used to live on the island of Mospheira, before the humans landed, and now because we Ragi gave the island to humans, they live on our coast, which the Marid used to think they owned."

"*Did* they own it?"

He knew that answer, too. "No, honored Father. The Marid

claimed the whole southern half of the west coast, but an association of local clans owned it. The Marid had tried to bully all
the clans that were here. Then the Edi came in, and the Edi got
along with the local clans well enough, especially since the Edi
helped throw the Marid out and back into their own territory.
Then the Edi fought among themselves, mostly, until Great-
grandfather put a Maschi clan lord in charge of the coast and
created Sarini Province. And now that Lord Geigi of the Maschi
has been in space all these years and his nephew has turned out
to be a total fool, the Marid thinks they can get back onto the
west coast, which is what nand' Bren and Great-grandmother
just stopped. And the Edi are all upset with the Marid, but they
are grateful, too, to nand' Bren and Great-grandmother, which
is why they wanted to talk—nand' Bren is their neighbor, and
they feel an association there, and they really respect elder people, especially elder ladies, and, besides—" He was getting too
many "ands," which Great-grandmother said was undignified,
so he tried to amend it. "Besides, Great-grandmother has influence with you, she is an associate of Lord Geigi, too, and her
own province is on the other side of the world, so she would be
a very smart alliance for them. They know *she* would not want
their land. And she is associated with nand' Bren, so there is a
local connection."

His father bent an absolutely dispassionate face toward him,
which, since he doubted his father had reason to lose his temper further than he had already lost it, probably meant that his
father was actually amused at his account. One might take offense at that, because he had tried hard to understand what was
going on—except it was certainly better than his father losing
his temper.

"Tolerably well-reckoned," his father said. "But there is risk
in staying here, boy, which agitates your great-uncle considerably. Not to mention your mother."

"If the Edi fall out of the aishidi'tat and the Marid starts
fighting them, there will be a lot of assassinations, and *you*

could be in danger, honored Father, even in the capital, not to mention other people who will get hurt all over the place. If the Edi clan protects this coast and it allies to the Gan and to Great-grandmother in the East, that will annoy some people, but it will make this coast stronger, so the Marid can never come in here again. And if nand' Bren had *not* found out the Marid were plotting to take Kajiminda, then the Taisigi of the Marid would have gotten a claim to it. And they would have killed off the Maschi one at a time until they got somebody else stupid like Baiji to make a treaty with them. And then you would have to come in and fight them and it would have been a *much* bigger mess than having the Edi as allies and letting them have a house of their own."

"Clever, clever boy. All your great-grandmother's arguments in a pleasant package."

It was not time to be pert with his father. Not at all. Cajeiri made a judicious bow.

"Do you already know you are about to become the elder of my offspring?" his father asked him then, which took a second thought, and rapidly three and four. "Is that what has prompted this current adventurism?"

Elder? As in—two? And with the same mother? Surely with his mother! He would be very upset if his father ended the contract with his mother and she went away. And Uncle Tatiseigi would be furious.

"No, honored Father. Is the mother *my* mother?"

"The same," his father said, immediately relieving him of one huge concern.

"Am I to have a brother?" That could be good or bad. He had no idea. It could be fun.

"Or a sister," his father said.

Among humans, one apparently had a way of telling. But either was important news. It affected his place in the world, but not too much, since the parentage was all the same two clans, Ragi and his mother's Ajuri clan.

And having a baby of the same heritage might divert his mother *and* his great-uncle from excessive worry about him, which could be good.

But—

—which would not be good—

Great-grandmother would have another great-grandchild to fuss over, who would get all the favors.

That was not to be tolerated. That thought got his blood to racing.

He really, *really* did not want to share Great-grandmother's attention. Or nand' Bren's. He was not going to share. No.

"We would rather have told you under calmer circumstances," his father said, "and we would have done so in very short order, in fact, so you would not hear it first from other sources. But you left the capital "

"Does Great-grandmother know it?"

A snort. "There is nothing your great-grandmother fails to know. Study that woman's information-gathering. It is highly efficient."

"She did not know we were going into a trap at Kajiminda."

His father flung up a hand. "Say no more on that score! One has heard quite enough of that argument!"

He bowed, not knowing what had annoyed his father, but he was sure that something had, something to do with that incident.

And whatever it was, it had nothing to do with the truly important fact—namely that his parents were having another baby.

That possibly made him a little less valuable to some people. It meant if someone did away with him, his father would still have an heir. He supposed that was a good thing.

It meant somebody else would be available for people to watch and fuss over, which was definitely good. His father only had so many security resources. And that meant more freedom for him.

But it also meant he had to be *better*, in everything, or people would say his sib was better, which was already unfair.

It meant he was going to have to *work* and stay ahead forever. Or else. *That* was a threat . . . a threat a lot more personal than the Marid posed by shooting at him. He never, ever wanted anybody to say his younger sib was better than him at anything.

Great-grandmother said if he was able to deal with the Edi because of meeting them and talking to them, that would be an asset for the future. And he was very sure that if they could settle the Marid's ambitions that would be an asset for everybody's future.

And he was not going to give up any assets he had. Not now. Not with competition on the way.

"Your great-grandmother says you can use common sense when you understand a danger is real," his father said in that no-nonsense voice he had. "One suggests you consider that the danger in this entire district is quite real."

"One has very well comprehended that, honored Father."

"Continue to comprehend it," his father said. "And obey knowledgeable elders!"

He was going to get to stay! "Yes," he said triumphantly— but not too triumphantly. Nothing was safe until his father actually left him here in his great-grandmother's keeping. And then he could *do* things to secure his future and the aishidi'tat's. He would be important. He would make himself important— given a head start.

"Behave!" his father said, and he bowed and his father nodded an end to the matter and that was that. His father left, taking his bodyguard with him, and he—

He looked at his intimates, his aishid, his bodyguard, who had necessarily heard all that exchange. He was gratified to see they all looked very respectful, even impressed . . . even Lucasi and Veijico, who were complete snobs about everything. He had come off rather well in that exchange, he thought, except being surprised by the information that he had a sib coming.

Still, one's aishid had to be privy to moments like that. And they had to keep quiet about what they knew. It was part of what they were.

"We need information, nadiin-ji," he said. "We need to know what my father said to my great-grandmother, for one, and to nand' Bren. Find out."

Jegari and Antaro were equal with Veijico and Lucasi in that mission: the two young Taibeni, who had reasonable access and credit with house staff, were able to get things from the servants, who heard almost everything. And the two newcomers, being real Guild, could gather information among senior Guild in the house. Both sets looked at him very soberly.

And then they dispersed, Antaro leaving Jegari on duty with him, and Veijico leaving Lucasi with him. Two sources, two kinds of inquiries—neither leaving him alone with the other for a moment—because the two halves of his aishid were *not* in good agreement.

That was the problem his father had given him *along* with his two real Guild members.

Well, that was all right. At least all his bodyguards were primarily *his*, not spies for Great-uncle, for his father, or even for Great-grandmother, and he would work it out. Veijico and Lucasi would take orders: they had said so, and they had better mean it.

He had been doing some talking with the two new members of his aishid over the last couple of days, and he had arrived at a fair understanding of their position. They *were* good, they *did* understand Guild operations, and they would take the lead in defense. They had been very frustrated at having to live in the Guild house where nothing *ever* happened that the seniors did not take care of, and they realized that being attached to him was a great thing, and they looked forward to being in action . . .

But they also understood that they had to take general orders from Antaro and Jegari as the two who best knew his mind on what Great-grandmother would call "staff policy."

They had readily agreed they would not tell tales unless they feared he was making a serious, serious mistake—and he was determined not to do that, given their experienced advice. Which he promised to hear, at least, on any important question. He assured them of that, and they seemed happy.

So he had his household in fairly good order. Jegari and Antaro ran staff things and most of the defense planning for the room and all was done by Veijico and Lucasi, who could also get some information out of nand' Bren's bodyguard and some even from Great-grandmother's.

And even his father had had to admit his presence here was an asset to the aishidi'tat, if he was learning things and making a good impression on people. He was proud of that.

So everybody agreed he would stay in nand' Bren's house, and he was so happy he could run through the halls shouting. But he did no such thing, because he was being proper.

He would be helpful. He would *get* the man'chi of the Edi *and* the Gan, the way Great-grandmother planned, so that someday when he was aiji, he would have the whole coast secure.

The Ragi? They ran the whole aishidi'tat, all the Western Association, and they might be upset with him dealing with the Edi, but they were always arguing about something. One thing he knew for certain: he had Uncle Tatiseigi backing him, which was the Central Clans; and he had Great-grandmother, who was the East; and he was fairly sure of the Isles and the North; and certainly of the Taibeni, who were Jegari and Antaro's clan; and if he got the Edi, too, then they could flatten the Marid, and nobody was going to overthrow his father's heir.

No little brother was going to get ahead of *him*, ever.

3

Tabini-aiji did *not* pay a visit to Lord Geigi's nephew Baiji, in the basement. Nor did he linger for tea, let alone lunch.

In the main, Bren could surmise, this had nothing to do with Tabini's irritation at the local situation, and was entirely due to security concerns and the insistence of his bodyguard. The less time the aiji spent in this chancey region, the better his bodyguard would like it—and, unhappy truth, the better the Edi residents of the area would like it, too. Ragi clan atevi, which the aiji was, moving in with orders and decrees and consequent upheavals and relocations, was the unhappy history of the Ragi clan with the Edi people and their northern cousins the Gan. The Edi district remained as skittish about the aiji's actions as they were about Marid plots. Tabini, being no fool in such matters, and his guard likewise, they had kept his presence quick and relatively quiet.

What would be noted among the Edi and other observers was that Tabini's son had stayed, evidently with the blessing of his father, and his grandmother Ilisidi stayed, and the paidhi-aiji stayed, all with their Guild bodyguards, all of them having already established a dialogue with the Edi at some little cost of life and current risk to themselves.

That, Bren hoped, would resonate clear up the coast to the Gan, who were very likely following the proceedings here with some interest.

It would resonate southward, too, around the curve of the

coast to the bottom of the continent, where the Marid, that little aggregate of five clans around a deep bay—a little private sea—had strung out a long history of conspiracy, internecine warfare, and general ferment. Members of the aishidi'tat? They were. But enemies of the aishidi'tat? They always had been.

So he could look for his Bujavid apartment back. Soon. The Farai could start packing and take themselves back to the Marid, ending any pretense of negotiations and new agreements for that region. That was one good thing to come out of Tabini's visit. Given current circumstances, the Farai might get nervous enough to quit the premises without the aiji ever saying a thing. *That* would be nice.

And under other circumstances, he would intend to be back in the Bujavid in short order—except for the matters he had inadvertently stirred up on the coast, namely the *rest* of the business that the Farai and their fellow Marid were involved in . . .

Namely the plot to marry into Lord Geigi's clan and inherit Lord Geigi's estate—*with* its property rights and treaty privileges on the west coast.

The defunct Maladesi clan, through which the Farai claimed that prime Bujavid apartment, had also been the previous owners of Najida. One wondered, one truly, truly wondered whatever had made the Farai hesitate to claim the estate as well during Murini's days in power.

Possibly a little reluctance on the part of Murini, himself from the central clans, to have the Farai, and thus the Marid, get too powerful too fast? The Farai had already claimed the Bujavid apartment. Maybe Murini had rebuffed their more important claim to the old Maladesi west coast estate—or told them to wait for that.

Maybe Murini had had enough common sense not to want to stir up the Edi in his first year in power. If the Edi-Murid feud had gone nova, Murini would have had his most important ally, the Marid, distracted with that old quarrel—and having the Marid's main force pinned down in a guerilla war would have weakened Murini's hold on the capital, and thus on the aijinate. It had been rumored, at the time, that Tabini was dead. It had been rumored, at the time, that Tabini's heir was lost somewhere in the heavens along with the aiji-dowager and the paidhi-aiji and never would come back—but there would have been claimants soon enough, if Murini had at any point looked distracted.

Timing, timing, timing. Contrary to Murini's expectations, the dowager had returned from space, Tabini had launched his counterattack on Murini, and Murini had gone down to defeat . . . *before* the Marid had wormed their way into their hearts' desire . . . namely the west coast.

So—with Murini gone—the Marid had just kept working toward their goal while trying to stall Tabini with promised new agreements. The marriage offer to Baiji predated Tabini's return to power: so the Marid had been quietly pursuing their objective regardless of who sat in power in Shejidan. Murini might not have known what they were up to, offering Geigi's foolish nephew a Marid wife, or had turned a blind eye to it because he did not want a public break with his allies.

But certainly the Edi had understood what was going on. The Edi servants in Baiji's house had found a stream of Marid agents visiting the estate—agents who had set up shop in the township that neighbored the estate. Agents who had evaporated following the failed attempt on the paidhi-aiji's life—and now were rumored to have set up again.

Tabini's men were, one hoped, discreetly ferreting out that little nest, which had fled from Kajiminda estate down to Separti Township.

Possibly the Edi people were helping the aiji's men find those cells—though one doubted it: the Edi historically had blamed the Ragi for the treaty that had lost them their homeland, over on Mospheira, and they had only marginally attached to the aishidi'tat. The old, old resentment had never died, and they particularly did not cooperate with the Assassins' Guild.

Which made it all the more remarkable that the Edi people had approached both the paidhi and Tabini's grandmother— herself an Easterner, from another region dragged somewhat unwillingly into the continent-spanning modern state.

So Tabini had just paid a personal visit? The Edi would have known it even while it was in progress. The paidhi had absolutely no doubt of that—since there were Edi servants under this roof. They would know, they would be concerned, and they would certainly have an opinion, based on whatever those servants reported, which might well be the whole content of the conversation with Ilisidi—the conversation had hardly been quiet.

Considering the fragility of lines of communication just ever so tentatively reopened, it did seem a good idea to be sure the Edi did not feel the paidhi had been communicating their closer-held secrets to the aiji . . . in a conversation which had been much lower key.

So the paidhi went out into the hall and located, with no trouble at all, his majordomo, Ramaso, who was his most reliable link to the Edi. Ramaso was standing between the servants' wing and the dining hall, a high traffic area in the house, and a very convenient place to watch who came and went in the main hall: its view included the master suite, the library, the office, the dining hall, and the doors to all the guest suites and formal bath.

Not an accident, that position: Ramaso kept himself informed on all sorts of matters: it was his job to do that. And Ramaso very politely bowed when accosted. His dark face was absolutely innocent of motive, which was to say, expressionless, in the best formal fashion.

"Rama-ji," Bren said. "This has been an interesting morning."

"Indeed, nandi."

"The aiji asked no questions into Edi business. His visit seems a signal, and the aiji's specific decision not to pull his heir back to Shejidan seems so, too. He knows the contact with the Edi people took place and knows what was said. Tell the Grandmother that. If the Edi wish to meet formally again, their neighbor the paidhi would be willing to come to the village— or we would welcome the Grandmother or her representative here, should she wish."

Ramaso read him quite well, Bren thought, and signals were not lost on him. A hint of expression touched the mouth and sparkled favorably in age-lined amber eyes. "Very good, nandi."

Signals. One of the things at issue in the district was the dowager's suggestion that the Edi should seek a lordship of their own, and establish themselves, after two hundred years of limbo, as a recognized presence in the Ragi-dominated legislature. There would certainly be a bit of a fuss about it, when the aishidi'tat had to accommodate a new presence and new interests—but there it was. That was the situation which Tabini had walked in on, and only mildly mentioned, in his dealings with his grandmother. It was the aiji's lack of comment, ergo tacit acceptance, that needed to be communicated to the Edi.

Others of the staff, too, had witnessed the meeting and knew exactly what they had seen and heard. Ramaso had had his clarification on that. But it was not the only issue the aiji had brought into the household.

So Bren walked on back to the furthest suite, where the hall bent gardenward, next to that fine stained-glass window— darkened, only its hammered surface sparkling inkily in the hall light, since they had put the storm shutters up. The whole estate still had the feeling of a fortress under seige, and right next to that huge window was the nerve center of house operations in their state of siege—the suite where Banichi and Jago, Tano and Algini, and occasionally Cenedi, the dowager's chief of security, met and observed, via their small roomful of sophisticated monitors, everyone who came and went in the house, on the grounds, and out on the road.

His personal bodyguard—his four constant attendants, his aishid—kept the suite door open, as usual, and the monitor room door itself stood open. He walked in, not unnoticed in his approach, he was quite sure—as he was sure the whole progress and tenor of the aiji's visit had been a matter of intense discussion in this little room, especially once Banichi and Jago had arrived to debrief to their teammates. Banichi and Jago occupied the left half of the little station, Tano and Algini had the right, and they accepted his presence with a little nod toward courtesy—he disliked formalities in his bodyguard—as he perched on a fifth, vacant chair in their midst.

"Bren-ji," Tano said. That was a question.

"One has invited the village Grandmother to discuss the visit," he said, and heads nodded solemnly—his aishid entirely understood that matter. "One conveyed this suggestion through Ramaso."

"Wise," Banichi said. That was all.

That Lord Geigi was arriving tomorrow, and that they had that very astute help coming—and the pressing problem of where to put him—Banichi and Jago would have covered that matter with Tano and Algini.

"One still has no idea how we shall settle Lord Geigi's staff—or how many people may come with him. But we have to do something by tomorrow. The Edi may well wish to move back into Kajiminda. They will have no wish to see their lord guarded solely by Guild."

"The premises of Kajiminda will be compromised if they refuse all communication with us," Algini said, momentarily diverting himself from his monitors—and, like a piston-stroke, Tano's attention went onto those screens. "The Edi might expect to undertake his security arrangements, yes, nandi, but they are inexpert in modern systems and they would be going into a seriously compromised environment with questionable equipment. One doubts, too, that the aiji's guard will willingly vacate the grounds until they have secured the estate, and that operation is not yet complete. A further difficulty: Lord Geigi's Guild bodyguard has no current knowledge of systems here on the ground, and *they* will need to be brought up to date on what capabilities we do and do not have."

"Best keep them here at Najida as long as possible, Bren-ji," Banichi said, "and let the aiji's guard have as long a time as possible to go over the premises there."

"Regrettably," Bren said, "nadiin-ji, you know this is the only suite of rooms left. And while it is not my desire to see my bodyguard housed in the basement . . ."

"Better to move our operations to the library," Jago said.

That was a thought: it would be closer to the front door—though one of the dowager's favorite sitting spots, it was a thoroughly sensible suggestion, there being only this remaining suite remotely accceptable for a lord of Geigi's rank.

One last suite to be had—this one, small as it was, with only three rooms; and if Geigi brought more than four Guild with him, it was going to be a squeeze. But Geigi could handle that. He was adaptable—hence his success governing the atevi side of the space station.

"We must move this afternoon, then," Tano said.

"We do *not*, Bren-ji," Algini said quietly, "propose to give Lord Geigi's aishid, Guild though they be, close access to our own operations. We hope for your firm support in that position."

"Without question, nadiin-ji," Bren said. That posed another sticky little question. Lord Geigi was—one never said *friend* among atevi, who had neither the concept nor the emotional hard-wiring to feel that sentiment. But certainly he was a personal ally, a very closely bound ally of many years, through many very difficult circumstances. There was *nobody* more reliable than Lord Geigi, and they owed him profound gratitude and a feeling of absolute acceptance and trust.

But one could not rely on staff, Guild or otherwise, who might have suffered a confusion of man'chi—that warm emotion in atevi which attached individuals to other individuals

of greater power. Man'chi, the glue that held atevi society together and made households function, had a certain tendency
to weaken—given long absence or political upheaval.

And Lord Geigi, while only a phone call away from the
planet, had spent the last decade up on the space station. The
Guildsmen with him had been long out of touch with whatever
ties they had had here in Sarini Province, or elsewhere.

Given those circumstances, staff's sense of precaution was
entirely reasonable, by atevi lights.

More, that absence had left Geigi's estate—and his once-
close relationship with the Edi people—to suffer the effects of
two caretaker lords: first his sister, and then his nephew Baiji—
whose flaws of character had been extreme, and whose staff
had ranged from questionable to Marid-based.

No knowing, in effect, what Lord Geigi would be walking into
over at Kajiminda if he imprudently tried to go there straight
away; and no knowing—a worse thought, which popped into
Bren's head quite unwelcomely—no knowing what odd influ-
ences might have gotten onto Geigi's staff even while he was
on the station, slowly and over the years. Tabini had been very
careful who got into orbit—and with the shuttles grounded all
during Murini's administration, *nobody* in Murini's man'chi
had gotten into orbit—but man'chi was always subject to revi-
sion, given changed circumstances. Houses onworld had risen
and fallen: allegiances had rearranged themselves clear across
the continent. Certain clans had fallen. The Guild itself had
suffered upheaval, including the overthrow of one Guildmaster
and the assassination of another. Relationships on the planet
had undergone profound change—and that might affect a whole
range of things that could make a once-reliable relationship
unstable.

No, he decidedly did not want Geigi's current staff having
free rein in his security operations. Algini was very, very right
about that notion. They would have to research Geigi's bodyguard, learn who their relatives were, how placed, how con-

nected, during the usurper's regime. Matters which could hang fire forever so long as these men served in orbit could reach out to change loyalties, once they were on the planet. Geigi himself would know that, and likely had been very careful which of his staff he picked to go with him—but would he have done it with perfect information?

God, what a mess!

"Are we, however, yet admitting the heir's two new guards to trusted levels?" he asked, a point of not-idle curiosity.

"Not in any particular way," Tano said, and Bren nodded slowly. Lucasi and Veijico, whom Tabini had installed in addition to Antaro and Jegari, came to the household with high-level credentials, too. But by that statement, his aishid was not turning over the house codes to them, not yet admitting them to decision-making, apparently not even letting them give orders to the servants. The dowager's staff, yes, could do all those things. Cenedi, absolutely; but Cenedi was a long standing exception. His staff was clearly running a very tight ship.

So Geigi's staff was destined to be under-informed until the investigation ran its course.

"I concur," he said. It was not a lord's business to critique security decisions unless he found serious fault—and with his aishid, he didn't. Ever. He was damned lucky, he thought. Very damned lucky to have this bodyguard. He would not be alive, if they had been in the least lax, but they had not, not even when they had arrived on what they had expected to be a working vacation. They still smarted over the ambush at Kajiminda . . . when their domestic sources had given them bad information, and when their lord had not picked up on the clues that should have warned him.

"Do what you need to do," he said. "Staff will move anything in the library that you want moved out." Staff would not be allowed to touch Guild equipment. But historic porcelains and small tables and sitting chairs were definitely something staff could handle, and should, with their own sort of care.

So he went out and gave the orders to the servant staff. The household security station, in the advent of another guest, was about to be remade as a visiting lord's residence.

All of which meant the paidhi's office now became his last refuge, the last secure, quiet place where he could work and answer correspondence and prepare arguments for the coming legislative session . . . which was what he had been doing when all hell had broken loose in the district.

But the legislative documents, regarding a proposed cell phone installation, lay underneath a stack of research and maps of the west coast, which was pretty well the situation in reality. He was no longer sure he would make it back to the capital for the session . . . but then, he was no longer sure the cell phone controversy would make it to the floor, thanks to the nest of problems he'd stirred up. He *should* be in Shejidan for the session.

But he was likely to be here, on the west coast, trying to comprehend Edi interests and figure exactly how the dowager's proposal was going to work in practicality.

Oh, the debate in the legislature was likely going to be loud and nasty.

Another armed set-to with the Marid?

Well, on the one hand, another Marid flare-up was the one thing he could think of that might draw the Padi Valley clans back together—fragmented as that local association had been since Murini's clan, the Kadagidi, had seized power in alliance with the Marid. The Marid was generally detested now. By everyone—including the Padi Valley.

But, ironically, and on the other hand, a proposed Edi seat in the house of lords could see the Padi Valley *and* the Marid united in opposition. The Padi Valley would oppose it because they were the old nobility and ran the legislature, and liked it that way. The Marid—

Well, the Marid needed no excuse at all to oppose the Edi.

Not to mention that certain conservatives in the legislature blamed the paidhi's influence for the recent troubles. Now he would be associated with offering the Edi equality and a voice in politics.

He really, truly *needed* to preserve this one little sanctuary in the house, where he could get his thoughts together and figure out what to say when he finally did have to face the legislature.

And facing that moment with an acceptable solution already worked out would make life so much easier.

There were two keys to getting the Edi representation accepted. One was Lord Geigi, who, being the real lord of Kajiminda, and a good man, had long enjoyed the man'chi of the Edi people—before he had gone to space and left his estate to his sister and her fool son. If Geigi could sort out his domestic problems and regain that man'chi, his influence over the Edi could make the proposal a great deal more palatable to several factions.

The other key to the situation, oddly enough, was Ilisidi's sometime lover and Cajeiri's great-uncle—Lord Tatiseigi of the Atageini, that hidebound old man who didn't approve of trains, telephones, television, space travel, humans, Southerners, Taibeni, west coasters, or anything ever imported from those sources.

Uncle Tatiseigi ran the Padi Valley Association, with its powerful sub-associations, on the sheer force of his antiquity. No, he didn't want Tatiseigi here at Najida, physically, but dealing *with* Tatiseigi was inevitable . . . and possibly to the good, since Tatiseigi swung a big weight with the conservatives—and since Ilisidi, above all others, could reason with the old man.

Especially since *she* had evidently wanted to do this fifty years ago—bringing the disenfranchised majority of the west coast into the house of lords. Depend on it, ultimately Ilisidi tended to win her arguments, and knew Tatiseigi like a well-read book.

The wonder to him was that Tabini, the cleverest and most underhanded politician the continent had witnessed in centuries, second only to Ilisidi, had just walked in, passed that issue by with fairly moderate comment, and let his eight-year-old son stay in the middle of the situation.

The paidhi, who rated himself the *third* cleverest politician on the continent, was left wondering what had just happened, how many Marid agents there might be in the vicinity that Tabini's agents *hadn't* ferreted out—and whether he, the human who didn't have atevi senses to read the currents, was going to be blindsided twice in this war of towering egos and ancient agendas.

First on his own agenda, definitely, had to be making sure the Edi didn't put an unfavorable intrepretion on the aiji's visit.

And that meant making sure the Edi knew the aiji-dowager hadn't changed her opinion.

That meant dealing with Ilisidi when her blood was up.

A fool would do that. He wrote out a message, went out into the hall and gave it to a junior servant to give to Cenedi, senior of the dowager's bodyguard. It said:

> *Certainly the Edi have noted the coming and going of the aiji-dowager's grandson. The paidhi-aiji has accordingly sent an informal message to the Edi leadership offering a consultation should they wish one. The paidhi-aiji willingly takes all responsibility for such a meeting, whether on the premises or in the village, unless the aiji-dowager wishes otherwise.*

The answer came back in a few minutes. It read:

> *The paidhi-aiji may assure the Edi leadership that our statements stand.*

And from the Edi leadership, within the next hour, a young man, definitely not the Grandmother of Najida village, arrived in the little office, escorted by Banichi and Jago, and bowed respectfully. Dola, he said his name was, and one recalled seeing him the night of the village council meeting.

"Nand' paidhi, the Grandmother asks if there is any change in the understandings."

"One can assure the Grandmother that there is no change at all. The aiji had heard of the agreement." That was a diplomatic understatement. "He issued no instruction about it. He was persuaded that his son was safe and that his grandmother was comfortable in her situation. The paidhi-aiji attended that meeting and knows these statements to be true. And the aiji-dowager particularly asks me to assure the Edi that the understandings have not changed."

A bow and an immediately relaxed countenance. "Nand' paidhi, one will say so."

"One is grateful, nadi." He bowed in turn, and that was that. The young man left, and he went back to his papers.

One matter handled.

The five clans of the Marid would be—doubtless having gotten wind of the visit by now—furious.

Beyond furious. If a leader of the Marid had had his schemes go this far astray—not only losing their smoothly running plot to marry their way into control of Kajiminda, but now provoking the aishidi'tat into establishing their historic enemies the Edi as a new power on the coast—that leader had to fear his own neighbors, whom he regularly held in check by threat and judicious assassination. In the last half-year that young man, who had loomed as the dark eminence behind Murini's takeover—thus poised to assassinate Murini and take over the whole aishidi'tat—had lost the west coast a second time, thanks largely to the paidhi-aiji's visit here, and was about to see the Marid's old enemies gain legitimacy. If somebody attempted to take out Machigi, it would *not* be somebody who favored the Edi taking power. It would most likely be somebody else from the Marid, incensed at his failure.

Perilous times indeed.

"The move to the library is proceeding, nadiin-ji?" he asked Banichi and Jago, when they came back after escorting the latest visitor to the front door.

"Proceeding rapidly," Jago said. "We shall not break down all the equipment at once. Part of it will be set up and running in the library before we move the rest."

A good idea, he thought, that they not be blind at any given moment. Matters had gotten that dicey over the last few days. There hadn't been this concentration of high-value targets on the west coast in two hundred years . . . all sitting in Najida, which was a sprawling country house, not an ancient fortress.

And Machigi of the Taisigin Marid?

Machigi was going to move. He had to.

Bet on it.

4

One of the mundane tasks of the paidhi's residency in Na-jida had been finding a replacement for the estate bus—which had lately come to grief—along with the service gate, the garden utility gate, the garage door, the garden wall, and part of the arbor.

And while the lord of Najida naturally *wanted* to patronize local businesses, the only dealer in such vehicles in the region was down in Separti Township, a district in which Tabini's forces were still ferreting out the last of a Marid cell—the same cell that was indirectly *responsible* for the disaster to the gates, the garage door, and the garden premises.

So the paidhi had regretfully sent his business elsewhere: a call to his office staff in the Bujavid in Shejidan—and to his bank—had reportedly solved the problem, and the item had been acquired with no delay at all, and shipped. He had had his Shejidan staff select a stout, security-grade vehicle from a random choice among three such dealers in Shejidan, one with ample seating for, oh, about thirty persons.

His chief secretary had called back yesterday asking if he wanted to outlay extra for blackout shielding on the windows—no actual protection, but a way of making life more difficult for snipers.

Yes, that had seemed a good idea, all things considered.

Weight mattered. A totally secure vehicle, involving bullet-proof glass as well, was a very slow-moving vehicle, and gulped fuel, a dependency which became its own vulnerability in attempting to maneuver across Sarini Province, which had very few fueling stations. He had fared well in the past by relying on agility. So, no, he would not prefer the armor-sided version, which was more apt for city use.

But the blackout shields would certainly be nice.

It was an expensive vehicle, far exceeding the ancient rattletrap of a bus they had wrecked. And an extravagance—but the old bus had been the same vintage as the village truck, the same as the grading and mowing and harvest equipment, warehoused and maintained down in Najida village—along with a firetruck, a pumper, for anyone in the district who needed it—all of these antiques inherited from the previous lord of Najida, now deceased. The village constabulary and its deputies were the usual mechanics, drivers, and operators of all these vehicles in Najida . . . and they would have to urgently read up on the manual for this one, one supposed. The new bus would be larger, air-conditioned, modern at every turn: and God knew there would be a learning curve—but they were adept mechanics, no fools at all, and at least the learning would be on country roads, not in winding city lanes.

Outside of the local market traffic between Najida and Najida estate, or either of those places and Kajiminda, or on down to Separti and Dalaigi, there were, in fact, very few roads in all the province, except those that went to the railhead or airport—and those were mostly mowed strips in the grass, with a few persistently bad spots graveled and the local streams bridged. You wanted to go to Separti? You went to Kajiminda, and took the road on from there. You wanted to go to the Maschi estate inland? You went to the train station, then took the train station road to the airport, and then drove across the end of the airstrip to pick up the Maschi Road.

Any people and baggage that had to go long distances on the continent moved by air or by train. And today, as happened, the morning, crack-of-dawn train originating in the capital was bringing them that fancy new bus, specially loaded onto a flat-car, to arrive a few hours before the airport would bring them Geigi.

That was about as tight scheduling as one could imagine, but just in time. There was a small fuel depot at the train station. That would get the bus rolling. Painting the Najida emblem on the new bus door? That would just have to wait, since it had its first job immediately after arrival, and had to pick up the welcoming committee and U-turn back up the road to the airport.

So everyone was up early as the new acquisition came purring nicely down the road and onto the drive. It pulled up under the portico with—Bren winced, watching it skin just under the portico roof—barely enough clearance—which he was sure staff *had* checked. There was not, thank goodness, a central light fixture under the portico: light came from fixtures on the five stonework pillars. And it missed them, too.

It stopped with much less fuss than the old bus, no wheeze or cough, and when it opened its doors, it exuded a new smell, an impressive sense of prosperity. It was a rich red and black—Tabini's colors, not what one would have wished in this province, but there it was. It was red, it was shiny, it was—staff reported happily—very elegant inside.

Bren stood at the house door with Banichi and Jago and watched the proceedings in lordly dignity. The dowager had entirely declined to come outside, saying she trusted the bus would be everything it was promised to be, and that she would felicitate the acquisition from her warm fireside.

Cajeiri, however, with his whole bodyguard, was outside. Cajeiri managed to get right up to the bus doors, trying for a peek inside, obviously itching to go aboard and look it over.

The young lord did, however, defer to the owner, and came back to ask. "May one go aboard?" Cajeiri made a diffident, proper request, all but vibrating with restraint, and Bren indulged him with a laugh and a beneficent smile. He was curious about the interior himself, but dignity insisted he wait, and he simply stood and looked at it, and awaited his staff's prior assessment of its fitness.

"It is very fine, nandi," Ramaso reported to him. "The seats are gray leather, and the carpeting is gray."

Not quite in harmony with local dust and mud, he thought. He hadn't expressed a preference on color. He'd left that to staff and chance, willing to take any color that happened to be ready to roll onto a train car, roll off at Najida Station, and provide him and his staff with some transport that was not the sniper opportunity of an open truckbed. Red. Hardly inconspicuous, either.

"Stock it for a proper reception of our arriving guest," he said to Ramaso. "Fruit juice, at this hour. The traditional things. And the bar. The space station's time is not our time, so one has no idea what our guest will desire. One understands there will be a call advising us when Lord Geigi's plane is about to land, not before then."

That arrangement was for security's sake. Geigi, they now knew, was coming in at Najida's airport, which was hardly more than a grass strip and a wind sock—and from what prior landing they had had no information, for just the same reason of security. Separti Township, which had a much larger, round-the-clock airport, was not a thoroughly safe place, and one thought it just possible Geigi was coming in direct, taking a prop plane clear from Shejidan Airport. One was sure that if he did land at Separti, it would be with the aiji's security in place to assure the safety of any plane he boarded there . . . but one had still had no word where exactly Geigi was, even yet.

Such grim thoughts kept the paidhi-aiji from quite enjoying the novelty of his big new bus. And upon Ramaso's report, and without so much as a personal look inside, in proper lordly form, he retreated to his office to deal with the invoice that came with the bus, a thick bundle of papers which a servant brought him on a silver tray. The invoice, in six figures, debited his personal finances, not the estate—the bill would have upset the annual budget considerably, right when they wanted the books to look their best, in any upcoming legislative scrutiny of the Edi region.

At that point, Banichi and Jago traded off their duty with Tano and Algini—the latter reporting, as they arrived in the office, that the security office had finished the move to the library, and were set up there.

So he did the accounts and filed the papers while staff loaded the bus with necessary things. At a very small side table, Tano and Algini settled down to a quiet card game—a variant of poker had made its way to the mainland a decade ago, and atevi were quite good at it. Superstitious atevi put far too much ominous freight on its nuances, but atevi who weren't at all superstitious about numbers were frighteningly adept. When those two played, it was a spectator sport.

And just a little distracting from the far more important numbers he was dealing with.

But he had ample business to occupy him: the finances regarding the bus were one account. Plus the estate needed to order in a delivery of fuel, what with all the recent coming and going . . . and that delivery was, under current circumstances, a high security risk. The fueling station for the whole peninsula was in the village, a supply the village truck and the fishing boats and the estate bus all used. He wrote out orders for the fuel purchases, too, to be billed to his personal account. And he made a note to staff to consult security all the way on that delivery and to have several of the dowager's staff overseeing it from the depot in Separti all the way to Najida.

He was not in the habit of spending money in such massive amounts. He generally let his finances accumulate, had let them ride for the last number of years, and was shocked to find the bus did *not* put a cautionary dent in his personal accounts. He only needed to move money from one account to another.

He had to do something with that personal excess. New harvesting machinery for Najida village. A modern fire truck, to serve Najida and Kajiminda. Maybe even a new wing on Najida that *would* allow more guests. Construction of that sort would employ more Najida folk. The estate occupied all the land there was on its little rocky knoll, without disturbing the beautiful rock-lined walk down to the shore, but the estate *could* spread out to the west, by creating a new wing, along the village road.

That would solve a problem. He had thought about expansion before; had considered siting the garage across the road . . . but that would require a walkover arch for the road, which would require a second level on any structure to meet it on this side of the road, which would destroy the felicitious symmetry of the ancient house . . . Not to mention, it would impose a part of the house between Najida and their market. And *that* was an unwarranted disturbance in the people's daily lives.

But by putting a whole new wing where the garage was, with no walkover, just the pleasant walk through the garden . . .

Though an underground connection beneath the garden walk, for the house servants to get back and forth from that wing conveniently at all hours and in all weather would be useful.

Another plus: the garage, which the occupants of the house did not routinely visit, would *not* be taking up a garden view. Instead, the garage would be relegated farther out into what was now scrub evergreen and some rocky outcrops, an area of no great natural beauty.

Brilliant solution. It would be minimal disturbance to the ancient garden, it would connect directly to the house—it would put the garage beyond a blank wall, and yet allow easy access to it.

He liked that.

Pen moved. He sketched. The new wing would have a basement connecting to that underground access, beneath the garden walk. So would the restored garage, also joining that underground passage; and the new wing basement could accommodate new staff quarters as well as storage—while the upper structure could be made with the same native stone construction and low profile as characterized the rest of the ancient house. The same terra cotta tile for the roof. And a double-glazed window—greater security than a plain one—overlooking the garden and the main house, the architecture of which had always gone unappreciated except from the garage door.

Excellent notion. A second window, looking out toward the harbor, where the rocks dropped away in a hitherto-unused prospect on the ocean. Maybe use *that* for a dining hall.

He could use local labor at every stage. Najida folk were clever, could learn anything necessary, and the income would flow from the estate to the village, as it ought to.

And if the Edi people did build a hall for their own lord over in Kajiminda district—likely for the Grandmother of Najida village, but no one but the Edi quite knew where Edi authority truly resided—the skills of construction and the prosperity in Najida village would both feed into that project.

He liked his idea. He had a brand-new bus sitting in the driveway and a very useful air-castle rising in place of his wrecked gates.

Beside him, Tano and Algini still played poker. He sketched out his plan, derelict in his legislative duties. A new—second—ground floor bath. And a second, larger servants' bath, with two sides, two baths, below. *That* would be very useful.

Plumbing—he made a vague squiggle on his design. That detail was for experts to figure out. But another hot water tank on that side of the house would certainly be useful.

God, he was spending money left and right this morning, and he was in uncharted territory now, having no practical knowledge of the costs of such a construction.

He should talk to—

A rap at the door interrupted both the card game, and his daydream of easy, sweeping solutions.

Jago opened the door and slipped inside. "Lord Geigi's staff has just contacted us, Bren-ji. He is in the air at Mori, and will land here, we estimate, within the hour. The new bus is fueled and stocked and in order. The guest quarters are available now, and furnished with linens. The truck is on its way up from the village. We are ready."

"Excellent." He looked at the wall clock. So Lord Geigi, having landed at Shejidan, had come into an airport near the Isles by jet, and was coming down the coast from the Isles by prop plane . . . inventive route, possibly with time for contact with old allies on the northern coast. "We should be moving, then."

The card game had ended, unfinished. Jago gave a single hand sign to Tano and Algini that simply amounted to, "Banichi and I will go with Bren," and that was that: all arrangements made. Tano and Algini would stay with the monitoring, along with Cenedi and his men, and Banichi and Jago would go with him to the airstrip.

Certain house staff would go with them, too, particularly to handle the luggage, additional of which might be coming in a second plane—one would not be at all surprised at that arrangement. Personal baggage could go into the underside of the fancy new bus; but the village truck would be a prudent backup, so as not to leave any of Lord Geigi's belongings exposed at the little airstrip, begging the kind of michief they had had.

Moving an atevi lord anywhere was an exercise in complex logistics, but what a lord saw generally went smoothly—thanks to staff.

And all he needed do was go to his bedroom, put on a nicer coat—Koharu and Supani helped him with the lace and the pigtail and the fresh white ribbon, the white of neutrality being the paidhi-aiji's heraldry and sign of office. That was his choice for the meeting, a politic choice considering the color choice of the bus.

Then he walked out and down the hall toward the front door,

picking up Jago and Banichi along the way, along with four of the dowager's guard, for a little extra security. One of the dowager's men would drive, this trip—Banichi and Jago were, on his orders, taking it a little easy the last several days.

It was a wonderful bus, on the inside—new-smelling, modern, and clean, with very comfortable seats, its own lavatory, and a well-stocked galley. *Now* Bren finally got to enjoy it, and enjoy it he did, in a seat of atevi scale, plenty of room for a human, new upholstery, and deeply cushioned, responsive even to a human's lighter weight, and with a place for his feet. "No, nadiin-ji," he said, to the staff's offer of fruit juice. "I shall enjoy it with Lord Geigi when he arrives. Kindly serve it once he is aboard."

The bus had, besides the luxury of a galley, air conditioning and the very nice protection of windows that appeared black to the outside, even without using the pull-down shutters.

The engine positively purred with power.

And the front seats were arranged by opposing pairs, so that he and a guest, or, at least on the way out, Banichi and Jago, could sit facing one another. There were pull-out trays in the arm-rests, like those on a transcontinental jet. And footrests—the paidhi was particularly happy with that arrangement, usually having his feet dangling in atevi-scale transport. He settled back in utter comfort and watched the slightly shaded landscape go past in backwards order, while Banichi and Jago, similarly comfortable, and armed to the teeth, casually watched for trouble on the road ahead.

None developed. They crossed the tracks at the station and kept going on a reasonably maintained gravel road—thank Najida village for that convenience—which led to, one and a half fairly smooth kilometers from the train station, a small, flat-roofed building with a fueling station, a recently mowed grass strip, and a single windsock.

They parked and waited.

And in time, delayed a little, perhaps, by the soundproofing, one of Ilisidi's young men thought he heard a plane.

The driver opened the bus door for that young man to listen. Everyone else agreed they heard it.

Finally Bren did . . . by which time the sharp-eyed young men, gathered at those side windows, said they actually saw it coming. Atevi were just that much keener of hearing and sight—night-sight, in particular. The only area in which humans had the physical advantage was in spotting things when the sun was at its brightest.

In this case, the sound grew until, yes, the human heard it, too. And sure enough, what appeared in approach was a fair-sized plane, a twin prop, a model that served the smaller towns and the outlying islands, where short strips and high winds were the rule. It wasn't the sleekest of craft that came in, fat-bodied, with high-mounted wings and a blunt, broad nose, but it managed the single strip handily, even in the mild crosswind. Landing gear came down, and it touched down reasonably smoothly, then taxied about and maneuvered back toward the small building and their waiting bus.

The engine slowed to a lazy rotation of the props. The plane's door opened, lowering as a set of steps. Two of the dowager's men from the bus and two Guildsmen from inside the plane stepped out—numbers mattered in a situation, and what that read was not an infelicity of two on either side, but an implied felicity of three: they each represented someone protected by their immediate company.

Now it was for one more of them on the bus to create a new felicitous number.

He didn't need to say so. Jago got up and went out, down the steps, solo, felicitous seventh in the arrangement; and hers was a face and form that Lord Geigi's guard would recognize in an instant.

Lord Geigi was indeed the arriving party. His considerable

bulk immediately appeared in the doorway—which demanded a response.

Bren got up and went out himself, quicker on the short descent from the bus than Lord Geigi, who had further to go, and whose rotund shape needed a little caution on the narrow steps. Two more of Geigi's men came out. Banichi and one of the dowager's men followed Bren.

Beyond that, once lordly feet were on the ground, superstition went by the wayside, neither he nor Geigi doing more than observing the forms; and now numbers ceased to matter. Staff poured out on both sides in brisk application to business. Baggage compartments opened up on the plane and the bus. The truck, which had also pulled up behind the bus, started up and trundled closer to take its own share of whatever was not to go on the bus.

None of which activity was at all the lords' business. Bren walked forward and bowed, Geigi bowed, and then they bowed again, in lieu of hugging one another, which would have been the human response to the meeting.

Broad smiles, however, were definitely in common. They were old allies.

"Geigi-ji," Bren said. "One is delighted to offer transport."

"Bren-ji," Geigi said, "one is ever so pleased at such personal courtesy. One delights to see you well despite all the to-do I hear of."

"Will you come aboard, nandi, and accept the hospitality of my house tonight?"

"Gladly, nandi. Very gladly, my own house being, I understand, in some disarray. One also understands Najida has a relative of mine imposing on its patience, in consequence. One very earnestly apologizes for that necessity."

They had started walking toward the bus steps.

And Bren nodded acknowledgement of the courtesy. "One is gratified, however, to see Kajiminda safe in allied hands. The aiji's men have things there in good order, as I understand. But do postpone such stressful business, Geigi-ji, in favor of a pleasant ride and a leisurely reception and dinner under my roof. My staff will be delighted to make your visit an occasion in the household tonight and as long as you wish. And the aiji-dowager would never forgive me if I let you say no to it."

"One very much looks forward to Najida's hospitality," Geigi said, laboring up the bus steps. Then he paused to glance down at Bren. "And I will have somewhat to say to my nephew."

"At your convenience, " Bren agreed, and followed him up into relative security, behind darkened windows.

Were they not such close associates, two of Geigi's people— Geigi had four Guild bodyguards and four Edi-born domestics bustling about—would have gone up first to look the situation over . . . but only one of his black-clad Guildsmen joined them. Aboard the bus only the fourth of Ilisidi's men, the driver, and one of the Najida servants awaited them. Banichi and Jago were busy outside with the rest of the guard.

Such was the level of trust between them.

There were bangs and thumps from below as baggage went aboard. "Please take the seat opposite mine, nandi," Bren said, and: "Nadi—" This to the sole remaining staffer. "Refreshment for our guest, now, if you would be so kind. —What will you have, Geigi-ji? Fruit juice, tea, perhaps spirits at this hour?"

Lord Geigi named his drink, a local fruit juice impossible to obtain on the station, a choice which Bren had guessed; and the young servant in charge turned and looked questioningly in Bren's direction: the juice Geigi had chosen was alkaloid-laden, bad choice for a human. "Orange, if you please," Bren added, for his own order. "Thank you, nadi."

Lord Geigi, poised at his seat, meanwhile, looked admiringly about the new bus, floor to ceiling, and about the tinted windows and array of leather seats.

"Extraordinary. Very elegantly appointed, Bren-ji," Geigi said. He sat down and ran his fingers over the gray leather. Extended his foot rest. "It smells new. You have prospered, Bren-ji. None more deservingly."

Geigi was a man who appreciated his luxuries, wherever met.

"We are honored to have you as our first passenger. One regrets to say, the last bus, and Kajiminda's portico, jointly came to grief. One does need to tell you so, with great regret."

"Piffle. The matter of the portico—" Geigi waved a dismissive hand as Bren settled into the facing seat. "One is only glad you and your companion escaped unscathed, Bren-ji, and regrets to know your driver was not so fortunate."

So Geigi had gotten most of the details, likely directly from Tabini.

"The driver is recovering well, however."

"One rejoices to hear so." A sigh. "One hopes my Kajiminda has not suffered too many bullet holes. Ah, for my porcelains—and no staff to protect them. Damn my nephew."

"The house itself looked in fair order when I was inside, just before the incident, and one hopes the aiji's forces have operated with some finesse since. Kajiminda is a district treasure, and one is certain they will attempt to respect that."

"One wonders," Geigi said with a second sigh, "one wonders whether I am still fit to maintain it in my trust, Bren-ji."

Such a sad assessment, and no time to answer it, except to say: "One believes you are very fit, indeed, Geigi-ji. And the province so very desperately needs you right now." There was a final, louder thump as the baggage door shut, the essential luggage evidently now taken below. Directly after that, Banichi and Jago came back aboard and the rest of Geigi's bodyguard arrived behind them. Domestic staff arrived, too, filing to the rear, Geigi's servants with them, four men in clothing that had everything to do with the efficiency and economy of the space station, and nothing at all with the natural fibers one would buy in Najida village. It was a little breath of the filtered, synthesized and highly organized culture of the space station that had arrived with Lord Geigi—and how these four cousins would be received by the rustic Edi of the coast remained to be seen.

Geigi and his household were all sea-changed. The Guildsmen attending Geigi would have grown much more reliant on intercoms and were accustomed to computers monitoring everything that moved. And all this staff spoke a patois of station-speak and Ragi, words drifting past that Bren understood, and his aishid certainly understood, but most of the staff at Najida would not.

Too, unhappy thought, it had been a long time since Geigi's bodyguard or Geigi's servants had had to deal with any threat of assassination.

Geigi's household needed to adjust its attitudes and its reactions to local reality, and that lack of practice was worrisome. Geigi's personal bodyguard would catch up, fast, once back in a Guild environment. Their trained attentiveness would reassert itself under the influence of top-level Guild staff like the paidhi-aiji's and the aiji-dowager's guard. But the personal attendants—

There was an accident waiting to happen, from kitchens to front door.

The driver revved the engine softly and the bus gently began to move, backing and turning past the sole building of the airstrip, before it headed back down the road.

"Anything Najida can do to assist," Bren said for openers. "Indeed, Geigi-ji, anything the paidhi-aiji personally can do to assist in Kajiminda's recovery, one will be honored to do. And one absolutely insists, for a start, to repair the portico . . ."

"No such thing, Bren-ji! You were assaulted by a member of my household! Should you pay the damages, too?"

"One refuses to consider Baiji's failings in any way connected to my old associate, and one charitably hopes the attack was not even by Baiji's direct order. No, Geigi-ji, I blame my enemies and yours. So do please allow me to make that gesture of repairing the premises, to salve my memory of such a calamity."

"Your generosity is extreme, but, yes, it is welcome," Geigi said, "since you have local resources, and I have few. And one day, Bren-ji, I personally shall reciprocate such a favor . . . ."

"One hopes in no event more severe than wind and weather!" Bren said with a little laugh—then soberly: "And in one sense, Geigi-ji, and to give him due credit, your nephew prepaid the debt. He was instrumental in rescuing the aiji's son . . . ."

"For reasons one fears may be entirely dishonest," Geigi interjected glumly. "One has heard about the incident. One very much doubts his intentions, under the circumstances."

"Oh, I do give him at least credit for the attempt, Geigi-ji; and possibly for a little courage in doing so. One believes he even thought of making a run for Najida. But he was surely not alone on that boat. And it was possibly at some personal risk that he called me to tell me where the boy was. For that, for even the remote chance that was the case, I forgive him other things. But not all of them." The bus joined the road, and now nosed toward home.

"I rather fear the aim was to draw you into proximity," Geigi said. "I forgive him nothing." A small silence. "I should have had no illusions about him. I should have made the trip down to the world long before now."

"I fear you would have come to grief, Geigi-ji. One hates to say it, but the enemy had gotten their foothold in your house, even if they were not there in force. One is very glad you delayed a visit."

"I have the most terrible fears what my nephew may have done to the estate over the last year. My collections. My antiques. The boy's earliest request of me was for money, when the phones first worked again. When I heard my sister had died and learned *he* was in charge, I was shocked. I gave him latitude, however. I drew money from Shejidan to supply him, fool I!"

"Likely some of it did go to the estate. Surely it did."

"I trusted my staff was still in place, to report any untoward actions. And now I suspect they were justifiably out of sorts with me for leaving them. I had left them to bad management. They left without advising me. Kajiminda was deserted to its enemies with, as I gather, absolutely no warning."

"Alas," Bren said. "One understands your distress. But one does not see it as a mark of disregard by the Edi folk, rather of their confusion in our situation. Many people were still in fear, even after the aiji came back to Shejidan. Many people, to tell the truth, are still in some fear that the trouble has gone underground, and may still come back."

"Did you see none of my old staff at Kajiminda, Bren-ji? Not a one?"

"None that I clearly recognized: in truth, I think they all went, and fairly recently. I did not succeed in getting plain answers from the Grandmother of Najida on what happened, or why, but one surmises they found themselves suddenly up against Guild, Geigi-ji, and I believe that answers a great deal. There was a new bodyguard arrived, the same people I blame for the attack on me and my staff. I think your Edi staff realized who these new people were, they did not trust the house phones, they feared Marid agents; and they ran, advising no one—possibly not even the people of Najida, possibly fearing to draw trouble down on them—or I truly think my own staff would have been certain enough of danger to warn me off, and they did not do that, Geigi-ji. You were not the only one to be caught by surprise. I was. I was, and the aiji-dowager was."

"One is shocked by that!'

"I have had time to consider it. I do not think badly of the Edi, or of my staff. I think the desertion of the last staff from Kajiminda happened as I said, very recently, even days ago, without notice to Najida, and one only hopes they all made it out alive."

"I have brought four of my house staff with me. They may

extract some answers locally. I must say, this is such dismal news, Bren-ji. And Najida village cannot inform you? This is very grim."

"Grim, indeed," Bren said, "and I do urge you tell your people to use greatest caution in searching about the district after answers. Sarini Province is not safe. When I say we need you—we do most urgently need you, and your local connections, *and* authority. Your staff must trust no one, not even other Edi, until the whereabouts of former staff *have* been entirely explained. One does not believe the Marid could suborn Edi to turn against their own—but threats against family are hard to resist. Or local Edi might well be trying to deal with the threat without my knowing—which would bring the Guild into things the Edi may not want known. They have had their own operations during the Troubles, up and down the coast and including the Gan people. One hardly knows what touchy situations one might stumble into, or where covert things lie buried."

"One follows your reasoning, Bren-ji. Unhappily, one does, and we *have* had such a discussion among us, my staff and I. My staff insists none of their people could be traitors, even under the greatest threat. But they still have deep concerns, and know where to inquire, or hope they do." Geigi heaved a deep sigh. "Such a world. Such a world." And another sigh. "I must ask— such a petty question, among such large considerations: but my orchard. I was so fond of it. How did it fare in all this? Did you notice at all?"

"I glanced that direction, and saw the trees through the gate, apparently well, though this early in the season, my eye cannot readily tell. This I did observe: the estate roads were not at all kept up. The outlying walls could certainly do with painting. Details—again, I have no idea, Geigi-ji. I noticed no sign of damage there, but I was paying most attention to the oddness of your nephew's behavior."

"Understandably so. The wretch!"

"One hoped to do a favor for my old ally and neighbor and solve a local problem discreetly. I very little thought it would come to this." He shook his head. "I have had time to think about it, and I suspect, do you know, that my staff was hinting hard, believing, possibly, that my arrival had something to do with the local problem, that the aiji was investigating, through me, and that *I* was being reticent with them. I took the aiji's son with me—that had them convinced, I fear, that I was up to something, in light of other covert operations, as Tabini-aiji's return has restructured the north coast. So they were *not* involving themselves, not when they thought it was a clandestine move. They expected trouble from it, and perhaps expected Guild to sweep down from the heavens. That old mistrust between Ragi and Edi, Geigi-ji. You understand that better than I do. Am I amiss in my speculation?"

"One would concur, if they thought it was Guild business. That would be their great fear, that with the disappearance of Edi staff, they might be suspected of wrongdoing, and *their* doings would be questioned and investigated . . . some of which one admits may not be quite—legal. And, to be fair, by all past history, the Ragi presence would turn everything on its head, then quit the province and go back to the capital—leaving them prey to Marid retaliation."

"The aiji-dowager herself arrived, and I persisted with my plans to visit Kajiminda. I surely confused them."

"One thing you can rely on," Geigi said. "Even if they trust your intentions, and even if they highly regard certain Guild members, the Edi people will not trust the Guild. In this district, in past administrations, the Guild's operations have been the Guild's operations, beyond even the power of the aiji to steer them. And the history between the Guild and the Edi is grim. I did discuss it with the aiji: he says freely that his intelligence failed you. And failed the dowager, too. He greatly regrets it. My nephew declined to go to court this fall. My nephew told *me*, when I heard and reproached him for it, that he thought he had no authority to represent me, the damned little slink. And Marid spies were doubtless into the house by then."

"I surmise," Bren said quietly, "that he truly deluded himself that he still ran things. And as we entered the house, and the Guild who had become his bodyguard suddenly maneuvered to take us out, they suddenly broke all pretense of taking his orders, and began to behave differently. At that point he wanted rescue. I do believe that."

"Ha!" Geigi said. "You are too generous. He wanted to keep himself safe!"

"That certainly was in it. He brought us into the sitting room. My staff had an increasingly uneasy feeling and at their signal I got up to leave. He was increasingly distraught, and followed us to the door." A sigh, and the unpleasant truth. "He declined my suggestion to order his own car and follow us: that was just. They would have held him from it. He wanted to go with us, he said. And I declined that, because the heir was with us. In that regard, I fear I put him in a terrible position. And when we left, under fire, Banichi threw him onto our bus and restrained him."

"Baji-naji," Geigi said. "My sister was a good woman . . . industrious and sensible in all respects, except her doting on that vicious, *stupid* boy. He may have asked you for rescue, Bren-ji, but he had had chances before that, and I think it was fear of discovery of all his little connivances that prevented him appealing to Shejidan. I think it was greed for more that drove him closer and closer to the situation in which you discovered him. I have the notion all sorts of things will come to light, not least of them financial. He had not thought it through—he saw his misdeeds called into question, if you or the aiji-dowager got onto the case. He feared the Marid. He was, perhaps, about to double-deal them, fearing the aiji would come down on him. But they would kill him in a moment to keep quiet what he knew. And if he has a brain, he knows that now. If they had killed you—he would have turned coat again and continued dealing with them until the next crisis. If *they* have a brain among them, they *know* he swings to every wind!"

Refreshment fortunately arrived at that moment. It arrived nicely served on a tray, in fine glasses. And one did not continue a deep discussion, least of all a heated one, past the arrival of any service or the attendance of staff. Geigi heaved a sigh, took the generous glass, and calmed himself with several deep breaths. Bren took his, and quieted his nerves.

"Fresh juice," Geigi murmured reverently, and lifted his glass and took a very small sip. His eyes shut. "Bliss. Ah, Bren-ji. This is purest liquid bliss. So good. One had forgotten how good."

Juice reached the station only in frozen concentrate, and not even that, in the priorities of shipment since the coup. It was a traditional welcome in the capital, this early in the day: One had anticipated it would be a treat, and Geigi savored it with a delicate sip and closed his eyes for two sips, and three.

"Ah," he said. "Ah, Bren-ji. Now I am home."

"Have you anything else coming in by rail, Geigi-ji?" Bren asked; the road was passing near the train station.

"No," Geigi said. "Only what we carry. One hesitated to make extravagant demands on the shuttle, coming down, no matter the aiji's kind indulgence." A deep sigh. "This may not have been a wise decision, to rely on Kajiminda's resources—if my fool nephew has plundered the place."

"Najida stands ready to assist in whatever resupply Kajiminda may lack," Bren said. "We shall send linens over, food, everything."

"You are beyond generous. I thank you, I profoundly thank you." A moment of silence then, and afterward, a refill on the juice. That glass went down. And: "One can bear it, Bren-ji, now that one is fortified. *Tell* me now. You have told me the exonerating moment. Tell me the very worst you suspect of my nephew. The imagination of Baiji's misdeeds has quite depressed my appetite. Financial damage. One is certain of it. Harm to my staff. Can there be worse?"

Gentle, plump Geigi had a temper, and a hot one when it finally stirred. And it was very grim, indeed, what he himself suspected. But Geigi asked. One could not lie to him. And delivering the truth, before Geigi could hit the house uninformed, was why he had undertaken this trip out to meet Geigi.

"I do fear worse," he said.

"Say it," Geigi said.

"One suspects, Geigi-ji, one suspects—not, indeed, of Baiji, but certainly of his allies—your sister's decline in health—"

"Gods unfortunate! I knew it!"

"Forgive me, Geigi-ji. This is only my surmise."

"No, go on, go on, Bren-ji! I want to hear this! I want to hear it all!"

"Her death was too opportune for the Marid. Your sister was astute in most matters. Not so your nephew. *That* may have drawn them in."

Geigi heaved a mournful sigh, shaking his head. "She was not in good health. One had not thought. And that boy, that unspeakable boy—"

"Forgive me, nandi, but I rather blame his gullibility."

"Gullibility and greed together. His mother, in my last calls to her, and hers to me, had been allowing him certain duties, and she claimed he was fulfilling them with some promise. Now one suspects—gods, one suspects—she allowed him some management, and he brought a Marid Assassin under the roof! Murder, Bren-ji! His own mother! Gods above, one does not wish to believe that, even of him!"

"One does not believe he knew," Bren said. "I think that he was genuinely grieved at your sister's passing. And very much alone at that point. But he had associates to rush to him and console him and advise him . . . in those months when communications with the world were cut off."

During Murini's administration, when Tabini had been overthrown, and the shuttles had stopped flying, and communication with the space station had stopped.

"We were receiving intelligence relayed up from Mospheira," Geigi said, "but from the south coast, we had nothing in those days, nothing but reports of unrest and resistence action. He was claiming her post—he was all I had in place. I had no way to intervene."

"One so regrets it, Geigi-ji."

"And I so *worried* for that boy's sake! I sent him letters of advice and encouragement the moment the blackout ended. I actually sent him my understanding this winter when he missed the court session. He must have laughed at that."

"One thinks, rather, nandi-ji, he grew afraid, and perhaps had the wit to be afraid not only *of* you. Perhaps he grew afraid *for* you should you come down to the world and walk into the situation he had created. He fears you to this day. He fears you extremely. He is terrified at the dowager's apprehension of his crimes; but he is mortally terrified of you. So far as a human can possibly judge, he still does not understand the magnitude of what his allies have done, let alone what they still intend. Mostly, in his eyes, as I suspect—he would still find greater importance in the world by this marriage with the Marid girl. The status of that match would somehow make you respect him. The implication that these people may have assassinated his mother—I did tell him what I suspect—has hit him hard, if a human is any judge of that at all."

Geigi's eyes, deep set in, for an ateva, an extraordinarily plump face, were both quick and thoughtful. He pursed his lips and nodded. "You need not deprecate your perception of us, Bren-ji. The paidhi-aiji is *not* without skill in reading us. I can accept he is grieved: she doted on him, all but fed him from her plate as if he were three, and told him every move to make. She greatly exaggerated his accomplishments in her calls to me: I knew that, if nothing else. Now he is alone and unadvised. Consequences he thought he would never see are coming down on his head and his mother is not here to cover his sins. Miss her? Infelicitous gods, of course he misses her!"

A deep, deep breath. "What else do you read in him, paidhi-aiji?"

"That he has to this hour no real apprehension that the world has changed." He drew a deep breath. "For the Marid's help in seizing power, Murini did not reward Machigi of the Tasigin. Whatever Murini's failings, he was never that great a fool. Murini apparently told the Marid to keep their hands off the west coast—I have no proof, but suspect it—and the Marid decided to proceed in their usual way, by stealth, to get their way—they were already moving. Your sister was only their first target. They were plotting to take the whole west coast. I think they had been after that, even before they prompted Murini to seize Shejidan."

"Building a power base, by doubling the size of their lands, that would almost equal the central and northern clans combined. At that point—they would be as powerful as the aishidi'tat."

"Murini would not have been able to withstand them once they had that secure," Bren said, "and if they should succeed now, even with Tabini back in power—they would *still* pose an immense threat. *That* is what the aiji-dowager sees, I believe. Tabini-aiji will not quite admit it, but I think he has been playing the Marid, trying to figure what they are up to, where the next strike will come, and has seen every complicated possibility *except* the rural west coast. And the key to controlling the west coast is—"

"My clan's treaty with the Edi people."

"Exactly so. Murini's supporters—notably the Marid—did *not* attack my estate during the Troubles, when small coups had taken the mayoralties of little fishing villages clear up in the Isles. *That* is what I find most suspicious . . . two large estates, and no move from the Marid against the property of either of us, who were most notably their enemies. The Edi say it was because the Marid was afraid to start a war with them. I think differently. I think the Marid objective was always Kajiminda, for themselves, and they were going after it covertly, against Murini's orders. When Tabini retook the capital, the Marid suddenly took a very soft approach with Tabini-aiji, claiming they had a revised view of the world—but from what we see here, they kept right on going with their plan. They were going to marry their way into Kajiminda, your nephew was going to fall ill, the Marid wife would run things, and *then* the Marid, behaving ever so nicely in Shejidan, was going to claim Najida through the same inheritance connection with the Maladesi that won them my apartment in the city. Nobody in Shejidan thinks the rural coast is that important. The revenge on me, putting *me* on the losing side of Bujavid politics, would be particularly pleasant to them—but the fact is, they really do have that distant claim. It is at least arguable. The legislature might insist, to settle the peace for good and all. And there we would be, with the Marid quietly, one step at a time, taking over the west coast, never making a fuss, becoming so, so agreeable and always appearing to be working within the laws. I would be shifted over to some other property the aiji would give me to compensate, probably in another district, and *nobody* would be set up to handle the Edi's interests, except the newly reformed Marid, who are their worst enemies—and does the Ragi center of the country think that a problem? No. Tabini-aiji has had to rebuild the association brick by brick. *Every* little interest has some little claim they want addressed, out of the aiji's gratitude for their support, of course; but the aishidi'tat is a maze of conflicting claims—an absolute mess, in fact. The Farai claim on the Maladesi inheritance—my properties—is one of a hundred such. How can they be more suspect than any other, after all this upheaval?"

Geigi stared at him, thought it over, and finally heaved an angry sigh. "It makes sense. Gods less fortunate, it makes awful sense, Bren-ji. Have you told all this to the aiji?"

"*I* have not told the aiji, but my aishid and the dowager's have surely relayed our suspicions to the aiji's men." Information necessarily flowed through protected channels. One did not make pronouncements without proof behind the statement: one hinted, and it was the Guild that investigated such things. "And now you are here. We are so very glad, Geigi-ji."

"One begins to understand."

"Here is the concrete proof we have: my aishid has informed me, and the aiji now knows, that the Guild that had operated at Kajiminda were not Maschi. They were from the Marid. Second: there was an assassination in Separti Township. It was unattributed. Baiji claims to know it was Marid agents. The turning point of his understanding, so he said to me, was when he tried to put the first visitors off. He falsely claimed he had a verbal understanding with a young lady south of Separti—and that whole family was assassinated."

"Gods less fortunate!"

"Indeed. He claims he has constantly found other ways to stall them, claiming he was in mourning for his mother, claiming various things, but the Marid were insistent. You, on the station, were dropping relay stations from space during the Troubles. You were setting up a satellite network to threaten Murini's regime. You were bringing cell phone technology to Mospheira—it was quite clear that you were trying to encourage someone to take out Murini. So fearing that the tide might turn at any moment and possibly fearing the rumors that Tabini was not dead, the Marid accelerated their demands on your nephew and set up a base in the township before we returned from space. At a certain point, they were going to force that marriage, and your nephew, do him credit, was still stalling even after Tabini-aiji turned up alive. Was still stalling, even this late, when I came to visit. If he had had the courage, he could have gone out on the boat, sailed over to Najida and trusted *my* staff to get him safely to Shejidan. But he did not. I admit my affairs are complex—and confusing even to my staff, who did not know where I stood, but—"

"One is absolutely aghast and appalled, Bren-ji."

"The dowager has promised her support of a house and a lordship for the Edi—you do know that."

"The *dowager* has made this proposal?"

"One was certain the aiji would have told you."

"The aiji mentioned there was some local proposal sent up for such a move. I thought it was you!"

"It was the dowager's proposal and her idea from the beginning. I had no idea she would do it."

"Well, well. I am not, myself, opposed to it." Geigi's face grew sad, the offering of true feelings between old associates, as he dropped any pretense of impassivity. "I have my household on the station. There is my best service to the aishidi'tat, for now and in the foreseeable future. They cannot do without me up there, Bren-ji. Perhaps I *should* cede Kajiminda to the Edi. They would treat it well. Certainly better than my nephew has done. Those things that are Maschi treasures—let them go back to the clan estate at Targai."

"Wait on that," Bren said. "Wait, to be sure of your feelings in the matter, honored neighbor; and if I must plead the aiji's case—preserve the aishidi'tat's options by holding the treaty as it stands. The relationship between your Maschi clan and the Edi is a great asset in the aishidi'tat. That Kajiminda remain in Maschi hands—is part of that treaty. Building an Edi house, however—this would be my suggestion . . . supposing, of course, that the aiji does grant this lordship. And I do think he will."

"The firestorm in the legislature can only be imagined," Geigi said with a great sigh, and that was the truth. "The inland lords will certainly oppose it. Ragi clan itself will have apoplexies. The Marid—"

"Indeed, the Marid."

Geigi's eyes had widened. "They will bolt from the Association. They will declare war. Is this 'Sidi-ji's desire?"

"It is certainly the likelihood. Things *will* change when this becomes public. The relationship the Marid has to the aishidi'tat has given us several wars and a coup, and in my opinion, things *must* change, so that we have no future coup. Perhaps I am too reckless. But the dowager supports this notion, and I am with her on this matter. See what you have walked into, Geigi-ji."

"Bold. Bold, to say the least."

"Should you wish to return to the capital—"

"By no means! I wish to be part of this!"

"We will weather the storm," Bren said. "This region will weather it, and the aishidi'tat will emerge from this, one hopes, with the addition of an ally it can truly trust—the Edi *and* the Gan peoples—rather than the South, which has attempted to break up the Association from its outset. So if the five clans of the Marid bolt from the Association, good riddance. That is my view, and the dowager's, I am convinced. Your support in this matter would speak with a definitive voice—and I personally, would be very much relieved. I value your good opinion, and your judgement, and *this* is why I have come out to meet you here, and not in Najida, and to have this talk with you: to tell you what has gone on, and what is being arranged, personally to beg your help—and to give you the opportunity to catch the train back to Shejidan without setting foot in Najida under these circumstances, should that be your choice."

Geigi looked at him with a directness and emotion rare in his class *and* his kind. "One will never forget this gesture, Bren-ji. One will not forget this extraordinary respect."

"To a greatly valued associate, in a relationship which has stood many, many tests, Geigi-ji. I have the utmost trust in your wisdom and your honesty. Our mutual connections to the aiji and to the aiji-dowager can do a great deal to stabilize this district—at a time when, we both know, in events in the heavens, stability of the aishidi'tat is absolutely critical."

"There was a time you had great reason to distrust Kajiminda; and there was a time *I* had a Marid wife, and there was a time when I myself trod the outskirts of the aiji's good will. And yet you have consistently trusted me, Bren-ji. You bewilder me."

"I have trusted you despite those things. And still do, Geigi-ji." He added, in Mosphei', which they had not used: "Humans are crazy like that."

"Crazy," Geigi echoed him, "means so many things. Now I am an aging lord, with my estate in disarray. *Why* have you trusted me? You cannot think favors buy favor when clan is involved. You know us far better than that, and you are above all no fool, Bren-ji."

He smiled. "A few months ago some would have called me a fool to stand by Tabini-aiji. The odds were everywhere against him. I have this most irrational pleasure in your company and this perfectly rational trust in your judgement. You could have declared yourself aiji, in the heavens. And yet you did not, did you, Geigi-ji?"

"I love my comforts too much to be aiji. It is a *very* uncomfortable office."

"You see? You saved the whole aishidi'tat, Geigi-ji. Had Tabini actually been lost—you would have held fast. And that proposition has no doubt."

"Ha! If I had been put to it, I would have found an aiji and named him."

"And the world, I have every confidence, would have listened. Your power is inconvenienced, but not at all in ruins. You are held in greatest respect, not alone among atevi."

"You are very generous, Bren-ji."

"I am accurate. Why do you suppose the aiji-dowager favors you?"

"Ha!" Geigi laughed outright. "What was between me and 'Sidi-ji certainly does not apply in your case, Bren-ji."

"Then say we both favor her, and we both know that if we were irrelevant she would not bother with us, and if either one of us merited her disapproval, neither of us would breathe the air. *She* is our ultimate judge, Geigi-ji!"

A laugh, silent, and thoughtful. "'Sidi-ji. Yes." A flicker of the eyes. "There is 'Sidi-ji. If she does not yet call me a fool, then I suppose I may indeed weather this."

"You shall. One insists on it!"

"She came. With the young lord."

"The young lord came to visit me. *She* came to see to him. Likewise my brother and his lady, who were visiting when this whole untoward situation presented itself."

"Shall I see them all, then? I have longed to meet your brother!"

"My brother and Barb-daja will come up to dinner, very likely, which I assure you will be extravagant in your honor. One has given those orders." He had, in fact, ordered every local delicacy Geigi would have missed all these years. "The actual accommodations I fear are cramped: Najida is a small estate, and my bodyguard now lodges in the library, and my brother and his lady stay on their boat in the harbor."

"One trusts my nephew is by no means honored with a suite, under such circumstances!"

"Nandi, we have lodged him in a servant's room in the basement, where there are no windows."

"Good!" Geigi said, taking a sip of the new drink that had turned up under his hand. "I shall be extremely grateful to stay under your roof tonight, Bren-ji, myself and my staff. We may have no little work to do at Kajiminda, but I am indeed feeling fortified, hearing how things are taken care of."

"One delights to hear it."

"The young lord, whom I saw so briefly last year—the boy must be approaching his fortunate birthday."

"In two months," Bren said. Nine, following the unnameable eighth, was a very felicitous birthday, and at times they had despaired of Cajeiri ever reaching that happy year. "He has grown in very many ways, Geigi-ji, even in the months since you saw him. He has lately become quite the young gentleman, with encouraging signs of keen judgement."

5

It would have been far, far more fun to be on the new bus looking out the windows and trying out all the interesting features.

But Great-grandmother had nipped that notion before Cajeiri had even laid his plans.

"Nand' Bren will deal better with his neighbor without a distraction present. They have distressing matters to discuss." Great-grandmother meant about Baiji-nadi being locked in the basement and them being shot at and almost killed. He could tell nand' Geigi a thing or two about *that,* first-hand.

But probably that would be pert. That was his great-grandmother's word for it, when he got beyond himself.

So his information was not welcome on the bus.

And there was *nothing* to do, at present, since they were all locked in the house, nothing that was really interesting, because he could not draw back the slingshota to its full stretch, not without risking ricochets that would hit nand' Bren's woodwork, which had already had enough damage from bullets.

So he grew bored with that, and even when he gave turns with the slingshota to his bodyguard, his aishid—they could get no real practice at it in such limited circumstances.

They all wanted to go out into the garden, where they could really let fly—but the doors were kept locked, even when there were village workmen repairing the portico out there (one could hear the hammering all morning.)

He so wanted to be on the bus. But he was forbidden even to meet the bus when it came back. Great-grandmother had thought of that, too, and had forbidden him before he could even think of it. "These two lords have serious business under-way, almost certainly. You are not to meet the bus when it ar-rives. Dignitaries from the village will be arriving to meet Lord Geigi when he gets here and, mind, you are *not* to enter into an indecorous competition for attention on Lord Bren's doorstep, young gentleman. You will make yourself politely invisible and do your homework."

Gruesome. His current homework was court language verbs. Which was not too exciting.

But his father's visit loomed large in recent memory and it was clear to him he was very lucky to be left here in nand' Bren's house, instead of being packed back to Shejidan and his tutor. Sitting in his father's apartment while his Ajuri clan aunt was visiting and while his Atageini clan great-uncle was living just down the hall—that would be awful. Not to mention that his mother would be upset with him for the mischief he had been in, and if his Ajuri grandfather heard about the train and the boat, through his aunt, he would have his *grandfather* fuss-ing about his supervision and demanding more guards, too, pos-sibly even demanding to install some of *Ajuri* clan with him, which was just too grim to think about. Even if he thought he and his aishid could get the better of anybody Ajuri clan had, it was just too many guards, and more guards just got harder and harder to deal with.

He understood his situation. He understood the threat hang-ing over him. He had to behave here, and learn his court verbs beyond any mistake, or he would be back in the Bujavid with grown-up guards at every corner.

So after a little while he grew entirely bored with the sling-shota and the circumstances they had, and took his aishid back to their suite to think about what they *could* do in the house. Lucasi and Veijico being still new to his service, they were getting used to things, though they really *were* Guild, unlike Antaro and Jegari. They were brother and sister like Antaro and Jegari, and everybody older said they were very good . . . but.

There was always that *but* . . . with Lucasi and Veijico.

The *but* that did not let them find out everything they wanted to from senior Guild.

But . . . that made Cenedi look grim when he talked about them.

But . . . that made Banichi and Jago sigh and talk together in very low voices.

If Lucasi and Veijico had been younger (they were felicitous nineteen and the year after) people would probably call them what they called him: precocious—which was a way of admiring somebody while calling him a pest. Precocious. Pert. Sometimes, even toward him, they were stuck-up; and they were far too inclined to tell Antaro and Jegari they were wrong about something, even about how they sat and how they stood at attention, even when Antaro and Jegari were not allowed to wear a Guild uniform yet. It was just a pest, their know-it-all manner, and it made him mad, but Antaro said, with a sigh, when he mentioned it: "We need to learn, nandi."

It really was true: having two real Guild in his aishid meant Jegari and Antaro were learning things around the clock now, not just going out for a few hours to the Guild hall. Even he could see a change in how they stood and just the way their eyes tracked—which was probably really good. Jegari and Antaro seemed glad to talk about Guild stuff with Lucasi and Veijico, even if the newcomers *were* snotty about it—snotty was one of Gene's words, up on the ship, or the space station, now, where Gene lived; and it was a good word for those two. Snotty.

And full of themselves. That was another of Gene's expressions.

The fact was, though, they were *smart*, they knew they were smart, and they were short of patience with other people, which was going to get them in trouble if they were not just very careful. He was just a year short of nine and *he* could see it on the horizon . . . but not Veijico and Lucasi, oh, no, they were far too smart to take personal criticism from somebody who was infelicitous eight.

Well, *he* knew they were not smarter than Banichi and Jago and Cenedi, or Tano and Algini—and Cenedi and Algini in particular had no long patience with fools. Algini had been very high up in the Guild before he sort of retired from that job, and one could just see Algini's eyes looking right at Lucasi's back in a not-very-good way.

"We did not authorize them to ask!" he had almost blurted out on one occasion, when those two had repeated a request to which Banichi had said no. He had witnessed that second request, and Algini had looked mad. But they were his aishid, and he was responsible for anything they did, so he had only said, later, "You made Algini mad, nadiin-ji."

"We report to your father, nandi," Veijico had said quite smoothly and with a shrug. "Not to them."

"You will not disrespect them!" he had shot back, very sharply, and that had backed them up just a bit. "And if you do it again, nadiin, *I* shall report to my father!"

That had set them back for at least an hour.

The thing was, there was a fairly fine dividing line between precocious and *fool* . . . he knew that better than most, having crossed that line a few times and having had to hear Great-grandmother tell him where that line was in great detail, interspersed with: "Tell *me* where you made mistakes, boy. Go think!"

Maybe the Guild instructors had told Lucasi and Veijico that exact same thing a few times, too, but Lucasi and Veijico were never going to listen to Guild instructors the way he knew to listen to Great-grandmother—who had used to thump him on the same ear so often he swore it was larger than the other. Great-grandmother probably still made his *father* think of ear-thumping: she was that fierce.

But clearly the Guild instructors had not set the proper fear in Lucasi and Veijico, and by the way they carried themselves, maybe they had lacked a great-grandmother, up in the high mountains, where they came from.

Maybe, he thought, he should maneuver those two afoul of his great-grandmother and sit back and watch the outcome. That would be interesting. But he was not sure he would ever get them back if they did. So he kept that in reserve.

And thus far he was managing things. At least today Lucasi and Veijico seemed to be showing a little improvement, and being much more polite to everybody all morning. So maybe his threat yesterday had worked. He hated being mad at people. It was like the business with the slingshota. *They* were so sure they would never miss that they thought they could shoot it in the garden hall, never mind the woodwork. Never mind Ramaso would scold them all and *he* would get in trouble for it.

And never mind Lucasi had stolen five teacakes from the kitchen this morning, when they had no need to steal at all: Lucasi had rather steal because, he said, it kept him sharp—never mind that some servant might get in trouble for the miscount. It was not Lucasi's habit, to think of things like that. Great-grandmother would thwack his ear for not thinking about it—if she knew it. But tattling to her was hardly grown-up.

He had a dilemma, was what. He had to make Lucasi and Veijico care.

More, he had to make Lucasi and Veijico care what *he* thought.

His father was very clever. His father was a great strategist and absolutely ruthless, which was what his father's enemies said, even though his father was really good to people who deserved his good opinion. His father was so smooth that sometimes people had trouble telling which he was being at the moment—ruthless, or good.

He had thought, a few days ago, that his father had given him two very good guards, despite the suddenness of the surprise; and they were real Guild, and young, and he was going to like them just the way they were and everything was going to be splendid.

Not so easy.

It was like dealing with Great-grandmother. About the time one thought one had her figured out, Great-grandmother proved to be a few moves ahead. Dealing with his father was like that, more than anybody else he had ever met, and he thought about it, sitting in his little sitting-room at his desk, parsing his verbs, and watching Jegari and Antaro over in the corner with Lucasi and Veijico. Jegari and Antaro were listening, all respectful, to something Lucasi and Veijico were telling them—and he thought—

I was stupid when I thought I could ever bring somebody that smart in that fast. I was too nice.

These two are not easy to manage and they come with no ties to me the way Jegari and Antaro have. These two cheat. They lie. They sneak. And that would be all right, except—they disrespect *me*. They annoy *me*. One has to be smarter than they are to make them behave themselves, there is *no* kinship between us, and the fight has to go on all the time—because their man'chi is *not* to me nor to anybody in the whole midlands— maybe not to anybody up in their mountains, who knows?

It *would* be easier if I were older. If I could impress them—I could get their man'chi. But they left home to join the Guild. So one supposes man'chi is no longer there. And right now they belong to nobody except maybe the Guild. They say they report to my father, but I doubt they really feel man'chi toward him, or the Guild, or anybody in the world, even their own clan, which is small—too small for *their* ambitions. One can see that. They have probably always had trouble.

Which was not to say they were bad. Or wrong.

They were just going to be *work*. A *lot* of work. Running them, he would need to be sharp all the time, or he could never trust those two to do what he said—until he got old enough and powerful enough to get their attention. His father probably thought if they were going to make a mistake they would make it so senior Guild saw it and fixed it, but that was not necessarily so. They were sneaky. And everybody in this house was busy. And there was something his father might not have seen: these two were upset, and maybe they thought they were being disrespected in being given to a child, even a child who was the aiji's son and heir. They happened to be wrong to think that—he bet his father bet that he would duck out on them and give *them* trouble the way he had always done.

But that kind of behavior was for guards that people set *over* his aishid. Part *of* his aishid—that was something else, and it had stopped being fun, was what, because inside an aishid—there had to be trust. There had to be man'chi holding the whole thing together. And that was what he was *not* able to get out of these two.

He had escaped his tutor, escaped his lessons in the capital, and come out here to go on nand' Bren's boat and go fishing with Jegari and Antaro. Life was going to be easy and good and constant fun.

Now they had been shot at, the windows were all boarded up, both the boats were out of commission with repairs, and his father had sent him a gift to protect him, as if he was that same boy who had ducked out of the Bujavid to get away from that old fool of a tutor?

Hell, nand' Bren would say. Bloody hell.

And he could call those two over right now and tell them exactly what he was thinking, but they were too self-assured to take any shame of it.

And his father might *think* those two were naturally in awe of the aiji of the whole aishidi'tat, and that they would follow his orders, if nobody else's . . . but they were, in fact, just too smart to be impressed. They would absorb any warning the aiji's son gave them and come out of it just the way he would, thinking he still could get the better of the situation and run things the way he wanted. They were more than twice his age and they had had a long time to get into bad habits. And they had every fault Great-grandmother said he had.

Which made him mad, because it meant maybe his father saw the same thing—

Was it possible? Would his father do that to him?

Things he was involved in were serious. Lucasi and Veijico thought they knew how serious and just how much they could get away with.

But he was Great-grandmother's student, and nand' Bren's, and Banichi's and Cenedi's and Jago's, and he was not going to be found at fault for their misbehaviors.

They *thought* they had his father figured, and they could just run things in his household until *he* grew up, and that they could get past Jegari and Antaro and be senior. On a second and third thought, probably everything had been fine with them until they had found out he was going to prefer two Guild trainees to *them*, and then they had gotten their backs up—gods, they *might* even have the notion of getting *rid* of Jegari and Antaro, if they were really ruthless.

And they were real Guild, and had no orders about that . . . and no scruples.

That was a terrible, terrible thought.

He hadn't thought it when, of course, he had told them how the household was to be ordered.

He had told them that back when he had made assumptions they would automatically have man'chi to him . . .

It was just not good, when he thought about things from the side of two very ruthless, very determined, almost-adult Guild.

Algini, who let very little slip, had given him a direct warning: *They are not all good.*

When Banichi and Jago and Cenedi had all been with him in deep space, Algini and Tano were the ones who had stayed on the space station. Algini in particular had helped reconstitute the Assassins' Guild after the coup.

So Algini's letting slip that one small expression was no casual remark. It was a very purposeful warning. Had he been asleep? He did not think Algini ever was.

So *he* had to get control of his own aishid, fast, before somebody got hurt. He had given orders maybe his elders would not advise, and he had either to give up control of his own household to them—or get these two to change their ways.

Gods, mark it down to remember: annoy his father the way he had done and his father was eventually to reckon with. Had his father *known* what might happen? Did he still predict it?

Did his father *care* whether his son and heir could rely on his own household—when a mistake could get people killed?

His mother and father were having another baby, a *safe* baby they would bring up themselves, and who would not have been off in space with Great-grandmother and nand' Bren, that was what. Succeed or not. Obey or not. Rule or not. Make these two obey—or not. There *will be* an alternative to you.

Damn it!

Lucasi and Veijico were *homework*, was what. They were capable of becoming a real major problem.

And he could solve it one way by asking Great-grandmother to take them away and put them in *her* guard. She would make an impression on them, and she was almost the only person who could—because Guild who had served high up in the aiji's house could only go to a related aishid; or they had *nowhere* to go. And in the Guild—that could be fatal. Were Lucasi and Veijico thinking about *that* at all when they acted so snotty with Antaro and Jegari?

Or with him?

He *could* go to Great-grandmother, and she would assign them tower duty in Malguri, which was about as far from talking to anybody as you could get . . . for the rest of their lives.

If they were as smart as they thought they were, they would

be afraid of that eventuality. They would have figured out that if this assignment went bad, they would know too many house secrets to be let loose into someone else's employ.

So Lucasi and Veijico were in a bit of a trap, whether or not they figured it out. He was ahead of them in that.

And he was not ready quite yet to go to his Great-grandmother, but he had thought out his alternatives. He scowled at them, thinking this, and they noticed, and pretended not to, and then he smiled at them with his father's nastiest smile. They would ask each other, later, "What was that look about?" and they would probably not come up with the right answer.

Which proved that they were not quite as smart as they thought they were.

He had to impress them and get them to *take* orders from Antaro and Jegari. That was the first thing on the menu. And he could *not* sit around playing with the slingshota and being told that he could *not* meet the bus and could *not* find out what the important business was between nand' Bren and Lord Geigi. He had a rival. His father had warned him about that. And maybe his father had even thought he would go on playing games while things were happening that were serious, even after being warned. Maybe his parents had decided he was stupid.

He was not Baiji. Maybe if he were, having Lucasi and Veijico around would not matter at all and he could just sit back and let them run his life.

But he was *not* Baiji. And his father regarded him enough to challenge him, really challenge him. That was an encouraging idea.

So he got up, he had Jegari go get his better shirt and best coat, and Antaro help him with his pigtail and ribbon, to look absolutely his best.

He was, first of all, going to go call on Great-grandmother, because he was sure Lord Geigi and Lord Bren would both be talking to Great-grandmother among the very first things they did, and if he were there when they came back, and in very good graces because he showed up looking like a gentleman, he might be able to stay with Great-grandmother once the bus arrived. And it *should* be coming soon. The airport was about a quarter of an hour past the train station: he had heard staff say that.

And he would have Jegari and Antaro for a presence inside mani's suite so *they* would get the information first-hand. Even better, all the information Lucasi and Veijico could get would have to be second-hand, from them. Which served them exactly right.

So when he had dressed, he found a moment to pass close to them, and said:

"You should stay here, or in the library with Tano and Algini, if they permit. What Lord Geigi says when he gets here will be important. And his presence here will upset the Marid. So possibly they will attack us again. But attacking my great-grandmother is not a good idea. So learn from what you hear."

"Nandi," Lucasi said, with a little bow of his head. They looked just a little put off—maybe because they had not had outstanding success getting to sit in the security station with Tano and Algini.

Too bad for them.

He left his apartment, then, and went just next door, to Great-grandmother's suite, and knocked. Nawari opened the door. That was good. Cenedi was there, behind him. And that was not.

He bowed. "Is mani receiving, nadi-ji?" he asked, in best form.

"Perhaps soon, young sir," Nawari said.

He had made his move little early then. Damn. Very damn.

But then Cenedi said, with unexpected generosity: "You might come in and wait in the sitting room, should you wish, young lord. Is there some particular business?"

It was the immaculate clothes and proper form. It had to be. He straightened his shoulders.

"Nothing in particular," he said to Cenedi. "One came to be

very quiet, and to learn. We are not to meet the bus and we are not to interfere with nand' Bren and nand' Geigi. But surely we can be very quiet and listen."

Cenedi looked him up and down, looked at Antaro and Jegari—and showed him right in.

Maybe it was the fact Lucasi and Veijico were *not* with them. Was *that* not a thought?

He set himself in the lesser chair by the fireplace, and Jegari and Antaro properly positioned themselves, standing, along the wall.

So! They were *in*. And he would be particularly on his best behavior when Great-grandmother laid eyes on him— absolutely proper. Great-grandmother would be sure, just the same as Cenedi and Nawari, that he was bursting with curiosity, and that sometimes annoyed her. But that was not all that it was. He had very serious matters to deal with, himself, and no one had figured that out and told him what to do.

Or had he figured out Great-grandmother's riddle? He was not supposed to meet the bus. He was not supposed to be outside.

But he was admitted *here*, in his proper best clothes, to hear things the lords said.

Just getting here had been—his father's lately favorite word— educational.

6

The bus pulled up under the portico and made a quiet stop—its soft, powerful sigh very much more impressive than their thirty-year-old estate bus, which had always come in gasping and squealing. And the staff did Najida proud: they turned out in their party best to welcome Najida's long-absent neighbor.

But not just staff had come in, Bren saw as he descended, with Banichi and Jago, and with Geigi's two senior guards. Clearly defying the risks of travel in the district, a whole truckload of festively dressed Edi people had arrived up from the village, all resplendent in their bright colors, pouring in to wonder at the bus *and* to welcome Lord Geigi, who was their lord and long-time protector. In Edi eyes, things were surely looking up, and power lately had descended on Najida—in the form of the aiji's visit, the aiji-dowager's residence, the local victory over the Marid intruders, the fall of the detested Baiji, and now the return of the Lord of Sarini Province from orbit. Geigi descended the steps to a great deal of applause.

Geigi looked about him, at that, and indeed, despite the grey hairs, not much changed from the Geigi who had left all those years ago. Geigi's two-man guard had moved in to be close to him: that was of course as it should be.

But one absence was remarkable.

Cajeiri was not outside to meet them. *That* was downright worrisome.

"One does not see the young gentleman, nadiin-ji," he remarked to Banichi and Jago, while waving to the assembled onlookers and smiling.

"The young gentleman has set up to be with his great-grandmother," Jago said—his aishid was in contact with each other short-range, information likely pouring back and forth. "He has assigned his two new guards to be with Tano and Algini. Antaro and Jegari are with him."

"Well," Bren said in some surprise. The young gentleman declined a noisy, exciting event in order to be strategically positioned and in on everything important. *There* was a little advanced thinking, when the boy of not too many months ago had achieved strategic thinking only in his lulls between motion.

"Indeed," Jago said dryly, clearly in the same train of thought.

Ramaso stood to the fore of the staff, and Geigi made clear to him he would say a few words. Ramaso held up his hands, and a silence descended on the happy gathering, starting with house staff and extending to the visiting Edi.

"My welcome here at Najida," Geigi said, looking about him, "is a great comfort to the distress of Kajiminda. So many things remain to be done, but with the help of good neighbors I shall do them in short order. I have heard the aiji-dowager's proposal and shall be hearing more details. I shall be sending to Maschi clan and consulting with them, with the aiji-dowager, with my neighbors, and certainly with the people of Kajiminda, a meeting one most earnestly desires at the earliest. One hopes to meet with the Grandmother of Najida: one hopes to do that tomorrow, if at all possible. Only bear with me today: I have had a long journey, however rapid, and I am still catching my breath. But tomorrow I shall get down to business, with the kindness of my neighbors. One hopes to do the best possible for Kajiminda and to restore the good relationships Kajiminda has always enjoyed with Najida. Thank you very much for your welcome. One thanks you with all depth of feeling."

He gave a little bow to the crowd, and Bren bowed in gratitude, too, before he directed Geigi inside, into the quiet and shadow of the inner halls.

"Be welcome," he said, the formula. "Geigi-ji."

"One is dazed, Bren-ji, simply dazed. One thinks of things on the planet proceeding slowly, but the changes I see have been astonishing."

"Not all to the good, one fears. We have been very fortunate in the aiji-dowager's presence. One cannot estimate what might have happened here at Najida were it not for the reinforcement her visit entailed. Our enemy's plans would have been quite adequate to have disposed of either or both of us—without her fortunate intervention. Is the dowager ready for us, nadiin-ji?" he asked his bodyguard, and Banichi nodded in the affirmative. "Then we shall go to her for a start. Have you need of anything, Geigi-ji?"

"We are perfectly prepared," Geigi answered him.

"Excellent," he said, and Banichi and Jago led the way to the dowager's door and knocked. Cenedi, no great surprise, opened it for them.

"The dowager is expecting you, nandiin-ji," Cenedi said, and that often-sober face lighted with an honest smile for Geigi. "Welcome, nandi."

"Indeed, indeed, Cenedi-ji," Geigi said. "You know my senior guard: Haiji and Cajami."

"One knows and welcomes them," Cenedi said, and made room for them to pass, all of them, inside.

Which was a fair complement of Guild, besides Antaro and Jegari, who stood quietly in the far corner.

The dowager had the fire going in the fireplace, and had her chair there. Cajeiri sat with her, and got up immediately to bow and offer his hand to his great-grandmother, in lieu of her cane, since she elected to stand to meet an old ally—an honor she paid to very few.

She took her cane in hand to walk forward to midroom to meet them, stopped there, leaning on the cane, nodded deeply and said, "One is pleased to see you, Geigi-ji. How are the legs?"

"Oh, holding me up, 'Sidi-ji. They are, still. But the far horizons all are flat! It is so strangely disconcerting."

"One is sure your eye will adjust in a day or two," she said. "Come, sit with us. Will you take tea?"

The dowager became the hostess in whatever house she lodged, a matter of rank and custom, and Bren needed not even signal his own staff—Ramaso had come into the room, and Ramaso had quite naturally anticipated the order. They had scarcely found their seats near the fire—Cajeiri moved to the farthest, to make room for Geigi next to his great-grandmother—when the servants came in bearing enough tea for the purpose.

The talk then was all of the journey, the rush to make space on the shuttle—several commercial loads would be a week late, and probably all that the human companies knew of reasons was that the highest-ranking atevi lord had taken a yen to visit his estate, with no hint of the urgency involved. Secrecy had been invoked, and the four captains on the station were in Geigi's confidence, but the information did not go much lower than that.

"One wishes it truly were a whim that brings this visit," Geigi said over their second round of tea. "One wishes, indeed, that I had made this visit while my sister was still alive."

"One cannot mend the past," Ilisidi said sternly. "And you never got along with her, Geigi-ji. Remember it accurately."

"Well, true, true, 'Sidi-ji, we fought. And a good part of our disagreement was her perpetual doting on that boy. One knew, one knew when news came that she had died, that the estate would be in trouble, but there was nothing I could do from the station. If I had used the very first opportunity after the shuttles were flying again to come down here—"

"That graceless brat's associates would have assassinated you on your very doorstep," the dowager said bluntly, "as they likely assassinated your sister, one regrets to say. We do not at all wish you had come down here before now. What we *do* regret, in the general scarcity of good intelligence—that scoundrel Murini having utterly disrupted the Guild's networks—is that my own information was just as lacking as my grandson's. Cenedi."

"Nandi?" Cenedi answered.

"You have taken an unacceptable blame for the paidhi's situation and my great-grandson's near calamity—when the fault lies in the Guild itself, in its concentration on the central clans since the Troubles. *That* is how our very competent security received bad information. 'Is the district quiet?' One is certain my Cenedi asked that question of Guild headquarters, as he would ask of any district. And what answer did you get, Nedi-ji?"

A slight bow of Cenedi's head. "That there was no hint of trouble in the district, aiji-ma."

"And when Banichi asked?"

"The same," Banichi answered, with the same slight bow, "aiji-ma."

"And when *we* asked my grandson's office if there was a difficulty regarding Kajiminda?"

"The same," Cenedi said.

"So," Ilisidi said definitively. "You see the state of affairs. Do not take the word of either the Guild *or* my grandson's office." Click went the dowager's teacup onto the marble side table. "Well, indeed. There is blame to go around including to my grandson, who went off to Taiben while the Kadagidi were plotting their coup in the first place: it saved his life, however, and Damiri-daja's. Baji-naji, we in this room are all alive when our enemies wish us dead. That is a cheerful point, is it not?"

"Indubitably," Geigi said firmly.

"So, well, Geigi-ji, and in consequence, we are holding your nephew, to whom we refuse any title or courtesy. We reserve all such titles and honors for you, whom we greatly esteem. And we damn him to our great displeasure. *We* are settled on the fate of Kajiminda, understand. And on the fate of your nephew. Will you hear it?"

"We shall certainly hear it, aiji-ma."

"You yourself, esteemed ally, will be of greatest use where you have been. And we should not reward you for your service by settling Kajiminda estate on any other person, and we will not support such a notion should it ever be made. Kajiminda should remain in Maschi hands, tied to the aishidi'tat. The treaty is valuable, particularly now. You will, however, cede the seaward end of the peninsula to your Edi neighbors, as I shall ask the same of Najida."

"Readily, aiji-ma," Bren said. "One anticipated such a request."

"The same, yes," Geigi said, "but I am getting older, and with this disaster, I have no successor, aiji-ma. You know my disposition. Even in my own clan—"

An impatient tap of the cane. "Oh, pish, with that boy, you *had* no successor! And we shall find you better prospects. What is old and tested under adversity should not be yielded up to a momentary situation. *Our* disposition of your misbehaving nephew is direct to that point. His marrying began this crisis. His marrying can settle it. *We* have a girl in mind, a strong-minded *Eastern* girl, of a family *we* approve. Ardija clan."

"Ardija," Geigi echoed in some surprise. Bren had not heard the name in that context either. Ardija was a neighbor of the dowager's own Malguri holdings, a tiny clan, but one with historic ties to the dowager's line.

"We know the young lady well, a strong-minded young woman, well-bred and intelligent. The East would be salutary for your nephew and keep him out of trouble until there is a child. After that contract produces a child, we care little where he lives, so long as Ardija clan has the upbringing of the offspring, who may spend some time under your tutelage on the station or at Kajiminda when he—or she—reaches an appropriate age. Maschi clan will get its heir out of a politically advantageous line."

Geigi listened through all of this and finally drew a deep breath. "You have spent considerable thought on this, 'Sidi-ji. Your solution, an Eastern tie, will shake Maschi clan to the roots."

"Do not be modest. It will shake the aishidi'tat itself, linking the west coast with the East. Your Maschi clan has occupied a delicate position, poised between the Marid and the west coast. They were dutiful enough, and they have paid all courtesies to my grandson on his resumption of power. But we have remarked their curious silence regarding your nephew's flirtation with the Marid. Not a word of warning came from them—and we assume they were surely not ignorant of the situation. Or should not have been."

"This has indeed crossed my mind, aiji-ma."

"Then we agree on that suspicion."

"One cannot say with any certainty. I have no current knowledge of my own clan, embarrassing as it is to say so. First my long absence, then the year without communication with the world at all, and all the changes since . . ."

"Do not apologize. It was incumbent on *them* to approach you. Let them feel the weight of your hand, Geigi-ji. We greatly suspect the quality of their leadership and we suspect the head of Maschi clan of doing much what your nephew has done, neither joining the Marid in its schemes nor reporting them to my grandson. If you wish to know the *real* fault that allowed your scoundrel of a nephew to continue his flirtations with the Marid, look to the failure of Pairuti of Maschi clan to be forthcoming to my grandson."

That was news. So communication in the southwest had broken down in a major way. The old web of information had not totally reintegrated after Tabini's return to power. That was a fact. Maschi clan leadership sat poised between the Marid and the coast, supposedly communicating with the capital. And had Tabini been getting *no* alarms from them?

A thump of the cane on the floor punctuated the dowager's

assessment. "The aishidi'tat has *never* solved its problems in this district. Your leadership, Geigi-ji, your personal efforts, brought peace and laid the foundations for an association on this coast. And the world may have urgently needed your talents on the station, where you have done remarkable things for us all; but with your departure to that effort—a keystone fell out of the association here. Your own clan has grown weak, at best, and we fear, at worst, quite as much as your nephew, Maschi clan has been playing both sides of the recent civil disturbance."

My God, Bren thought, and two and three pieces of the situation clicked into place. Not just the nephew. The *clan* seat . . . poised physically between Kajiminda and Marid territory.

"One is appalled," Geigi said somberly. "Their communications to me have been routine."

"So have their communications to my grandson in the capital. It does not say those communications have been truthful."

"Aiji-ma!"

"Pish, Geigi-ji. Where is 'Sidi-ji?"

" 'Sidi-ji, forgive me. But one is—appalled, entirely. Thunderstruck. Embarrassed, extremely. Pairuti—before the Troubles, he was a dull fellow. He collected *sisui* figures. That is absolutely the only distinction he had. He kept meticulous books. He—"

"—is absolutely dutiful in attending court sessions, for both Murini *and* my grandson, of course. Whoever has been in power, yes, Pairuti has been obedient and attended court. But his proximity to the Marid during such uneasy times has required more talents than collecting porcelain miniatures. And what troubles me, Geigi-ji, is that he has *not* distinguished himself lately in providing information. Cenedi-ji?"

Cenedi said, "Nandiin, a query to Shejidan has *not* produced any but routine, formal communications of a mundane nature from Lord Pairuti to the aiji since his return. Guild communications are equally sterile, reporting everything in the district tranquil, and the district prosperous throughout. There is *no* fluctuation in the provincial tax records, be it Murini or Tabini-aiji in Shejidan."

"One would expect something more of disturbance," Ilisidi said in a low voice. "Considering the situation in this district of the province, which *we* have turned up inside only a few days' residence, its mundane character becomes entirely damning."

"Gods," Geigi said. Geigi, the Rational Determinist, who relied on reason. "Gods. I know the tone of his letters, up and down. Pairuti discusses his acquisitions. His figurines. He offers his felicitations on whatever good fortune has attended, his sorrow for any ill—of course his willingness to be of service, when he is so remote he knows he will never be called upon in the least. I have dealt with him for years. He is the most boring man in the aishidi'tat."

"He surely called you on the station, once my grandson returned to power."

"He did. He did. Never an indication of Marid pressure on Sarini Province, no hint of the nest of Marid lurking in Separti. He offered condolences for my sister's death—he promised to look in on my nephew. I took it in the way of every promise from him, something one means very well, but one never intends to get around to . . . unless he should extend his travel a little on his way to the airport, for winter court. And one was all but certain he never would actually do it. Those are my correspondences with Pairuti. But his people thrive. He has been a decent administrator. His extravagances are all for his collections."

"And he has written faithfully to Tabini-aiji," Cenedi said. "Nothing suspicious at all—except *we* know situations in *this* district that the lord of the Maschi should have known."

"The Edi did not inform him," Banichi said, "that we know. But he did not inform himself of the situation at Kajiminda and at Separti and Dalaigi? With whom is the man trading?"

"With whom, indeed?" Ilisidi muttered. "Is this the pattern

of a man who keeps good books and succeeds in the markets? He was *at* winter court, making excuses for your nephew, Geigi-ji. He was either ignorant, or complicitous in the situation here, nandi, forgive my bluntness."

Damn, Bren said to himself. He hated surprises. And *surely* the lord of Maschi clan had not been under suspicion when he came here: he could not—

Not until the paidhi-aiji encountered the local situation and stirred up a nest of trouble, which, in turn, proved the aiji's information had been lacking.

The dowager had applied directly to Shejidan for her information, been told wrong in a way that had nearly gotten them all killed, and now had narrowed down the logical source of misinformation inside the province.

Damned right the dowager had had her staff asking questions, direct ones, ever since Tabini's visit yesterday, when staff had met staff and information had passed—to her people, and to his. In Banichi's eye he caught an indefinable glint of expression. Banichi *had* been on it, or at least Tano and Algini, left behind today, had been briefing themselves.

"One had no idea," he murmured to Geigi, chagrined, "or one surely would have said something of it on the bus. I would personally have *trusted* Pairuti."

"So would we all," Ilisidi said grimly. "So *did* we all, until it came clear to us that if my grandson lacked facts, it might not be that he has failed to gather information from Sarini Province . . . but that those who should be advising him—have directly *lied*."

"One still—" Geigi said. "One still cannot entirely conclude . . ." A breath. "Did you come here suspecting this?"

"We did not." She gave a dismissive wave of her hand. "We shall cease to amaze you, nand' paidhi. We sent to Shejidan last night, in the dark hours. We called our household staff at that unsavory time of night. We asked certain questions, and this morning while you, nand' paidhi, were otherwise occupied with estate business, my staff in Shejidan was busy phoning certain offices and locating records. While you were at the airport, your staff and mine received their report, a complete *lack* of extraordinary information in the court record of missives from Lord Pairuti. He reports the sad death of your sister, Geigi-ji, and the accession of your nephew, to whom he says he has written offering assistance. He reports everything quiet in the province, and reports, at court, the restoration of trade. He provides exquisitely balanced books for the whole district. Nothing is the matter. Which is exactly the thought that interrupted our sleep last night. The prospect that someone of Maschi clan might call on us in Lord Geigi's sojourn here, or worse, with our Lord Geigi understaffed at Kajiminda, suddenly occurred to us, *hence* my calls to Shejidan, which I assure you were deeply coded. We used the night hours and this morning to ask a range of unpleasant questions—and to notify my grandson, who—*if* he had asked such questions immediately instead of assuming the vector of attack on us had been entirely southerly, out of Separti Township—would have turned this up. As it is, he has deployed his forces southward. The Marid infestation south of here may be a mere decoration. A deliberate distraction." A waggle of the fingers. "Of course we could be wrong. But we rarely are."

"One is appalled," Bren said. "One is utterly appalled, aiji-ma."

"Ha. So you agree." The ancient eyes that had seen a good deal of treachery in a lifetime sparked fire. "And we shall not sit here inert."

"'Sidi-ji," Geigi said. " 'Sidi-ji. What can one say to this?"

"That you will take action, Geigi-ji. That you have been a long time removed from this arena, and your presence here as lord of Sarini Province can only be salutary."

"One had planned to return to the station, but—"

"Oh, you shall. You must. You have done far too well in that position. Considering the situation we face, with foreigners apt to arrive, we need you there. But certain things need your attention."

"Absolutely, aiji-ma. Whatever one can do—"

"If my grandson steps in and takes action, it is another heavy-handed Ragi seizure—such an unhappy history on this coast. If the Guild does—the same. Things here are delicate. You appreciate it in unique ways. And coming at proof may not be easy. Lord Pairuti may have destroyed records . . ."

Geigi held up a finger. "May have. But I would wager not, aiji-ma. Not that man. His disposition is compulsive—a passion for details. He will have them. And I can get them. I shall need to take back Kajiminda with some dispatch. Clearly, so doing, I shall need to interview certain of my own clan. Which makes my calling on Pairuti obligatory. He will expect it. He will be in a dither to hide the records, but he will not destroy them, not that man."

Go there? Good God.

"We are understaffed, Geigi-ji," Bren protested.

"We have taken measures in that direction, nandiin," Ilisidi said smugly. "We will *have* force at our disposal—granted my grandson understands our position. He will *not* permit Lord Geigi to come to grief. He may fuss about the situation. But he will move to protect the treaty that binds the coast to the aishidi'tat . . . and you, Geigi-ji, are its living embodiment. He *will* move."

Read: Tabini hadn't agreed to Ilisidi's demands. Tabini hadn't jumped to relocate his forces from Separti. He hadn't come rushing to Ilisidi's conclusion, perhaps, or he had something else going on that he wasn't happy to leave.

Which could mean there were complications.

Najida's perspective on the immediate threat, however, were different than Tabini's. If Pairuti was colluding with the Marid, Najida was staring up the barrel of a gun. Problems could come at them right down the airport road. Or arrive en masse by train.

And Tabini, mind, had just yesterday left his son and heir *and* the aiji-dowager *in* this position.

Damn, he didn't like it when Tabini turned as inscrutable and ruthless as his grandmother. Especially when he and people he cared about were in the target zone. He had to get Toby and Barb out of the harbor, as early as possible. He'd *like* to ship Cajeiri and his young company back to Shejidan . . . but that meant exposing the movement in Najida. They'd had their chance to get Cajeiri moved out—and his father had left him behind, perhaps—dared one even think it—as an intentional *proof* of his lack of alarm?

"We need the help of the Edi, aiji-ma," he said. "We need everything they can bring to bear."

"Oh, we shall have help," Ilisidi said with a small, tight smile. "And so much the better if the Edi will protect the grounds here, and protect us all. I have requested it. I have asked Ramaso to relay it to the Grandmother, and I have received assurances."

God, leave the house for a few hours and come back to war preparations.

"We shall deal with it, 'Sidi-ji." Geigi gave a little bow, distressed of countenance, but not about to retreat, no, not with that look. "I shall do everything in my power, aiji-ma, and your recommendations, allowing me to deal with this myself, are generous. And I shall want to speak to the Edi on your staff, with your kind permission."

"You certainly have Najida's full support, Geigi-ji," Bren said, "so far as lies in my hands."

"And I shall see my nephew." Geigi drew in a long, long breath. "The wretch. I will meet with him tomorrow after breakfast. Tell him I am here, Bren-ji; and let him stew tonight."

It had been interesting. Interesting was what Great-grandmother would call it. Cajeiri had been just very quiet and respectful, and heard all kinds of news about the neighbors, and scary hints that nand' Geigi was going to have a talk with his relatives inland.

The talk he meant to have with Baiji, down in the basement— *that* was one Cajeiri very much wanted to hear. He was already thinking how to get in on that interview, even if he and his aishid just had to be casually walking through the downstairs— repeatedly.

But he had been right in his approach. He and, he was sure, Jegari and Antaro, had sopped up a lot of what was going on with the seniors; and maybe Lucasi and Veijico had learned something useful, too—if Tano and Algini had been in a good mood.

So very quietly, after nand' Bren and nand' Geigi had left— Cajeiri paid his own little bow to Great-grandmother. "One is grateful, mani. One did learn."

"See you stay within the house, Great-grandson. And stay within call."

"*Yes*, mani." A second bow, a deep one, in leaving. "I shall."

What was going on outside mani's rooms was preparation for a formal dinner this evening, and nand' Toby and Barb-daja insisted they were coming up from the boat, which had security and staff running about—not mentioning the ongoing process of getting Lord Geigi fully installed in his suite, which had been the security office, and fed a light late lunch—everybody in the house had already eaten—to tide him over until supper.

And Lucasi and Veijico had been in the library with Tano and Algini—who might have let them hear all of it, he supposed— glum thought—or maybe not.

He gathered his aishid in his own apartment, himself sitting by his own fireplace and its comfortably warm embers. "Sit down," he said, "nadiin-ji." And they took the other chairs, all four of them.

"How much did you hear?" he asked Lucasi and Veijico. "And how much did you understand?"

"We heard," Lucasi said, "that they are hoping Edi will function in the place of the Guild in protecting this region, and that Lord Geigi intends to move into Kajiminda faster than the aiji's Guild occupying it would like. We heard that Maschi clan leadership may no longer be reliable."

That was certainly an aspect of it. One could gather Tano and Algini had somewhat discussed that problem in their own terms. And one also gathered Lucasi and Veijico clearly did not think Geigi was being smart.

"The Edi know everything that moves on the coast," he reminded them. "And they are used to managing this area, nadiin-ji."

"They failed to advise nand' Bren there was a problem. That was wrong."

"Talking to the Edi is a problem. You know they have a rule against talking to outsiders. Nand' Bren has gotten past that now. So has my great-grandmother. And Lord Geigi is their lord—besides, mani is already talking about putting the Edi in charge of part of this coast. So the Edi are talking to us now. And they are part of the protection of this house."

"They have no skill against real Guild," Veijico said. "And should not be relied on. Your father ought to know this, nandi."

"One is certain he will know it," he said, annoyed at their pertness with opinions. "But the Marid Guild did *not* succeed in taking this house, or in holding onto Kajiminda. So they are not as smart as they think they are. And the Edi are not doing badly."

His older bodyguards looked more than a little offput. Then Lucasi said, "That is no measure of success, nandi. The Guild does not *hold* positions. Holding positions is a lord's business. Holding is politics, and the demonstration of power."

Well, *that* was a recitation from some book.

"So it is my business to hold things," he said. "And yours to take them. When I say so."

Silence, from the troublemakers. "Yes," Antaro said quietly. Jegari nodded. But not the other two.

Useful to know the Guild's opinion of its uses.

"The Edi," he said, "have done very well."

"*Not* well," Veijico said.

"Better than the Marid Guild," he said. Tag. Point for his side. He liked winning an argument, too. "Some of them are dead. The Edi were smart. They sided with Great-grandmother."

"Still, nandi," Lucasi said, "they are irregulars."

"They are alive," he said, "and the Marid's Guild have been trying to take over for years."

"Kajiminda's Guild has prevented it, nandi. It is *not* irregulars who have defended this coast."

He liked the notion that his bodyguard would talk back to him: Cenedi talked back to Great-grandmother, and Banichi talked back to Bren. But Lucasi and Veijico were being stupid. And that made him mad.

"That was," he said shortly, "after Kajiminda's Guild went off and got killed in the Troubles, or never even got to Shejidan, for all we know. They died."

"Possibly the Edi that served Kajiminda all died, too," Veijico said. "Since they are missing."

"Nandi," he corrected them sharply. "You say 'nandi.'"

"Nandi," Veijico said.

"And you are to mean it, nadi!"

A bow of the head and *no* openness of expression from her or her brother. Mani would never put up with it. They thought he had to, being a year short of nine.

"I have been in space," he said, just as nastily. "I have been on a spaceship and on a station *and* the shuttle, and I have seen people who are not atevi and not human, either, where we all could have gotten blown up. So I know things, nadiin. I have gotten myself out of trouble. And Antaro and Jegari and I all three were in a war. You were not. So you should listen."

"We listen, nandi," Veijico said glumly.

"You are rude."

"*No*, nandi, we are *not* rude. We are advising you, for your safety."

"We do as we please, nadiin! *You* do not. *We* get away with things because we are not loud about it and we do what our guards by no means expect, but also because we *listen* about what is dangerous and what is not and we do not go some places. We are not stupid, nadiin! You think anybody not Guild is stupid. You think the Edi are stupid. You probably think everybody in the staff is stupid. Superior thinking, mani says, does not consist of thinking oneself superior. We think you should reconsider who is stupid."

There was a moment of deep, uncomfortable silence.

"We stand corrected, nandi," Veijico said coldly.

"You should," he said. It was as good as mani could do—almost. And they had deserved it. He was still mad. Which was not satisfactory. He hated being mad. He hated having people see that he was. *Face!* mani would say, and thwack him on the ear until he mended his expression. Which he did—mended all the way to a tight, small smile. And got up, so they all had to.

"It will be a very formal dinner tonight," he said, meaning whatever bodyguard attended him had to eat beforehand or after. The little dining room was going to be wall-to-wall security—literally shoulder-to-shoulder Guild, considering nand' Bren's little estate had so many important guests.

And maybe the boredom of standing about this evening, while Antaro and Jegari ate at leisure in the suite, would give Lucasi and Veijico enough time to think about the seriousness of the situation, and about the fact that they were in among very senior security who had earned the right to respect.

"You two will attend me," he told them. "All day." He planned to do his lessons, which was the most boring thing he could think of, and not to let them off. "You can stand at the

door and keep an eye on things. Jegari and Antaro will be helping me with my homework."

For the paidhi-aiji, it was a formal evening coat, light green,
and freshly pressed, with only a moderate amount of lace—
comfortable, a country style. It was one of Bren's favorites,
comfortable across the shoulders, unlike the court-style that
was intended to remind the wearer about posture—constantly.
He slipped it on and went down to the front door to welcome
Toby and Barb into the house. It was an exposed walk, coming
up the hill, and he breathed easier when the door opened and
let them in.

"I gather Lord Geigi made it in all right," Toby said. "We
saw the bus. Fancy!"

"Everything in order," Bren said. Toby didn't bow. He didn't.
And they didn't touch, in front of staff, which they always were,
in the hall. "Barb. Good evening."

"Are we proper?" Barb asked in a low voice. Toby's lady—his
own ex, which was an inconvenience—but one he was determined to ignore. And do her credit, Barb tried. Toby and Barb
had come up the hill wearing good Mospheiran-style clothes—
that was to say white trousers, light sweaters, Toby in blue,
Barb in brown with a little embroidery, and in Toby's case, a
dress jacket, the sort one might wear to a better Port Jackson
restaurant. It was as formal as two boaters got, within their
own wardrobes.

"Perfectly proper," he said, in good humor, and led them
on down toward the side corridor toward the dining hall, with
Banichi and Jago in attendance.

But just down toward the end of the hall, Lord Geigi exited
his quarters, and they delayed to meet the portly lord and his
two bodyguards . . . Lord Geigi resplendent in gray and green
brocade and a good deal of lace.

To Lord Geigi, surely, the mode of Barb's and Toby's dinner dress might be a little exotic—yachting whites weren't the

mode among the numerous humans on the station—but Lord Geigi was an outgoing fellow and went so far as to offer his hand, station manners, to the complete astonishment of the household servants standing by at the hallway intersection.

"My brother Toby and his companion Barb," Bren introduced them both. They both knew Geigi by reputation, no question of that: but a formal introduction was due. "Lord Geigi of Kajiminda, Lord of Sarini Province, third holder of the Treaty of Aregorji, Viceroy of the Heavens and Stationmaster of Alpha Station. Nandi, my brother-by-the-same-father nand' Toby, an associate of the Presidenta of Mospheira, and his companion Barb-daja."

Barb and Toby had never heard the full string of titles rattled off, and seemed a little confused. Toby bowed. Barb stared with her mouth a little open.

"Very glad to meet you," Geigi said, using very idiomatic ship-speak, as they pursued their walk toward the dining room. "A pleasant surprise, your presence here."

"Honored," Toby said. "Very honored, sir. My brother has always spoken extremely highly of you. One is grateful." The latter in fairly passable Ragi.

"Well, well," Geigi said, still in ship-speak, "and eloquence runs in the family. I do very much regret displacing you from your quarters."

"Oh, no way, sir. We're very comfortable on the boat. The same as being home."

"Gracious as well." Geigi was at his jovial best as they reached the door and he half-turned, hesitating at another arrival behind them in the hall. "And the aiji-dowager joins us."

"Do go in," Bren said to Toby and Barb, while Geigi's attention and his courtesies passed smoothly to Ilisidi. Personal staff had neatly coordinated the arrivals by inverse order of rank, and the paidhi-aiji in particular did *not* enter the dining room after the aiji-dowager. Toby and Barb went first, least in rank; he came second, and as host and holder of the estate he took his place and bowed to Lord Geigi, who entered next, and found his chair at table, at Bren's left.

Immediately after, Ilisidi arrived with Cajeiri—hindmost.

And what with Banichi and Jago, Cenedi and Nawari, Lucasi and Veijico, and Geigi's guards, Saoji and Sakeimi, the wall around the dining table was solid black and armed to the teeth . . . not that the guests present didn't trust each other. It was the house itself that was in jeopardy: dinnertime was absolutely classic in the machimi, as the most convenient time to sneak up on a house—what with servants coming and going, everybody gathered in one place, and maybe not paying attention . . . and perhaps a little buzzed with alcohol.

Their bodyguards, however, *were* paying attention. Constantly.

Poison? Not in his kitchen. Not with his cook.

Not with off-duty security having their supper next door to the kitchens.

And not with a household staff that came from Najida village. He had too many eyes, too many people on alert for any intruder to get that chance.

And dinner began, first of all, with wines, fruit juices, liquor. One knew what things their guest had been in the way of missing.

"Do choose, Geigi-ji," Ilisidi said. Ordinarily staff would seek her choices first. She gave Geigi that honor.

And Geigi chose a delicate white wine for openers . . . Cajeiri opting for a sparkling fruit juice.

After that, then, came a succession of courses, especially the traditional regional dishes of the season. The cook had announced a seventeen-course dinner, which, even for atevi appetites, amounted more to a leisurely and lengthy tasting event than a dinner in the usual sense. There was a constant succession of plates and dishes—fish, shellfish, game of the season, imported curd and sauces of black bean plant, greenbud, orangelle, too many to track. There could not be a utensil in the kitchen not being washed and reused. There was black bread, white bread, whole-grain and soft bread. There were three kinds of eggs; and preserves and pickles. There were gravies, light and dark. There were vegetable sherbets—palate cleansers—between the courses. Bren had had particular warning from the cook about the lime-green sherbet, and he had a servant hovering anxiously by to be absolutely certain neither he nor Toby nor Barb got into that dish, which would have probably dropped them to the floor inside the hour.

There were souffles, and patés, there were crackers, four different sorts, and there were, finally, oh, my God—desserts, from cream fruit pudding with meringue to cakes and tarts, and a thirteen-layer torte with a different icing in each level.

Bren pushed back from the table in near collapse.

"If you'd like to go back to the boat—" Bren said to Toby in a very low voice, "staff can see you down. It's dark already. But if you would like to attend the session in the study, where we shall drink brandy, or pretend to drink it at least, and observe courtly courtesies—"

"Barb?" Toby asked.

Barb looked on the verge of pain, but her eyes had that bright, darting glitter they got at jewelry counters. She looked at the lordly company, and at him, and at Toby, all in three seconds.

"When could we ever have the chance?" she asked. And then said, quietly: "If it really isn't an intrusion for us to be there."

Give Barb credit—and at times he truly struggled to give his ex any credit—she really was trying to absorb the experience she and Toby had fallen into, and she was on best behavior. She'd gathered about five Ragi phrases she could use, she'd bought herself a beaded dinner gown—itself a scandal in Najida village, but he didn't tell her that—which she was not, thank God, wearing tonight. And after she'd helped Toby sink a boat in the harbor on the night when the whole place had erupted in gunfire—he'd actually had to admit Barb had been trying through all of it. Harder still, he had to admit that her help to Toby had mattered when it counted. Tonight she'd picked up cues very well, and Toby was happy, which mattered even more.

"Wouldn't be a problem at all," he said. "Mind, Lord Geigi handles our language on a regular basis up on station: you've heard. Just don't be too informal with him. There's some good brandy for us—don't touch the dowager's brand. Or have an orange and vodka. Those things are safe."

"I'll just sip at the brandy," Barb said. "God, I'm stuffed."

"Goes twice," Toby said, "but if we won't be trouble, we can go down late to the boat, your staff willing."

"They'll be up for hours, cleaning. And someone will be on duty. You're welcome to join us." He wasn't Ilisidi's escort this evening: Lord Geigi filled that post. He saw he'd inherited Cajeiri, who hadn't said a word this evening, not one. "Are you coming too, young sir, or will you retire?"

"I shall come, nandi."

The dinner party broke up. The dowager and Geigi went out together. Cajeiri stayed right with him. Lucasi and Veijico stayed right with Banichi and Jago. The young lord had been amazingly proper today—one was tempted to compliment him, but one always wondered what he was up to.

Gathering the gossip, Bren rather suspected, in the legitimate way, which meant sitting with the adults and listening even to things that didn't really interest him, in hopes of some bit of mischief he could get into.

As for Toby and Barb, they were truly overfed, and had had perhaps just a half glass too much already.

But Geigi had come in from a long, long flight, endured all manner of inconvenience for a man of his girth, met with Tabini, hopped two flights, and since had a long bus ride, a meeting with Ilisidi and now a massive supper, so one rather suspected the brandy service would not stretch on into the small hours.

*   *   *

"Delightful, positively delightful, Bren-ji," Geigi said to him as they were settling in to the admittedly cramped sitting room. "I have not had such a dinner in ages!"

"You are very kind to say so," Bren said; and took a brandy himself, if only to moisten his lips with it.

Talk ran light for the while: Cajeiri was as quiet as Toby and Barb, and Bren himself had little to say, once the dowager and Geigi took to discussing the Marid.

Now that *was* interesting. One knew, but didn't *know* the intricacies of the Marid relationships the way Geigi did.

Geigi had himself been married to a woman of the Marid—"I committed my own folly," was Geigi's way of putting it, "so I cannot wholly fault my fool nephew on that point, except that when the man ahead of you has fallen into a pit, it is entirely foolish to keep walking down the same course."

"It is what we said from the beginning, nandi," Ilisidi said. "You were doing, yes, much the same as your nephew did in listening to the Marid; but there is a difference. You hoped to stabilize the west coast, which was in a very uncomfortable balance at the time. Your staff served you gladly; you had the confidence of the Edi, despite your unfortunate marriage, and despite your wife's best attempts to bankrupt your fortunes. Your nephew, in these dangerous times, was more concerned with stabilizing his own fortunes—no, not even his fortunes: he is not that foresighted. His comfort. One scarcely believes young Baiji ever had a thought in which his own convenience and comfort were not preeminent."

Geigi nodded solemnly. "One hoped he had changed. I lamented my sister's passing—we were often at loggerheads, but she had virtues when it did *not* involve her son. And she *was* my sister." Geigi sighed. "Marriage has been very problematic for my house, nadiin-ji. A reef on which my branch of Maschi clan may have finally shipwrecked."

"Say no such thing!" Ilisidi snapped. "Your management will resurrect Maschi clan's fortunes. As for heir-getting, *Baiji* will produce an heir with a lady of advantageous birth, his mother will have his rearing up to fortunate seven, and then we shall simply pack him up to the station so you may have the pleasure of bringing up your nephew in a proper way."

A little smile. "You have it planned, aiji-ma."

"Enough of aiji-ma. 'Sidi will do, I say. Speak to me. Voice your opinion about this course."

"I would wish my heir to grow up at Kajiminda," Geigi said wistfully, "and I would wish to have my nephew as far away from any impressionable child as possible."

"Ha. Bring your nephew up to the station, then *marry* the young woman I suggest, and install *her* as lord in Kajiminda."

Geigi's right brow lifted. He took a sip of brandy. "Do you have a name for this theoretical young woman?" he asked.

"We have two possibilities. But we lean most to Maie of the Calrunaidi. A brilliant young scholar. Her brother will inherit Calrunaidi, and she has no shortage of prospects. She is sensible, good at figures, a credit to her parentage, which is Calrunaidi and Ardija. She is no beauty, but it is not beauty that recommends her."

"Ardija," Geigi said, nodding slowly. The aged lady of Ardija, as Bren well-rememered, was Drien, Ilisidi's closest living relative in the East. It was a connection with her own estate of Malguri that Ilisidi proposed for Geigi.

"The young lady has rights there, but no inheritance: Drien of Ardija has a brother-of-the-same-mother whose son will inherit *that* estate. So young Maie has better connections than she does prospects. She is a well-dispositioned child who could do far, far better than temporarily marry one of my neighbors and produce *them* heirs with her connections . . . frankly, a potential inconvenience to my house, which has no heir but this young gentleman, and *he* is too young for her."

"Great-grandmother!" Cajeiri said in shock.

"Continue to be young," Ilisidi said, brushing the matter aside. "Too young, I say, and the young lady is far too bookish for your taste. Not, however, for Lord Geigi's interests, perhaps. Geigi may marry her."

"*Marry*," Geigi said, still in shock, himself; and Barb and Toby were looking in Bren's direction in some small concern, but it was no time to provide translations.

It was a brilliant piece of dynastic chess—if the individuals involved could be persuaded. The sticking point was persuading any young lady of taste to bed down with Baiji long enough. But *that* marriage could be contracted to last just as long as it took to produce an heir, then evaporate as if it had never been. The young woman would find herself quickly married to Lord Geigi, who might even visit the planet for the occasion—and thereafter, if one could read Ilisidi's plans between the lines, young Maie of the East would occupy Kajiminda, deal with the Edi, and bring up a suitably educated heir for Geigi's branch of Maschi clan. Maybe two heirs, if she and Geigi actually took to each other . . . though the unspoken matter in the background was that Geigi was rumored to have very little interest in young ladies, and no success in getting an heir of his own.

"With adequate security for her residence here," Geigi said quietly, "that above all. She would be an immediate target of our neighbors in the Marid. So would her child."

"The Edi will be establishing their own house somewhere neighboring both Kajiminda and Najida," the dowager said. "And one does not doubt they will become a force to be reckoned with."

"But is that a certainty?" Geigi asked. "One believed it would still be under debate in the legislature."

"Oh, pish," Ilisidi said with a dismissive wave of her hand. "My grandson has a brain. He will agree with me, given the other circumstances. And he will see that the legislature agrees. The arrangement gives no great advantage to any single *western* house, which would be the greatest sticking-point. So it will pass."

It wasn't going to be as easy as the dowager said, but with the possibility of a renewed set-to with the Marid looming in the immediate future, and another round of Marid-directed assassinations aimed at destabilizing the aishidi'tat, then counter-moves by the aiji, the house of lords might be inclined to give in and support the proposal. Even the hidebound traditionalists of the center, like Tatiseigi—who was a staunch ally of the aiji-dowager on other points—might be persuaded. One had the feeling of watching a landslide. Boulders were coming downhill, in the dowager's planning, and damned little was going to stand in her way.

Certainly not one young bookish girl in—what was the clan? Calrunaidi. Nobody in the west had ever *heard* much of Calrunaidi.

But one had certainly heard of Ardija. That, tied closely to Malguri, and involving relatives of the aiji-dowager, was a bloodline of some potency.

And that alliance would tie the west coast firmly to Malguri, which was *Cajeiri's* inheritance, until he produced an heir for it.

God. On the chessboard of politics, that was a potential earthquake. The great houses employed not only numbers experts, they employed genealogists to track this sort of thing. They would see it—but they likely would give way to it, in the interests of peace.

"One would agree," Geigi said, "if this can be arranged."

"Good, good," Ilisidi said. "So you may think on it and tell me your thoughts when you have had time to mull it over. Perhaps we should have our last round and let you get to your bed, Geigi-ji. You must be exhausted."

"One admits to it," Geigi said. "And I shall indeed think on your proposal, 'Sidi-ji. I shall think on it very favorably." He turned then to Toby and Barb, and said, in very passable ship-speak: "We discuss politics. Unavoidable. One wishes a more tranquil conversation."

"An extravagant honor, nandi," Toby said, one of his courtly phrases of Ragi. "One is gratified by your notice."

He got it out without saying *orange drink*, a close thing, with the word *notice*. Bren was astonished.

But then—Toby had spent the last couple of years running messages between the Resistance and the Island, and his vocabulary hadn't exactly rusted.

"You speak a fair amount of Ragi, nandi," Geigi said.

"About boats, navigation, hello, and goodbye, nandi."

"*-se,*" Bren tossed in, the felicitous false-one, since Toby had given a list of infelicitous four. It was natural as breathing.

"*-se,*" Toby added in the next breath. "We hear, but do not talk, nandi."

Geigi laughed. "*Very* well done!" And continued, in ship-speak: "The station knows you as *Frozen Dessert.*"

Toby and Barb both laughed.

Frozen Dessert? Bren wondered.

"Our code name," Toby said to Bren, "when the authorities had to refer to us."

Bren translated that for the dowager, and for Cajeiri. "That was the word referring to them and their boat, during the Resistance, aiji-ma, young gentleman. When they were running messages."

"And bravely done!" Geigi said. "The enemy would appear and the dessert would melt in the sun."

"Little boat," Toby said in Ragi. "Hard to spot."

"Very good work," Geigi said in ship-speak, and in Ragi: "Tell them that they will be welcome as my personal guests in Kajiminda, when I have done a little housecleaning."

"He says you're welcome as his guests at Kajiminda when he has things there under control," Bren said, thinking the while that Geigi could not possibly follow through on that, and, please God, would never have to give up his station post to do so. But there was another round of polite sentiments, all the same.

Then a tap of the dowager's cane. "We must let this gentleman get to his bed, paidhi-ji."

"Indeed, aiji-ma." As host, he made the suggestion. "Geigi-ji, please let my staff escort you to your rooms."

Geigi's bodyguard, among other things, had to be bone-tired, exhausted, after standing the last while, and those two still needed to brief and debrief with the rest of his aishid, and with the aiji-dowager's people. *They* had several more hours to go before they saw their beds.

"We are quite weary," Geigi said obligingly, and in a series of small signals, the dowager gathering up her cane and signaling Cenedi; and Bren, as host, making a sign to Banichi and Jago, Geigi gathered his considerable bulk up from his chair, everyone got up, and there were goodnight bows all around as he left. Cajeiri and Barb and Toby hung back until the dowager and Geigi had gotten out the door.

For Bren, exhaustion came down on him, not just for this day, but for several days before. He waited while Cajeiri joined his bodyguard on the way out; and then heaved a deep sigh, feeling the effects of just about two sips too much brandy. "So sorry you have to hike down to the boat," he said to Barb and Toby. And added: "Very well done, extremely well done. Frozen Dessert."

They laughed, assured him an after-dinner hike wasn't at all a hard thing for them, and he walked them to the door.

Then, in an attack of unease, and thinking of that long, dark set of steps amid the scrub evergreen, and that exposed dock below, he said to Banichi and Jago: "Nadiin-ji, one hates to ask, but would you go with them?"

"Yes," Banichi said. "Let us pick up some equipment, and we shall be glad to do so."

"I hate to bother them," Toby protested. "Surely just house staff—"

"—is in no wise equipped to take care of untoward situations," he said. "Indulge me. Geigi's just arrived, with all that means. If our enemies aren't asleep or more disrupted than we think, they'll know he's here, they'll know meetings are going on, they'll want more than anything to know what we've said, and I'm almost inclined to move out some more staff and house you two in the basement with Baiji tonight. Frozen Dessert, indeed. You're too well informed. Scarily well-informed. And I don't want the Marid getting their hands on you."

"Is *that* all?" Toby laughed. "I thought it was brotherly concern."

"That, too, is somewhere in the stew. Just take the protection. And if you're harboring any *more* secrets, bring me up to date on them."

"Oh, you knew we were running messages. Most of the time we didn't have a clue about the content. At least on *this* side of the water."

"But you did know what Mospheira was up to."

"Nothing not well-known now."

"The Marid may not think so. You're just a bit more fluent than makes me comfortable, brother. Unguessed talents." That Toby had never outright told him how fluent he was getting—that bothered him; but Toby worked for Shawn, the President of Mospheira, the way he himself had once worked for Shawn in the State Department, and there were secrets and secrets in government employ.

"It's getting better," Toby said lightly. "I haven't been around people talking before. I'm starting to pick out words. Figure out others."

"I still can't put a sentence together," Barb said. "Toby's far braver about that. But we absorb things. I'm picking up a lot about the boat from the work crews."

"Well, you just be careful going down there, and get the hell away from dock if you don't like the look of what's headed your way. Even if you just get nervous. Stand off from shore and be ready to get out to the middle of the bay if you don't like the feel of things at any time you're down there. Better a little in-convenience than a mistake the other way."

"Got it," Toby said, and by then Banichi and Jago were com-ing back, carrying rifles, and with their outdoor jackets on—bulletproof and heavy as sin.

No surprise to Toby or Barb, who were used to Guild work-ing gear. Bren saw them all out the door.

"Kindly go straight to the room and stay there, nandi," Jago said.

"I shall," he promised her. "Immediately."

And he walked straight in that direction the moment the front door shut.

His two personal staff, Koharu and Supani, weren't long ar-riving in his suite, a characteristic knock on the outermost door. Staff in the hall would have reported he was retiring, and his valets showed up almost before he'd gotten his own coat off.

He handed the garment in question to Supani, who hung it on a hanger, and that on a hook on the door: the coat would go away with them and come back refreshed and pressed by morn-ing. Likewise the shirt and trousers and the ribbon that tied his queue, which he finger-combed out. He automatically sat down and let Koharu apply a brush to his past-the-shoulder hair.

Felt good. Took away tensions of the day.

Pop-pop-pop from outside. From down the hill.

Gunfire. He leapt up, headed for the other room and the door. Supani chased him down with a dressing gown and insisted on helping him.

"Tano and Algini!" he said, and Koharu understood and ran, outpacing him as he made the hall along with four of Ilisidi's men and Cenedi himself, Cenedi giving directions as more of that company showed up from the lower hall.

Bren reached the library, where Tano and Algini still sat at stations and the two assigned to Cajeiri hovered by. "Get to the young gentleman!" Bren snapped, and those two went, leaving him room to reach Tano and Algini in the cramped quarters.

"Movement, nandi, down by the dock," Tano said, "and up by the house."

He didn't distract them with questions: Algini was talking in code, probably to Banichi and Jago, maybe to units disposed about the grounds, and Tano's eyes never left his screens.

"Sector 14 now," Tano said into his own microphone.

Whether intruders were incoming or outgoing in sector 14 one had no idea, but it was too near the downhill walkway. Bren hovered and kept quiet. He could see that blinking sector for himself, some distance off the walkway where Banichi and Jago would be.

He didn't know who had been firing, except the one from Ilisidi's young men on the roof. He hoped it was Banichi and Jago taking a few shots at intruders and not the other way around. He hoped Toby and Barb kept their heads down. They hadn't had time for it to be just Banichi and Jago on the return.

"Somebody should check the boats," he muttered.

"Someone is doing that, Bren-ji," Tano said. "Both boats. And our own perimeter." His eyes never left the screens. "It may be diversion. We have called the village and set them on alert."

Damn, he thought. The aiji's men *hadn't* cleared out all the problem. They'd gotten Kajiminda cleaned up, they'd gone after the lot down in Separti Township, but very possibly people had gotten out of Separti. Some might have escaped by sea, and some might have headed overland, to take the long land route to the Marid. Some might not have left at all, but gone to set up bases in the wild lands, the hunting reserves, between the coastal villages of Sarini Province and the Maschi territory . . . bases that could continue to be a problem until hunted down.

How many Guild agents might the Marid have deployed in the district? Unfortunately, a lot, if one counted any Guild who had been supporting Murini . . . who might have headed down to the Marid as a way to escape retribution.

He really, really didn't like that line of reasoning. He stood very still, just watching the retreat of intrusion in a series of lit-up squares. Which could be a real retreat, or simply designed to divert attention from something breaching their perimeter elsewhere.

He stood still so long his arm, leaning on Tano's chair, began to tire, and his eyes, focused on those screens, to dry out from want of blinking. He shifted position slightly and did blink.

The Guild's actions were like that. Patient waiting, interspersed with a few moments of adrenaline.

They were back to the patient waiting. Which was almost as bad as the adrenaline.

"Are our people safe?" he asked.

"All reporting, Bren-ji."

Our people included his brother, Barb, and the two people he loved most in the world.

And the fact Tano and Algini were sitting there dead calm and completely unemotional meant only that they were on the job and not sparing a thought to personal relationships with anybody. They continued nonstop observing, listening and, with small key-clicks, aiming sensors and communicating with various people about the grounds . . . all of whom were evidently reporting in or responding in some fashion.

Bren waited for another length of time before saying, very quietly, without inflection: "If it is safer for Banichi and Jago to bring their wards back to the house tonight, we shall certainly find room."

"It may indeed be safer," Algini said, and plied keys, a series of fast clicks. He said then: "They agree."

The next while, extricating two valuable and highly visible targets, namely two pale-skinned humans, from a difficult position on the lower walk—that took some time, and Bren stood and listened for part of it.

But then he decided he could be of somewhat more use than that, so he went out to the hall, and asked Ramaso, who had appointed himself to hall duty during the disturbance, to make ready two beds belowstairs.

"Indeed," Ramaso said. "Please delay them with hospitality upstairs, nandi, and there will be space for them as fast as possible."

"One doubts they will sleep immediately," he said, and turned to find Antaro and Nawari both, one an emissary from Cajeiri and one from Ilisidi, and then Lord Geigi himself coming out into the hall, to find out what was going on. Lord Geigi, like him, was in his night-robe, but not, like him, with his hair undone. Bren felt a little heat touch his face, a little embarrassment at that, and so surely must Ramaso, but there were more important things afoot than a little impropriety. "Geigi-ji," he said. "What a welcome we have given you!"

"My staff informs me your brother and his lady are turning back."

"Indeed. It seems safer."

"It must," Geigi said. "Infelicity on the Marid and all its houses! No one will sleep for hours, and my fool of a nephew should not be the exception. Let your staff inform him I shall speak to him directly after breakfast and that the activities of his associates tonight have placed me in no good mood toward him! I would deal with him tonight, except I want my wits about me!"

The middle door opened. Cajeiri turned up, putting his head out. "Are we safe, nand' Bren?"

"At the moment we appear to be, young gentleman. Go back to bed."

Cajeiri likewise was in a night-robe, and barefoot, with *his* hair streaming over his shoulders.

And Ilisidi's door opened. Cenedi himself arrived, in boots and trousers, and with braid intact, and obviously wanted answers.

"Nand' Toby and Barb-daja are coming back to the house tonight, Cenedi-ji." Which was stupid to say: of course Cenedi knew that part of it already. Guild in protection of their lord were never out of touch with the rest of their number. What Cenedi didn't know was the arrangement he had just ordered in the household. "We are lodging them downstairs. If the dowager would wish a quieting cup of tea in the study, we might arrange that." It came to him that, besides his study, which he needed for his own urgent business in straightening this mess out, they *did* have the sitting room they could convert to sleeping quarters.

But that had its own necessary function in the house, the meeting place, the only place besides the dining room that could accommodate them all; and the dining room was just—not the place one discussed business. Impossible, he thought distractedly. And *any* room downstairs was bigger than the cabin Barb and Toby shared on the boat.

Two beds, he had told Ramaso. Were they going to think he was making a statement?

"The dowager will take tea," Cenedi said, "but will not receive visitors tonight, nandi."

"Mandi-ji." Bren snared a passing servant, who skidded to a fast halt. "Tea for the dowager. Tea for any guest who wants it."

"I shall take some myself," Geigi said, "with teacakes, should there be any at this hour, nadi."

"So would we like teacakes," Cajeiri said. "My staff would, too."

Where a boy Cajeiri's size proposed to put more food after that supper, God only knew. "See to it," Bren said to the servant, and as Samandri took out at all decorous speed: "Cenedi-ji, can your people supply security to the front door while we open it for Banichi and Jago?"

"We are already in position, nandi. And they are on their way."

"Of course." He found himself exhausted. "Forgive me, nadi-ji."

"We are glad the paidhi has an accurate sense of these things," Cenedi said diplomatically. "I shall see to the front door myself," he added, "being in the vicinity. By your leave, nandi."

"Please do," he said. The others had gone back to their rooms. It was his job, as the lingering visible civilian, to get himself out of the hall and back out of the Guild's way. The one moment that might provoke renewed attack, were there any enemy still in position, would be a door opening, and their guard needed no distractions in protecting them from more dings in the woodwork.

So he went back to the library, where Tano and Algini reported Banichi and Jago were now at the portico, and then that they were coming in. He watched the lights that indicated the opening and then the safe shutting of the front door, he heard the thump of the bar going into place, and headed back out into the hall again.

Banichi and Jago looked unruffled. Barb and Toby, in their company, were dirty and disheveled, their boating whites scuffed and bearing traces of dirt and evergreen. It was likely Banichi and Jago had landed on them, or thrown them into the bushes with a force they would have considered only adequate.

"Well, here we are again," Toby said with a shaky laugh, "like bad pennies. Sorry about that, brother."

"Just thank God you made it—and thank God I sent Banichi and Jago with you! Who fired?" The last he asked in Ragi, and Jago said:

"We did, nandi. We had a security alert, and a sure target. The dowager's men are searching the grounds. They will report. We stayed with our principals."

"One is profoundly grateful," he said. "Are *you* all right?" Jago was nursing a stitched-up wound from the *last* fracas. And one didn't ask Guild to admit to injuries in outsider hearing, but Barb and Toby were not exactly outsiders, and Jago nodded with, he thought, honesty.

"One remains a little sore," she said, "nandi. But their return fire was not accurate."

"It might have been, without you. Thank you. Thank you profoundly, nadiin-ji."

"Thank you," Toby added in Ragi, on his own behalf, with a correct little bow, and Barb echoed, in fairly bad Ragi, but with the correct addition of a third—consciously or not, "Thank you two, and Bren."

"Indeed," Banichi said, returning the bow.

"Go where you need to go," Bren said. There was debriefing yet to do, and two of Cenedi's men had come into the hall. "Rest. We are guarded, here."

Banichi smiled, a little amused at him, but he frankly didn't care. He was tired, his guard was tired, and Barb and Toby had just been through enough to keep them awake the rest of the night. Servants had shown up. He said to them: "I shall see nand' Toby and Barb-daja in my study while staff prepares their bath. Send another pot of calmative tea to my office. And brandy. They will surely wish to sit a moment."

"Nandi." Two servants sped on different missions, and Banichi and Jago had headed for the library/security station. Bren directed Barb and Toby to his office door, opened it, and brought them inside.

They took chairs, gratefully but cautiously. "I'm afraid we'll get dirt on the carpet," Toby said. "Let alone the upholstery. Is my backside clean?"

"Honorable dirt," Bren said, a rough translation of the Ragi proverb. "The staff will gladly clean it, and the chairs are tougher than they look. There's a bath downstairs. They're setting up. I've ordered a sedative tea. It's fairly strong. Harmless to us. And a very good thing at times. Add a shot of brandy and you won't wake til morning."

"I wished I'd had my gun," Toby said, "which is, of course, down on the boat."

"Well, well, but you're on the mainland, where professionals handle that sort of thing," Bren said. "Unfortunately it means professionals on the other side, too."

"That's certainly a downside," Barb laughed. She moved to brush back her hair and she was shaking. She looked at her hand as if it were a foreign object and made it into a fist, resting on the chair. "I guess the other side isn't through trying, is it?"

In that moment he forgave Barb a lot. He looked at the two of them, his quasi-ex and his brother, and saw a pair . . . not the woman he'd have picked for Toby, but then, Barb lent Toby just enough of her predatory selfish streak to keep him from flinging himself on grenades and Toby lent Barb enough of his sense of stability and loyalty to keep her better side in the ascendant. Toby the rock. Toby the damned self-sacrificing fool. Barb wanted somebody who'd always be there—even if she had to follow him in and out of irregular harbors under fire, as it appeared: this the woman who'd lived for nightclubs and fancy gowns.

"Good for both of you," he said, and meant it fervently.

"Just so damned glad you sent Banichi and Jago."

"I assure you, you and whoever else went with you would have been under watch the whole route down to the boat, but you don't have my skills at falling flat in the dirt on cue."

"I'll be faster at it, after this," Toby said. "*Banichi* shoved me flat. I think I'll remember that fact tomorrow morning."

Bren laughed, well familiar with that sensation, which involved the relocation of every vertebra in one's neck and back, not to mention the meeting with the ground.

And just then a knock at the door heralded the servant with the tea service, the very historic tea service—the others must be elsewhere disposed—the cups of which Toby and Barb took with dirty fingers, ever so carefully.

"This is beautiful," Barb said, looking carefully at the cup. Barb had an eye for assessing things. "But my hands are shaking."

"They won't, in a moment. Thirteenth century, that service. Best the house has. —Thank you, nadi," he said to the servant. "Please wait." And took his own sip of tea. "Your boat will be safe. Someone is checking out both the boats, yours and mine, just to be sure."

"So grateful," Toby murmured. "You think of everything, brother."

"I have no few brains working on problems for me," he said. "So I don't have to be brilliant."

"I never appreciated a house like this," Toby said. "I'm starting to understand it. In all senses. It's not all tea and cookies, is it?"

"It's a village of its own," he said. "It defends itself pretty well, and we all take care of each other. Staff smuggled most every stick of furniture and set of china, even whole carpets, out of my Bujavid apartment when the Bujavid was being taken over. They got it on trains right under the opposition's noses and had it and key staff members collected here at Najida before Murini's people knew they were missing. And some of my staff, Murini's people would particularly have liked to lay hands on, but they weren't about to come in here to get them . . . Najida being part of Najida Peninsula, which is part of the west coast, which is Edi territory, Murini didn't want his agents cracking *that* egg, for fear of what might hatch and raise holy hell. But you know that, Frozen Dessert."

"Even the Marid," Toby said, "was scared to take on your staff."

"I think so. They'd organized. That was everything. Favor Ramaso for that. Ramaso and his connections. No small advantage to me, in all this."

One cup gone, and Barb stifled a yawn. "Oh, my God. I'm sorry, Bren."

"That's the intent," Bren said. The sedative was hitting his system, too, and he set the precious cup aside on the desk. The attending servant, part of the furniture until that moment, instantly collected it, collected Barb's, and Toby finished his in a last swallow and handed the cup over.

"Nadi," Bren said, delaying the servant a moment, and gave him the incidental instruction to inform Geigi's nephew that his uncle was annoyed as hell and would talk to him in the morning.

"So we're downstairs," Toby said.

"Two of the youngest servants will have given you their quarters," Bren said. He could guess the names. "There's the servants' bath, down there, servant's kitchen, where you may find snacks at any time of night—but just ask the staff. They'll be happier to provide it for you on a tray."

"Better than Port Jackson's best hotel," Toby said, and then realized: "I don't have my shaving kit. Or either of us a change of clothes, what's worse. Everything's on the boat."

"Trust staff. They'll see to you. Pile your clothes outside the door and they'll turn up clean by dawn."

"God," Toby said. "Thank the staff for us."

"I have," Bren said, and got up, as Toby and Barb levered themselves up with considerably more stiffness. "Soak in a hot tub, mandatory. Atevi manners. Then bed. You're sleeping in a fortress. Let staff do the worrying tonight, too."

"Good night," Toby said, and hugged him, and Barb did, sister-like. Brother-like, he wanted to ruffle her hair, he was so pleased with her at the moment, sedative tea and all, but Barb was perfectly capable of building that gesture into a fantasy, and he didn't want to upset the sense of balance they'd found, at least for the night.

"Good night," he said, and showed them out into the hall, and pointed them the way to the downstairs, down by the dining hall, before he headed for his own room, and found his two valets on his track before he got there.

"Nadiin-ji," he said, feeling warm and cared-for and very, very lucky. He let them rescue his clothes, and flung himself into bed on the aftereffects of the tea, eyes shut immediately.

Jago would come to bed soon. Her sleeping with him was the arrangement that let his staff fit into the library with their equipment. But he was too sleepy to wait for her.

7

Lord Geigi might have interviewed his nephew in his nephew's room downstairs, and Bren had expected he would do so. But that venue would have been a bit cramped for the interested audience it turned out to have drawn—himself among them. Geigi had indicated the dowager would of course be welcome; and of course the paidhi-aji, and then Cajeiri had managed to attach himself to his grandmother, and they all came with their requisite security, six persons—Tano and Algini were on active duty with Bren this morning, while Banichi and Jago, avoiding formal uniform after a long day yesterday, stayed at the consoles in their station.

"There is the sitting room," Bren said to Geigi, so the sitting-room it was, a natural enough retreat after a good breakfast—in which Baiji did not share. Geigi did not let anticipation hurry him at all. They quietly took tea once they reached the sitting room. They waited, and chatted about affairs on the station.

The mood was jovial, even—so pleasant that when the dowager's guards—her personnel being in greatest abundance for such duties—escorted Baiji upstairs and into the sitting-room, Geigi scarcely paid him attention, savoring a last cup of tea, apparently indifferent.

Baiji was in a sad state this morning—sweating, as pale as an ateva could manage, and abjectly down of countenance. He gave a very deep bow to his uncle, who did not so much as acknowledge the fact, and quietly subsided into the chair the servants had placed central to the arc the other chairs, made the potential focus of all attention, if anyone had looked at him.

No one said anything for a moment. Baiji kept his mouth shut. Then:

"What happened to your mother?" Geigi asked directly and suddenly, and as Baiji immediately opened his mouth and started to stammer something: "Be careful!" Geigi snapped at him. "On this answer a great deal else rests!"

Baiji shut his mouth for a moment and wrung his hands, which otherwise were shaking.

"Uncle, I—"

"Who am I?"

"My uncle, lord of Sarini province, lord of Kajiminda . . ."

"I am less than certain you may call me uncle," Geigi said mercilessly. "I have not yet heard my answer."

Baiji bowed his head over his hands. "Uncle, I—"

"My answer, boy! Now!"

"I fear now—one fears they may have killed her."

"Do you, indeed? And is this a recent realization?"

"Only since I came here. Nand' Bren said it, and I cannot forget it. Day and night, I cannot forget it! I am sorry, Uncle! I am infinitely sorry."

"You disrespected your mother. You disregarded her good opinion when she was alive. You ignored her orders. You did everything at your own convenience or for your own benefit, with never a thought about her wishes or her comfort, or her respect. Am I mistaken?"

A lengthy silence, while Baiji studied the carpet in front of his feet.

"I regret it. I regret it, honored Uncle. I wish she were alive."

"So do I," Geigi said grimly. "But I would not wish her the sight I now have of her son, nadi."

"Uncle, —"

"Do not appeal to me in her name! You used up that credit

long ago. Muster virtue of your own. Can you find any to offer?"

"I see my faults," Baiji said weakly. "Uncle, I know I am not fit to be lord of Kajiminda."

"No, you are not. Have you any interest in becoming fit for anything?"

"The aiji-dowager has suggested—"

"I know what she has suggested."

"One would be very glad of such terms."

"I daresay you should be. Liberty there will not be, not until we have unraveled this mess you have made. Have you any excuse for yourself?"

One sincerely hoped Baiji had the intelligence not to offer any. Bren sat biting his lip on this untidy scene and watched Baiji bow repeatedly.

"One gave the papers to nand' Bren. One saved every shred of correspondence with these people in the Marid."

"Self-protection and blackmail hardly count. Had you attempted to use such things from the position you had made yourself, you would have been dead by sundown. You hardly have the courage to have taken them to Shejidan and given them to the aiji. Did you attempt that?"

"One feared he would not view them in any good light."

"One doubts there is a light in which to view them that would cast you in any credit whatsoever. I shall offer you several suggestions, the first of which is that you abandon any illusion you ever will rule anything."

"Yes, Uncle."

"The second is that you do not attempt to negotiate with anyone in secrecy from me and from the aiji-dowager, who has offered a handsome marriage for you, and the saving of your life."

"One would be grateful, Uncle."

"Did you hear the first part of that? Do I need to break it down for you?"

"I shall never deal with any other people, Uncle."

"The third is that you take pen and paper to your room and begin a list of every name you know in the Marid, every person you have had contact with directly or indirectly, including subordinates and Guild. Have you had any message from my former wife?"

"No, Uncle. Not directly."

"Indirectly."

"She—she vouched for the first person to contact me."

"Who was?"

"Corini of Amarja."

"How good is your memory, nephew?"

"I can remember the names, uncle."

"I suggest you go do so. The marriage that will be your sole salvation depends on the output of your memory and the speed and accuracy of your writing. Do you understand that? Make every connection clear. Provide us your best estimate of these connections and differentiate the ones you know from the ones you suspect. Provide us a list of the things they offered you, and the dates so far as you can reconstruct them, and no, you may *not* have access to the documents you provided to nand' Bren. Let us see the quality of your memory and the functioning of your wit. It may be instructive for you."

A deep bow, clasped hands to the forehead in profound apology. "I shall, Uncle. I shall. Thank you. Thank you. Thank you."

"What have been your dealings with Lord Pairuti of the Maschi?"

"None." A deep breath and shake of the head. "He commiserated with me about my mother and wished me well on my taking up Kajiminda. That was all. He never helped me. He never came to call."

"Nor did you call on him? It would have been courteous."

"I intended to, Uncle."

"Appalling," Geigi said with a shake of his head, and looked toward Ilisidi. "Does the aiji-dowager have any questions for this infelicitous person?"

"One believes you are setting him on a useful program," Ilisidi said, and looked at Cajeiri. "Great-grandson, this is a bad example. Have *you* any advice for this wretch?"

"He should obey his uncle," Cajeiri said.

"Good advice," Ilisidi said. "Very good advice. —Do you *hear* it, nadi? One recommends you hear it!"

"One hears it," Baiji said faintly. "One hears it, aiji-ma."

"Go," Geigi said with a wave of his hand. "Go downstairs! Begin your writing! Immediately!"

Baiji gathered himself up and bowed three times, to Ilisidi, to Geigi, and to Bren, then headed to the door—Guild instantly positioning themselves inside and outside to make sure he made it to the door without detours. Ilisidi's young men gathered him into their possession in the hall, taking him back to his cell in the basement, and Geigi let out a long sigh, shaking his head.

"Time has not improved him. One hoped, during the time we had no communication. One hoped, having no better choice when the shuttles were not flying—but that I believed his unsubstantiated reports that things were in order—it was my fault, aiji-ma. I left him in charge too long."

"If you had come back to Kajiminda while he was in charge, you would surely have died," Ilisidi said, "whether or not your nephew was in on it. About that, we make no judgement—yet. One only offers belated condolences for your loss, Geigi-ji."

"It will be my highest priority, aiji-ma, to find out what happened—starting with my staff. There is no word of them? No word, perhaps, from the Grandmother of Najida? One hopes she is not too put out with me."

Bren started to say he had had no word. Ilisidi said, crisply: "After lunch, one believes."

After lunch, Bren thought in some disquiet. Ilisidi had done more than take over the estate. She had taken over communication with the village. And, one hoped, security for the coming and going involved.

"I shall go to my rooms and have my thoughts in order, then," Geigi said. "One will expect the Grandmother of the Edi at whatever time she chooses to visit. My gratitude, aiji-ma, nandi." He gathered himself from his chair, moving slowly, looking, at the moment, very sad.

One wished one could do something. But what could be done—seemed out of the paidhi's hands at the moment.

So for the next while, they had one very worried Baiji down in the basement with a stack of paper and a pen. They had Geigi relaxing in his quarters with a plate of teacakes and a pot of tea. They had the dowager busy phoning Shejidan and sending messages to Najida *and* over to Kajiminda, apparently couriered by the village truck.

So . . . it was a chance for the paidhi-aiji to get to his office and do some fast research in the massive post-coup data files he had gulped down months ago and had only moderate time to sort through . . . what lord was currently in charge of what province, since the Troubles; what was the situation of the clan and family, and what were the affiliations and associations—all these things—notably regarding the west coast and the Marid. In a land that knew no hard and fast boundaries, among people who viewed overlap of associational territories as entirely ordinary, allegiances shifted in total disregard of physical boundaries.

Impossible to draw any meaningful atevi map except in shades of those relationships, in which the likelihood of various families having ties outside, say, a province, increased markedly as one approached a quasi-border—and so did the likelihood of various families having bloodfeuds on the other side of the almost-border.

The west coast was a case of shells within shells within shells, all overlapping circles of territory and past agreements. The whole district had a long history of warfare, sniping, assassinations, political marriages, and simple trade-marriages, where two families made arrangements for business association in the only coin that lasted centuries: blood-ties. Marriages.

Exactly what Ilisidi proposed for Baiji . . . and what Geigi was interested in, not only for Kajiminda, which he ruled; but also for Maschi clan. The current head of Maschi clan was Pairuti. That, Bren knew.

Records confirmed that Pairuti had come to formal court in Shejidan during the days when Murini was in power, paying the expected visit to new authority, and probably really worried about getting back home alive.

Pairuti had come to Shejidan when Tabini had come back to power, paying the expected courtesy, and had probably really worried about his life then, too. Pairuti had not written a letter to Shejidan when Geigi's sister had died—had let Baiji step right into the lordship with never a protest *or* a request for external review of the succession, during Murini's rule; evidently he had simply approved the inheritance.

It would have been so useful if Pairuti had had the sense and the nerve to do something, considering Lord Geigi stranded in space and no shuttles flying, with a spoiled brat about to take over the administration of Kajiminda, in its strategic location.

But then, Pairuti was . . . over ninety years old, with four sons and two daughters by several marriages . . . all mature and married.

More searching of the database. Two sons by a wife from the northern clans. One daughter by a remote relative of the Taibeni Ragi, central district. One daughter and a son by a local wife, out of the Koga, a Maschi subclan, no useful power games there, at least for the Maschi, unless the game was stabilization or paying off a local debt. Maybe it had been honest attraction on Pairutii's part. But interspersed between the Ragi wife and the Koga, back when Geigi himself had had a marriage into the Marid, Pairuti, then in his seventies, had contract-married one Lujo, daughter of Haiduni, in the Senjin Marid.

The Senjin. Neighbors to the Farai, who were currently sitting in *his* apartment, pending Tabini throwing them out . . .

Geigi himself, in the old days, had had very troublesome associations: had been an associate of several people in the Samiusi district . . . had had a wife out of the Samiusi clan of the Taisigin Marid, a woman—the names floated past, jostling old memory—affiliated with Hagrani clan of the Taisigi, who was (he needed no help to remember this one) related to the current bad piece of business in the Marid—Machigi, who was clanhead of the Taisigi and lord in Tanaja at age twenty-two.

That was a coupling of power, intelligence, and raw inexperience . . . bad business, which Geigi had shed very definitively. Geigi had fallen out with the Marid when he discovered his Samiusi wife had been playing games with the Kajiminda books and trying to bankrupt him. *That* had driven Geigi straight into Tabini's camp, where he had stayed ever since.

God knew what Pairuti's Marid wife had been up to on the other side of the shared quasi-border, what kind of financial mess and political tangle Maschi clan proper had gotten into because of that tie—

And it was a fairly delicate matter to bring up with Geigi. Forgive me, Geigi-ji . . . when you divorced your wife, what did you advise Pairuti to do about his?

Pairuti hadn't divorced the woman. The contract had eventually ended and she had gone home to her clan. But a lordly marriage—servants came into the household with the arriving spouse, and melded with household staff, and got children of their own, and lines mixed, and connections lasted for generations. It wasn't just the lords that needed watching.

There'd just been too much going on for the aishidi'tat as a whole to keep a very close eye on the Maschi, in their critical position. Geigi, who was actually far more powerful in the aishidi'tat than Pairuti, had probably been wielding his worldwide influence with a little delicacy when it came to dealing with his own rural clan. Geigi hadn't involved himself in Maschi affairs . . . had drawn his servant staff from among the Edi, who did *not* marry outsiders, or much associate with them. Even when Geigi had had a Marid wife, infiltrating his staff would have been very, very hard for the Marid.

Not so, with Pairuti.

Most troublesome of all, the Maschi clan lord hadn't given Baiji any help or advice at all, to hear Baiji tell it—whether thinking that it was Geigi's business who ruled in Kajiminda—or just being scared of Baiji's suitors.

They needed to know. They needed either to support Pairuti, and help him clean house—or to deal with Pairuti's situation. An aging lord, perhaps having accumulated a lot of problems on staff—they could sit here at Najida trying to fix Kajiminda, which had ceased to be a threat—but ignoring Pairuti, given what they had learned, that was a potential problem.

He jotted down the text of a letter:

The paidhi-aiji, neighbor to Kajiminda at Najida, newly arrived in his estate after long absence, wishes officially to extend salutations to the clan of his neighbor Geigi of the Maschi.

We are informing ourselves and Tabini-aiji of the dangerous situation that has placed Kajiminda in difficulty and would be interested to hear the opinions of the lord of Maschi clan regarding the situation.

We rejoice in the safe return of Lord Geigi to rule Kajiminda and will be assisting him wherein we are useful.

We wish to arrange a meeting with Maschi clan as soon as possible.

That should scare hell out of the old fellow, if he had been playing both sides of the table. Let him wonder what had happened to Baiji . . . if his wife's former staff connections didn't tell him.

So the Marid had made their move: Machigi, the twenty-two-year-old head of the Taisigin Marid, had used his neighbors like chess pieces, and likely had inherited the game from his predecessors.

Machigi had assumed power at twenty-one, meaning that he had *not* arranged Pairuti's marriage, but he *had* come into his office with Murini's rise—had fairly well come into his power right when Murini had taken over in Shejidan.

So he would have been directing Marid moves, and if somebody had intended Murini's assassination when he ceased to be useful, that would be Machigi.

Another small search, instant to the screen.

Guild reports on Machigi agreed he dominated his advisors and not the other way around. The latest report said two of his advisors were now dead, who had mildly argued against him.

That seemed fairly definitive, didn't it?

Machigi had been in power during the probable assassination of Geigi's sister, the courtship of Baiji, the assassination of the girl Baiji had claimed to be interested in—and her whole family—the establishment of Marid Guild in Separti and Dalaigi Township, the takeover of Kajiminda, the attempt on the paidhi's life . . . and probably collusion with the Farai in keeping the paidhi out of his Bujavid apartment, while setting up in that apartment at least to spy on Tabini, if not to attempt to assassinate him.

For twenty-two, young Machigi was developing quite a record.

The paidhi-aiji's proper business was to interpret human reactions to atevi actions, and to let Tabini-aiji determine policy and do the moving. But paidhi-aiji was not all he was. Tabini-aiji had appointed him Lord of the Heavens *and* Lord of Najida: and Najida was under seige.

He found himself no longer neutral, no longer willing to support whatever authority turned up in charge on the mainland. He had started with a slight preference, and it had become an overwhelming one. He had long ago stopped working for Mospheiran interests. Now he moved a little away from Tabini-aiji. He wanted certain people currently under this roof to stay alive . . . and he had to admit to himself his reasoning was not all cold-blooded, logical policy. He *cared* about certain people. He *believed*—at least on some objective evidence—that their survival was important to policy. But *cared* and *believed* were not words his professional training encouraged. He walked cautiously around these affections, which atevi would not even understand, outside the clan structure. He examined them from all sides, examined his own motives—he didn't trust his loss of objectivity, and he didn't at all trust his personal attachment to the individuals involved . . .

But, damn it, if anything happened to certain people he'd—

He wasn't up to filing Intent on Machigi. He didn't want to put his security team in that position, for one thing: he didn't have the apparatus necessary to take on a provincial lord who had five tributary regions attached to him, each with its own force of Assassins. It would be suicide—for the people he was most attached to. And that course of action wouldn't help the situation.

And he wasn't wholly sure he wanted Tabini-aiji to file Intent on his behalf, either, even if he could manipulate the situation to make that happen. Going after Machigi in an Assassins' war would be messy. It would cost lives, as things stood now, and Machigi had far too many assets. Those had to be peeled away first.

Add to that the fact that Tabini was relying on a new security team—good men; but Tabini had lost the aishid that had protected him literally from boyhood, a terrible, terrible loss, on an emotional scale. He had lost a second one, which had turned out unreliable. The emotional blow *that* had dealt someone whose psyche resonated to loyalties-offered and loyalties-owed, he could only imagine.

So Tabini himself was proceeding carefully since his return to power . . . trusting his new team, but only step by step figuring out how far he could rely on them, both in how good they were, and how committed they were. Extremely committed, Bren thought; but Tabini might be just a little hesitant, this first year of his return, to take on the Marid, who had defied him from the beginning of his career.

Caution wasn't the way he was used to Tabini operating. Reckless attack wasn't the way Tabini was used to the paidhi-aiji operating, either. Of all people in the world—the paidhi was not a warlike soul. But the fact was, of persons closest to Tabini, the ones with aishidiin that absolutely *were* briefed to the hilt and capable of taking on Machigi—amounted to the paidhi-aiji and the aiji-dowager.

God, wasn't *that* a terrifying thought? He was grateful beyond anything he could say that Tabini, lacking protection, *hadn't* yanked Banichi and Jago back to his own service. He couldn't imagine the emotion-laced train of atevi thought that had persuaded Tabini *not* to do that—well as he knew the man, when it got down to an emotional choice, he *couldn't* imagine and shouldn't ever imagine he did. Just say that Tabini hadn't taken them. Tabini had left the paidhi-aiji's protection intact and taken on a new aishid, himself. Man'chi, that sense of group and self that drove atevi logic, had been disrupted in the aiji's household, and had to be rebuilt slowly, along with trust. And until that could happen—Tabini was on thin ice, personally and publicly. Tabini *needed* help. Tabini was, damn it, *temporizing* with minor clans like the Farai, when, before, he would have swept them away with the back of his hand.

Meanwhile, starting during Murini's brief career, Machigi had almost won the west coast, a prize the Marid had been pursuing for two hundred years. He'd come damned close to doing it, except for the paidhi-aiji taking a vacation on the coast. And now things were happening—the Edi organizing and gaining a domain, for one thing—that were not going to make Machigi happy.

Damned sure, Machigi was going to do something—and they were *not* strong, here. Tabini's organization was weakened. The paidhi-aiji was understaffed, always, and the aiji-dowager was operating in a territory completely foreign to her, taking actions she'd wanted to take for decades, but risking herself and the whole Eastern connection to the aishidi'tat.

At least Geigi had returned to the world to knock heads. He hadn't come down with his full security detail either, but whatever operations the Marid had been undertaking to draw Maschi clan into its own orbit were going to suffer, now that Geigi's feet were back on the ground, and that posed a threat to Machigi's plans—to his life, if they took him down. Marid leaders did not retire from office.

All hell was going to break loose, was what. And there was no way the paidhi-aiji could request a major Guild action in support of his position. Tabini might not be eager to get himself visibly involved in this venture—he had a legislative session coming up in very short order, and likely didn't want to involve himself in Ilisidi's controversial solution for the west coast— even if he personally wanted to agree with her.

So it devolved down to *their* problem. They had to solve it with the assets they had packed into Najida estate . . . while Machigi had the whole South to draw on, probably including every member of the various Guilds who had too enthusiastically joined Murini's administration. The various Guilds' leadership had suffered in a big way during Murini's takeover, from politically quiet ones such as Transportation and Healing, to politically volatile ones like the Messengers and, God knew, the Assassins. The way Murini's people had purged the Guilds, the Guilds' former leadership now being back in power had purged Murini's people out of their ranks, and those people had run for protection to the one district that had supported Murini. The South. The Marid.

Machigi. Who consequently might be able to put into the field as many assets as Tabini-aiji.

No . . . he didn't want to challenge that power to a personal shooting match. No more than Tabini did.

Not yet.

He sat, elbows on the desk, with his hands laced together like a fortress.

One unlikely force had sat like a rock for centuries in the tides of Marid ambition: the displaced peoples of the island of Mospheira; the Edi, and the Gan. And the dowager—God, that woman was shrewd—had offered that force a prize it had never thought it could win.

And offered it with real credibility.

A knock at his door. Jago came in.

"The Grandmother of the Edi is on her way, Bren-ji. We are not interfering, but we are covertly watching, with Cenedi's cooperation."

"Good," he said. "Lord Geigi?"

"Is aware."

Which meant his security staff had informed Geigi's.

Bren got up and picked up his coat. Jago assisted him to put it on. She was in house kit, augmented, however, by a formidable pistol that rode low at her hip: the ordinary shoulder holster might be under the jacket, but that thing looked as if it could take out the hallway. "House rules: we respect her security."

"Yes," Jago said. And added, in a restrained tone: "Barb-daja is asking to go into the garden at this moment."

"No," he said. Two people in the house were *not* in the security loop, and didn't have staff to inform them there was a major alert going on. The movement of the Edi lady was a serious risk. "Tell Ramaso to attach two senior staff to my brother and Barb-daja. They should not let them out of their sight—and they should stop anyone who attempts to exit the house."

"Yes," Jago said with some satisfaction, and plucked his pigtail and its ribbon free of his collar.

He took the time to fold up his computer, lastly, and put his notes away, and locked the desk, not against *his* staff—just his personal policy, and precaution, under present circumstances. They'd had the house infiltrated once, and he didn't take for granted it couldn't happen twice.

Jago said, head tilted, pressing the com into her ear, "The Edi are arriving."

Time to go, then.

8

Only the chief lords in a gathering sat to meet, in Ragi culture. Among Edi there was no such distinction. Every person present was entitled to speak on equal footing; so the household had prepared the room with every chair that could be pressed into service—including one large enough for Lord Geigi's massive self, and three others small enough that the aiji-dowager, Cajeiri, and the paidhi-aiji would not have their feet dangling—Bren had made the point himself with staff about seating humans, and staff had cannily and tactfully extended the provision to the diminutive aiji-dowager without a word said.

The Grandmother of the Edi, whose name was Aieso, was a lady of considerable girth, but like most Edi folk, too, small of stature. The weathering of years of sun and wind and the softness of her well-padded body allowed deep wrinkles below her chin. She was a plump, comfortable lady—until one looked in her eyes. And no knowing which of the two, she, or the dowager, was older, but one suspected that honor went to Ilisidi.

Aieso sat, as Geigi rose and came to offer a little bow. "Aieso-daja. We have met many years ago. I am Geigi of the Maschi."

Aeiso regarded him with a little backward motion of her head, as if she were bringing him into focus. "Lord Geigi. Many years we have been allies."

"One is honored," Geigi said. "And I am extraordinarily appreciative that you were willing to come up from the village."

The Grandmother nodded, rocking her whole body amid her fine embroidered shawls. "And have you come back to stay now, Maschi lord?"

"At least to finish my usefulness here, honored lady. I have come back to remove my nephew from any position ever to deal with the Edi, and in the interests of setting the tone of this meeting, let me say at the outset that I wish to make thorough amends to my neighbors and to my staff before I go back to space."

"Huh." The Grandmother made a low sound in her throat. "*Will* it change, Maschi lord?"

"The understanding of the treaty will not change, one hopes," Geigi said levelly. "Some things, however, nandi, ought to change. We are not in disagreement with the aiji-dowager's proposal. And with that said, one hopes this will be a productive and harmonious meeting of old allies." Lord Geigi bowed, waiting not at all for a comment from the lady of Najida, and went over to resume his own chair, leaving the canny lady nodding thoughtfully to herself, with her hands folded on her lap.

Tea went the rounds. And it took every cup and every pot available in the house, considering the Najida Grandmother's contingent. There was a decided dearth of Guild security in the room: Banichi and Jago had stationed themselves just outside, in favor of Cenedi and Nawari, and Cajeiri's young guards were also outside. Geigi's bodyguard, however, most directly in need of briefing, were standing in the far corner of the room.

"Welcome to our Edi guests," the dowager said, when the tea service was done to satisfaction. "Welcome to Lord Geigi of Kajiminda, who is residing here at Najida for safety's sake, until something can be done to guarantee Kajiminda's security. We hope present company can assist in that matter. Gratitude to the paidhi-aiji, our host for this auspicious meeting. We have spoken to our grandson, meanwhile, and he has received news of our proposals without comment as yet, but he is listening with interest. Lord Geigi may have a comment on this."

"One would wish to speak, yes, aiji-ma," Geigi said, still seated. "And one can only regret the mismanagement of my nephew in his care of Kajiminda, and one must say—my own acceptance of his lies as the truth. He has been dismissed from his honor and remains under close guard. He will not return to Kajiminda under any circumstance and only remains in this district because he may still hold useful information. Tell me, neighbors, nand' Aieso, is there any news of my staff? Are they safe? One understands this may be a veiled matter, but one earnestly wishes to hear good news. One would instantly offer them their jobs back, if they could be persuaded to return. Certainly, for those who may have retired during my absence, under a reprehensible administration of the estate, one foresees issues of recompense and pension . . . all things I would wish to see to."

"Regrettably," Aieso said, "certain ones have died violently, Maschi lord. Others have gone to Separti Township. Some few are in Najida village and some will reside in your own village, when you go there. Certain ones, indeed, have grown old in your service and have not been fairly dealt with by your nephew."

"Tell me these cases and ask them to come to me for redress, nandi, one earnestly asks this."

A nod from the lady, a lengthy and meditative nod. "You have a good reputation, Maschi lord. Your clan has not, at the moment, and your sister and your nephew have not. Your surviving staff is waiting for word, waiting for the Ragi to clear out of Kajiminda. When you go to your own house, you will have staff and you will have protection enough in the fields round about. Dare you rely on it?"

"One is greatly relieved to hear so," Geigi said. "And one has no hesitation in relying on it. These four Guild will still attend me. These men—" He indicated the Guildsmen in the corner. "These men are attached to me, of long standing. Never be concerned about their man'chi. It is to me."

A long, slow intake of breath on the Grandmother's side—

a difficult issue, and one would suspect the Edi would like to detach Geigi from any Guild presence at all, but Geigi's firm statement indicated this would not happen.

"The matter of an Edi house," Geigi said further, "I strongly support. One assumes the Grandmother of Najida would be in charge of such an establishment—and should you, nandi, at any time wish to be my guest in Kajiminda until this is a reality, you are welcome. Kajiminda estate will welcome you as resident. Kajiminda will remain Maschi, so long as the treaty stands, but will cede all the peninsula south of the brook, all those lands and the hunting and fishing in them—it does this unconditionally, looking forward to the construction of an Edi estate."

It was an astonishingly generous offer. It stripped Kajiminda of all income except a little hunting and a little fishing, and, most importantly, put Kajiminda village itself under Edi control. There was a quiet buzz of interest in the room.

And the paidhi asked himself—was it legal? *Could* Geigi do that, without the authority of his clan lord? Never mind he was the holder of Kajiminda—did he have the authority to sign part of it away?

Muted tap, from Ilisidi's cane.

"We also support Lord Geigi's offer."

More comment in the room, people perhaps asking themselves the same question. And two more taps of the cane.

"Cenedi," Ilisidi said sharply, and Cenedi walked from behind her chair to the midst of the gathering.

"A word from the Guild that protects the aiji-dowager," Cenedi said, "and from others of the Assassins' Guild involved here at Najida, regarding our intent and purpose. We will bring armed force where necessary to protect the lords of the aishidi'tat. We will *not* move against forces that may be defending Edi territories. We count such forces as allied to the lord of Kajiminda according to a treaty approved by the aishidi'tat. Our Guild supports Lord Geigi's decision to rely on local force, and will cooperate."

Technical, but that was major, even speaking only for Guild presently in the area. The Assassins' Guild had historically taken a very dim view of militias and irregulars . . . and Ilsidi's chief of security promised cooperation with the Edi.

"Nadiin," Cenedi said then, and four more Guild walked to mid-room: Geigi's, from the station. "Nand' Geigi's bodyguard."

A little bow from Haiji, the senior of that association. "We are here *with* our lord. We will work with Edi staff and with Guild here at Najida. Cooperation with the people of the region is our lord's standing order."

With which, with quiet precision, the five Guildsmen separated and went back to their places, leaving a little buzz of talk behind them.

"We invite the Edi to choose a building site," Geigi said. "Anything is negotiable. We are at a point of felicitous change. Baji-naji, there will be adjustments and perfection of our understandings, but let us establish that there will be an Edi seat in this district, whether or not the lordship is declared this year or the next. You will begin to make it inevitable, and *having* a place to which communications may come and from which statements are understood to be official—the aishidi'tat understands such things as important. To what degree you use this place for your purposes, or in what way you use it, or how you sanctify it—that will be *Edi* business."

There had been a lukewarm response up to that last sentence. But Geigi, whose whole business on the station was maintaining a smooth interface between atevi and humans, and making things work, had just delivered something that did matter, deeply, with that last *how you sanctify it*. Old Aeiso rocked to and fro and finally slapped her stout hands together, twice and a third time.

Feet stamped. Faces remained impassive, but the racket had to be heard throughout the house; and it went on until Aieso got up and wrapped her shawls about her.

"Will it be agreed?" she asked, and at a low mutter from her people, she nodded, folded her arms tightly and looked at Geigi and at Ilisidi, and straight at Bren. "Kajiminda will be under our protection, the same as Najida, and our hunters range as far as Separti Township and report to us. Guild are welcome under the direction of our allies Lord Geigi and Lord Bren and the Grandmother of the Ragi."

That was a damned major concession, and rated an inclination of lordly heads.

"Najida hopes to be a good neighbor, nandi," Bren said.

"So with Kajiminda," Geigi said.

"The Grandmother of Najida knows our disposition," Ilisidi said, and Aieso nodded, rocking her whole body.

"So. We will walk," Aieso said, "we shall go walking seaward of the brook on Kajiminda, Maschi lord, and see if there is a spot the foremothers favor."

"Indeed," Geigi said. Bren only remotely construed what Aieso intended, but one recalled the monuments of the Edi on the island of Mospheira, the monoliths incised with primitive, slit-eyed, slit-mouthed faces and the hint of folded arms: the Grandmother Stones, left behind—one could only imagine the trauma. Such stones stood on an isle to the north, in Gan territory. Ragi atevi, inveterate tourists, who would undergo amazing hardship to view something historic or scenic, were not welcome there, and, in turn, pretended no such stones existed. They were *not* on the official maps.

One thought of those stones, in territory where no outsider was welcome.

One gathered the old woman would, indeed, go hiking about the peninsula, likely with a contingent of her people—testing Geigi, among other things. Maybe establishing lookouts and arrangements of their own, for future defense.

It would be a far walk for the old woman. And a hard one. By the placement of such statues, the Edi favored difficult places.

"Najida would lend the bus for transport," Bren said, "should you wish, nandi."

That won a soft chuckle from Aieso, who seemed in increasing good humor, even brimming delight. "The old truck will suffice us, Najida-lord. But mostly we shall walk." And to Ilisidi: "Grandmother of the Ragi, speak to your grandson and advise him what we have agreed. Advise him when we walk in Kajiminda, we will assure our own safety."

Ilisidi nodded. "We wish you well, Grandmother of the Edi."

Aieso gathered her shawl about her. Her company stood up, and Bren did, and so did Geigi and Cajeiri. There were bows on both sides, a second nod from Ilisidi, who accepted Cenedi's arm to rise, slowly, using her cane, and the visitors quietly followed Aieso out, leaving a room full of slightly disordered chairs and a portentous silence.

God, Bren thought, done was done. The Edi were going to pick out a building site on what amounted to their half of Kajiminda Peninsula, and one could figure, up on the north coast, their fellow exiles from Mospheira, the Gan, were going to start making their own demands on the aishidi'tat for full recognition and, one hoped, membership in the aishidi'tat—*that* point was one on which he intended to work hard.

Well, well, the aishidi'tat was still suffering aftershocks from the earthquake of Tabini-aiji's fall and his triumphant, popularly driven return, and in some ways that popular mandate was still empowering the regime to fix things.

It was an old, old wound, the two exiled atevi peoples from Mospheira, essentially being the west coast of the aishidi'tat, yet being governed by other, continental, clans—while coming under perpetual assault from their old enemies in the Marid—

Well, things were going to change, if change didn't kill them all.

Certain interests were going to have a howling fit.

"Well done, Geigi-ji," Ilisidi said. "Bravely done."

Geigi gave a small, dry laugh. "Now we have only to inform Maschi clan," he said, "that I have given away half the peninsula."

"Let Maschi Clan be very careful," Ilisidi muttered ominously. "We will speak to them, Geigi-ji, should the Guild of Maschi clan at Targai want more information."

"Aiji-ma," Geigi said quietly. Ilisidi was taking actions in which her grandson had not been consulted . . . actions that could shake a quarter of the continent.

But then, her grandson had left her here. *With* his heir. Tabini was just about on Ilisidi's scale when it came to forcing his way on the world.

Bren had personally dreaded the upcoming legislative session, and his own part in it—which involved the proliferation of cell phones. Now he was less sure they were even going to get around to debating cell phones, once the matter on the west coast hit the floor.

And Lord Geigi said: "'Sidi-ji, I must deal with Maschi clan, *and* the Guild that serve there. One owes one's clan that, at least, amid the honors Ragi clan has given. I must be the one to deliver this news."

"Then do it by phone!" Ilisidi snapped—an earthquake of a statement from one of the most conservative, traditional forces in the aishidi'tat.

Geigi shook his head. "'Sidi-ji, you know I cannot. I must tell him. I must tell him soon. That was the price of so advising the Grandmother—and one knows Pairuti will not be pleased with me."

"If he is wise, he will be pleased!" Ilisidi said. "Or you will *take* the clan, Geigi-ji. We *need* the vote!"

"Aiji-ma," Geigi began to protest.

"The Marid will take him," Ilisidi said, "or we do. Pairuti is a weak stick. This arrangement cannot lean on his good behavior."

"Aiji-ma," Geigi said in despair.

"And you may advise him of *that* by phone, if you take our advice! And summon him to Kajiminda!"

"One cannot, one cannot, aiji-ma, for my own honor, and Maschi honor, most of all, one cannot. I must give him a chance, with his dignity, for his honor, and mine."

"*His* honor!" Ilisidi said darkly, and leaned on her cane and frowned at him, and frowned at Bren, and then at nothing in particular. She drew herself up then, and the cane tapped softly, once, twice, three times, and her jaw set. "He surely knows that you are back on the earth, he surely knows that Kajiminda is in distress—oh, we cannot believe that he is under-informed, and where is any message from him? We see none."

"There has been none, aiji-ma," Bren said.

"Well, if you must do it, Geigi-ji, prepare to do it in style. And nand' Bren will assist. He is a persuasive sort. Will you not assist, nand' paidhi?"

Bren bowed his head, said, "Aiji-ma," and thought to himself—Ilisidi had just gone secretive on them.

"The lord of Kajiminda must *sit* in Kajiminda again, nandiin-ji," Ilisidi said. "From *there* he most reasonably would depart to visit Maschi clan. Nand' paidhi, you have a bus."

"At nand' Geigi's service, and the aiji-dowager's, of course."

"We have some few things to arrange," Ilisidi said, flexing her fingers on the knob of her cane. "We have some calls to make, but, Geigi-ji, *you* must simply rest and let us arrange them."

"Aiji-ma," Geigi said with a little bow. "But I must send messages."

"One is certain they will be discreet, and wise. Nand' Bren will assist you, making any contacts you need."

"Without doubt, aiji-ma," Bren said, but was not certain she even heard him.

Ilisidi was already, in her mind, setting something in motion, and it was a fair guess that Geigi's honor would not like to know too much right now.

That, or Geigi had just made the requisite formal protest—for his honor's sake—before undertaking something his honor found difficult. He *was* a Rational Determinist, a philosophy which relied less on Fortune and Chance, that baji-naji attitude of the traditionalists. In his beliefs, he could shove Fortune into motion; and he had just made his own proposal to the Grandmother of Najida, generous beyond anything reasonable.

And, what was more, one suffered more than a slight suspicion that Geigi had not at all surprised Ilisidi when he had done it.

9

Lucasi and Veijico were not entirely happy. They had, of course, been listening at the door during mani's session with the Grandmother and Lord Geigi, but they had not been pleased with being relegated to the hall.

And they had had their heads together at least twice since they had gotten back to the suite. Cajeiri noted that fact. He had very good ears—too good, Great-grandmother often said—and he knew a good many of the Guild hand-signs he was not supposed to know, because Banichi and Jago had taught him, and so had Antaro and Jegari, whenever they learned them.

There was no sign for *our seniors are out of their minds* and there was none for *we are superior to all these people.* But that was rather well communicated without their saying a thing.

"Luca-ji. Jico-ji," he said, in the process of shrugging on a light daycoat Jegari held for him. "Are we possibly discussing my great-grandmother's business?"

That got their attention. Instantly. And he thought, *If they lie to me, they will be in trouble.*

Lucasi bowed slightly, a little more than a nod. "We were discussing the events in the house, yes, nandi."

"Do we form policy, nadiin-ji?"

A small silence. A slightly seditious silence. *Seditious* was one of Great-uncle's words. *Conspiratorial* was another.

"We do not," Lucasi said with a second bow.

Cajeiri wished he had a cane like Great-grandmother's. It would be very useful with manners like that.

"You are much too smooth," Cajeiri said. "Smoothness is just a little step from lying."

"We do not lie, nandi!"

"What is a lie?" he asked back—seguing right to one of Great-grandmother's little lectures.

"We do not lie."

"Answer me! What is a lie?"

A deep, annoyed breath. "A falsehood, nandi. And where have we uttered a falsehood?"

"You try to give me a false impression. *That* is a lie. You talk in signs and you discuss my great-grandmother. That is *stupid*, by itself! And lying to me does not improve it!"

A sullen bow in reply. "If you choose to regard it that way, nandi."

"Do you see a difference in it, nadiin? *I* do not. You may be called upon to lie in my service. But never lie to me. Never lie to Antaro and Jegari. And never conceal your opinions from me! But be *very* careful of my great-grandmother!"

They both looked as if they had a mouthful of something very unpleasant.

"Well?" he said. "Say it."

"We are concerned," Veijico said. "We are greatly concerned that your elders are making dangerous decisions. Your great-grandmother is aiji-dowager, but she is *not* the aiji. We are bound to report to him."

"And I say you do not! Who do you think you are, nadiin? Higher than Cenedi? Higher than Banichi?"

"We report to the aiji, your father!"

"Regarding me! Regarding when I break one of nand' Bren's rules or get lost on the boat! But you do not make calls to my father about my great-grandmother, or you will be very sorry for it. You do not meddle! Do you hear me?"

"We hear," Lucasi said in a low voice, and not a shred of remorse was in evidence. "But we have an opinion, nandi."

"State it."

"These are foreigners," Veijico said after a moment of silence, "with their own man'chi."

"*Who* is a foreigner?" he asked. "Do we mean the Edi?" Deeper breath. "Or do we mean nand' Bren? Or do we mean nand' Geigi, who comes from the space station?"

Another silence. Then, from Lucasi: "We are concerned about the welfare of this house, nandi. Your great-grandmother is attempting to replace the lord of Maschi clan. This will upset the whole aishidi'tat. It affects every lord. It will not be popular."

"Maybe," he said. "But it may be smart, if Pairuti is a fool like Baiji, or if he has made bad bargains with the wrong people."

"And Lord Geigi and Lord Bren are considering going to the Maschi house! That is stupid, nandi!"

"We doubt it is."

"*You* are eight years old."

Oh, *there* it was. Antaro and Jegari took in their breath. He saw their heads lift, and saw them both like wound springs, ready to say something. He signed no.

And smiled, just like Great-grandmother. "Yes, I am at an infelicitous age," he said, not personally using the insulting and unlucky *eight*. "But I understand when not to touch things. You should learn it."

Two very rigid faces. "We were put here," Veijico said, "because we have a mature understanding, which you, young lord, do not yet—"

"*You were put here,*" Cajeiri said, "because I make guards look bad and tutors quit. The only ones who can keep up with me are Antaro and Jegari. See if you can, if I get mad at you."

That got frowns. "We can keep up with you," Veijico said. "Never doubt that."

"Good," he said. "Baji-naji, nadiin. People have been

wrong. And you do *not* call my father to report on my great-grandmother. Sometimes my great-grandmother is scary. So are her associates. You should get used to this. My father is used to it. So should you be, if you are going to try to keep up with me."

Sullen silence from Lucasi, and one from Veijico. A scarcely perceptible bow from Lucasi.

"Are you honest with me?" Cajeiri asked. "Do you still think I am stupid and have to be lied to?"

A little pause additional. Then a slow bow from Lucasi and from Veijico, nearly simultaneous. "No," they said.

Not: No, nandi. Just no. They were saying what they had to say. But he realized something right then that he should have felt much sooner. There was no connection. There was no man'chi. And there was no inclination toward it. They might feel it toward his father. But who knew where else—if it was not to him?

But *everybody* who was not his father's enemy felt man'chi toward his father. To decide that *was* their man'chi—that was more than a little presumptuous on their part. Presumptuous. That was what mani would say. They thought they were in his father's guard. They found fault with his great-grandmother and practically everybody, including him.

A lot of people in the central clans were like that. But *they* were from the mountains. They had made up their minds to be like that.

And he was mad.

He was very mad at them. And they knew it. It was in the stares they gave back, and they were not in the least sorry.

"You know far less than you think you do," he said. He would *never* dare say that to the least of Great-grandmother's men. He would never dare say that to the maid who cleaned the room. But he said it, and meant it, and glared at them.

He had finally disturbed them. Good.

But they were not sorry about it.

He did not like that. People in one's guard who were not in one's man'chi were dangerous people, people he did not want near him.

But his father had given them to him, and he was stuck with them.

He could give them one more day and let everybody cool down, and *then* call his father. Or tell mani. They would not last long if he talked to mani, who would talk to Cenedi, who would find someplace to put them, no question.

He was not quite ready to do that. Just upset. And sometimes his upsets went away in an hour.

"You have made me mad," he said, "and that is stupid, nadiin."

"Nandi," Antaro said quietly, "they *are* Guild. And you did put us over them, and that is hard for them."

"We do not need defense, nadi," Veijico said shortly.

"Twice fools!" Cajeiri said, and set his jaw. "Give *me* that face, nadiin!"

It was what mani would say when *he* sulked. And it got their attention.

"I could turn you over to mani," he said. "But I am mad right now. And when you do something involving my great-grandmother you had better mean it. So I am giving you one more chance. You take my orders."

A deep breath from Veijico. A little backing up, from both of them, as if, finally, they had had better sense, or saw a way out. If you corner somebody—Banichi had told him once, and he had always remembered it—you can make them go where you want, by what escape you give them.

"You go," he said, "and keep an eye on things in the house, and if anything happens about what we heard today, or if anything changes, or you even suspect it is changing, you come back to me and tell me. But do not follow me about, and do not ever be telling me what to do. You can give me your opinions. But you *cannot* give me orders."

"Nandi," Veijico said, and finally bowed her head and took a quieter stance. Lucasi did, too.

"Go do that," he said, fairly satisfied with himself, even if he was still mad.

Only when they had gone and he was alone with Antaro and Jegari, he let go a lengthy breath and let a quieter expression back to his face.

"Do you think they will do it?" he asked them outright.

"One is not sure," Jegari said. "But you scared them, nandi."

"Good!" he said. "*You* are senior in my household, nadiin-ji, and will always be, no matter how high they are in the Guild. And for right now, none of the Guild under this roof are happy with them."

"One has noticed that," Antaro said.

"But we are obliged to take their orders in Guild matters," Jegari said, "unless we have orders from you not to."

"You have, nadiin-ji. We *order* you to refuse any order from them you think is stupid. Or wrong. And we want to know what they said and what they were doing. Their man'chi is *not* to us!"

"One perceived that, nandi," Jegari said.

"One perceived it," Antaro said in a quiet voice, "and was not that sure, until now. One is a little concerned, nandi. We were prepared to be careful what orders we took. At least to go to Cenedi or Banichi."

Two of his aishid had political sense and discretion. The same two of his aishid had learned from Banichi and Cenedi, and that put them forever ahead of two who had not, in his opinion.

Two of his aishid had a real man'chi to him, and he cared deeply about that. The other two—it might yet come. If he got control of his temper. His father's temper, Great-grandmother called it, and said she had none.

But he rather hoped it was hers he had, which was just a little quieter.

He had not shouted, had he?

And he thought he had put a little fear into those two. More than a little. He might be infelicitous eight, but he was nearly nine, and he was smarter than almost anybody except the people his father had left in charge of him, which he thought might be why his father had left him here—unless his father was tired of him getting in trouble and wanted to scare *him*.

Fine, if that was the case. He was only a little scared . . . less about what was going on outside the house than about the two Assassins his father had given him to protect him.

His father had given him a problem, was what. A damned big problem. And for the first time he wondered if his father knew *how* big . . . or had these two so wound up in man'chi to himself that he never conceived they could be that much of a problem where he sent them. Maybe they were to be perfect snoops into *his* aishid, and into nand' Bren's household and into mani's.

Would his father *do* a thing like that?

It was what mani said, Watch out for a man whose enemies keep disappearing.

Well, that was his father, damned sure. Most everyone knew his father that way.

But then, one could also say that about Great-grandmother.

Both of them had been watching out for him, all his life. Now he had to look out for himself.

If he could *take* the man'chi of two of his father's guard, that would be something, would it not? He had gone head to head with these two, and scared them.

The question was, did he want them? And could he get them at all, the way he had Jegari and Antaro? Did they have it in them, to be what Jegari and Antaro were?

Mani had told him, when she took him away from the ship and his human associates, that there were important things he had to learn, and things he never would feel in the right way, until he dealt with atevi and lived in the world.

Was this it?

His whole body felt different, hot and not angry, just—overheated, all the way down to his toes. Stupid-hot, like a sugar high, but different. Not bad. Not safe, either . . . like looking down a long, dark tunnel that was not quite scary. It had no exit to either side, and no way back, but he knew he owned it, and he suddenly conceived the notion *he* was the danger here. He wondered if he *looked* different.

He needed to be apart from Veijico and Lucasi for a few hours, was what. Antaro and Jegari were all right. They steadied him down and they could make him laugh, which was what he very much needed right now. He very, very much needed that.

10

Thus far, probably bored out of their minds, Bren thought, Toby and Barb were dutifully keeping to the basement, through all the coming and going in the house.

He went downstairs into the servants' domain—Banichi and Jago stayed right with him despite his assurances that everything was calm and they could take a little rest; and they walked with him through the halls, two shadows generally one on a side, except where they passed the occasional servant on business. It was a bit of a warren down here, rooms diced up smaller than those above, and the floor plan much more humanish, having a big square of a central block and a corridor all the way around. The main kitchens were down here, with their back stairs up to the dining room service area; and next to them the laundry and the servant baths all clustered together at a right angle—sharing plumbing.

Beyond that side of the big block, beyond fire-doors and sound-baffling, was the servants' own recreation hall, their own library and dining room, and beyond that, again another fire-door, the junior servants' quarters.

Baiji occupied one of these rooms. One of Ilisidi's young men, on duty at that door, had been reading. He set down his book so fast he dropped it, and got up with a little bow, which Bren returned—though likeliest it was Banichi and Jago whose presence had made him scramble.

"Your guest is not my concern," Bren said mildly. "One

trusts the fellow is busy at his writing. My brother is down here. Where would he be?"

"The third left, nandi." The young man walked ahead of them, escorting them that far, and knocked on the door for him before retreating and leaving Banichi and Jago in charge.

The door opened. Toby saw him with some relief—stood aside as he entered, and left the door open; but Banichi and Jago opted for the hall, and shut the door, likely to go back and pass the time sociably with Ilisidi's lonely and very anxious youngest guard.

Barb sat at the little table, where the light was best, doing a little writing herself. The disturbed second chair showed where Toby had likely been sitting before he heard the door and got up. The bed, just beyond the partial arch, was made and neat: the servants would have seen to that; but maybe two ship-dwellers had taken care of it themselves.

"Are we being let out?" Toby asked hopefully.

"Sorry. Not yet." Bren dropped into the chair by the door and heaved a heavy sigh as Toby sank back into the second chair at the table.

"Ah, well," Toby said. "Any idea when?"

"Well, it's stayed quiet out. We haven't had any further trouble. And Geigi's talking about going home to his estate—that may provoke something. Likely it will. But *if* it does, it may shift the trouble over to Kajiminda—and that may get your upstairs room back."

"That still throws you short," Toby said. "If you can get Geigi home, you can at least get us to our boat."

"Sorry. The bus doesn't go down the hill. You're safer here."

"You can only play so much solitaire," Barb said, and Toby said nothing, only looked glum.

"You're exposed to snipers down on the boat," Bren said. "It makes me nervous, your being there."

Sighs from both of them. "We can't go into the garden, I suppose," Barb said.

"No," he said. "But it's not forever. There's movement in the situation."

"What kind of movement?"

"Best not discuss all of it. But things are happening."

"We're not pacing the floor yet. We've threatened murder of each other if we get to that."

"The room is bigger than the boat."

"There's no deck," Toby said. "And there's no window. —I'm not complaining, Bren. Honestly not."

"You're complaining," he said wryly. "And I'm honestly sympathetic. Just not a thing I can do to make it safe out there."

"We're just blowing off steam," Toby said. "Honestly. We aren't complaining. Being alive is worth a little inconvenience. We're grateful to be here—grateful to the servants who gave up their room for us. We're here, we're dry, we're not full of holes—"

"I'll relay that to the fellows who live here," he said, with a little smile. "But I can at least give you a day pass. Things have quietened enough you'll be welcome upstairs at most any time. Just don't wait for directions. Duck down here fast if there's an alarm of any kind. I'm afraid the library's off limits now; just too crowded in there. But you can use the sitting room, what time we're not having other meetings. Staff will signal you. I'll advise them to tell you that."

"We've become the ghosts in your walls," Barb laughed. "Spooks in the basement."

"That's it," he said.

"Staff has been really good," Barb said. "They won't let us make our own bed. We tried, and the maid had a fit."

He laughed gently. "The juniors have that job and if they don't do it, the seniors will be on them. Don't object." Which said, he got up to go.

"What?" Toby protested. "You're not staying for a round of poker? We play for promises."

"I'm up to my ears in must-dos. I just want you to know

there's some movement in the situation, and so far, so good. We have people watching your boat round the clock. No worries down there."

"Can we possibly help?" Toby asked. "Can we actually *do* anything around the place? Can we hammer nails, carry boxes, help with the repair?"

He shook his head. "That's the downside of having an efficient staff. They have their ways. Just relax. Rest. Take long baths."

"Can I at least get some coastal charts?"

Those were slightly classified. But he did have them. And Toby was in Tabini's good graces. He nodded. "I'll send a batch down."

That brightened up his two sailors. He felt rather good about that.

So he took his leave, collected Banichi and Jago, and went back upstairs to his office, while Banichi and Jago, secure in the knowledge of exactly where he was, in a fortified room with storm shutters shut, got a little down time of their own.

"Coastal charts," he recalled. "Toby wanted coastal charts." He went over to the pigeonhole cabinet, unlocked the case and pulled out several. "Have these run down to him, nadiin-ji. I take responsibility."

Jago went to do it. Banichi diverted himself to somber consultation with Tano, Algini, and Nawari.

And he sat down with the database again, trying to discover how Pairuti's bloodline—and Geigi's—connected to the world at large, over the last three hundred years.

Meticulous research on kinships. Who was related to whom and exactly the sequence of exterior and internal events— negotiations in which certain marriages had been contracted and when they had terminated, and more importantly with what offspring, reared by which half of the arrangement, and with what claims of inheritance. Dry stuff—until you discovered you had a relative poised to lodge a claim or engage an Assassin to remove an obstacle.

One of the interesting tactics of marriage politics was infiltration of another clan: marry someone in, let them arrive
with the usual staff. That staff then formed connections with
other, local staff—and even once the original marriage had run
its course—it left a legacy in that clan that *could* be activated
even generations down.

And there the paidhi ran head on into that most curious of
atevi emotions: man'chi. Attachment. Affiliation. When it triggered, by whatever triggered it, be it the right pheromones or
a sense of obligation or ambition or compatible direction—one
ateva bonded to another. When it happened properly, in related
clans or within a clan, it was the very mortar of society. When
it happened between people from clans that were natural enemies, it could be hell on earth.

There'd been a lot of marrying, for instance, of Marid eligibles out and around their district, begetting little time bombs—
people never quite at home in their birth-clan, longing, perhaps,
for acceptance; and one could imagine, ultimately finding it—
because the Marid clans were not stupid.

So the web grew, decade by decade, and that sort of thing had
been going on for a lot of decades all up and down the coast and
somewhat inland. Sensibly, a stable person was not going to
run amok in the household at the behest of some third cousin
down in the Marid. But take a little unscheduled income from
that cousin for some apparently meaningless datum? Much
easier. If you were a very smart spymaster, you didn't call on
people for big, noisy things or life changes. You got bits and
pieces from several sources and never let any single person put
two and three pieces together.

If you were a lord like Geigi, who'd actually married into the
Marid, or drawn a wife out of there, you sensibly worried about
the safety of your household—but that household being Edi,
the likelihood of any lingering liaison was not high at all. It had

surely frustrated the Marid, and perhaps made them wonder who was spying on whom. Geigi's ex-wife had not risen high in her life, nothing so grand, after Geigi. She'd gone off to the Marid taking all Geigi's account numbers with her, but Geigi, Rational Determinist that he was—had not been superstitious. He had immediately changed them, and the Marid's attempts to get into those accounts had rung alarms through the banking system, a defeat that had greatly embarrassed Machigi's predecessor.

It had been an elegant, quiet revenge that had done the wife's whole family no good at all. Doubtless they took it personally.

Paru was the subclan in question, on the ex-wife's father's side. He wrote that name down, then got up and walked to the security station, the library, walked in after a polite knock and laid that name on the counter.

Jago, who was nearest, looked at it, and looked up at him curiously.

"This is the clan of Geigi's wife," he said, "who was greatly embarrassed in her failure to drain his accounts. And they *do* own a bank in Separti Township: Fortunate Investments. One simply wonders if they have any current involvement."

"Paru," Algini mused. "Fortunate Investments, indeed."

"Certainly worth inquiring," Tano said.

"Bren-ji is doing our job, nadiin-ji," Jago said, amused.

"One does apologize," he said, though the reception of his little piece of information was beyond cheerful. It clearly delighted his aishid.

"Permission to discuss with Geigi's staff," Banichi said.

His bodyguard had a new puzzle. They were cramped in these quarters, they were operating nearly round the clock, and Banichi and Jago had bruises and stitches from the last foray, but they had a puzzle to work on. They were happy.

"I leave it in your hands, nadiin-ji," he said. "Whatever you deem necessary."

And they thought his small piece of information was worth

tracking. Nobody said, as they usually did, oh, well, they had already investigated that.

So he went back to mining the database with a little more enthusiasm.

When one was put out with half one's aishid and not speaking to them, it was a grim kind of day. Everybody in nand' Bren's house was serious and busy. Cajeiri was *bored, bored, bored,* and tired of being grown up, which he had been all morning and most of the day, but it was not *his* fault half his aishid were obnoxious, and he was tired of dealing with them, so he just found excuses to keep them elsewhere and away from him—it was no cure, but it at least made him happier.

There was a beautiful bay out there, probably sparkling in the sunshine, with boats and everything—but one would never know it, in the house, with all the windows shuttered tight.

There was a garden out there, with sky overhead and things to get into that they had never had time to investigate.

But it was off limits, because there could be snipers.

There was the garden shed, and the wrecked old bus, and all sorts of things worth seeing, not even mentioning there was Najida village not too far away, about which they had only heard, and which they had never yet visited.

And there were fishing boats and the dock and all the shops on down the beach toward the village, from a blacksmith to a net-maker. The servants talked about the net-maker's son, who was about his age, so he gathered, and it was all off limits, because of snipers and kidnappers. The net-maker's son could be outside in the sunshine. The aiji's son was stuck inside, behind shutters.

The Marid was a damned nuisance to him personally, along with all the real harm they had done to completely innocent people, including one of mani's young men being dead, which was just hard even to think of and terribly sad. When *he* was aiji, he was going to be their enemy, and they had better figure how to make peace with him or it would turn out very badly for them.

Probably his father was thinking the same thing, by now, and one was sure Great-grandmother was not going to forgive what the Marid had done, but he wished he knew what his father was doing, and one *never* knew entirely what Great-grandmother was going to do, but it could be grim.

It was a scary, worrisome thing, to send Guild out on a mission. Nand' Bren had had to send Banichi and Jago out, and Jago had gotten hurt, which he was really sorry about. And if things got really bad, they were going to have to send a lot of Guild out, and people he knew could get killed. He hated even thinking about that.

He just wished the Marid lords would do something really stupid and that his father's men—mostly strangers—would go in and settle with them before somebody he knew got hurt.

But the Marid sat down in their land and had their fingers in everything, including, apparently, trying to finagle or bluff their way into Geigi's clan, if what Lucasi and Veijico occasionally reported back was true. The Marid had possibly infiltrated the Maschi, and Great-grandmother was making a lot of phone calls, but his informants had no idea what she was saying or who she was calling, except it was code.

And Lord Geigi and nand' Bren were planning to go take Kajiminda back.

And the Edi thought they were going to replace his father's Guild, who were occupying it at the moment.

And meanwhile Guild was investigating things on the other side of Kajiminda, down in Separti Township, because Marid agents had set up down there.

But that was not all that was going on, because once Lord Geigi had taken Kajiminda, he was going to go inland and visit his cousins in the Maschi stronghold, and it was possible he was going to tell the current Maschi lord to retire so Lord Geigi could take over the whole clan. How this was going to work, one was not certain, but it sounded risky, and people were likely to say no to that . . .

And if the Maschi lord agreed, and Geigi moved in at Targai, there was the Marid right next door. It looked to him as if Lord Geigi was setting up to be real trouble to the Marid, and if it looked that way to him, being a kid, one could expect the Marid was going to figure it out—and figure they had one choice at that point: give up annoying the west, or go after Geigi.

He really hoped the Marid would decide then, just like in chess, that they really should not make the next few moves. That was the way he saw it: just like the chessboard—which he played pretty well, but not as well as mani, not nearly as well as mani. And there was nand' Bren, being the Advisor; and Geigi, being the Rider and moving by zigs and zags; and the Marid could see them maneuvering.

The piece they knew they needed to watch—that was the Consort. And if they were not stupid, they would know that.

Which was *why* they had to have everything shuttered up, and *why* everybody was so grim. If they were stupid, they would try to go straight for the Consort, that was mani. And mani knew it.

Mani had taught him that game on the ship. She said it was a human game, but atevi were generally better at it. And he had thought—he had been just six, then—that it was funny that mani ever played games. But she and Cenedi played, sometimes, and early on he had thought all that sitting and staring was just boring.

Sit down, she had said when he said so. And she had proceeded to teach him. He played it with Gene and Artur, the both of them against him, and then they had gotten Irene to join in, so it was him against all of them. Just occasionally they had won, and when they did, he would have learned something.

And once he knew what was going on, watching Cenedi and mani play was not boring. It was hard work. It was very hard work.

It was like that, now. Things were going on, and he was handicapped by having two fools for bodyguards, and he sat and stared at the homework he was trying to do and kept seeing nand' Geigi and the Grandmother of Najida and mani all building something, and nand' Bren, who for a human, gave away very, very little with his expressions . . .

If he went to nand' Bren and asked, he probably would not get all the truth. Nand' Bren would tell him just about what he could guess for himself, and that was that his father was sitting back in Shejidan being safe, which was what the Aiji usually did in the game; and one could lay a bet that his father was going to act as if he had no information from mani at all.

He did bet he knew who mani's phone calls were to.

He knew who, besides Bren, was very good at not telling all the truth.

He bet, too, that, the way both nand' Bren and mani talked about Lord Geigi and swept him right into their plans, Lord Geigi was a lot more than he seemed, too, and probably not as easygoing and jolly and defenseless as he looked.

That meant he would be a good ally to have on *his* side.

He had never, personally, dealt with Lord Geigi. He wondered how to make an approach to him. The brat kid pose was not the way. The curious kid pose was probably not the way, either. Geigi liked to eat. But Geigi would suspect a bribe if he brought him cakes or the like.

Geigi was interested in his estate, in his clan, in the Edi, in the station, and in business. That was what he knew about Geigi. And Jago had told him once upon a time, about getting information out of somebody, Some people like you to do them favors. Some people like you to ask them favors. The one wants things. The other wants power. You can read people by that.

He thought, Geigi certainly enjoys food. But he expects *that*. He always does things for nand' Bren and for mani and for my father. That could make him the second sort.

What favor can *I* ask him that he can do? Is that the way to get to him?

He thought about that for several whole minutes. Then he sat down at his desk and took pen and paper and wrote.

Cajeiri to Gene and Artur and Irene and all.

I have written a lot of letters but I never get one, so I have become suspicious. I am sending this one a different way so maybe it will get to you. If you write to me by the same route and I get it I will send you a long letter because I have been doing a lot of things you will like. We are all fine but people are still shooting at us for now. I hope it will be safe for you to come down to the world before long. It would be good if you could come to my next birthday. I have very many things I could show you if you could.

He folded it twice, having no proper seal, nor a waxjack. He put it in his pocket, then walked down the hall, knocked on Lord Geigi's door and met Lord Geigi's junior servant.

"I am Cajeiri. I wish to speak to nand' Geigi, nadi."

"Nandi," the servant said respectfully: even the new servants knew who he was. And the servant did not go to announce him, but took him directly into the sitting room, where Lord Geigi was busy at his desk.

"Nandi. Nand' Cajeiri wishes to speak to you."

"Indeed?" Lord Geigi asked, pausing in his writing, and turning his chair. "May I help you, young lord?"

He had chosen exactly right. He put on a pleasant and hopeful face and took the letter from his pocket. "Nand' Geigi, one has had a very great difficulty sending letters to the station or getting them back. Someone is stopping them, and one has no idea whether it is someone here, or there. This letter is to Gene of the Parker house, who came on the ship, and he will be living on the station with his family. We are very close associates.

And probably you will ask my father if you should take it for me. If you do ask and he says no, please at least tell me."

Lord Geigi was a very big man, and sat fairly well back in his chair; his dark gold eyes, deepset, holding a lot of secrets, Cajeiri thought. On the surface he was not a scary man. But for just a second he was standing there with Lord Geigi looking at him very seriously and thinking.

"Is this a conspiracy, young gentleman?"

"Only I have written very many letters and gotten no answer, and if my father is stopping them, sometimes he wants me to find things out. One does not at all ask you to go against my father, or to do anything at all risky, nandi, only to tell me the truth. And if he tells you not to tell me, of course you will not. You can read the letter yourself if you like. I have no seal. But if you *can* figure out what happens to my letters and tell me, one would be very grateful."

A very, very serious look. Geigi took the letter from him and laid it carefully on his desk. "A reasonable request, young lord. I shall ask him, and I shall inform you of his answer, unless instructed otherwise. Naturally—if I do not inform you—" A slow and wicked smile came to Geigi's face. "You will naturally assume correctly."

He flushed a little and bowed, caught out. "Thank you, nandi."

"You are clearly your father's son, young gentleman. One would not willingly stand in *your* way."

He was not sure what that meant. A compliment, he decided, and bowed a second time. "One will leave you to your work, then, nandi, with great thanks."

"No, no, stay and have tea, young gentleman. Perhaps a teacake or two?"

His interest perked up. It was something to do, and it was even safe, to have tea with lord Geigi. Even Great-grandmother would approve.

"One would be delighted, nandi."

"So." Geigi signaled the servant, who had stood by. "Tea, nadi-ji." With which, he got up from his desk and walked over to a sitting area, where he lowered his bulk into a sturdy chair and waved an invitation at another, less substantial.

"One understands you took a tour of my gardens at Kaji-minda," Geigi said for openers.

"One did, yes, nandi."

"Tell me what you saw. Tell me everything. One understands it was a very clever escape."

He did that. Geigi interrupted him with questions about what the staff had done, how they looked, how old the servants had been, and how things looked inside the house and in the orchard. Gcigi was aftcr information, was what, and with any other person, he would have been very much on his guard, but Geigi had a perfect right to ask, so he poured out everything he could think of, between the tea service and the cakes, which ran on to a second helping.

"I think we broke the surveillance machinery," Cajeiri said at one point, "and I think the roof lost some tiles."

"Cheap at the price, one is sure," Geigi said cheerfully, "and roof tiles are replaceable. One congratulates you, young gentleman! You did very well!"

"Nandi." He inclined his head politely, and popped a quarter of a last teacake into his mouth.

"And about this slingshota," Geigi said.

"Oh." He gulped tea down in a fashion Great-grandmother would never approve, wiped the crumbs from his fingers with the other hand and reached into his other coat pocket, holding up his treasure. "Nand' Toby made it for me." He got up and offered it to nand' Geigi's inspection. Nand' Geigi put aside his own teacup, and he showed nand' Geigi how to hold it and aim it.

And that was how they ended up out in the garden, under the shade of the portico, defying all the security precautions, with four of Geigi's men sitting, two on the roof and the others where a tree overhung the old stone wall, and Antaro and Jegari helping them keep watch.

It was the best time he had had in days. They broke already-broken pots, and chased pot-chips across the garden flagstones. The Edi workmen who were repairing the portico began to lay bets, and some of the servants came out and watched.

He won the contest. "But I have used it longer, nandi!" he said. Great-grandmother had taught him always to salve feelings when he won.

"Pish," Geigi said, which was Great-grandmother's word. "You are indeed your father's son. You have a talent for hunting. I, alas, have a talent simply for consuming good dinners *after* someone has done the hunting."

He laughed, seeing Lord Geigi was joking with him, and maybe saying something deeper: Geigi was that kind of man. This is a very, very smart man, he thought to himself, and then: Geigi sits and watches and just collects power when people give it to him. Besides my father and my great-grandmother and nand' Bren, this is the most powerful man there is. And people want to give it to him, because Geigi has no ambitions for his own clan. He is disconnected from the Maschi.

The Maschi clan lord is a fool. Geigi does not want to be clan lord.

The grownups talked about the Maschi and the Marid, and how Geigi had a Marid wife until he got the idea she was plotting against him. And he made a fast move to my father's side.

Geigi is not a stupid man. Whatever he does, puts more things in Geigi's hands. And me being who I am, he is very glad to do me a favor. He is storing that away for when I am grown up. When Geigi does you a favor, Geigi will always be very smart how he uses it.

One has never met a man like Geigi. He is different. He moves slowly on his feet, but is way ahead in his mind. And he would put up with a lot before he would want to be the lord of the Maschi.

He runs Sarini Province. How does he do that, from orbit?

A lot of phone calls. And when the phones were all shut down during the Troubles, Sarini Province had no lord and things got in a real mess. The Marid moved right in. And the Edi stopped them. So the Marid got to Baiji.

"You are thinking, young lord," Geigi said.

He was caught with his solemnity-face. He put a smile on it, the sociable face. And still kept his thoughts inside. He gave a polite bow. "Nand' Bren says you are very smart, nandi. I think you are."

He somewhat surprised Geigi. Or Geigi put that kind of face on, and gave a little nod of his own. "You flatter me, nandi."

"You had rather not be clan lord, had you, nandi?"

That did surprise Geigi. He was fairly sure of it.

"Far from it, young lord."

Cajeiri raised the slingshota, put a stone in it, and further pulverized a potsherd. He handed it to Geigi, who made a creditable shot himself, and handed it back.

"And you want to go back to the station, nandi," Cajeiri said. "You like living there."

Now it was a very sober face Geigi offered him. "The station is my domain, young lord. I have business there."

"You really like it, however," Cajeiri said.

A heavy sigh. And Geigi looked at him in a curious way. It was the way adults looked at adults. "The world has its pleasures," Geigi said. "But I—quite honestly, young gentleman, I have a certain peace in my station post. A certain confidence in waking up in the morning. And a certain skill in getting atevi on the station to stop squabbling over clans and prerogatives and do their jobs in a sensible, civilized way. I derive a certain pleasure out of seeing Maschi and Edi, Taibeni and Atageini and all the rest sitting at my table and behaving themselves in a way they would *not* do on the planet."

He had seen it, in his time on the ship. He had seen it with his human associates. "Like myself, and Gene, and Artur. They are my associates, nandi! Nobody will say they should be, but they are, the same as Jegari and Antaro, who are Taibeni, and people think they belong back in Taiben, but they are *my* associates, and Gene and Artur and Irene would get along with them very well. I know what you mean."

Geigi smiled at him. "So you do, young lord, so you do."

"One wishes one could just make everybody do that down here!"

The smile became a gentle laugh. "One does indeed. One only wishes one had fruit trees up there."

He saw something else about Geigi. "I bet you could have one in a pot."

Geigi laughed, and then looked thoughtful, and very thoughtful. "Young lord, that is a very interesting idea!"

He passed the slingshota to Geigi, who scored on a potsherd, before Geigi passed it back and said that probably they had defied the precautions too long as was, and that they should go back in so his bodyguard could get down off the roof.

So they did.

He understood a lot more about Geigi, then. He had things to think about when they went back inside and Geigi went back to his work.

One of the first things he thought was that, within his aishid, two would understand perfectly everything he and Geigi had said; and two, who had come out at the last to stand and look worried about it all, would be completely appalled.

He was less bored now. But no less frustrated with what he had. He had a crystal-clear idea of the way his own aishid could work—that one-table idea Geigi had talked about. The thing that did not work on the planet.

Except that Geigi and Lord Bren and Great-grandmother were doing something of the like, inviting the Edi in, so maybe it was not a stupid idea for the world.

*   *   *

The boy had been exemplary for days. The worst he had done lately was entice sensible Lord Geigi to violate security precautions. The whole house had stood to attention while Lord Geigi and Cajeiri had destroyed pottery in the garden; but with security all about, on the roof, on the wall, and about the premises—at least it had let young Cajeiri—and their visitor from space—blow off a little steam.

Toby and Barb had taken their own little turn at freedom, coming upstairs to the sitting room, which was, if only psychologically, far more comfortable than the basement. They had procured a deck of Mospheiran-style playing cards, so staff reported, and were pleasantly engaged.

The dowager was doing a little reading, after a spate of phone calls and coded requests. Her staff was resting.

The paidhi's bodyguard was resting again, too, since the two escapees to the garden were safely back inside—while the paidhi was still sifting through names, names, names and whereabouts and histories and genealogies and business arrangements . . . and reading through the first pages of Baiji's sorry account of the last few years. Baiji's writing—God! Every line was *I*, I-this, I-that, and I-thought and I-felt, and damned little information. There were asides, in which Baiji described, to his own credit, one was sure he thought, that he had planted fruit trees in the back of the orchard. That he had enlarged the dining patio. That he had built a new stairs on the dockside. He had built an elaborate gazebo in his mother's memory. He seemed bound to list all his credits, never mind the information they were really after.

The account finally got to a visit from a representative of a trade office from Separti Township, and the proposal, convolutely related, for a further meeting.

That had been the foot in the door. The trade organization in question had Marid ties. They had talked finance—clear that Baiji had a very weak grasp of that subject—and cited refer-

ences from various south coast companies, which Baiji claimed
not to remember, except for one vintner. God! Hardly a nest of
espionage there. But there was, buried deep within the account,
mostly implied, the notion that Baiji had been scared the world
was ending when Tabini had been replaced by Murini, and had
been very relieved to receive this contact with people who represented money.

Money. Something which Baiji had been spending wildly in
his first few months in his stewardship. One had not seen the
monument to his mother, but there was talk of marble columns and siting the thing up on a scenic cliff with a permanent
light. One could only imagine.

And who had built it? He had not hired the Edi. He had
called in a company from Separti, who ended up presenting
him with more bills than he had planned, and said that supplies
were short because of interruptions in shipping—there was a
deal more about Edi engaged in piracy and sabotage, but not,
of course, the servants, who were grateful to him for his good
management and his looking after their interests.

Amazing. Baiji had the cheek to say he had thought his staff
was being infiltrated by spies. And he had secured a loan "at
advantageous interest" to support the estate and keep it "in
the style my uncle would approve" despite the downturn in the
general economy during the Troubles. He had arranged to buy
fish from a company in Separti, when Kajiminda had not been
paying its debts to Najida for that commodity—a detail which
he had somehow not written down—did he think the lord of
Najida would miss that little detail?

Baiji had made all these brilliant moves and secured money
which he put on interest "at the bank," while paying interest
to the trading company which had lent it to him—"to encourage good relations" because the trading company had "very advantageous ties" to "people in power."

Of course they did. The account mentioned names, none of

which meant anything to him, but which his staff would be looking up in a different database.

He was building up a good head of blood pressure when Ramaso came knocking at the office door to report there were nineteen people at the train station wishing to see Lord Geigi.

Two blinks. Three.

When one's mind had been deep in Baiji's illogical account, one found just a little difficulty focusing on that statement.

"Staff, nandi," Ramaso said in uncharacteristic excitement. "Kajiminda staff. They are coming back!"

My God! "Have they transportation, nadi?" Najida ran the local bus service, for all this region. It was, originally, why they *had* a bus. But it was too good a piece of luck to be landing in their lap. Could they *trust* these people?

Sending Guild out to investigate Edi who were on their way home after what they had been through—that would not be the most politic thing to do, even if the Guild and the Edi had trusted one another.

"They hope Najida will send the bus," Ramaso said.

"They will not accept Guild surveillance, Rama-ji; but how shall we know all these people are uncompromised?" Threats against relatives, hostages taken, held under extreme duress— were not the only possibility. "One is extremely distressed to say so in such happy circumstances, but one can think of no better way to breach Najida's security."

Ramaso took a deep and sober breath. "Indeed, nandi. But other Edi can judge them. The Grandmother of Najida, with her people—she will get the truth."

"Would she consent to go meet them? Ask her, Rama-ji, and if she will, arrange to have the bus pick her up in the village."

"Indeed," Ramaso said, and bowed, and hurried out.

Which left him worrying about the Grandmother's safety. But where Aieso went, her wall of young people went with her, and any Edi would-be assassin would be daunted by her mere presence.

Well, he thought—at least one hoped so. It was the best they could do. They had to rely on the lady.

So he went out and down the hall to advise Geigi of the event personally.

"News," he said when the servant let him in, "Geigi-ji. Nineteen of your former staff have arrived at the train station."

"Excellent!" Geigi exclaimed, getting up from his chair, and immediately called for his coat and his bodyguard.

"One has requested the Grandmother of Najida to meet them on the bus," he said. "In the interests of security."

Geigi was not slow. He froze for a moment, absorbing that, then: "One will meet them here under the portico, then, with your permission, nandi."

"Absolutely," he said.

"I shall have to go home today," Geigi said. "And our plans have to accelerate, Bren-ji. Your house can absorb no more guests, and they will want to go there immediately."

"A dangerous situation, potentially very dangerous."

"One has no doubt of that. But one must, Bren-ji, one simply must do it. Our plan must go into action, to that extent—depending on what these people have to tell me. I have no choice but to do this. They expect to be able to go home."

And bringing these people under Najida's roof—or declining to do so—both courses held risks. On the one hand—bringing them in would expose them all to the danger Geigi intended to deal with, that one of them was a threat. On the other—it would insult the Edi to treat this as anything other than a happy event and a homecoming. Geigi saying *I have to do this* had a whole wealth of meaning, and much as he would like to argue with it—there was no argument.

"The wreckage is at least cleared away from your front door," Bren said, "so the workmen report, and work has begun on resetting the pillars. Najida workmen come and go there, but the place is otherwise under the aiji's seal, with his guards. One believes the dowager has been in contact with Shejidan on that score. They can be urged to leave as you come in. They must be."

"Must be, indeed," Geigi agreed.

"Supply—Outside of what the aiji's men brought with them, there likely is a want of most things. And vehicles and communications. We have not arranged that. This has caught us all by surprise. We are not ready to have you there, Geigi-ji."

"Now we shall draw on my own financial resources," Geigi said, "which are not inconsiderable. If my staff feels safe to do so, they can go down to Separti and buy what we need, even a truck, if we may borrow transport from Najida to get that far."

Rely on the Edi to check things out and to be sure of the security of the sources and the items from Separti, where they knew there were Marid agents?

He was entirely uneasy about that, too. Guild could be damned clever at their work, and one had far rather rely on other Guild to figure out the likely ploys, when it came to high-level operators.

"One worries about this," he said plainly. "One worries extremely, Geigi-ji. One is quite sure the Marid will try something when this news gets to them. They will have been embarrassed—granted they did not arrange this."

"My aishid will be with me," Geigi said with a little shrug. "For the rest—I shall simply trust my staff. I always have. Without them—there is very little point of my existence as the lord of Kajiminda, is there?"

"One can think of extraordinarily many points to your existence, Geigi-ji! Please remember that you are an associate the dowager and I and the aiji himself would be extremely grieved to lose. You are a target. You are a high-value target! If the Marid could take you out—"

Geigi laughed. "I shall take no chances, Bren-ji. I do trust the Edi. From the beginnings of my life I have trusted them. This is no different. I know their faces. I know their expressions, of all my people. I speak their language that they use among themselves. If I detect a problem, I shall signal you immediately."

"I shall go talk to the dowager," he said, "and hope we can arrange this smoothly."

They had about half an hour or less to arrange things smoothly—somewhat more for the Guild inside Kajiminda to arrange their situation.

And the dowager was—depend on it—already aware of what was going on. Even smug about it.

"We shall manage, paidhi-ji," had been her word.

There was a steely twinkle in her eye. Accordingly one had the sudden feeling that certain movements and timing were not wholly outside the dowager's control—and yes, the aiji's men would readily clear Kajiminda the moment Geigi arrived to take possession of the house. Guild would hand off to Geigi's Guild, all quite regular, very quick, very quiet, and with no reference to the Edi wishing the inlander Guild generally in hell.

There were a thousand questions one would like to ask Ilisidi about her phone calls this morning, and probably Banichi and Jago could say *exactly* where those calls had gone, courtesy of Cenedi and Nawari—but Guild would talk to Guild, for any information that had to be passed, and meanwhile the paidhi had other things on his hands, imminent things.

The bus, for instance, and the need to give specific orders, with nineteen people standing on the platform at the train station, exposed to snipers and God knew what until they could get there.

The bus was reported to have pulled out of its garage and indeed, the Grandmother of Najida *would* go out to meet the incomers, along with all four of lord Geigi's Edi domestic staff. The bus pulled up under the portico, picked up those four, and set out on its run, kicking up a cloud of dust on the road in its haste.

Ilisidi ordered a pot of tea and a snack, and the paidhi decided to spend his time coordinating a list of supplies for Kajiminda, including some essentials to go with Geigi.

And to grim looks from his staff, he ordered his own bags packed, because Geigi's security had been years on the station, out of touch with what the planet had to offer, for far too long.

There was one graceful way to get additional help over there—for the paidhi-aiji to pay a courtesy visit to Kajiminda, and incidentally to have his bodyguard go over the arrangements and provide backup firepower so long as the paidhi was under that roof.

"Are *you* leaving, nand' Bren?" Cajeiri caught him in the hall, and interposed a very worried question. "What does mani say?"

"Your great-grandmother I am sure is perfectly aware, young gentleman," Bren said with a bow. "I shall not surprise her."

"We would go with you," Cajeiri said, "if we were older."

"One appreciates the sentiment, young gentleman, and one assures you—we shall be very careful. Remember your father's guard has been days in the place."

"I regularly escape from my father's guard," the young rascal said with a contemptuous lift of his chin, "and I do it very casily. Please be careful, nand' Bren! My father's guard is *not* up to Banichi and Cenedi!"

He was amused, and tried not to show it. "We shall check everything, young gentleman."

"May we come out to see you off?"

Difficult question. A hazard. But everything was a hazard. "You may stand by the door—only by the door. If there should be trouble you should dive right back inside: set that in your head. Do you agree?"

"Yes!" the young rascal said, and was off, attended by, one noted, Antaro and Jegari. His other two bodyguards had been making pests of themselves today, probably at the young rascal's orders, at the security station, and were likely still there.

But Cajeiri had hardly left before he was back again, not

bothering to knock. "The bus is coming, the bus is coming, nand' Bren!"

"One is gratified to know it," Bren murmured. "Have your bodyguard advise Lord Geigi and your great-grandmother."

Gone again. On a mission. Bren put on his coat and walked out into the hall first to meet Banichi and Jago, who were on their way to him, and then to intercept Lord Geigi and his bodyguard. They started on their way to the front doors, and the dowager appeared, walking with a greatly sobered and proper Cajeiri, and with Cenedi and Nawari.

The house doors opened just as the bus pulled up and sighed to a stop. Its doors opened, and disgorged first the venerable Grandmother and the local folk, who gathered into a knot near the front of the bus—and Lord Geigi's servants, who came to him, while the bus continued to pour out passengers. The new people were mostly older, with a few young men and women— there had been standing room only on that bus.

"Peisi!" Geigi exclaimed in sudden recognition, and walked out to meet an old man, who bowed, deeply affected, and Geigi bowed, and soon they were the center of a cluster of older folk, the younger hanging back in uncommon solemnity.

It was not all good news that was relayed, Bren surmised, watching that exchange and the sad nods. Geigi surely asked after absent staff, and did not get, apparently, a happy answer in all cases. Bren hung back with the dowager and Cajeiri, in company with their security, not to forget that there were others of the Guild up on the roof, maintaining a watch and a vantage over the whole situation.

There must have been a phone call gone out to the village, too, because in not too long a time, people came walking up the road, meeting old acquaintances with a great deal of bowing and politeness. Some of the villagers had brought small gifts, packets of, perhaps, food; or items they thought might be in scarcity at Kajiminda, like tea, and pressed these little packets on the Kajiminda staff.

Geigi was quite moved by it all. And came to present his elderly majordomo to the dowager and to the young gentleman, and to Bren: "I remember you, Peisi-nadi," Bren said, and did. The good will was palpable, in all present, and made all their precautions seem excessive.

One recalled it was exactly the mood evoked in the machimi plays—before the last act. They now had to get back on that bus, he and everyone involved.

He had not—God!—remembered to tell Toby where he was going. He had been in the atevi world, lost in it, and he had outright forgotten. But it was too late. Barb and Toby had not come out. They were probably back in the basement, oblivious to what was happening above, until some servant might inform them they now could move back upstairs.

And with a certain misgiving, and a look back at his own front door, Bren paid his parting respects to the dowager and Cajeiri, bows.

"One anticipates," he said, "at least a stay overnight." The baggage compartment of the bus was open, and staff was loading on his baggage, including supplies, and his entire aishid's gear, and Geigi's four, which took some shoving. "One regrets to withdraw any support from your safety here, aiji-ma. But—"

"We shall manage," the dowager said. "Take care, nand' paidhi."

And to Cajeiri he said: "Bend all your energies to protecting your great-grandmother, young lord. See that the doors stay shut and people stay within the house. And one asks a personal favor. Go downstairs and explain to nand' Toby that I shall be gone just overnight and that nothing is wrong. One absolutely relies on you."

"Yes, nand' Bren," Cajeiri said soberly. And: "We so wish we were going."

"The young gentleman knows . . ."

"We know," Cajeiri sighed. And added helpfully: "We jammed the surveillance in the second tower. Perhaps my father's men have fixed it. But it could still be broken. You should check that!"

"We shall indeed, young lord," Bren said, and took his leave and went to escort Lord Geigi up onto the bus.

He had all four of his bodyguards going with him; Geigi had his four, and his four domestics, and that meant many of the younger returning staff had to stand in the aisle, but it was all in good, if solemn, cheerfulness. People carried aboard their gifts, tied with colored string, and, wrapped in colored tissue, even a bouquet of seasonal household flowers and some stones and a small winter branch, a token of alliance, no matter the season, for display in the house.

Their Najidi driver got on board and started up the engine, closing the doors. Villagers and staff cleared away slowly from the path of the bus.

The village truck was waiting out on the road, loaded with such bulky things as flour, preserves, and other foodstuffs and basic necessities from Najida estate—there was no likelihood the aiji's men would have allowed anything to remain in storage from the prior resident when they were clearing the place, for fear of poison, and just as a matter of policy. The search and clearance would have taken the pantry down to bare shelves, Banichi said, and so the truck would go on back to the train station, not down to Separti, and pick up a double supply of groceries they meant to order in, some for Kajiminda, and others for Najida and its village. It might be slightly short commons this evening, give or take what Najida sent, but supplies would be coming in tomorrow.

There was a load of lumber coming in, too, on the train; not to mention Lord Geigi's new truck—that was already ordered. And a bus. Kajiminda would need its own bus, and fairly soon.

Kajiminda was coming back to life, and took all manner of supply. It *was* a cheerful prospect they had.

And somewhere out there across the meadows and small woods, Edi were out doing their own survey of sites, which would mean more building supplies coming in from the south. Businesses down in Separti and Dalaigi were going to be happy about that—without quite figuring, yet, perhaps, that the way politics had run on the west coast for two hundred years was about to undergo a sea change.

The truck traveled ahead of them, too, for a very practical reason—it protected the bus. Though Ilisidi's young men had kept a very close eye on the district, one never forgot there were some very good Guild doubtless under orders to infiltrate and cause harm of various sort. Guild rules protected non-Guild from involvement; but one had, Algini had once said, no confidence that the Guildsmen in Marid employ were going to be as observant of the rules.

"Some Guild in Southern employ now are outlaws," Algini had said on that occasion, a rare revelation about internal Guild operations, "who did not report in to Guild headquarters after the aiji's return. Some are reported dead, which the Guild very much doubts. We have been quietly hunting these people. Some are suspect of crimes and illegal tactics."

Chilling memory, on this occasion.

But thus far the Guild was handling the whole district with tongs—because of the Edi.

He would bet a great deal that Algini had communicated personally with Guild headquarters, to relay to Guild leadership certain very unpleasant observations . . . and possibly to receive certain orders from Guild leadership. Algini had said he was no longer operating at that level of the Guild, but the fact was that those who *did* operate at that level of the Guild were inclined to develop a cover story, so no often meant no, but it sometimes meant one was not talking.

Geigi had settled opposite him, with his security standing just behind, as his own sat and stood near him; and the bus moved quite slowly, pacing itself behind the truck . . . which had not yet run into any undermined culvert, or other such illegal trick.

"I am nerving myself for what I shall see, Bren-ji," Geigi said. "The devastation of my grounds, my orchard . . . my collections. I wish this were a happier moment in that regard. But I have recovered my people. *My* people."

"Be assured about the orchard," Bren said. "One has just read part of your nephew's account, and he claims to have planted new trees in the west of the orchard."

"Gods know what he planted," Geigi said with a deep sigh. "But that does offer some hope. And my boat. I hope it has survived intact."

"When last my staff was there, it was riding securely at anchor, and they handed matters directly to the aiji's men. One hopes they have checked it out."

"Baji-naji," Geigi said. "One hopes so, too."

Bump. Even the modern bus springs had trouble with that one.

The road had seen a bit more traffic since their last visit— the Najida truck traveling back and forth had actually worn down the grassy track here and there. The bumps, however, were little improved.

But when they came to the turn off toward Kajiminda estate, and when they had reached the gates, the view of the harbor showed Lord Geigi's yacht riding serene and safe on the dark water. That heartened Geigi no end, enough to lift his spirits even in the face of conditions inside the estate grounds: the neglect of paint and edgings about the walls, the sad state of the gates, hanging crooked on their hinges, and notably the portico being completely missing—except two and a half pillars with the beginnings of a timber frame between two of them.

"Najida is doing a grand job, Bren-ji," Geigi said. "You are a most excellent neighbor."

"One will relay the compliment to Najida village," Bren said, himself heartened to see what progress the carpenters had made. The estate at least had the look of a place being improved, not a place in complete ruin: they had done that much for Lord Geigi.

A small dark van was parked on the circular drive, just beyond the building. Two men in Guild black came out of the house to meet the bus as it pulled up to the side of the construction zone. Banichi and Jago, along with Geigi's men, got off the bus to meet them—Tabini's forces, Bren said to himself, watching the handoff of keys and a small booklet. The book contained, one suspected, codewords or perhaps technical specs on equipment that might have been installed for the estate's protection.

There was a solemn exchange of formalities, Banichi bowed, the leader of Tabini's lot did, and then they headed off for the van and Banichi gave a small hand signal toward the bus.

"We may go, nandiin," Tano said, standing up behind Bren's seat. Bren got up, Geigi did, and the rest of the company took it for a signal, waiting, however, for them.

Down the steps, then, Bren descending very cautiously behind Lord Geigi. The last thing they needed was a bad omen like falling down the bus steps on an arrival like this, and he was more than a little on edge descending to the cobbles, mentally hearing the gunshots and the crash that had accompanied the fall of the former portico, unconsciously scanning the peripheries of the drive and building for any threat.

He didn't waste time getting to the side of the building, which afforded major protection. Geigi stared about him a moment: it was his first time home in a very long time, and he was clearly trying to catch a view of his orchard, off behind the wall to the left—but Geigi's bodyguard moved him very quickly to the open front door and on into the house. Bren followed, and Jago and Banichi stayed close as they entered the front hall. Tano and Algini went on past them, past Geigi and his guard, back into the further recesses of the house, evidently on a program of their own, and probably having consulted with Geigi's men.

Geigi's stationside major domo, Barati, came to him, bowed, and asked, with brimming excitement in his old eyes, whether the lord would care to take tea in the sitting room.

"Yes, Bara-ji," Geigi said warmly, and then to Bren: "Will you join me, Bren-ji?'

Staff, for one thing, wanted the lords contained, amused and out of trouble for the hour. One couldn't blame them for that. "Delighted," Bren said, and went with Geigi to the sitting room he had lately occupied with Baiji. There they settled down, while the house quietly resounded with footsteps. Banichi and Jago stayed outside, and would be very busy right along with Geigi's guard and Geigi's four station staff, checking things out in the transition from Tabini's men.

That was going to take hours. And a lot of tea.

But at least it was quiet in the house, and the likelihood of anything turning up to threaten them was not at all high, considering the handoff from Tabini's men. The serving staff proudly arrived with tea and cakes from the supplies brought with them.

And he and Geigi had a lot to talk about, now that the matter of the estate seemed settled—not imminent business, nothing so dark as that; but the state of affairs on the space station—the likelihood of the promised visitation by the kyo, the aliens they had met in deep space; the state of affairs in his own stationside apartment, and the cherished staff he had left there, staff that had passed all but unnoticed in his lightning-fast transfer from the ship to the downbound shuttle. How were they? Well, it seemed, and happy enough. There had been a marriage on staff, and a baby was expected—fine news, but the couple and the baby very much needed passage to the world again, to present the new arrival to the respective clans.

Their talk wandered on to the station's decision to build and drop the mobile stations: the decision to set up the cell phone network on the Island—a means of collecting observations from Mospheira during Murini's takeover, and a means of reassuring and distracting a nervous Mospheiran population that they were still protected from a now-hostile and dangerous regime on the mainland.

It had worked. Mospheira had been utterly—and completely—distracted by the phones. They were protected from mainland troubles. But they walked off curbs into traffic, arguing with their girlfriends.

A sigh. And now the cell-plague threatened the mainland.

It could be useful here and there. He was starting to admit that. He still thought it too potent a change to loose in atevi society, wholesale.

Which he didn't say. Geigi was the consummate gadget-addict, even more than Tabini, and that was saying a bit.

And while they discussed station politics and station gossip, Kajiminda quietly took on an actual semblance of its former life.

Then Geigi's security reported the arrival of a number of lightly-armed Edi folk from further out on the peninsula, seeking permission to establish a surveillance post in the farther extent of the orchard and out by the estate wall.

"Yes," was Geigi's answer. "Coordinate with them, nadiin-ji."

And hard upon that good sign was not-so-good news from the majordomo: there were certain valuable artworks missing. They were still taking account, but the absence of a famous porcelain was significant.

"The scoundrel," Geigi muttered, over a renewed cup of tea. "The unprincipled young scoundrel. That is a famous piece! Did he think I would never notice? Or did he not know what it was?"

"I think we may surmise the district who dealt with him," Bren said grimly. "And someone there undoubtedly knew its value. Or possibly some individual not in the district paid the price for it, someone who did not attend to its provenance."

"Or my nephew forged the attendant documents."

"Either way, one is certain the Artists' Guild will have a certain interest in the matter, and I have some confidence in the integrity of that guild, throughout. One understands they came under some pressure during the Troubles, and did not buckle. They may turn it up."

"One will prepare an inquiry," Geigi said grimly. "Banditry. This is banditry. And Kajiminda, I am sure, has not lost so much as others. Except my sister. Poor woman. She was not stupid, Bren-ji, except in her doting on the boy."

"Her protection did not improve him," Bren said with a shake of his head, and then they fell to discussing the Marid, the rise of Machigi to the lordship over the region, and his ambitions—not least of it certain things he had gathered from files, who was now in charge of what township, and who was in favor and who not.

Banichi came in with another report, along with two of Geigi's bodyguard, detailing the findings, progress in stocking the necessities for the estate, and the meeting with the leader of the peninsula's Edi residents—who were armed, setting up camps around and about, and with shelters and camouflaged blinds.

It was not a regulation Guild operation, to say the least.

"Irregular," was Banichi's judgement, "but not easy to infiltrate, nandiin."

"How is the interface, nadiin-ji?" Geigi asked his own security, who had come in with Banichi, and with a shrug, his head of security said: "Information flows, thus far, nandi. We have no difficulty."

Excellent news, that the Guild and the irregulars were communicating. Banichi left. Jago, Tano, and Algini had not put in an appearance in hours, and did not reappear by supper, which turned out to be a one-pot dish, but savory and a great deal of it—admirable under the circumstances. The cook was one of the local Edi women, who reported she had told the paidhi's staff exactly her secret recipe, and had substituted two spices at their request.

That was the terrifying problem—the herbal possibilities in the countryside were unusual, traditional cooks were not chemists, and had no idea which were poisonous to humans. Bren ate cautiously, a few spoonfuls, then a period of conversation and concentration on the bread, then a few more, pleading that he was full, thank you, nadi-ji. So very good and rich, one dare not overindulge . . .

Dessert was a cheesecake and compote, and he, for once, ate the whole atevi-scaled serving.

And retired for an evening of nothing but light and pleasant converse with Geigi on boats, local fishing, and the markets.

He was aware, however, keenly aware, that his bodyguard was *not* relaxing. At a certain point, toward dusk, Banichi and Jago arrived in the sitting room with Tano and Algini, who went out into the hall and disappeared, to rest, possibly, but more likely to be watching the irregulars, the house staff, *and* Geigi's guards.

Security was not going to have a restful night.

Bedtime arrived, and Geigi's Kajiminda majordomo showed him to a room where staff had put his luggage. His next day's clothing was pressed, hung, and attended to, and two of Geigi's staff showed up to assist him with undressing and to attend to necessities. He took a fairly quick bath—having no desire to be caught in the bathtub by a general alarm, which was more and more likely, counting the hour and the likelihood the Marid was highly annoyed at their reclaiming the place.

His second concern, and the one that went to bed with him, was Najida. He was sure his security would tell him if anything were remotely wrong there, or if they'd detected anything to worry about. But they had spent the whole day waiting for the other shoe to drop here at Kajiminda, and he was sure there was one due to drop somewhere—given the shift of Tabini's forces down toward the township.

So he stared at the ceiling now, and fretted. No distracting conversation. Nothing to do. Nothing he *could* do but get up and wander the halls, annoying staff, who were working in shifts through the night trying to set things to rights.

He had quietly brought his pistol with him—had it on the bedside table, and Jago had, also very quietly, when his staff at Najida was packing, included one of her jackets for him, which had added considerably to the weight of the suitcase. He had hung that on a chair right beside the nightstand, just in case, and was glad to have it. If shooting did break out, the paidhi-aiji would at least have that between him and a body-aimed bullet, freeing his staff to take care of themselves. Among his thoughts tonight, given this new breakout of civil unrest, was that a bulletproof vest his own size would not be a bad item to own and take with him when he traveled. Uncomfortable—yes. But he kept getting into these places. Or places he went kept erupting into chaos.

And *he* was supposed to be the peacemaker.

Jago came to bed, finally, well after midnight, tired and trying not to wake him.

"Good evening," he murmured, rolling over.

"You should not be awake, Bren-ji," she said.

"One was awake thinking on our situation," he said. He had no wish to imply his insomnia was anything she could cure, or she would scant other needful things. "How are we doing out there, Jago-ji?"

"Very well so far," she said, peeling off her shirt. "We are in contact with Najida, which is spending a quiet night. We have spoken with Edi folk in the encampment, which has no difficulties tonight. The aiji's forces in Separti Township have had a less restful evening, but they may have put some of the Southern Guild to inconvenience."

"One is delighted with that."

"It is the plan," she said, "for the aiji's forces to keep our enemies busy and pinned down in the township, if possible, for at least the next number of days. They will be encouraged to flee southward or to sea, not in our direction."

"An excellent plan," he said. What they least wanted was to have their enemies move in on Najida.

But there was by now, one hoped, considerable Edi presence in the field across from his estate and up on the train station road.

"One would appreciate just one restful night," Jago said, and hung her gun within reach of her side of the bed, which was between him and the door.

"How is the returned staff?" he asked. "Are they in good mind about this risk?"

"They are determined," Jago said, and sat down on the bed, turning toward him. "Likewise the Edi in the camp. The Guild does not approve of amateurs, understand. But these—the better name is irregulars—are not entirely in that class, and we should make certain agreements with them in areas where they know their resources. Algini intends to make a firm point of this with the Guild. We cannot bring them into our operations, nor would they accept it, but we can create a mode of reasonable cooperation, within certain difficult districts. This is long overdue. Since the Troubles, it has become more important. This is all secret, of course."

He withheld comment. Rare that even Jago discussed Guild policy. It was certainly not the paidhi-aiji's business to pass on it, though she apparently considered it need-to-know. He mentally labeled that piece of information as privileged, like their cook's secret recipe, and let it rest.

For what else they did in bed, absolutely no discussion was necessary.

11

It was exciting, Cajeiri had thought at first, after nand' Bren left, to know one was on one's own—almost. Except for Great-grandmother's guard.

Cajeiri had gone down to visit nand' Toby and Barb-daja. And, with the staff, he had helped them move upstairs to the suite that nand' Geigi had now vacated in favor of his own estate. It was funny how everybody kept changing rooms. Even nand' Toby thought it was funny.

But after that, nand' Toby and Barb-daja were busy settling in to the upstairs suite and trying to talk to the servants, and then they were sitting about and moping and worrying about their boat being down in the harbor and about nand' Bren being over at Lord Geigi's estate where it was dangerous. They did play a game of cards with him. But they moped until dinner.

Moped. That was another of Great-grandmother's words, and a state of being he was to avoid. Only bored people moped, Great-grandmother said, and only boring people could be bored.

And *he* was not to be boring.

Great-grandmother herself was alternately busy and out of sorts, though she did not mope. Great-grandmother herself *never* moped. She did play a board game with him after dinner, but won, persistently, so that was no fun. One always knew when Great-grandmother was on the hunt, and she was now, and just did not let him win.

So he and Antaro and Jegari taught his two new bodyguards
to play poker when they got back to the room, and then proceeded to win a few hands. That was good. Veijico and Lucasi
were behaving much more respectfully after he had had them
out working with other Guild all day.

They were respectful for a while. Then they started winning,
and were not polite about it. He grew disgusted, and took all his
guard out into the hall and down to see if Barb-daja and nand'
Toby were doing anything interesting, but there was no sound
from that suite.

The only place still alive at this midnight hour was the
kitchen, so he went there, back behind the dining room, and
hung around Cook, who, with his staff, was cleaning up. He
wanted to see how that worked, since it was the only entertain-
ment going, and how the kitchen ran. There were treats. There
always were if you hung around the kitchen: there were spare
pastries from supper, and Cook said he was making up a snack
for the guard change, when the guards on the roof came down.

Veijico and Lucasi were still with him, along with Antaro
and Jegari, but Veijico and Lucasi got bored and stopped paying
attention. They went off into the dining room without permission, and were talking to one of the house staff. Cajeiri put his
head out and looked, and they said, "Just a moment." Without
even "nandi."

That made him mad.

That made him very mad. He waited that moment. And
waited. And they went on talking with one of the serving staff,
who was Edi, and who did not want to talk to them, because
the servant was supposed to be helping Cook.

"Nandi," Antaro said quietly, close by him, "shall we go get
them?"

"No," he said, and then he thought he would just teach them
a lesson. He made a sign for silence to Antaro and Jegari and he
took them both out the back way, using the servants' passages,
just to see how long it would take Veijico and Lucasi to figure

out he was missing. He could have taken the back way all the way around and gotten all the way back to his suite without coming into the hall at all.

But about that time the guard changed. He watched from one of the side doors as some of mani's guard went outside to the garden, where there was an easy way up to the roof, and there was noise overhead, as the guard that had been up there began to come down for hot sandwiches and tea.

Which would probably give Veijico and Lucasi someone else to talk to and another excuse to ignore him. He was disgusted.

So he went down to the lower hall, where nand' Toby and Barb had been until they had moved upstairs.

From there they walked way around past the kitchen store-rooms into the residency hall, where most of the servants had their rooms. They did not go to the hall where Lord Baiji was. That would run them straight into two of Great-grandmother's young men and he had the notion of not being findable.

"Nandi," Antaro said. "We two should go up and advise Lucasi and Veijico. We do not need to say where you are. But they will be worried up there by now."

"Good," he said. "They should be."

So they found a storeroom to explore, and looked through it, just to see the fishing tackle and odd things that hung about, tools he had never seen—it was just interesting to poke about the house when most everybody was asleep.

But then he heard the distant thump of one of the big doors.

That was a little worrisome. It was *after* the time for the guard change. Something was going on upstairs.

"Maybe someone has come from nand' Bren," he said, and they left the storeroom and went out into the hall, where they ran straight into one of nand' Bren's valets.

"Nandi! They are looking for you! They are looking for you everywhere! They are even searching outside!"

"Gods less fortunate." It was his father's favorite bad word.

"Fools!" That was his great-grandmother's. He headed down the corridor, heading for the servant accesses to the upstairs, and Antaro and Jegari were close behind him.

They burst up into the main hall and saw only one of the servants, who exclaimed: "Young lord! The Guild is looking for you!"

"Did someone just now go outside, nadi?"

"Several people, nandi. Nand' Toby, the lady, two of your young guard, and two of the aiji-dowager's—"

Disaster. Complete disaster. "Run, tell my great-grandmother we are safe, nadi!" He ran for the door, Antaro and Jegari with him. He flung up the floor lock. Jegari got the top locks. By then another servant had run up and started trying to keep the door shut, crying out that they were to stay inside.

"Stand *back*, nadi!" he snapped, and they got one side of the doors open, enough to rush out under the portico in the dark. The walk led around beside the house, and down a series of zigzags in scrub and rock to reach the harbor.

He stayed close by the front house wall and ran as far as the very top of that walk, cupped his hands about his mouth, and yelled down the hill at the top of his lungs: "We are up here, nandi, nadiin-ji! We are safe! Come—!"

Shots erupted, flashes off in the dark to the right, shots from across the slope. Then shots banged out from off the roof, shots came from everywhere at once, and he and Jegari and Antaro all dived for cover against the house wall.

The house door opened, throwing light and servants' silhouettes out onto the cobbled drive.

"Go back, nadiin!" Cajeiri yelled back from his hiding-spot. "We are safe here! Shut the door! You are lighting us up!"

The door thumped shut. Dark fell on the portico again. One did not wish to be responsible for enemies getting into the house, into Great-grandmother's vicinity. At least *Cenedi* would be with Great-grandmother, not leaving her for anything—which was good. So all he and Antaro and Jegari needed to do was just stay flat and not get into any more trouble until the Guild handled the problem.

People shouted, far downhill. One was nand' Toby, shouting in Mosphei': "Barb, where are you? Somebody help! Somebody help! Barb's not here!"

Nobody could understand him. Cajeiri did.

"Barb-daja is in trouble," Cajeiri said, and wriggled onto the flagstones, but he could not see Toby. He decided to risk it. He yelled down the hill: "Veijio! Lucasi! Everybody! Help nand' Toby! He cannot find Barb-daja!" And in the sudden thought that nand' Toby might be carrying a gun: "Nand' Toby, keep down! I have sent my guard down to help you!"

Shots were still going off, sporadically.

Then someone yelled out faintly, from far, far below: "Along the waterline! Someone is down there!"

"Don't shoot!" Cajeiri yelled out. "It could be Barb-daja!"

It was a mess. It was a terrible, mistaken mess.

And he had started it, making everyone think he had done something stupid—because that was what people always assumed he would do.

More shots went off, all the same. On both sides.

"Barb!" nand' Toby yelled. His voice cracked. There was no answer. Guild were surely moving out there, and it was dangerous for Toby to keep shouting. *"Barb!"*

Then there was quiet for a few moments, just the whisper of the wind and the sound of the water up from the harbor, the bump of something hitting wood, in the rhythm of the waves, from far, far down at the dock. It was that quiet for a moment. Several moments.

Then somebody, one of Great-grandmother's aishid, called out: "Nand' Toby has been shot! Assistance here!"

12

Bren sighed into soft, cool pillows, next to Jago's very warm company—after a session of what Jago called good exercise. It was blissful contentment—not without, however, the awareness that very many people were spending the night in somewhat less comfort, on guard around the estate, even on its roof. A little wind had started up, audibly whistling around the eaves, and there had been clouds in the west, good indicator of weather to come before morning.

Bren sighed, rolled over, and rested his head against Jago's shoulder.

A knock came at the door.

Jago rolled out of bed so fast his head hit the mattress. An atevi knock meant somebody was opening the door, and that didn't exclude assassins. Jago met the opening door stark naked except for a gun.

The intruder, limned in the dim light from the sitting room, had a Guild-uniform outline. And said, "Excuse me, nandi, but there is trouble at Najida."

God. That was Tano. Bren bailed out of bed in no different condition than Jago and grabbed a robe. "What trouble, Tano-ji?"

"An attack, nandi. Your brother is injured, and Barb-daja is missing."

His heart went leaden. "Did they get into the house?"

"No, nandi. They were outside. They were driven off."

"How badly is my brother hurt?"

"Seriously, nandi, not fatally, is the report. They are bring-
ing him to the house. The dowager's physician is standing by."
Tano's voice trailed off slightly as he pressed a hand to his ear.
"There is a phone call from the house. Ramaso is reporting.
The house is secure."

Toby. God. Toby wasn't his first duty. "The dowager," he
asked. "Cajeiri."

"—was thought to be outside, nandi, but turned up in the
house. Lucasi and Veijico, however, are failing to report."

"Damn!" he said, and raked a hand through his hair. Complicitous? Tabini-aiji himself had assigned those two—they
could *not* be working for the Marid. Tabini's organization could
not be that compromised.

And Toby . . .

They could need blood at Najida. Human blood. Barb was
missing. He was the only human on this side of the strait. "I
have to go there," he said. "I am Toby's blood type. I have to get
there as soon as possible."

Jago nodded, once, affirmatively. "Yes," she said, with no
argument. And to Tano: "Wake Banichi. Safest we *all* go back,
nandi. We must wake Lord Geigi."

All their plans were thrown upside down. It would look
like retreat, which had its own impact on the situation for the
whole region. But they had no choice.

Banichi had shown up before Tano even cleared the room.
Four or five handsigns flew between them, and Banichi said, "I
shall wake Lord Geigi. Haste is paramount. Packing can wait."
Two more handsigns and Banichi was gone.

"Algini will negotiate this with the locals," Jago said, "and
with the Guild. Dress, Bren-ji."

Dress. Fast. He *couldn't* go over the emotional edge. He had
Guild under his direction: he had Geigi's plan for the situation
left exposed and fragile. He couldn't put them at risk by flying
about in a mental fog. He had his professionals opposing other

professionals who were intending to do all the damage they could, and he had to get his thoughts in order.

Getting that bus back down that road in the dark was not going to be safe. But they'd made a mistake coming back here earlier than they'd expected, relying on the Edi irregulars to hold back Guild professionals—political decision in a military situation, which was *still* right, politically, but potentially, now, they had exposed a second target, depending on how many resources the Marid had left on the coast . . . and how far Tabini's men had retreated.

They'd expected the strike to come at Kajiminda.

But Barb missing—and Cajeiri's two new bodyguards with her—

God, that was damned suspicious, no matter Tabini had appointed them; and he hoped that Algini, who had major clout with the Guild, and Banichi, who had major ins with Tabini, could give them some information.

Which didn't make damned sense. If they were infiltrators, why in hell go after Barb, and not the aiji-dowager, for God's sake? Why not Cajeiri?

No, it sounded more like Cajeiri's two guards were themselves in trouble. And if that was the case, either the enemy had been very lucky, or Najida was facing somebody very, very good, and *that* didn't augur well for the safety of anybody, here or there.

He threw on his rougher clothes, sturdy coat, minimum of lace, and he put the gun in his pocket. More, over the lot, he put on Jago's spare jacket—it was far shorter than his coat, and still weighed like lead, but he felt safer with that on, undignified as it looked. Jago ducked into the bedroom, helped him zip the jacket, grabbed up her own gear, and had him out into the front hall before Geigi and his majordomo arrived.

"An outrageous situation," was Geigi's word for what had happened. "One is devastated, Bren-ji, devastated at the attack on your household." And to his majordomo: "We must support our neighbors, Bara-ji. My bodyguard will stay here with half of nand' Bren's guard to defend this house and my staff. We are calling in support from Najida and the township, and we are going with nand' Bren in the care of his bodyguard, as quickly as we can, to bring nand' Bren to his brother-of-both-parents. One asks, one asks fervently, Bara-ji, that you keep close, trust to your defense, and hold the house safe. Do not attempt to defend the grounds! Reinforcements are coming from the capital in a matter of hours. We are assured of it."

Tabini knew what had happened, then. It was word he had not had, but expected.

And Tano and Algini were electing to stay at Kajiminda? It was a Guild decision. He didn't meddle.

"Yes," the old man said, bowing. "No one of ill intent will cross this threshold, nandi."

Outside there was the sound of the bus engine, as it pulled up to the front door. Banichi and Jago were there, household servants had a small amount of gear, and there was no time for more farewells or expression of sentiment. They moved forward, the small party they had assembled. The majordomo opened one house door, and as it opened, Jago flung an arm around Bren, and hurried him for the bus door—which this time faced the house door at very short range. He scrambled up the tall steps at all the speed he could muster, Geigi boarded with Banichi, and Jago herself took over the driver's seat while the assigned driver, a Najida man, took the seat behind.

The door shut. They rolled. Immediately. The bus whipped around the U of the drive, gathering speed as they headed down the long estate grounds road for the gate.

Bren didn't ask whether he should be on the floor. Banichi had set Geigi on the floor in the stairwell, ordered their erstwhile driver to the floorboards and crouched on the floor beside Jago, holding on to the rail with one arm and keeping a heavy rifle tucked in the other while the bus roared along the road.

They slewed around what had to be the turn onto the main road and Jago opened it up for all it was worth, no matter the condition of the road.

"We are not using the bridge," she warned them. "Hold on!"

God, Bren thought. He knew why not. The little bridge was a prime candidate for sabotage—but he wasn't sure the bus could make it across the intermittent stream below.

It did. It scraped, but Jago shifted and spun the wheel, and they bounced, but they cleared it and kept going, breaking brush and throwing rock as they rejoined the road and opened up wide.

Banichi said one word into his com. That was all Bren saw of communications between their bus and anywhere else, but at very least Najida's defenders were not going to mistake the bus for any other vehicle—even the irregulars couldn't make that mistake.

Nor could their enemies, unfortunately. Bren maintained a death grip on the seat stanchion nearest, tried to keep his foot from contacting Geigi, who was having as difficult a time maintaining his place against the door.

It was no short trip. And they were going where they *knew* the trouble was. Guild tactics were rarely those of pitched battle; but they were making racket enough it was likely to make their attackers think, one hoped, that they were coming back in full force, maybe with reinforcements, and leaving Kajiminda open.

It would not make it easier on Kajiminda's defenders—but it would take their enemy time to change targets, overland. Few forces, but stealthy, preferring ambush if they could—that was Guild. And thus far the bus had met nothing to oppose them. Jago was risking herself, driving, but it was driving of a kind their village driver wouldn't—probably couldn't handle.

Jago slacked speed in a series of fast moves, took the bus around the turn onto the east-west road, the one from the train station, slewed it straight, and gathered top speed, just about as much as they could handle on the downhill.

"One thought the shuttle quite the worst," Geigi muttered, from over his arm. "One is impressed with your bodyguard's driving, Bren-ji. Quite impressed."

They slowed again. This time it was the estate drive, and Jago made the corner without sending them into the culvert. They'd made it.

Shots raked the front windows on the driver's side. Jago ducked and a dozen pocks erupted across the glass.

A fusillade of shots came from the other side, and Jago, upright in the seat and spinning the wheel with all her might in Bren's upside-down view, pulled them into the yellow glare of the porch lights.

"Douse the porch lights," Banichi snapped into his com, vexed. And nearly simultaneously shot to his knees and hit the door mechanism, sending it open onto the porch.

They had to move. Bren scrambled up to his knees, shoved at Geigi's bulk to help him get rightwise around on the steps of the short stairwell, and helped steady him on the way down as armed Guild showed up to assist from outside. He thought he was going to descend the steps next. Banichi simply snatched him by the jacket and hauled him down—set him on his feet on the cobbles and shoved him toward the door.

Jago had to be all right. Bren couldn't see her, but she had gotten them in—they had bulletproof glass in front. He hadn't known they had. Thank God, he thought. Thank whoever did the details on the bus—

Banichi shoved him ahead. He was right with Geigi in passing the doors, past a small knot of the dowager's men, all armed with rifles, and, Banichi letting him go, he turned half about to see Jago and their driver both inbound.

The door shut. Bars went into place.

"The dowager," he asked on the next breath. "The young gentleman."

"Safe, nandi," Nawari said, "Toby-nandi is resting in the dowager's suite. Siegi-nandi is attending him."

That was the dowager's physician. And in Ilisidi's rooms. He heard with immense relief that Toby was alive—in what condition was not yet apparent, but alive. He began to shed the heavy jacket, and two of the staff assisted.

"Barb-daja?"

"We have not found her," Nawari said. "Toby-nandi says she ran up the walk. She did not arrive at the top of the hill. Local folk are attempting to track her, but thus far have no indication of her whereabouts. And the two of the young gentleman's bodyguard are still missing. They may be trying to track the attackers. We are devastated, nandi."

"You have done everything possible," he answered. Damned sure the house was upset. But he was not assigning blame at the moment. He looked back at Banichi and Jago, who were debriefing two of Cenedi's men—Cenedi personally attending the dowager, he was sure—and saw that Jago had blood running down her cheek, a chip off the windshield, almost certainly.

That made him mad. His brother's being injured made him mad. Whatever decision had sent his people out of safety and on to the hill in the dark made him mad, and at the moment there was nothing he could do about it, except see to Geigi's comfort as best he could and attend to his brother.

Ramaso had come, standing quietly by the side of the Guild, waiting for instruction.

"Please arrange everything available, Rama-ji, to accommodate Lord Geigi, whatever you must do."

"Your brother will have more need of the room than I shall, Bren-ji," Geigi said. "And I brought neither staff nor bodyguard with me. Please let me not discommode him. I should rather share quarters downstairs with my nephew."

"Then take my suite, nandi. I shall not need it tonight. Ease my mind by accepting." He stifled a gasp as the heavy jacket at last slid free. "Now I must go to my brother."

*   *   *

Resting, Nawari had said, with the physician still in attendance. Bren swallowed hard as Ramaso knocked for him, and opened the door on the dowager's sitting room.

It was not a pretty sight: they had appropriated a buffet and a side table for surgery, and Toby was unconscious, looking pale under the light the physician's attendants held aloft.

With an upward glance the physician saw him.

"I am his blood type, nandi," Bren said.

"Good." The physician, nand' Siegi, gave a jerk of his elbow, and said, to an attending servant: "Chair."

A servant helped him with his coat and his shirt sleeve. He sat down, and nand' Siegi's assistant arranged the equipment, found a vein—he ignored the procedure except to follow instructions and to try to quiet the pulse that had hammered in his skull ever since he had heard the news. On the table, Toby looked like wax, very, very still—sedated, one hoped.

Didn't need to be shooting Toby all this adrenaline, he said to himself. Calm down. They were linked now. Direct transfusion. It wasn't optimum, he guessed, but it was what they had. It was at least doing something—when there was, otherwise, damned little he could do.

At some point, Ilisidi put in an appearance. He was at disadvantage, far from able to stand up, and a little light-headed. He just stayed still and listened.

"We are doing well, aiji-ma," he heard the physician say to her. "His vital signs are improving. The transfusion will be helpful."

That was good then. He relaxed over the next while, except for the persistent paths his brain took about Guild business, the security of the house, and of Kajiminda.

And the dowager came back a second time, this time with Cajeiri, who looked at him and at Toby gravely and with very large eyes.

"One is exceedingly sorry, nand' paidhi," Cajeiri said.

"You were not outside, were you, young gentleman?"

"I was downstairs. I was quarreling with my bodyguard all day. They were not paying attention, so I left them to teach them a lesson. Everybody thought I had gone outside and down to the boats. And nand' Toby and Barb-daja went with them to help find me, but they could not understand well enough . . ."

"That is enough," the dowager said. "The paidhi-aiji has other things on his mind. You will rest, nand' paidhi!" Stamp went the cane. "Sweet tea for the paidhi! What are you standing there expecting? You, young gentleman, may go to your rooms. See you stay there! It is an indecent hour of the night!"

There was motion. In short order there was sweetened tea. He drank it down, and shut his eyes and listened to nand' Siegi talking to his assistant. The dowager was safe. Cajeiri was. Nobody had gotten into the house, and if anything were going on, he thought his bodyguard would surely come in to advise him.

In time, nand' Siegi pronounced himself satisfied, and turned his attention to Bren.

"Take more tea, a little nourishment. Rest a few hours, nand' paidhi. Nand' Toby is doing well, much assisted by your effort."

"One is very grateful, nand' physician. One is extremely grateful. How will nand' Toby be?"

"He has been fortunate—fortunate to have had medical assistance at hand; fortunate in your arriving. We have repaired the damage. One foresees a good recovery. Tell him he should not exert, should not lift, and he will have no impairment. He should rest. My assistant will remain with him until he wakes. If you wish to stay with him to rest, that would not be amiss. He is greatly concerned for the lady."

"One understands," Bren said, and started to get up to bow, but Siegi prevented him with a gesture.

"Stay seated. Rest, nandi. If you wish to walk, use caution."

"Yes," he said. It was all there was to say, except, "My profound thanks, nandi."

So all there was to do was sit there, wondering. Siegi left. The assistant sat beside the light, and Toby rested very quietly.

A servant came, offering more tea, which he declined.

His eyes grew heavy, though his mind continued to race. Then Cenedi came in, quietly, and went into the interior rooms to speak with the dowager, doubtless to report. Bren wanted desperately to know what was going on.

And in a little time Cenedi came out to the sitting room.

"There is no sign of the lady, nand' paidhi," Cenedi said. "Two of my men have been attempting to find a clear trail, which is greatly obscured by the passage of the young gentleman's guard."

Both hopeful—and grim. "How do you read those two, Cenedi-ji?" he asked.

"We cannot read them," Cenedi said, "except in their man'chi, which is considerably in question. The aiji's men are investigating. These two were often in the operations center. We are not pleased, nandi, with that combination of circumstances."

Things were in an absolute mess. If there was now question about the loyalty of the two young Guild, there was no knowing how much those two could have overheard, with application of effort—and Cenedi, one could read between the lines, was beyond angry at the situation.

"I shall consult with Banichi, Cenedi-ji. One believes we must make some decisions this morning, and make them quickly."

"If we had the mecheiti we could find them," the dowager said grimly. She had arrived silently in the doorway, having gotten no more sleep than he had. "You should have a stable of your own, nand' paidhi. Someone in this benighted region should have a stable."

"One wishes we did, aiji-ma," he said, and stood up, gingerly, fully awake now, and only a little light-headed. It was true. Mecheiti could have tracked them. But the nearest were up in Taiben, near the capital, and bringing them in would take a day at least. "We can send to Taiben," he said, "but one fears delay under these circumstances."

"Speed is of the essence," Ilisidi said grimly, and lowered her voice as Toby stirred, responding to the voices. "Lay plans, paidhi-aiji. Talk to your aishid and talk to Lord Geigi. We *must* not only react to their moves."

"Yes," he said. Press them back, the dowager meant. And move to get firm control of the region *before* they could receive any ransom demands—even if it meant Geigi taking control of the Maschi clan. Damned sure it was not a time for retreating and waiting with hands folded for their enemy to dictate the next move—he agreed with that agenda.

Moving into questionable territory to do it—that wasn't so attractive, but the dowager was absolutely right. They could not back up and wait.

"I shall speak to Lord Geigi," he said, and went outside, where Banichi was talking to Ramaso and gathered him up, Banichi with a finger to his ear and likely in touch with operations, bringing himself current with what Cenedi might have relayed to ops. "We may need to draw in Tano and Algini, Banichi-ji. We are going forward with our own agenda. Immediately."

"Yes," Banichi said. "They will not likely have killed Barb-daja. They would be fools."

"They will have to find someone who can speak to her," he said. "And then she knows very little of interest to them. Her main value is in exchange." When he had started his career he had been practically the only bilingual individual on the continent. That had changed—partly, he was grimly aware, because of *his* work. He'd built the dictionary. He'd taken it from a carefully prescribed permitted word-list to a self-proliferating, auto-cross-referencing file that had gotten wider and wider circulation and contribution.

And with the atevi working on station and the station's

communicating with the planet, and Mospheira's develop-
ment of contacts on the continent just during the two years of
the Troubles—one couldn't rely any longer on there *not* being
someone who could interrogate a human prisoner.

He couldn't stay here with Toby while that happened. That
wasn't where he was needed. Not even the search for Barb
preempted the need to get onto the offensive and make their
enemy reassess Barb's value, if they for a moment doubted it.

And if Geigi was going to make the move they needed him
to make, Geigi needed support—undeniably official support—
not just a solo operation. And to stay alive where they planned
to put him, Geigi needed Guild resources familiar with current
onworld tech.

The dowager shouldn't do it. But somebody official had to
go with him.

It was a very, very short list of official people available to
back Geigi up.

He knocked on Geigi's door—his own, as happened—and
walked into a night-dimmed suite. "One will rouse him, Bren-
ji," Banichi said, and Bren, finding himself a bit light-headed,
subsided into his own favorite sitting-room chair.

In short order, Geigi came out, his considerable self wrapped
in the bedspread in lieu of a night robe.

"Banichi says your brother is recovering, Bren-ji. This is excellent news."

"One is greatly relieved. But impossible for me to stay here
with him, Geigi-ji. The dowager urges us not to let our enemy
seize the initiative. You and I—must continue—"

"Say no more! I am willing, Bren-ji. Outrageous goings-on,
and not a shred of help from Maschi clan in our situation! I have
lain awake thinking about it. I have thought about my sister,
and my nephew, and the situation all across this coast. If I had
been here, I would have been outraged. One cannot but help
but feel a certain responsibility, as lord of this province—"

"No part of it, Geigi-ji, no part of it attaches to you. You gave your orders, which I well know, and if Maschi clan had followed them, the situation would not be the mess it is! Maschi clan did not maintain ties with the Edi during the Troubles. They did not oversee the transition of power in Kajiminda—everyone on this coast knows that much. Nobody in the north will fault you for taking action. And the aiji and the aiji-dowager will explain it to the rest of the aishidi'tat."

"One regrets it, still," Geigi said. "Gods know I did not want this. I did everything conceivable to avoid it. But unless Pairuti proves a better man than he has proved thus far, I shall take the lordship from him. Gods witness Maschi clan did not *want* the clan lordship tied to Kajiminda! Not from the beginning!"

"Times have changed, Geigi-ji. Many things have changed. *We* have changed. And if the nation we met in space comes calling—we *must* have our house in order, Geigi-ji. We must. They have formed an impression of us as rational and stable people, with whom a treaty could be lasting. They are strange folk and accustomed to destroy what threatens them. Those of us who were on that voyage have not told all our experience of these people, not to anyone on earth but to Tabini-aiji . . . and for good reason, Geigi-ji. We have no wish to see every lunatic in the aishidi'tat break out in proclaiming they were right, that we have put holes in the sky and people from the moon have taken offense. We dare not meet them with the attitudes of a past age, Geigi-ji, and if it means that you must take steps—one regrets, one regrets extremely the necessity. But this coast, this whole coast is locked in a pattern with the South that originated with the landing of my people on this world. Nothing has changed. Attitudes have not changed. The Marid still thinks domination of this coast is their way to rip the aishidi'tat apart and settle the world as they want it. *These* are your reasons, Geigi-ji. We are fighting against people who believe the space shuttle puts holes in the sky, and who believe they can go on fighting regional wars and profit from them. We know better. And we have to do something."

"I am with you," Geigi said. "If I have to appoint a proxy in the heavens, this has to be dealt with. I see that. You could not have convinced me until I saw this stupid attack, Bren-ji, this abysmally stupid action, and not even yet has a single messenger or even an inquiring phone call arrived from Maschi clan! When shall we go, Bren-ji? And most of all—with what resources?"

13

They moved Toby to his own suite and out of the dowager's at the very crack of dawn. Nand' Siegi said he was doing well enough, and that was a relief. Servants hurried about, arranging this and that, about which Toby knew nothing.

Bren watched, standing in the hall, judging that things would go more smoothly if he stayed out from underfoot.

And there was one other early watcher in the hall, a forlorn boy, escorted by his two remaining bodyguards. Cajeiri could be stone-faced—his grandmother's teaching—but at the moment he was not. He looked very lost, very miserable, very short of sleep.

And for once, the disaster was not his fault.

Bren walked over to him, with Banichi attending, and Cajeiri bowed and looked at him about on a level—they were almost the same stature—and bowed a second time.

"One is extremely sorry, nand' Bren. One is so extremely sorry!"

"One by no means blames you, young gentleman. Your bodyguards behaved badly. Not you."

"We failed to manage them," Cajeiri said.

"That would have been difficult," Bren said, "where the Guild failed. No one blames you."

"But everything is a mess, nandi! And if I had not gone downstairs, and if I had not evaded my guard—"

Bren shrugged. "Yet rather than consult with those guarding

the estate, not to mention those who know you better, those two made a general and undisciplined rush to the boats and drew my brother with them. One may imagine my brother understood that one word and your name, young gentleman, if nothing else. Hence he went with them. And Barb-daja went with my brother. It was your guard's foolish decision that took them outside."

"Or perhaps a most ill-timed independence of action," Banichi said. "And one does not discount that possibility, young gentleman."

Cajeiri looked at him, confused.

"One does not believe," Banichi said quietly, "that your bodyguards were acting against you, young gentleman, or they could have done so at any time—against you, or nand' Bren, or your great-grandmother. I do not believe that motivated them. But Guild man'chi does not rush off into forbidden territory, taking innocent parties with them."

Confusion became consternation. "You are saying that they were . . ."

"One does not know what they were doing. But they were not acting in your interest, nandi. If they were acting in your interest, they would not have lost track of you at any moment. If they were acting in your father's interest, they would not have lost track of you."

One had to remember the boy had spent two formative years with humans as his closest associates. The instinct for man'chi was potentially disturbed in him. It was one of the concerns everybody had had. If Cajeiri missed fine points—it was only what they were trying to correct.

But two near-adult Guild were a separate issue. When Guild attached—they *attached*. By what Banichi was saying— attachment had never happened in those two. Regarding Cajeiri, a minor child, that was clear. But if they were working at cross-purposes with the household the aiji himself had assigned them to . . . that was potentially a far darker matter.

And yet, Banichi had also said they were *not* acting *against* Cajeiri—or his father.

"Banichi?" Bren asked, suddenly aware *he* didn't understand what Banichi was reading in them, either, wasn't wired to understand it—not the way Banichi picked up the clues.

"They were not focused on the young gentleman," Banichi said. "They have not *been* focused on the young gentleman. They did not regard the young gentleman's orders, or his anger. Or the aiji's. This has been the difficulty."

"Yes!" Jegari said suddenly, as if something had suddenly said the thought in his mind. And far more quietly, Antaro, under her breath: "Yes."

"Did you know this?" Bren asked, looking at Banichi, shocked if this should be the case.

"One knew they were not attached," Banichi said, "but not that they would never *become* attached, nandi. That was not evident until this incident. That they wished to be attached was evident, but wishing does not create a man'chi that does not exist."

So something had tipped across a line for Banichi in that incident. Cajeiri hadn't picked up on it. Jegari hadn't been sure, Antaro looked still a little doubtful, but Banichi was willing to say so, now, for some reason which didn't have clear shape to human senses.

"Explain," he said, and used the request-form, not the order-form. "Explain, please, Banichi-ji. What is going through their heads? What are they up to?"

A slight shrug. "Their interests are not the young gentleman's. They have reserved themselves. Now they have acted along those lines without consulting senior Guild in this house. The direction is not clear, but it is not in line with service to the young gentleman. They have laid their lives on this choice."

"Literally?"

"Literally," Banichi said grimly, and added a phrase from the machimi: hoishia-an kuonatei—a shooting star. Somebody flaring off. Sometimes it was gallant, admirable. And sometimes it was not. Often enough, in either case, it was fatal.

And it was one of those aspects of the machimi plays that never *had* made rational sense. His personal translation for it had been somewhere between suicide and irrational, emotionally driven sabotage.

"*Why?*" he asked. "Do you think they actually *asked* Toby to follow them into that mess, Banichi-ji?"

"Maybe they did," Banichi said.

"Was it aimed against *me?*"

Banichi frowned. "One hesitates to guess that, nandi."

The Guild did not guess. In public. He had to content himself with that, until he could get Banichi in private. But then Banichi said, in a low voice: "The young gentleman is involved, nandi. One surmises, surmises, understand, that while this household may seem ordinary to your staff—it seems vastly different to outsiders. —Is that so, Antaro?"

"Banichi-nadi." Antaro bowed a degree lower than protocol, and so, immediately, did Jegari. Both faces looked shocked.

"You have gotten used to your young lord," Banichi said, "have you not, nadiin? *And* you are Taibeni."

"One does not understand, Banichi-nadi," Cajeiri said in distress; and there stood the paidhi-aiji and an eight-year-old child, both left in the dark on that one. "Are we in the wrong?"

"They are from the mountains, nandiin," Banichi said, "and they are not Ragi. They are extraordinarily gifted, but they have been called out by their superiors in the Guild no few times for independent actions, and have not mended their faults. They entered their adulthood in the Guild during the Troubles, when Guild leadership did *not* take them in hand and when they were *not* attached to that leadership. This was the beginning of their fault. Second, they have seen the aiji restored, but they reached their adulthood *outside* the surety of his man'chi. One is relatively certain they did not attach to the Usurper. There is that. They could not have passed the Guild's security check, else. But they have not attached to the restored regime, either, nandiin. One has feared this. Algini and Cenedi alike have attempted to sound them out and have received indefinite answers. *Therefore* we have maintained some distance from them, which may have worked harm in itself. They reasonably expected high honor and considerable latitude here—they attempted to exert rank with *us*—and instead met a far stricter discipline in this household of humans and Edi and a far lower rank than they expected. If they were mature in mind, they might have applied to the aiji, who assigned them, and ask for transfer into his household. They did not. They flared off."

"Then what are they doing, Banichi-ji?"

"It is an important question, nandi, whether they requested nand' Toby and Barb-daja to go out—or whether your brother conceived the notion through misunderstanding. Certainly this pair did not consult Cenedi before opening the house door onto an area under watch. *That* was a serious breach of rules."

"One does not understand," Cajeiri protested with a shake of his head. *"Are* they traitors?"

"They are confused at this moment," Banichi said. *"They* do not know. That is the point."

"One is quite helpless," Bren said in frustration, "to grasp the logic in this. Did *they* shoot Toby, do you think?"

"One doubts it," Banichi said. "But there was a state of alert declared on the grounds just before they went out that door . . . with nand' Toby and Barb-daja. They were in receipt of that information. They knew they were running into fire. If they invited nand' Toby out there, it was in that knowledge."

"A panicked decision—with the young gentleman missing?"

"Perhaps," Banichi said. "That would be a generous interpretation. But panic has not been characteristic of their misdeeds in the Guild. They are separated from their own clan.

They have done a desperate thing. The answer to that question I posed, nandi, will say a lot. Did they themselves ask nand' Toby for help?"

"Perhaps Toby can remember that," Bren said, laying a hand on the door.

"Tell him, nand' Bren," Cajeiri said fervently, "tell him we are sorry. It is our fault. It is at least our fault that brought this on."

It was a great deal for a young aristocrat to say. And a great burden for a young boy to carry—in what might be a great deal of confusion to come, over the next number of hours. "Come in with me," Bren said. "You may be able to say so yourself. But do not say more than that, young gentleman. He may not remember that Barb-daja is missing."

"Yes," Cajeiri said firmly. "*Yes*, nand' Bren. One wishes to see him. One wishes very much."

A pair of servants rose and bowed as Bren brought Cajeiri into the suite, and stood aside as Bren, with Cajeiri, entered the bedroom, along with Banichi and the two Taibeni youngsters.

Toby's eyes were shut. Two others of the house servants attended him, and retreated as Bren moved a chair closer to the bed and sat down, Cajeiri standing next to him.

"Brother. Toby," Bren said quietly, laying a hand on Toby's shoulder. There was a tube draining the wound, running down off the side of the bed. A saline drip. "Toby. It's Bren."

Eyelids twitched, just slightly.

"I think he hears you," Cajeiri said.

"One is certain he does," Bren said, and squeezed Toby's hand. "Brother, don't panic. It's going to hurt like hell if you twitch. You're in Najida. In your bedroom. I'm here. So is Cajeiri. You're going to be all right."

Blink.

A grimace. "Barb."

Well, then he knew. "Toby, it's Bren, here. We've got a problem. Come on. Wake up. Talk to me. I know it's an effort. I know it hurts."

Toby's eyes slitted open, just ever so slightly. "I'm hearing you. Where's Barb?"

Bren tightened his grip on Toby's hand. "Alive, we're pretty sure, but she's not here, and good people are out looking. Just stay still. We'll get her back. I don't know how yet, but don't panic yet, either. When this sort of thing happens, it's usually a political move. It'll play itself out in politics, and we're good at that game. We're better than they are. Believe me."

Toby didn't say anything for a moment. But he was tracking. His lips clamped down to a straight seam. The eyes stayed aware and fixed on the ceiling a moment, then on him, and on Cajeiri.

"You got *him* back," Toby mumbled. "Good." He started to lift his head, and Bren put a hand on his brow and stopped that.

"Stay put. You're full of tubes."

"Have I got all my pieces?"

"Far as appears to me." He rested his hand on Toby's arm, which appeared undamaged. "What happened? What in hell were you doing out there?"

Vague frown. "I remember—something popped. Hurt. Barb couldn't lift me. I said run and get help. She ran. And at the turn up the walk, this guy, total shadow—Guild, maybe—he just grabbed her up, gone so fast—so fast I couldn't see. Just nothing there. People were shooting. I remember thinking—don't hit Barb—"

Toby's self-control faltered. Bren squeezed his hand. "We'll take care of it. We just have to do this the careful way. We're already calling in reinforcements. They'll want to get her out of the territory fast, likely going all the way to the Marid, before they send us any demands, if that's who's got her, and we think it is."

"What are my chances of getting out of this bed and being useful?"

"In the next twenty-four hours, zero. Our people are throwing a wide net, interdicting the port and the airport at Separti and Dalaigi, checking every plane and ship and truck and tracking it. Standard, during an incident. This isn't a private problem. The aiji-dowager has been on the phone with her grandson. Believe it. We are not alone out here. Shejidan knows what happened, and they're on it."

A momentary silence while Toby absorbed that. "Barb's not that important on their scale, is she? She's going to fall through the cracks of what's going on here. She's not that important to anybody but me."

"She's *gotten* important to the whole aishidi'tat. The attack was an attack on the aiji. He'll take it damned personally."

"That doesn't make her exactly safe, does it?"

"Safer. It's a test of wills and capabilities. Frankly, they probably mistook you for me, hoped they'd killed you, and didn't have enough people on the grounds to make sure of anything. They had a chance to take Barb, and they're sure any human here is connected to me somehow. But they'll find out fast she can't speak Ragi. That will mean she's useless to them here, but valuable enough to send on to their home district. Which is exactly what we're going to try to stop them from doing. Listen. I have one other question for you, and don't take this amiss. Why were you out there? *Why* did you go outside? This is an important quetion."

"The kid was lost. They said—"

"What 'they,' Toby? This is important. Was it your own idea, going out there? Or did they ask you to help search?"

"The kid's guard—said he'd gone to the boat. I—thought—I thought—I didn't think—enough. I thought—they don't know the dockside. I thought—"

"They *lied*," Cajeiri said in ship-speak. "They lied, nand'

Toby. It was my fault. I was mad at them. I deliberately lost them in the hall. And they went to you and lied. I was downstairs!"

"Downstairs," Toby said, growing a little muzzy. "They said—the boat. I couldn't understand the rest. Too many words."

"It was my fault." Cajeiri looked thoroughly upset, and blurted out in Ragi: "You are not to die, nandi! My great-grandmother will get a plane and send you to the hospital if need be! You are not to die!"

Toby looked entirely confused. He hadn't followed that last, likely.

"You're under orders," Bren said, "to lie here, do what you're told, and relax, that's what he just said. I know *rest* is a ridiculous suggestion at this point, but I've personally got a list of people to contact. And if you don't stay flat and take orders, Barb's going to let me hear about it when she does get back." Deep breath. He set his hand on Toby's. "She *will* get back, Toby. Hear me?"

"Double swear?"

Kid stuff, between them. "Double swear, brother. You mind your doctor's orders. And don't make trouble. Got it?"

"Got it," Toby said. His eyes drifted shut. Gone. Out cold, or verging on it. He still had the anaesthetic in his system. Bren got up and steered Cajeiri out into the other room, then out into the hall, where their separate bodyguard waited.

"Best go back to your room, young gentleman. Or better yet, to your great-grandmother's suite. Things are not safe."

"One wishes to do something, nandi!" Cajeiri said, and gave a deep bow. "They are my aishid! I could not manage them! I am at fault!"

At fault, for failing with two damned crazed fools on a mission to be heroes. There was no word for that in Ragi, but that seemed the sum of it. Cajeiri was not faultless, but he was, for God's sake, a kid who'd finally, once in his life, obeyed his instructions to stay in the house. And after all he'd been through—

Leaving this kid unassigned and going out that door was a guaranteed way to make this boy at least think about doing something stupid.

"I am about to make a request, young gentleman, a very serious request of you."

"What is it?" Cajeiri asked, bluntly as Mosphei' could phrase it. Young eyes gazed at him in desperate earnest.

"This: that while I am gone, and I may be gone some time, on a mission with nand' Geigi—you must take charge with my staff and take care of nand' Toby. Help nand' Toby even with getting a cup of water to drink, and translate what he says for the staff, because he cannot speak for himself. Stay with him. Speak for him. And keep your ears open to danger and report to Cenedi or your great-grandmother anything you think out of the ordinary about the house. *We* have Baiji. *They* have Barb-daja. The Marid would like to get their hands on Baiji before he says everything he knows . . . certainly before what he knows can be entered into a legal record. And I intend to find out what that might be . . . before the people who have Barb-daja, whoever they are, ask for a trade. Can I rely on you, young gentleman?"

Cajeiri's eyes were huge. "Yes!" he said. "We shall do that!"

"Then go get a pillow and a blanket, and you may have that chair by nand' Toby's bedside. I am going downstairs," he said quietly to Banichi, "the moment I have paid my respects to the dowager, if she is awake. I am going to talk to Baiji about one particular detail. Personally."

Banichi looked entirely, grimly satisfied with that proposal. "Jago is coming," Banichi said. "She will meet us downstairs."

"Good," he said, and made one side trip.

He led the way up the hall and received news from the servant attending the door that the aiji-dowager was still awake, but on the phone, and had given strict instructions to admit no one.

One could easily imagine who in Shejidan the aiji-dowager might be calling at this hour of the night, probably not for the first time, and one had, he assured the servant, no desire to intervene in that conversation.

"Advise the aiji-dowager, when she appears, that the young gentleman is in attendance on nand' Toby, with his bodyguard attending, at my request. Do not bother her otherwise."

With which he headed straight down the stairs with Banichi. Jago was waiting at the bottom of the steps, and silently fell in with them. Doubtless she had had a briefing from Banichi, and knew at least the essentials. She was also carrying a sidearm in plain sight.

It was dawn. He had had no sleep. But sleep was very far from his mind as he reached Baiji's guarded door.

"You may take a small rest nadi-ji," he said to Ilisidi's man, with whom they had shared many a journey in the last three years. "Go take a cup of tea if you wish. About a quarter of an hour should suffice."

"Nandi," the young man said, and left Baiji to him and Banichi and Jago.

Banichi opened the door on a darkened room. Baiji was peacefully sleeping, snoring away.

Until Banichi turned on the lights.

Baiji struggled bolt upright, blinking in alarm and tangled in the blankets.

There was, in the white glare of electric lights, the bed, a table, one chair, a scattered lot of paper, and writing implements—of which Baiji had made some further use, by the evidence of the papers.

Bren drew back the chair, sat down, gathered the papers into three stacks that seemed indicated by position, sat down with no reference at all to Baiji, and flipped through the first stack.

Baiji said not a thing to him, only sat on the edge of the bed.

The first stack—excepting one stray paper Bren incorporated

into the third stack, a list of names—was a lengthy letter full of courtesies and blandishments, addressed to Geigi.

Bren laid it aside, remarking, "This one will do you little good. Geigi is quite resolved in the opinion he has of you. One hopes you have produced something of greater value than the last lot of paper you gave me."

"Nandi, I—What does this mean? Is it daylight?"

"It is dawn and someone, attempting an assassination in this house, has kidnapped my brother's lady. It may mean they hope to exchange a member of my household for *you*. Do you wonder why these attackers would be so concerned for your freedom? Would the reason for that concern possibly lie within these papers? Or have you been that honest with us? One doubts it."

Baiji struggled to his feet, dragging the blanket about his ample middle. Banichi set a hand on his shoulder and shoved him right back down to sit on the bed. Jago took up her station in front of the door, hand on sidearm.

Bren hardly looked at the man, being at the moment occupied in the second stack of paper. Freeing two sheets which represented the opening of a letter to Tabini, full of blandishments and assurances, he crumpled them in his fist.

"Useless. The aiji will not be your ally against his grandmother. Be grateful. I have just saved you from offending him. You are a fool."

"Nandi!"

The third stack, the further list, contained all unremarkable names, names he would expect to be there, many of which duplicated the prior list. He swung the chair around with a scrape of wood on stone.

"You do not truly *intend* to be a fool, do you, Baiji-nadi? You surely do not entertain the notion that your arguments against my keeping you here will be heard by the aiji, the aiji-dowager, or—least of all—by your uncle. The aiji-dowager has offered you your sole escape. *Surely* you do not plan to reject it."

"No. No, nandi. We have accepted the aiji-dowager's offer. We do accept it!"

One did not detect sufficient humility in a young, arrogant brat who had grown into an adult, arrogant fool.

"You do not half understand," Bren said, "the situation in which you now find yourself. There are names I now know that I have not seen on the other list, or on this. A member of my household, my brother of the same parentage, was *shot* tonight, by someone possibly believing he was shooting at me. A member of his household has been kidnapped by persons who themselves are likely to be shot if the aiji's power over this coast survives—while the inhabitants of this coast and all the rest of the continent are entirely determined to shoot them on sight. So the fools who have attacked my household are in great danger. And the lord who sent them is in much greater danger. The Guild is involved. Are you following this? Are you understanding, finally, that your Marid allies do not want you to survive to tell us everything you know—that, in fact, they will be quite interested in killing you—partly in case you have *not* yet told us all you know, and for another reason—simply because you have become such a great embarrassment to their side. They will blot you from the face of the earth . . . an absolute, extravagant *failure* of their plans to marry their way into your house so that *then* they could kill you and inherit your post! Have you really understood that, this far? Do you believe it?"

Lips stammered: "One believes it, nand' paidhi."

"So believe this: very few people care about your survival tonight. I have never asked my aishid to eliminate a man, but you and the mess you have created are fast approaching the limit of my patience, Baiji nephew of my ally."

Hatred stared back at him. Anger. And fear. "My uncle—"

"Your uncle will not preserve you in the face of the dowager's anger. Or mine. Oh, I am indeed your enemy, Baiji-nadi. I have very many who consider *me* their enemy—of whom I can be tolerant, since I look to change their minds. But I have *two* that I consider my enemies in the world right now. The Marid aiji who directed this attack is one. And the other? Before I met you, and listened to you argue your case, I would have said there was only one."

Baiji was not the swiftest. Parsing that took a moment, and he screwed up his face and protested, "Nandi, you surely cannot equate me with—"

Bren got to his feet. "You protect Machigi of the Taisigin Marid with your silence and you protect his plans by your reluctance to admit your own part in the whole business."

"I had none! I was an innocent bystander!"

"Do not mistake me! I shall walk out of this room and leave others to persuade you to tell me—not the first truths that occur to you, but the deepest of the truths you own about this affair and those you even imagine! Do we understand each other? Who else in this district is helping Machigi? Who are his associates?"

"I have told you everything, nandi! I have written it down in those papers—"

Baiji started to get up and Banichi slammed him right back down.

"I have no doubt these papers are as carefully crafted as those letters of yours in my office upstairs. I have seen your answers. And the effrontery of your writing a letter to the aiji under these circumstances tells me I am dealing with someone too convinced of his own cleverness to *ever* believe he can be brought down permanently. You are down here laying plans for a future in which you hope to deceive everyone all over again and protect your remaining places of influence. You are so very clever, are you not?"

No answer. No answer became sullen defiance, more than Baiji had yet shown.

"Now I believe you," Bren said. "Now you show me your real face, and not a pretty one. You had your own plan for the future of this coast. Tell me *how* you planned to stay alive, granting you had the least inkling that you were bedding down with very dangerous people. *Who* was the support you counted on? There was someone else, was there not?"

Baiji sweated. His face was a curious shade. He towered over Bren, but Bren had the all but overwhelming desire to seize him by the throat and strangle him.

"There was someone who supported you," Bren said, "and one doubts this moral support was among the Edi. Who were your other recourses?"

"I—"

So, Bren thought—he was right. And considering Baiji's natural resources, ones he owned by birthright, there were not that many.

"This person should have been at the top of the list, should he not?"

Baiji did not well conceal his discomfort.

Baiji stared at him. Just stared, grimly saying nothing, but sweating.

"Jago-ji," he said, looking to the side, "you and I will go inform nand' Geigi we have no more doubts. It would be well, nadi," he added, addressing Baiji, "for you to dress. One believes you will get no more sleep tonight."

"Do not leave me with him!" Baiji cried, with a glance upward at Banichi. "Nand' paidhi!"

"Banichi-ji, would you ever harm this person?"

Banichi smiled darkly. "Never against your orders, nandi."

"So," he said, silently collected Baiji's documents, then left by the door Jago opened, and headed upstairs.

Upstairs was not calm, despite the hour that should have seen only the household assembling for breakfast.

There was a small turmoil, a little gathering of the staff at the front door—a gathering in which Cenedi himself was involved.

Jago said, quietly, in communication with operations. "The

Grandmother of Najida has just arrived, Bren-ji. She asks to speak with the aiji-dowager. Cenedi is agreeing."

Ramaso was involved at the doors, and spotting them, cast a worried and querying look Bren's way. Bren signed yes, and Ramaso ordered the doors opened, which admitted a small crowd of persons into their secure hall.

The Grandmother of Najida it was, indeed, a little out of breath, and flanked by two of her older men. Others crowded about. Bren made his way in that direction, walked up to the situation quietly, and gave a little bow.

The Edi were, at depth, a matriarchy, when it came to negotiation. They were fortunate to have the dowager accessible—and in no wise was the paidhi-aiji going to intrude into that arrangement.

"Please accept the hospitality of this house, honored Grandmother," he murmured with a little bow, and heaved a deep sigh of relief as Cenedi showed the lady on toward Ilisidi's suite . . . and one problem, at least, landed on someone else's desk.

He *wanted* to go sit by Toby, continually to reassure himself the only kin he owned—excepting a no-contact father somewhere on Mospheira—was still breathing at this hour. He wanted to stay there for days, until Toby was better, and he could get Toby onto his boat, call in a continental navy escort and get Toby the hell home.

But Shejidan's largest train station had less traffic than Najida estate at this hour, he thought glumly. The Edi were not going to be happy to have failed in their guarantees—and fail, they had, conspicuously . . . which was probably why the Grandmother had come up here personally to speak to the dowager, if the dowager had not called her here in the first place.

Tano and Algini and Geigi's four bodyguards were still over in Kajiminda, meanwhile, relying on Edi to hold the perimeters if another attack came, and he, at Najida, was about to pass an order to *all* Guild components under his control and Geigi's to come back to undertake a mission eastward—and that was going to leave the Edi in Kajiminda on their own, against God knew what. Kajiminda would be completely exposed, Najida considerably weakened. He was not a tactical thinker. Banichi and Jago were.

"Are we doing rational things, Jago-ji? One intends to pull all Guild from Kajiminda. One sees no alternative."

Jago's face was calm and unworried and he suddenly knew his was not. "Cenedi advises us," she said quietly, "that the dowager has indeed contacted Tabini-aiji. He is apparently sending Guild in some numbers, Bren-ji, to be under Cenedi's management. The dowager is going to make this situation clear to the Edi."

That was *not* going to make the Edi happy. But the Edi, dammit, had just failed them, and knew it. The whole ground underfoot had shifted, neither he nor his team had had significant sleep, and decisions had to be made—which Ilisidi had been making for them, left and right.

Calls to the aiji for some reinforcement—routine. But *in some numbers!*

Alarm bells rang. He had left Ilisidi in charge of Najida, with the implements to make secure calls. And Ilisidi had an agenda that, par for Ilisidi, ran solely on Ilisidi's opinion. The Grandmother of Najida, with her agenda, had been dealing with a past master. So had he. Dammit.

Likely the Grandmother of Najida didn't know yet that there were Ragi foreigners coming into the district. That was what she had come here to learn . . . probably at Ilisidi's pre-dawn summons.

And somehow—he was not going into that room for anything—Ilisidi and the Grandmother of Najida were going to have a meeting with reality and necessity and consider the rearrangement of power on the lower west coast. God knew, there were already Marid foreigners here. The Grandmother of Najida had *not* been able to deal with them alone.

The aishidi'tat could.

The Grandmother of the Edi was then going to have to explain those facts to her people.

Not to mention what Geigi was yet to find out—which he would lay odds Geigi was learning in bits and pieces.

He knew the name Baiji had not given them. He was sure of it even before Jago said, quietly, relaying it from Banichi, "Pairuti of the Maschi, Bren-ji. Banichi is getting it in writing."

14

There was a lot going on. Even nand' Toby knew it, and asked, or seemed to, what was happening outside.

"I'll find out, nandi," Cajeiri said, and sent Jegari out with orders to ask questions and eavesdrop.

Jegari came back. Cajeiri went out into the sitting room to hear the report, and Antaro came with him.

"Nandi, they are getting the bus ready. Nand' Geigi is going to deal with Maschi clan and nand' Bren is going with him, mostly because nand' Bren can bring senior Guild into it besides your father's name."

The machimi plays were bloodily full of such instances where one lord replaced another the hard way. And mani had seen to it that he was acquainted with very many machimi.

But lord Geigi had a place on the space station. Was he going to tie himself down to live in the country like Great-uncle Tatiseigi?

Besides, the Maschi were such a little clan: most people, asked to name clans, would have trouble thinking of them, except for Lord Geigi, who was famous.

He had grown up with Gene and Artur and nand' Bren and he had been able to predict what they would do, when he was on the ship in space. But mani had always said, and it had made him mad at the time—that when he was among atevi, he would find things making sense to him in an emotional way. He would understand things.

He certainly understood more today than he had yesterday. He could feel the directions of man'chi, and it made things clear in his mind. He was very sure that there was nothing queasy about Lord Geigi, and that there was a question about the man'chi of the Maschi lord. That lord should have shown up in person here at Najida, especially with Lord Geigi here. He certainly should have sent someone.

And he could feel the direction of the Marid, too. That took no more reading of man'chi than it did to look at clouds and say there would be a storm. There were storm clouds aplenty when one read Great-grandmother. Great-grandmother was not about to go back East without having things her way, he was absolutely sure of it—it was not mani's habit to leave a fight, and this was a fight that had cost her one of her young men.

Besides, she was on the hunt for something political—he could not quite understand what, and certainly the surface of it had to do with the Edi, but he thought it also had to do with his father and old history, and he was relatively sure it was tangled up with the Marid, with whom he knew mani had an old quarrel. He knew mani's moods, and he knew when she was up to something. He had felt the currents moving when his father was here and mani and his father were fighting. He had felt then that mani wanted something and mani had talked his father into it, which meant his father had been halfway agreeing with her before the argument ever started. They just shouted at each other because they always shouted at each other over little things, not the big ones.

And now Lord Geigi was in the middle of it, and so was nand' Bren's house, and now nand' Toby had gotten hurt, and Barb-daja was a hostage. So it could be a really, really big fight, once it started rolling, bigger than anything since they had taken Shejidan and thrown Murini out of power. He had been at Tir-namardi, with Great-uncle, when things had blown up left and right and there had been a lot of shooting.

So it could turn out like that. It was already showing signs of it. And just thinking about the Marid made his heart beat faster, and made him mad along with everybody else, that was what it felt like—not because he was a kid and a follower; but because these people had messed up *his* business and *his* intentions and then shot people who were attached to nand' Bren, who was *his* nand' Bren. Maybe his was not so big a piece of business with the Marid as mani had, certainly not as big as the Edi, or the aishidi'tat had. But he was very close to being mad, personally.

And it was a long way from being about his fishing trip.

One did not want the fight to turn out like Tirnamardi. One did not want nand' Bren's house blown up and people killed.

And there was something else he was mad about. He resented being mad about grown-up things because he didn't want to be grown-up yet. He wanted to go fishing and go exploring and messing with things. He just wanted an aishid that wanted to do fun things—Antaro and Jegari did.

But Veijico and Lucasi had brought grown-up business with them. And they had done things that dragged him into the adult fight. And he didn't want that. Damn them.

He was thinking in ship-speak again. He did that sometimes when he was upset and wanted to think his own thoughts, privately, just to himself. He thought thoughts that nobody else around him could think, and he was glad they couldn't.

And it would make Great-grandmother mad at him, because he was supposed to be atevi all the time now and forget about Gene and Artur and Irene and just be—

Grown-up. And mad. Along with everybody else.

No. That was not what Great-grandmother had said, more than once, often enough thumping his ear hard to make him remember.

Anger does not plan. When one Files with the Guild, one does not File Anger. One Files Intent, because one has thought clearly and seen a course of action. The Guild officers meet and decide to accept or not accept the Filing, and they will not accept it if the outcome destabilizes the aishidi'tat. That is their rule. It takes far more than anger to direct the aishidi'tat, boy. So do not sulk at me. Think! If you are a fool, your Filing will never be accepted. Your enemy's may be more sensible. Think about that, too.

He had objected, *But I shall be aiji, and they have to accept it!*

They do not! mani had said. *Fool!* And his ear had been sore for days after he had said something that stupid.

So was nand' Geigi on the phone Filing on the Maschi lord? Surely the Guild would *not* accept the Maschi lord Filing on nand' Geigi, even in self-defense. That would destabilize the whole heavens.

So the Maschi lord was really stupid for annoying Lord Geigi.

And was the Guild leadership meeting at this hour, and voting about that? Or was nand' Geigi actually going to go to the Maschi holdings to make Lord Pairuti make a mistake and get a clear cause for Filing? Did he need to do that?

There were so many questions he wanted to ask someone. The world was a more dangerous place than the ship, that was sure.

But getting underfoot of his elders when serious things were underway was a way to get another sore ear, or worse, to be shipped back to his father in Shejidan—and that would mean dealing with his tutor, who would have a stack of lessons, not to mention Great-uncle Tatiseigi, who had moved in down the hall.

That was just gruesome—besides having mani and nand' Bren in danger and not being able to know anything at all that was going on.

So he stayed good.

Mostly.

And fairly invisible.

He was not a follower, that was one thing; he was not designed to sit and wait. He would be aiji someday, and people would have to follow *him*, and that was the way he was born: mani said so.

And when he was aiji and the world was peaceful again he would go fishing when he wanted to and have his own boat.

Except his father never got to go fishing.

That was a grim thought.

He saw no way to change that. He wanted not to be shut in the way his father was.

But day by day he could feel atevi thoughts taking hold of him.

You will know, Great-grandmother had told him when they were about to come down from the station. *When you are only with atevi, you will know things that will make sense to you in ways nobody can explain to you right now.*

He had doubted it. But he *did,* that was the scary thing. When he thought of all of it, he got really mad . . . so mad he wanted to go fight Machigi, who was at the center of all this. Mad at Lucasi and Veijico for being so snotty and *not* being impressed by him.

Which was what he was supposed to feel, he supposed. It was what everybody expected of him. But in a way, it made him sad and upset.

Because he had much rather be out on the boat fishing, and not feel like that at all.

"Go back," he told Antaro, "and keep listening. I want to know everything going on."

15

It was the small hours, and with the house overburdened with guests and packing for what could either be a civilized argument or a small war prefacing a bigger one, there was, in a hot bath, one quiet refuge for the lord of the house. A folded, sodden towel on the marble tub rim became a pillow. Bren drowsed, was quite asleep, in fact—and wakened to a gentle slop of water and the awareness he was no longer alone in the ample pool.

He wiped his eyes with a soggy hand, and ran it through his hair. "How are things going, Jago-ji?"

Jago sighed, arrayed her arms along the tub rim, and tilted her head back, eyes shut. "One is satisfied, Bren-ji. Your cases are packed. As are ours. The bus is loaded. Tano and Algini have just come in, with Lord Geigi's bodyguard. And we now have eight of the aiji-dowager's own guard going with us."

Eight. That was a considerable deployment of that elite company. But a worrisome one—depleting the dowager's protection. The Edi might be an adequate backup over at Kajiminda, which had no attractive targets, but not at Najida, where the aiji-dowager *and* the aiji's heir were situated. "One is astonished," he said moderately, "and honored. But what about provision for the aiji-dowager's force?"

"Discreetly placed. They are here about the house, Bren-ji, is all we should say. Even here."

He drew a deep breath. He had run on too little sleep. The

cavernous bath seemed to echo with their voices. Or they were ringing in his head.

He had a dread of this venture upcoming . . . this venture specifically designed to provoke an attack from somebody—and they weren't sure who.

He wished he had any other team to throw into it besides Banichi and Jago, besides Tano and Algini. He didn't want to risk their lives this way—all for a pack of damned conniving scoundrels, and a clan too weak to say no to bad neighbors, too self-interested to have seen what kind of a game they were playing. He seriously considered, truly considered for the first time, Filing Intent himself and seeing if political influence could speed the motion through the Guild without it hanging up on regional politics.

But the paidhi *didn't* File Intent: that was the point of his office—he was neutral. He *had* no political vantage.

Until Tabini made him a district lord. Dammit.

Geigi didn't want to File on his own clan lord—even if he outranked his clan lord in the aishidi'tat. It was a point of honor, a sticky point, the long-held fiction of Geigi's being *inside* that clan. Bringing that fiction down would rebound onto clan honor—or make Tabini *have* to inquire, officially. And the plain point was—when there was a quarrel *inside* a clan, things were supposed to be settled, however bloodily, without recourse to the Assassins' Guild, except those already serving within the house.

So they were going in, with Geigi's aishid running the operation. They were going to *get* a provocation, or get a resignation, or get a direct appeal from Lord Pairuti for Geigi's support against the neighbors . . . and the matter was so damned tangled it was hard to predict from here just what they'd get from the man.

Things echoed back surreally. He had a feeling of being momentarily out of body, looking down on him and Jago, at a point of decision that he could critique, from that mental distance.

From here, he knew how dangerous their situation was, and how they could make mistakes that would cost their lives, cost the aiji the stability of the aishidi'tat, and leave the whole atevi civilization vulnerable. Civil war was the least of the bad outcomes that could flow from the decisions he was making—on too little sleep, too little information, and with deniability on the part of Tabini-aiji. Cenedi had talked about calling in certain forces under his own command: but Cenedi's focus was, when all was said and done, the dowager, and the heir.

The most important thing right now was Tabini's survival, Tabini's power. There was, God forbid, even a second heir. Or would be. The aishidi'tat would survive losing anybody— the out-of-body detachment let him think that unthinkable thought—*anybody* except Tabini, because in this generation there was no leader *but* Tabini that could hold the aishidi'tat together.

So Tabini had to survive.

All the rest of them were expendable, on that terrible scale.

He was exhausted. His mind was spinning into dire territory. He was scared, but he was so far down that path he didn't see an alternative.

Maybe it was a failure of vision. Maybe he should go to the phone, shove it all off on Tabini and let him deal with it.

But he couldn't see that ending productively.

And Geigi couldn't go in alone. Geigi was willing to do it, but *hell* if they could afford to wave that target past the attention of their enemies.

So there they were. They had to go in, hoping to frighten Pairuti into cooperating.

He leaned his head back on the towel-cushioned rim and shut his eyes, wondering if his mind and Jago's were on the same grim track. The water was going a little cold. He moved finally, reached, and turned on the hot water. The current flowed in, palpably warm.

"Has one been a fool, Jago-ji, to get into this situation?"

"Not a fool," Jago said. "Banichi does not think so."

"Do you?"

"No, Bren-ji. One would not think so—even if it were proper to think. This is overdue."

"On this coast?"

"In the whole quarter of the aishidi'tat—this is overdue."

"What is the Guild's temperature? Can you say?"

"Favorable, in this," Jago said. He had half expected she wouldn't answer. But she did. And he felt better.

"I have ceded our bed to Lord Geigi," he said apologetically. Jago had gotten no more sleep than he had—less, if one counted falling asleep in the bathtub. "But this is comfortable."

"I have located a place," Jago said. "A solitary place. In the servants' wing."

That was clearly a proposition. A decided proposition. He smiled wearily and decided maybe—maybe both of them could benefit from distraction.

So he shut down the hot water and looked for his bathrobe.

16

The bus was loaded with luggage and gear. It waited under the portico, sleek and modern, pristine except the track of bullet holes across its windshield. Lord Geigi's four bodyguards had caught a little sleep before breakfast—and Cook had scrambled to feed them handsomely, not to mention the rest of the household. The Lord of Najida and his guest would not go off unfed.

And, after breakfast, there were calls to make: on Toby, to be sure he was well. Cajeiri, poor lad, had argued to have his breakfast at his appointed post, and now was fast asleep in his chair, his bodyguard tiptoeing about to avoid waking him or Toby.

For Toby he left a note—in Ragi, in care of Antaro, for Cajeiri to read, since Mospheiran script was not one of Cajeiri's many skills. It said: *Brother, Ragi cannot truly express all the sentiments I have this morning. Please take care and follow instructions. We believe that the move we are making will turn up information on Barb's whereabouts and lead to finding her, though it may not be simple. We are sparing no effort and we expect eventual success. Think of me as I shall be thinking of you.*

He had a last look, in case Toby should have waked—he had not—and left quietly.

Last—a call on the aiji-dowager and Cenedi.

He walked alone into the dowager's sitting room, where the

dowager was having an after-breakfast cup of tea, and bowed very deeply.

"Aiji-ma," he said, and received, uncharacteristically, a gesture to approach closely. He did so, and knelt down at the side of Ilisidi's chair as if he were a second grandson. Cenedi stood up, by the mantel.

"This is very vexing, paidhi-ji," Ilisidi said. "Cenedi argues against my going with you and unfortunately his reason prevails, since that equally unreasonable great-grandson of mine will be entirely on his own if we both should go on this venture."

"I am only sorry to have been selfish, aiji-ma, in refusing to lend you Tano and Algini, but should one truly need them—"

A flick of the hand. "Pish. You are being sensible. Cenedi is the one being unreasonable, are you not, Cenedi-ji? He worries too much."

"Always, in your service, aiji-ma."

"One begs," Bren said, "that you will listen to Cenedi-nadi and take very great care. I leave my household and my trusted staff in your hands, hoping they may be of service. Your great-grandson has been in constant attendance on my brother. Both were asleep when I looked into the room, and one hopes you approve the young gentleman's absence. He has been very good."

Ilisidi arched a brow. "Your brother will be in our care, nand' paidhi, under all circumstances. Have confidence in that."

"One is extremely grateful." He bowed, hearing the implication of dismissal in that tone, and knowing he was delaying a busload of people. He bowed again, and with a little nod to Cenedi, took his course out the door and down the hall to the door, where Ramaso stood in official attendance.

Supani and Koharu were there, too, his valets, who bowed, and followed him to the bus. He had asked Ramaso, quietly, whether someone from the Najida domestic staff might volunteer for what might be a dangerous venture—servants were always exempt from assassination, but finding their way home could be lengthy and difficult; and shots strayed. It was, however, a great advantage for him and Geigi to have their own staff with them, those who would be closest and most intimate—an extra set of eyes and ears.

For himself, he had one intimate secret, as he boarded the bus, a very uncomfortable waistcoat he had just as soon not wear for several hours at a time . . . but that was the rule of the day. His staff had gone to great effort to put that item together out of one of Jago's very expensive jackets, and out of spares from several of the staff, in Geigi's case. The vest was heavy and it was hot; but the household had labored hard in that cause, and, in point of fact, produced two brocade vests, differently styled, that were more than they seemed. Others might think the paidhi, like Geigi, had been enjoying too many of Cook's excellent desserts—but Maschi clan had never met the paidhi-aiji, which was to the good in this instance, and they had not seen Geigi in years. Well-tailored coats had had to be let out, in Geigi's case—Geigi had laughed and said his seams were always generous. And staff and folk from the village had outright *made* three new coats for the paidhi-aiji to accommodate the protection.

He nodded to his own staff; to Tano, and Algini, Banichi, and Jago, and sat down with them on the bus. Geigi had settled with his bodyguard around him, and his senior two servants. That was the sum of twelve, counting Kohari and Supani; fourteen, counting a brave volunteer from Cook's staff, who was going to handle all food and drink for them; fifteen; and eight from the dowager's guard—twenty-three; with gear and baggage jammed under every seat in the bus and into the luggage area below. The bus was all but full—and then the door opened again and five more persons Bren did not know showed up—not the dowager's, not his, not Geigi's, but they wore Guild black, and Cenedi personally shepherded them aboard.

"Who are they?" he asked Banichi, who would be in contact with Cenedi, and Banichi said, simply, "Backup."

It was very, very likely they had just arrived from overland or from the airport: Tabini's, unofficially, he suspected, and did not ask. The five reached the back of the bus, some to ride standing, and staff somehow jammed more baggage into the underside of the bus.

The engine started.

They were a packed bus, they were probably full of ammunition and heavy as sin; and with Tano and Algini aboard, they undoubtedly had electronics and explosives stowed somewhere. He tried not to think overmuch about that—and remembered he could have ordered bulletproofing, and had settled on speed and fuel efficiency.

He drew in a large breath against the stiff vest and let it go, trying to settle his nerves.

Ramaso stepped briefly onto the bottom step of the bus to look inside and make eye contact with Bren, in the case there should be last-moment instruction. Bren just lifted his hand, a signal that he needed nothing, and Ramaso stepped back down again.

The driver shut the bus door and put them into gear, rolling gently over the cobbled drive and ponderously and slowly up toward the road. Fans cut on, a relief, just to have air movement.

"One might get a little sleep," Banichi said, "since it was scant last night. You in particular might, Bren-ji."

Geigi had settled deeper into his seat, folded his arms across his armored middle, and seemed intent on dozing.

Bren was not relaxed. His mind was racing in a dozen directions at once, whether they would meet trouble on the way, whether they were going to meet shut doors and problems at the outset of their visit to Lord Pairuti, or whether they would be welcomed inside. He had far, far rather have relations all blow up on the doorstep . . . except that one of their goals was information on Barb's whereabouts, and another was getting Pairuti to spill what else he knew.

So shooting their way in was not in the plan—unless they had to.

So, so much better if Pairuti would melt on their arrival on his doorstep, appeal for rescue and accept Geigi's intervention—after which they could remove any agents the Marid might have gotten onto Pairuti's staff, find out what they needed to, and hopefully negotiate something that would get Barb out of Marid hands, get the Farai out of his own city apartment, take Machigi of the Taisigi down a peg or two, and settle a few years of relative calm and peace.

Then they could dust off Pairuti's authority and set him back in power again with Tabini's blessing, so Geigi could get back to the station and get back to his real work—which would be the best outcome for everybody but Machigi.

There were a lot of ifs in their plan. They were, somewhere in the plan, making Tabini unofficially aware what they were doing . . . which was *why* they had those several strangers in the back of the bus, he supposed. Tabini's men, no question, though his own aishid had not explained their presence. Since they had *not* explained, he was apparently not encouraged to ask too much about them.

They *could* even be high-up Guild, along for their own reasons. When the Assassins' Guild sent its own agents into a situation, it was usually in the interests of keeping the lid on aftershocks and making sure no Guild members got ordered into some lord's suicidal resistence to the aiji's orders. He'd never seen it happen—possibly because Algini had served in that capacity, once upon a time.

And, Algini having resigned that covert capacity in favor of closer attachment to the paidhi-aiji, it *was* possible the Guild had sent observers to identify persons that might be on the Guild's own wanted list.

Most of the outlaw Guildsmen from up north were clustered around Machigi, as best he could figure, but it was possible they'd be running up against a few, considering Targai lay close to the Marid. Again, his bodyguard hadn't been too forthcoming about that aspect of the operation. Guild justice was *strictly* a

Guild matter and the paidhi-aiji was not informed at that level. Nor was Geigi.

The bus took the turn to the Najida-Kajiminda road. They would go past the Kajiminda turnoff and then onto what became the Separti market road, before they turned off toward Maschi territory.

Their Cook came up the aisle to ask, Would one like tea, or anything stronger? One was tempted, but—

"No, nadi-ji," he said, and looked across to Lord Geigi, who had waked. "Anything my guest or his staff wishes," Bren said, "my staff would delight to supply."

"The situation regarding my clan has quite depressed my appetite," Lord Geigi said. "Such elegant transport to such an unpleasant event. One is astonished by the comfort. And perhaps we could do with tea."

"Certainly," Bren said, and ordered it.

"One is grateful," Geigi said, across the aisle. "One is very grateful, Bren-ji. How far we have come, have we not, from the days we first met? Let us hope this goes smoothly. It only needs common sense."

"One concurs," Bren said. "One *hopes* he is under pressure that we can relieve. And if Barb-daja should be held there—"

"Baji-naji," Geigi said to that hope. "One is far from certain of his motives for paying social calls on my nephew, but in company with Marid agents? Introducing them?" Geigi heaved a massive sigh. "My clan has generated two fools and they have simultaneously gotten in power."

"In your nephew's case—not without Marid help. Perhaps we can relieve Pairuti of that problem."

"Well, well," Geigi said, "let us have a little tea and cease worry. The outcome of this now is my cousin's decision, not ours."

It was familiar scenery, down to Kajiminda. The road thereafter—Bren remembered from his earliest venture onto the west coast—cut through a small woods, and then a rolling stairstep of small hills and grassland that led on down to the coastal township of Separti, the larger of the two towns in Sarini province.

But at the divergence of the Maschi road, the track went off toward the east, through territory Geigi might remember, but Bren assuredly had never seen. The land gradually rose, became a meadow studded with large upthrusts of gold rock, and finally sheets and tables of stone where the road crossed a small river gorge that Geigi said was the Soa . . . much less impressive a river than it appeared on a map, but an excellent view of weathered stone that tourists might admire.

A man planning unhappy actions in the adjacent territory, however, looked on it as a chokepoint in any escape plan, one worth remembering, and Bren was sure their respective bodyguards took note of it.

Beyond the gorge, the road gently climbed again, to a high plateau, and wide grasslands and scattered woods.

"This is Mu'idinu," Geigi said. "My clan homeland."

If one had had no prior knowledge of the Maschi, then, one would still have understood a great deal about them, seeing that great grassy plain, with a handful of tracks branching off the main road that were more footpaths than real roads.

This clan hunted. From coast to coast of the aishidi'tat, there were no domestic herds, such as humans had had in their lost homeworld. There was no great meat distribution industry, though such had begun to appear, since airliners had made the impossible possible. An atevi district, aside from that—and traditionalists greatly questioned the ethics of transporting meat—ate local game supplied by local hunters, in its appropriate season, and not a great deal of it. There was fish, mostly exempt from seasonality, even by the traditionalists; and there were eggs, which were a commercial operation; and there was wool, but no meat came from that operation. One simply did not eat domestic animals. Even non-traditionalist atevi were horrified at the notion.

A hunting clan, and vast, undeveloped lands: that said a great deal about the psychology of the clan. They would be nominally independent, but very dependent on their markets for things they lacked, manufactured goods, and the like. They had, despite a cadet branch of their house being on the coast, been historically isolated from their neighbors, except in trade at appointed locations . . . one of which logically would always have been their common border with the Marid.

And their original good understanding with the coastal Edi had eroded over recent years—since Baiji had offended the Edi. That little detail had come clear in the various dry papers and accounts: mind-numbing detail, but the story was in them. Trade with the west had stopped and not resumed. The fish market had dried up. So if this district was not eating *only* seasonal game, it was getting its fish, that staple of various regional diets—from some other direction.

Like its eastern border.

The Marid.

Curious, the complexities that turned up out of such mundane information as the Najida market figures.

One began to form a theory on the Maschi's actions during the Troubles: that the Maschi had become a target of Marid diplomacy, economically and politically—they had been tied to the central district and Shejidan during Tabini's rule, but when Tabini had been out of power, and once Kajiminda fell into arrears on its accounts with Najida fisheries—

The Maschi clan estate at Targai had fallen right into the arms of the Marid.

Geigi had an unaccustomedly glum look as he gazed out on the broad plateau—remembering, it was sure; regretting, to a certain extent, the situation of his clan.

And Bren, looking out at that same landscape, thought about

Barb, and a lot of personal history; and Toby, and his promise, and how the data that had made things seem possible back in Najida were having an increasingly spooky feeling in all this untracked grassland.

There had been no ransom demand from the kidnappers. That, he found ominous. That said they were traveling—further than some nearby hideout. Or that somebody was figuring out what to do with a human hostage.

And that question would likely go right up the chain to Machigi in the Taisigin Marid . . . guaranteeing at least some period of safety for Barb. And . . . he could not but think it without much humor at all . . . Barb was as likely to make herself a serious problem to her kidnappers—which could mean she was not as well off as one would ordinarily hope. They would not likely hurt her—since it was unlikely they could figure out her rank or her right to pitch a fit; but she could push them too far. Knowing Barb, she would take a little latitude as encouragement to push. And that wouldn't be good. Not at all. He'd personally had an arm broken—by an ateva who didn't know how fragile humans were.

Not to mention food. God, they could poison her so easily without the least intention. Just one wrong spice . . . *Stick to the bread, Barb*, he thought desperately. *Please stick to the bread.*

The servant collected the teacups. Geigi sighed and seemed apt to drift off to sleep.

"Has there been any news?" Bren asked Jago quietly, not to disturb Geigi.

"None yet," Jago said. "Guild to Guild, Lord Pairuti has been informed officially to expect visitors. They have not phoned the Marid. We know that."

That was interesting. His bodyguard, over the years, had increasingly taken to informing him on things lords often didn't find out . . . things somewhat in the realm of Guild secrets.

"But then," Tano said, "the Marid Guild has its own network."

"Illegally so?"

"Oh, indeed illegally, Bren-ji," Banichi said in his lowest voice. "But then, they are no longer privy to our codes."

Tano said, from the facing seats: "The Guild has at least taken pains to keep them out. But *we* take care not to rely on that."

"If there is any Marid Guild in this district," Jago said, "they will not be minor operators. And they will not be taking orders from the Maschi."

"The Maschi lord," Tano said, "directs nothing regarding any Marid operation. If Barb-daja is there, she will not be in his hands."

"Therefore she will not be there," Bren said glumly, "and we may expect they will move her as rapidly as possible to the Marid, I fear too rapidly for us to overtake them."

"Plausibly so," Algini said. "The best we may hope for, nandi, is to settle the Maschi."

"By reason or otherwise," Tano added. "And one very much doubts reason."

"Nandi." Algini, who had had a finger to his ear, listening to something relayed to him, took on a very sober demeanor. "Go to the convenience."

At the rear of the bus. It was not better shielded back there. It was not the potential for gunfire that Algini meant, not so, if he was to be leaving Geigi behind. It had to be informational, a consultation waiting for him back there.

He got up and quietly walked down the aisle to the vicinity of the several strangers who had boarded with them. Algini was right behind him, and so, he saw, turning, was the rest of his aishid.

Which had to alarm Geigi's bodyguard. He cast a look back down the aisle and saw none of that lot stirring.

The next glance was for Algini, who said, in a low voice, "The aiji has Filed, Bren-ji. Word has just now come through."

"Filed."

"On Pairuti, on Machigi, on every lord of the Marid."

"One believes," Jago added dryly, "that the Farai will be quitting your apartment tonight."

The strangers near them could hear, surely. So could the domestics sitting nearby, and several of the dowager's guard.

"Lord Geigi—should not know this, nandiin-ji?"

"His bodyguard, nandi, is simultaneously receiving the same information," Tano said.

Then a glimmering of the reason came through. But he was not sure. "But Lord Geigi—"

"His honor and his position," Banichi said, "would require he advise Pairuti, Bren-ji. His bodyguard need not do so. They will not advise him."

"One understands, then." He almost wished *he* had stayed ignorant. Far better, indeed, if Geigi were not put in a delicate position. His own, human, sense of honor was hard-put with the information—how to approach Pairuti with apparent clear conscience—how to walk into that hall and betray nothing. It was not fair play. It was not honest. It was not—

It was not easy for his aishid, either, to breach Guild secrecy and bring their lord in on the facts—on Tabini-aiji's business. He had no good instinct for what had moved them to do so, except that he, more than Geigi, was adjunct to Tabini-aiji. Hell. He needed to understand that point.

"Why have you told me, nadiin-ji?" he asked outright.

"Tabini-aiji has specified you may be advised, nandi," Algini said. "But that Geigi should not be."

Use his head, then. That was what Tabini expected of the paidhi-aiji. Function in his official capacity. Think his way through. Advise the *Guild*, for God's sake . . . *nobody* advised the Guild, except he had Banichi and Jago in his aishid, who had been Tabini's; and Algini, who had been the Guild's; and

God knew what Tano had been, or why he had come in attached to Algini. His brain raced, finding connections, finding his own staff was a peculiar hybrid of high-level interests and that there was a *reason* his bodyguard told him things.

The west coast was a damned mess, was what. The dowager hadn't meant to get involved out here. She'd been on her way back to the East to spend a quiet spring. Tabini hadn't intended to have his son come out here . . .

"Is the aiji protecting Najida?"

A nod from Jago. "Yes. Definitely."

"And these four, with us?"

"Specialists," Algini said.

Don't ask, then. He didn't.

But Algini said, further, "There are many more moving in, from all directions."

Bren cast an involuntary glance at the windows. There was only rolling meadow. But they were not alone. Out in that landscape forces were moving, major forces . . . and he had told Toby they would get Barb back. He had believed it when he said it. But the operation had just mutated. Tabini-aiji was backing them, all right, but suddenly the dowager's phone calls to Shejidan and the Filing all made one piece of cloth. Tabini had behaved for months as if exile might have changed him, made him more timid, more willing to ignore longstanding situations, anything to avoid another conflict that might destabilize the government.

Negotiating with the Farai, who had occupied the paidhi-aiji's apartment and refused all hints they should quit the premises.

Negotiating with Machigi over old issues, as Machigi rose to power over the dead bodies of certain relatives who had supported the usurper Murini . . .

All leading to this.

Suddenly the argument between the dowager and Tabini about the Edi assumed a wholly different character. Reshaping the balance of power on the coast, hell! Reshaping the entire western half of the aishidi'tat, was what. Tabini had had an operation underway and Ilisidi had moved right into the middle of it with *her* agenda.

And co-opted the paidhi-aiji into it.

He felt a little sick at his stomach. He looked at four faces gone utterly solemn, four close associates who absolutely understood how the game had changed—and changed in ways that profoundly affected the mixed company on this bus.

"Indeed," he said, "I see." Pairuti, like Geigi, had no children. Baiji was, in fact, the governing line's main hope in that regard. So there was no family to get swept up into the order, but— "Is there a chance, still, nadiin-ji, that we can still go through with our plan and give Lord Pairuti the chance to resign?"

Banichi, Jago, and Tano all looked to Algini for that one. And Algini frowned.

"The order is without prejudice," Algini said, "regarding his situation. He *is* given that latitude."

"Is he viewed as complicitous, Gini-ji?" Bren said.

"As having cooperated with the Marid during the Troubles, nandi," Algini said. "Complicitous to that extent."

"Many did," Bren said. "There is that extenuation. The demise of Lord Geigi's sister, however—"

"He is not faulted in that," Algini said.

"Can we give him at least the chance, then?" Bren said. He had never participated in an assassination order. He had the most extreme qualms, even to the extent he wanted to order his own aishid to hang back and not get involved. "Nadiin-ji, the paidhi-aiji is neutral. I am an intercessor, not—not the lord of Najida, in this matter. But one cannot jeopardize the mission, either, to the aiji's detriment—or to the risk of his agents. One finds oneself in a most uncomfortable position."

Banichi said. "We should take the house. That must be done, efficiently and completely, Bren-ji. If you say preserve him, we shall do that."

"If," Bren said uneasily, "if you can do it without risk to yourselves." He took a deep breath and wiped his face with his hand. "This is *why* the Guild has a policy against involving outsiders, is it not, nadiin-ji? I am a fool. Forget everything I have said. I withdraw my statements. I place *no* such restriction or request. My intercession should have been with Tabini-aiji, *not* with Guild assigned to carry out his decision."

"Yet Lord Pairuti could provide useful information," Banichi said. "It is not an unwise choice, Bren-ji. But the decision must be politically supported. That is not our decision. If you say help him live, we can do that."

"What does Lord Geigi's aishid say?"

"They are willing to go in *and* to take down the lord," Jago said. "But they are *not* current with technology down here. It would be a risk we would not wish them to run. And they may have a personal connection with members of the household. That is another risk."

"We and the dowager's men can take the house," Banichi said. "We have no question."

"The aiji's men . . ." Bren began.

"We do not discuss that, Bren-ji," Jago said—which told the story. They were undiscussable and they were going to vanish at some critical point. It took no great wit to know they were going overland and across the local border, and in what direction, and why they were not lingering to assist his operation.

Bren absorbed that information, and Jago said, further: "There are others. Many others."

So *that* was how they were staying current with the situation. Relays—possibly something set up on Maschi land . . . and there were Guild out there—many others, Jago said, moving by stealth. Bren cast a look forward, where Geigi and his aishid sat—the bodyguard reading or with heads together in converse, Geigi still seeming to be asleep.

And one could not leave hanging the question of what to do with Lord Pairuti.

And one could not ask Geigi, either, nor get any useful opinion from Lord Geigi's bodyguard.

Though one had this most uneasy notion that Geigi's drowsiness might *not* be due to the schedule they had kept—that Geigi might be far more aware of things than he wanted to be, and intended to minimize what he did know.

The paidhi-aiji could have done the same thing—sit still while his bodyguard arranged things.

But his aishid had outright invited him into it—which meant, he thought, that they wanted him to make the political decision on what *was* left vague in their orders.

He went back to his seat. His aishid settled around him. Lord Geigi stirred somewhat, but never opened his eyes.

They sat, on a bus rolling along toward a major problem, and stayed in silence for a while, in a landscape no longer even relatively safe.

God, he had promised Toby. He had promised and offered assurances he had thought were reasonable, knowing the way political kidnappings usually ran, and now Barb's safety was nowhere assured in this. A whole quarter of the aishidi'tat was about to go up in major hostilities. Tabini was using their visit to the Maschi as cover for the wholesale movement of major forces . . . to attack the Marid in what amounted to war.

It was Tabini's right to do it to them, and Tabini would naturally regret doing it—but—

Damn!

There might be villages deeper in the folded hills; they likely were numerous, with market roads leading elsewhere. This road bore an overgrowth of brush, opportunistic plants that sprang up in the clear spot a road made . . . indicative of a road unused for a space of time.

Except that this growth of brush had been broken down by a recent passage that might or might not be intermittent trips to the Separti road. One rather thought of the appearance of Marid

Guild turning up at Kajiminda, and then at Najida, and Marid cells in Separti and Dalaigi.

Tabini's reinforcements would have gotten ahead of them, clearing out any ambush. He had to rely on that.

One had no idea what they might arrive to find at Pairuti's estate, Targai: the place in a shambles, or standing pristine and only this morning in reception of an official notice that there *would* be assassination attempts, an endless succession of them until one succeeded or until the contract was set aside. The Maschi were of course entitled to send *their* Guild members to assassinate the aiji without legal consequence, but it would be an enterprise little likely to succeed: the odds were somewhat lopsided.

The official notification of the Filing, which they had to pass to Geigi at some point before they stepped off the bus, would lend a certain flavor to their arrival. That was dead certain.

17

Mani had gotten a courier message. Jegari could not find out what it was.

That was interesting.

It was more interesting that mani ordered better dress and all of a sudden more men on the roof and had a private conference with Ramaso.

"You stay here with nand' Toby," Cajeiri said to Antaro, who was the more level-headed and the gentler of his aishid. "If he wakes up, say this." And he said, in ship-speak: "Cajeiri is talking with his great-grandmother," and made her say it three times so he knew she had it. "And if he insists he needs me, send a servant to find me. We told nand' Bren we would stay with him, so we can never leave him."

But he went and put on his best coat and gathered up Jegari, and went and asked permission to visit mani.

He halfway expected mani would say no and go away. But Nawari let him in, and told Jegari to stay outside.

Mani was sitting by the fireside in her usual chair. She was very formally dressed and very grim. Cajeiri went up to her and bowed very properly.

"Well?" she asked.

A second bow. "Nand' Toby is still all right, mani. He sleeps a lot. Why are we all dressed for court?"

"Because my fool grandson—your father—has launched a war and Filed on the lord of the Maschi!" Great-grandmother snapped. "A war long overdue, and one we have counseled long since, but it is highly inconsiderate of him to do so with the paidhi-aiji and Lord Geigi in such a position. We asked for support, not, baji-naji, a general conflict with the Marid! We are highly incensed!"

"Are they in danger, mani?"

"Oh, doubtless they are in extreme danger! The Maschi may by now have been advised that they will be attacked, they will draw an immediate conclusion when the bus arrives, and if they have Guild borrowed from the Marid, *those* clans will also have been notified they are to be a target. And if you were Lord Machigi, what would *you* do?"

"I would be very careful to keep Barb-daja alive and I would try to take nand' Bren prisoner, too."

"Brilliant! Unfortunately that is exactly what he will do. And your father did this in full knowledge of where the paidhi-aiji is going. Oh, he has committed an extraordinary number of Guild to protect them, but this is a high risk. One *assumes* the Guild has notified the Marid—or is in the process of doing so. And has it deliberated with *no* advance word getting to the Marid or to the Maschi?"

"They did not tell *you*, mani."

That stopped Great-grandmother for a breath, and made her look sharply toward the other room, which might be where Cenedi was.

"Also," Cajeiri plunged ahead, because the thought had occurred to him, "if I were Machigi, and I knew we were here, I would be *very* sure to try to catch you, mani, and me, even if my father *has* got another heir on the way."

Great-grandmother frowned at him, and Cajeiri decided he had just been scarily pert.

"Well," Great-grandmother said. "Well! Is my great-grandson possessed of any *other* thought?"

He bowed. That was always safest. And thought fast. "It would be good," Cajeiri said desperately, "if Machigi came here, since they would not be attacking nand' Bren with all their people, and *we* can be ready for them."

Great-grandmother suddenly laughed aloud, the grim lines fracturing into great delight. "Great-grandson, you have your father's nerve and, one is very glad to see, *our* wits! We have sent word to the Grandmother of Najida. We are about to call and thank your father for the *extravagant* favor he has done us all at this delicate time. And we are calling in the Gan."

"The Gan, mani-ma?" He knew about them. They were very much like the Edi, also from the island of Mospheira from when the humans landed, and they were independent like the Edi, but also allied to them, and lived on the northern coast near Dur.

"Relatives of the Edi, seafarers, who will be glad to be invited into a quarrel with the Marid. Your father will *not* approve, since they will be asking for the same privilege as the Edi, an estate, a state, and a lordship of their own, but we have another strong connection to them. Do you recall the young pilot, Great-grandson, who showed up at Tirnamardi?"

"Without a doubt, mani-ma!" He was immediately excited. It had been a beautiful yellow plane, and the young pilot dashing and gallant, and he had wanted to fly, too. "He is not Gan, however, is he, mani?"

"He is not, nor is his father, but in the way Lord Geigi has represented the Edi, his father represents the Gan, and stands for them, and he will immediately see the benefit in defending us. A threat to the paidhi-aiji will bring them here, we have no doubt. So go! Consider how you and your aishid will protect nand' Toby if we come under attack. We shall need to take shelter belowground and we have that pernicious nephew of Geigi's in our way."

"We could move the stored things up into the suites, mani, and clear the storerooms and then we would all fit downstairs."

"Good! Flexibility is a commendable trait. Send me Nawari while you talk to Ramaso and have it done."

"Yes," he said. He had never been given an important job until yesterday; and now mani handed him one, too, and he was supposed to be in two places at once. Mani clearly was short of people to take her orders, which meant she had everybody busy.

He stopped outside, where Jegari waited with Nawari. "Gari-ji," he said with a little bow. And another: "Nawari-nadi. Great-grandmother wants you immediately. Gari-ji, come with me."

"Where are we going, nandi?" Jegari asked.

"We are on Great-grandmother's business," he announced with some satisfaction, and headed off at a quick pace.

He was not sure he could get Ramaso to do what he said, and move all the furniture. But he intended to try, without any recourse to adult authority. He had gotten fairly good at getting his way.

It was becoming useful, even to mani.

18

The land had begun to rise again, as the bus entered a region of white rock and ancient, weathered evergreen, under a noon sun. One sat thinking about snipers, and watching those high rocks with some misgivings.

But it was, given other information, likely that those rocks were already cleared, and occupied by Tabini's forces. One didn't ask—only trusted that if their bodyguard were in the least suspicious, they would all be sitting on the floor.

Then the roofs of a village appeared in the distance—reminder that whatever force they could bring to bear, Maschi clan territory had a fair population. This village would belong to an affiliated clan, the Pejithi, who lived their lives and conducted their commerce with the capital, and likely with the Marid.

In the distance, around a bend in the road, and past an intersection with a better-used market road, rose a different outline, the sprawling roofs of a noble house of that same white stone, a noble house surrounded by a ruined remnant of its fortified walls, sign of great antiquity in this region.

Nowadays the breached walls, interspersed with zig-zag rail fence, would simply be keeping wandering herds of game out of the formal gardens that showed in those gaps. It was a picturesque house, with its two standing towers and its curved tile roof, a regional style. The television antenna somewhat spoiled the effect.

Lord Geigi stirred from his nap, or his pretense of one, even rising from his seat for a moment's better look out the front window.

"I have not seen Targai since I was a boy," Geigi said to Bren. "It has not changed. Not visibly. Except for the antenna. And the power lines."

One of Geigi's bodyguard said: "Best sit down, nandi. For safety."

Geigi sat down. The bus kept up its steady pace toward the gate.

At any moment, literally at any moment, they might come under fire. And as yet nobody had said that the non-Guild among them should get down on the floor.

"Should one not get down at this point?" Bren asked Jago.

"We have surveillance on the grounds, Bren-ji. But if you would feel safer, do so."

"The aiji's men are already here?"

Jago shrugged. It fell under the heading of not discussing Guild operations, but one began to regard those ancient towers in a different light. He had the very uncomfortable vest on—leaving his head vulnerable, but that was, he hoped, a significantly smaller target, and one did not expect the paidhi-aiji to be wearing body armor.

He sat where he was, behind opaque windows, as the bus pulled into the drive and trundled on around to the great house.

A pair of Guildsmen in black exited the house—placing themselves in great jeopardy. And if those were not the aiji's, Bren thought, his pulse racing a bit, they were likely native to the region, and deeply loyal, to be exposing themselves like that—granted they knew about the Filing.

Their own situation was potentially looking up—or getting far worse . . . because that brave gesture of peace politely required another, reciprocal gesture, which—he felt a rising tide of apprehension—had to come from Guild of similar rank, unless they meant to wade in shooting.

The bus braked. Banichi and Jago got up, and Bren bit his lip and *knew* who had to deal with this welcoming committee.

He leaned forward, himself. "Nadiin-ji," he said. "Tell Lord Pairuti he has a safe refuge with the paidhi-aiji if he will take it. Tell them so, urgently."

Jago listened, then inclined her head once, grimly, before the door opened and she followed Banichi off the bus—Tano and Algini taking up position with leveled rifles behind them in the doorway thus exposed.

The bus door faced the welcoming committee. There were weapons in evidence on the other side, but not drawn.

And wherever Tabini's men were, it was not, at the moment, here, where such a threatening presence would have been very useful.

One of the pair said—Bren could hear it clearly: "Stand there, nadi."

And Banichi answered her: "Advise Lord Pairuti, nadi, that he has an offer of safety and personal intercession from the paidhi-aiji. Your lord, we believe, is aware of the Filing of Intent."

"He is aware of it, nadi."

There was a moment of silence, then. Bren could not entirely see what was happening because of the doorframe, but he saw Jago standing quite, quite still, with her hand ominously near her sidearm.

"There is a signal passed, Bren-ji," Tano said without diverting his eyes from their potential targets. "Banichi has asked whether they are under duress. They have responded they are under internal threat."

Handsigns, that silent language of the Guild.

They had a problem, then. Marid agents—in the house. These two were out here in a desperate bid to negotiate . . .

Either that, or these two were lying and intended to set them up.

Tano said, sharply, "Bren-ji, up! Get off the bus. We are taking the house."

Damn! Bren thought, and flung himself to his feet and around the rail to reach the steps with Tano and Algini right with him. He thought he was going to run for the doors. But Tano seized him around the ribs in one arm and outright carried him to the front of the house, setting him down to the side of the entry as Banichi and Jago kicked wide the half-open house doors and fired one volley down the hall.

Then they were not alone. From cover of somewhere—the ornamental bushes down the drive, the ancient, crumbled masonry beyond, God knew—there suddenly appeared other black uniforms, guns lifted, signal of peace.

Tabini's men, Bren thought, heart lifting.

The two local Guild meanwhile turned their backs to the situation, hands held outward, a declaration they were not going to contest the takeover, Bren saw with a sideward glance. He felt sorry for them: they were in a hell of a situation, relying on *his* word there was a chance to save their lord.

But if the wrong word came out of the house, those two would fight. And die without a chance.

Geigi's guard had reached the door of the house just a little ahead of Geigi himself reaching Bren's position. The bodyguard had their rifles aimed generally up, but a scant heartbeat from going level and wreaking destruction down the hall.

Tano and Algini kept themselves in the way, cutting off view of any proceedings inside the building, while Banichi and Jago continued to issue orders from just inside. Nobody had touched the two local Guildsmen, who had not moved in all this, not a muscle.

"Lord Pairuti is offered the paidhi-aiji's intercession!" Banichi's voice rang down the hall. "Let him come out and surrender to the paidhi-aiji!"

There was silence inside. Bren was not in a position to see what was going on; there was a large bush and Tano's very tall body between him and the hall. Tano maintained a grip on his arm with his left hand, the rifle in his right, tucked under his arm. On the other was Algini, also armed, and partially blocking his view of Lord Giegi, who was similarly jammed into the bushes, with four or five of the newly arrived Guildsmen between their positions. The two still-armed bodyguards maintained their posture, waiting, arms outstretched, unmoving.

"Come out!" Banichi shouted down the inner hall, with Jago standing right by him—her rifle aimed right down that hallway.

Fire came back, a shot so loud Bren jerked; and in the same muscle-twitch their side fired back.

"Stay here, nandi!" Tano said, half a heartbeat behind Algini moving. They took up position in the doorway: Bren stood pat, heart pounding, wondering what had happened, whether Banichi and Jago were all right. He could just see Banichi down on one knee, with rifle braced to fire. Nobody was shooting now. And in a moment Bren saw Jago shift into view, standing, rifle covering the hall.

Algini moved, to insinuate himself past the open door and cover both Banichi and Jago, with no fire at all.

Then Bren became aware that Guild around them had moved—some vanishing from the driveway without a sound, just gone, when Bren looked back in Geigi's direction: the corner of the house offered a likely destination. Others had dragged the two locals out of the line of fire and applied medical aid to one of them—who must have been felled by that shot.

For a moment that gesture of mercy was the only movement, one of the two brought down by a shot presumably from their own side, and surgery being performed right on the driveway, in the cover of the bus.

Not a nice situation, no.

But it was over, he was thinking, starting to plan how he was going to get into the hall.

Banichi and Jago opened fire suddenly, a deafening discharge; and simultaneously moved, with Geigi's bodyguard at their backs. There was nothing Tano and Algini could do about the situation, not with two helpless lords in their care. Bren had the pistol in his pocket, but he left it there: they already had the example of friendly fire on the driveway. And he stayed right where he was, beside the open door, next to a row of bushes; and they daren't budge from here. Geigi was immediately behind him.

Get back to the bus? It was a sitting target, even if it hadn't gotten so much as a ding in its painted panels on this venture.

Better to be where they were. Unless things went very, very bad in there.

And God, there were so many ways it—

Blast from inside. Grenade, or boobytrap. There were wires that could take a head or foot off. There were a hundred ways the Guild could kill intruders in a territory they had prepared for invasion; and Bren stood there against the bushes trying not to think of that.

Then massive fire erupted inside the building.

Followed by a deafening silence.

Stinging smoke wafted out of the doorway.

And out of that smoke, Jago appeared on a leisurely retreat, spoke code into her com, and looked as if she had understood something in the instant before her eyes shifted for one split-second toward Bren and Geigi.

"The aiji's men have come into the house from the garden entry," Jago said, watching down that hall again, "meeting ours."

"Are they all right?" Bren asked in a low voice—not wishing to distract Jago from business; and in fact Jago's look of concentration never broke from the hall.

"They have asked the same of us," Jago said under her breath. "There are targets on the grounds. Probably it will be best to move inside the house, Bren-ji. Now."

Bren moved, jammed his hand into his pocket to find the butt of the pistol, and, with Jago, Geigi, and Tano and Algini, rounded the corner into the hallway.

Banichi, two of Geigi's men and a handful of other Guild were the only persons standing under a high pall of smoke in that hall. Two people in civilian dress were sitting on the floor, knees tucked up, against the wall—denoting their noncombatant status, and inconveniently far from any side door. Those were servants.

Two other Guild lay face down in a pool of blood. He and Geigi were still near the door, with their bodyguards; and Tano, stepping to the side, drew Bren against the wall there— a safer place than mid-hall, in case anybody should burst out of one of the side rooms firing, Bren thought belatedly. Geigi was in the same defensive position, their bodyguards arrayed as a living shield between them and anybody appearing from down the hall, and Algini, at their rear, guarding against anybody trying to retreat into the house and coming at them from behind.

Not an optimum approach, if they wanted to save Pairuti and what he knew. Bren looked at Geigi and saw distress: not an optimum homecoming, either, with dead in the hallway and house servants trying desperately to keep out of the line of hair-triggered Guild. Banichi signaled the two servants they could move to safety, and they quietly did so, getting into a side room, shutting that door.

So they were the only possessors of the hall, now. And the whole house grew very quiet for a moment.

Then shooting erupted outside, somewhat to the rear of the house, and again from the roof right over their heads. Footsteps sounded on the ceiling.

Attics. Attics in this district were a hazard, and this house, like Najida, like Kajiminda, was in the peak-roofed, sprawling style that had a full reach up there. Bren cast a worried look up, tracking that sound.

"They are ours up there, nandi," Tano said then.

That was a relief. What was going on out on the grounds was another matter. Fire kept up.

And their chances of finding Barb alive grew less and less—if she had ever been here in the first place.

One had, lifelong, become philosophical about Tabini's little surprises. Bren had told himself repeatedly it was how Tabini stayed in power. It was the way atevi managed things, and it was not the paidhi's place to critique it. The paidhi, however, *had* accepted appointments—had risen as high in politics as it was possible to rise, infuriating Tabini's opposition, astonishing his supporters.

And here he was, having involved himself in a district where peace had never existed, not since the War of the Landing, when the Ragi atevi agreement to pull two aboriginal peoples off Mospheira and settle them on this coast had thwarted their own major rivals, the Marid, in their grab for the same coast.

A quiet district, yes, under the threat the central region posed to any breach of order; but not peace, nothing like peace.

And the paidhi-aiji had been oblivious to the undercurrents sweeping toward an attack on the Marid, despite Tabini's personally reconnoitering the region, despite Tabini's curious engagement with his grandmother on the topic of Edi sovereignty. The paidhi-aiji had gone on assuming Tabini was going to stay out of it and just let his grandmother make her peaceful deals.

And it was Tabini, of course, who had *given* his resident human an estate in the plain middle of an old, volatile situation.

Tabini might well have known the district was a tinderbox when he'd cleared Bren to leave the capital and go vacationing on the coast. Tabini claimed not to have known. But that was not guaranteed to be the truth. Tabini was completely capable of sending somebody in to stir the pot.

God, at the moment he so wished he'd just gotten a hotel in town.

Another burst of gunfire, right out front. He *hoped* Tabini's men were enough. This was not a good position, standing here in the front hall with the doors open.

Better than standing out there in the bushes, however.

And Geigi—he threw a look Geigi's direction and caught a grim expression. Hell of a homecoming, all around, first at Kajiminda and now at Targai. Geigi and Geigi's bodyguard surely had their own sentiments about Tabini's actions—a human was not, possibly, wired to understand precisely that mix of emotions, the profound draw of man'chi toward Tabini and those aggressive urges of a born leader—literally, a born leader—and the draw of their own duty to Pairuti, who'd made a hash of his leadership of their clan. Grasp what a clash of emotions was going on in Geigi? Probably. Intellectually, he could.

Feel it the way Geigi felt it, in his gut? Not likely.

Have a clearer head than Geigi did at the moment? He might well. He didn't trust that gentle Geigi wouldn't order somebody shot.

It had gotten quieter outside all of a sudden. That was either good or bad. If bad, they were in the next place trouble would arrive.

"Nadiin-ji," he said very quietly. Tano and Algini were on high alert, watching any movement down the long hall, where Banichi and Jago, nearly back to back, were directing men probing other hallways. "How are we doing out there?"

"The aiji's men have the roof and the tower," Tano said, "and are reporting no movement on the grounds."

That was a relief. "Barb-daja. Any sign?"

"No, Bren-ji," Tano said. "Regretfully, not yet."

"The resistence is partly local," Algini said from behind him, without losing his concentration. "Partly outsider. Marid, likeliest, the first shot, that hit the man out front."

Thus starting a firefight—since all the local Guild, aware of the Filing, were going to assume they were under active attack. Their incursion had had everything under control, they'd been about to draw Pairuti out under a safe conduct and the local Guild had been taking it slowly, trying to get the best possible situation for their lord.

And then somebody had fired and hit probably the Guild senior of Pairuti's bodyguard, maybe not even aiming at Banichi. The Marid would be completely willing to see the place shot up, Pairuti silenced, his honest Guildsmen dead, and things in as big a mess as they could possibly be.

That added up to Marid infiltration. Pairuti had let these people in, the same way Baiji had done, and they'd taken over, the way they'd taken over Kajiminda.

After a long period of maneuvering to get himself in the right in public opinion, Tabini now had a provocation that would be evident to the whole world.

With his own grandmother right in the middle of it.

Maybe for once Tabini had even surprised Ilisidi. *That* would be a first in planetary history.

Deep breath. Tabini also trusted the paidhi-aiji wasn't going to get himself killed to no particular advantage. Tabini expected his people not just to sit still in whatever situation he'd engineered them into.

Damn him.

"Where is Pairuti at the moment, Tano-ji?" he asked.

"We believe, in the sitting room, nandi. But we have not gone in there yet."

"I need to reach him. I want him alive, Tano-ji."

Tano threw him a look.

"Pairuti can stop this," Bren said. "At least where it regards local Guild. Can he not? And he has things to say, in court. We need him alive."

"Yes," Tano said abruptly, order taken; he relayed that to Algini, whose attention was fixed on the hall, and Algini nodded abruptly in the affirmative. Communication drew a look from Banichi, and then from Jago, who nodded her own agreement. Geigi looked momentarily confused.

No time to think, then: Tano seized Bren by the arm and jerked him past Banichi, down the hall, with one of Geigi's men racing to the fore of them. His gun swung down, his burst of fire shredded the woodwork around the door lock—his kick opened it, and that man whipped around the door to the inside.

Fire erupted from inside—Bren had started to follow, and Tano snatched him back before he had so much as twitched. Then Jago appeared from the hall behind them, her gun spitting a volley of bullets as she went inside.

There wasn't time to say *help her*—Tano shoved him against the wall and dived to a knee, rifle around the edge of the door-frame. Then got up. Geigi's man came into view, moving side-ways, rifle still leveled, and Bren's heart skipped a beat, seeing Jago standing in the clear.

"We have him, nandi," Tano said, urging him forward, into the room; and Bren swore to himself he would never, ever, ever issue another order to his bodyguard.

The room was a shambles, three bodies on the floor, blood everywhere, openwork screens flattened and shattered by gun-fire, and a lone survivor in a brocade coat standing amid the carnage, a white-haired, lanky aristocrat looking not at all re-lated to Lord Geigi.

"Lord Pairuti," Bren said, mustering a breath. "Surrender and I can keep you alive. Do not do this to your staff. They rely on you, nandi."

The man turned away, looking ceilingward, seeming distracted.

And spun about with a pistol in hand. It went off.

The whole room went to ceiling in a burst of thunder. It was that fast, and it hurt, and Bren couldn't get a breath, lying flat on the floor with the feeling someone had just hit him, and he had hit his head, which hurt nearly as much as the punch in his gut. His whole brain was shaken, and his ears rang, and Tano had him by the hand and the arm and was hauling up on him, so he was supposed to get up—

He tried. He could not get a breath, and then got a little air: was aware of Tano on his knees trying to keep him flat, and Tano kept coming and going in a tunnel of dark.

Bad move. Thoroughly bad move.

"He is dead," he heard Algini say. And: "Good riddance," Geigi said, and another huge shadow obscured the light. A strong hand took Bren's shoulder. "Bren-ji."

"One is—" Bren tried to say, but ran out of air. It came to him that he had been shot, and that that was why the room had gone upside down, and why he had hit his head, but he was still alive, which was due to the vest. The vest now, as his numb fingers explored it, had a large frayed spot. He tried to get an elbow under him.

A halo of faces surrounded him, from his vantage: Tano and Algini left that halo, and Banichi and Jago appeared in their places. "I am quite all right," he assured them. And attempted to sit up, in which the stiff vest offered no help at all, and his ribs hurt abysmally. Banichi and Jago each took an arm and pulled him gently to his feet; but his head reaching vertical didn't help, not in the least. He felt sick, and dizzy, and was very glad when they let him down into a chair. He slumped back in the corner made by an arm, and surveyed the carnage in the room.

He'd given an order. Now Pairuti and four Guildsmen were dead on the floor and he'd risked Tano and Algini and Jago and everybody else who relied on him . . . all because he'd called it urgent.

"One has been a fool," he said in a low voice, and thought for a moment he was going to be sick and compound everyone's distress. He kept it down, however, and got two and three breaths. "Do what you need to do for the mission, nadiin-ji. I am far from dead."

"We are secure, Bren-ji," Jago said.

"As secure as we shall be," Banichi said, "until this situation is resolved. We hold Targai."

"An unwelcome gift," Geigi said glumly. "But mine to deal with."

"Can you sort out the staff, nandi?" Banichi asked, and Geigi shrugged.

"Perhaps," Geigi said, and then ordered his own guard: "Find me one of Pejithi clan."

"Nandi," that man said, and moved off. Bren shifted in the chair, sucking in his middle with a wince; but perhaps no ribs were broken—bruised, yes, but he had gotten off better than he had deserved, no question.

"Go do what you need to do," he said. "I am sure I am bruised, no more than that. From now on I *take* advice, no more of giving it, nadiin-ji. What is necessary, at this point?"

Banichi's hand closed on his arm, on the chair, commanding attention. "Lord Geigi must take control of the clan, Bren-ji. We must hold this place. The aiji's forces will do as they have orders to do. Beyond that—we hold here and trust Cenedi to hold Najida."

Some things came clear out of the fog: that the aiji's forces were dictating next moves, and that the next move beyond Targai was likely to be the Marid, and all-out war. They were sitting on the front lines. They were, in fact, holding a major piece of the front lines.

But the Marid was not limited to land. They had a navy and so did the aiji. There could be conflict striking at Separti Township, or coming into Kajiminda Bay, or Najida Bay—where there were very valuable targets . . . targets Tabini would want to protect; and he hoped to God that Tabini's forces were not going to start a feud with the Edi locals by going in there in force.

He had to think. Never mind the headache and the lump on the back of his skull, he had to think.

And just then every Guildsman in the room twitched: the door had opened, admitting a broad-shouldered Guildsman, with a solid grip on a younger man.

A very bedraggled, haggard and limping young man in Guild uniform, in the custody of a tall Guildsman with a red band about his arm . . .

"Lucasi," Bren murmured, and a dozen thoughts flashed

through his mind—Cajeiri's bodyguards: they had been near Barb, they'd disappeared, and they were here, where Marid agents had been running the place and where the local lord had shot at him. Bren sat up with a wince and started to get up from the chair, but bruised ribs said otherwise.

"Nandi!" Lucasi cried, and tried to reach him. The Guildsman holding him had another idea, and then Jago stepped into Lucasi's intended path, cutting him off. The young man protested: "Nandi, we tried to overtake them! We are *not* traitors!"

"I want to hear him, nadiin-ji," Bren said quietly, and did get to his feet, with Banichi's hand under his elbow. He got a breath and fixed Cajeiri's missing bodyguard with a steady stare and one question. "Where is Barb-daja, nadi?"

"Nandi, Veijico—Veijico—is still tracking the kidnappers. They were in a closed truck, four of them, with the lady . . ."

"On what road?" Jago asked sharply.

"The main road. East. I had put my foot in a hole. I could no longer keep up. But the truck stopped here. So we did not trust the Maschi lord . . . we hid. We waited. And then the truck went on. And Veijico went after them. And I was waiting for her—until Ragi Guild came in."

"And where was your communication back to operations?" Jago asked.

Lucasi cast a look at her and shook his head. "I—was not equipped, nadi. We have the short-range. We do have that."

"You left the grounds. You did not advise the officer of the watch. You did not take proper equipment. You went off without instruction."

We just . . . we thought—we thought, Jago-nadi, we thought—" Lucasi took a deep breath and wiped his face with both hands, shaking his head. "We had orders."

"From whom?" Banichi asked.

"From the young lord, nadi."

"From a child, nadi!"

"To whom we were assigned, nadi!" He made a profound

bow to Bren, a slighter one to Banichi. The ribbon of his queue had come half undone. He was dusty, dirty, and thoroughly wretched-looking. "I take all responsibility. Help my partner. Veijico will die before she leaves the trail now, and it is my fault, nadiin, entirely my fault."

"You involved the paidhi's brother and led him out of a secure house," Jago said.

"He came, nadi. We told him go back! We knew there was an alert in progress. We thought the young gentleman might have gone down to the boat—"

"So you took the extravagant action, you involved non-Guild, and at no time did you communicate with operations, though you had short-range available!"

Lucasi's face became pained. "The young gentleman despises us. He avoided us. We thought—we thought it was on our account, that he had gone out, to teach us a lesson."

"And why did you go to nand' Toby at all, nadi?"

"We were wrong," Lucasi said. "We know now. We were embarrassed. We thought—we thought we could get the young gentleman back, we could save him from a reprimand—we might mend matters. Intruders fired at us. Nand' Toby went down. We tried to get to position to return fire and protect him, but then the lady bolted uphill, across our line of fire. We *saw* them take her. We dodged around and got up as far as the road. Then we heard the young gentleman shouting at us from the porch. We moved to get between the intruders and him, and then we had his orders to retrieve the lady. We tried. We ran out onto the road and saw a truck in the distance. We tried to catch up with it. Then we thought—we need to know which way it will go at the intersection, toward the town or toward the train station, so we can report that. So we tracked them toward the intersection, and then—then we found ourselves out of range of house communications. The truck, nandi, had kept going east, toward the train station or the airport, and then we thought if there was a train, if they tried to take her aboard we could do something—but they kept going past the depot. We thought it might be the airport—but—then we thought—if we can reach Targai, the lord there will help us." The young man ran out of breath and shook his head. "We were wrong, nandi. And we just—all along, once we had left short-range, we thought if we could get her back—we could redeem some of our mistakes."

"Fools," Jago said. "Young *fools*. There was a phone at the train station and another at the airport."

The young man looked dismayed. "We—failed to think of that, nadi."

"Did you fail to think, nadi, or were you even thinking in terms of reporting? You were bent on following that truck. You knew what fools you had been and were bent on saving your reputations, to the lady's detriment."

"The truck was not going that fast, nadi, and we thought— we thought—it was trying to look ordinary. We could keep up if we cut across the land. We could find out where it was based. We were willing to die, if we could get good information on the lady! We at no time risked losing her!"

"So," Banichi said harshly, "you created the situation. Now you have somehow misplaced your partner *and* the lady."

Lucasi hung his head and looked miserable. "I put my foot in a hole in the dark. My own fault. Veijico kept going, and I came back for help."

"Finally!" Banichi said. "A thorough mess you have made of it, nadi."

"Yes," Lucasi said. "It is. We tried to do well for the young gentleman. But he despised us. And his order—"

"Enough of his order," Banichi said. "An excuse. An excuse, casting blame on your lord."

"It is not my intention!"

"Many things were not your intention, nadi!"

Lucasi turned his face toward Bren. "Nand' paidhi, let us at least finish this. The truck I think was going toward Taisigi territory. There still may be time."

He hadn't the hardwiring to read it. The words were one thing. But reading the boy—it took atevi to do that, and he looked from Jago to Banichi. It was by no means reasonable that that truck was not racing toward safety by now.

"Clever fool," Jago said, and nudged him with the rifle butt. "It would be bad form to shoot him."

"*Are* you lying, nadi?" Banichi asked.

"*No*, Banichi-nadi. I am not lying."

"And you think that truck is still loitering about for us to find?"

"We never ceased to observe it, nadi! My partner is still tracking it, wherever it has gone. She will not have given up. We were ordered, nadiin. We were ordered."

Banichi shifted the rifle that had been pointing straight at him, still frowning. "And do you not think you should have exercised more mature judgement on the young gentleman's behalf? Do you think you were sent to him to concur in every idea he might have?"

"Nadi, —"

"*This is your one chance, nadi.* Will you go on lying to the paidhi-aiji, and to the rest of us? Who *has* your man'chi, that you could leave your lord and leave him to two Guild-in-training, because a child told you to do it?" Banichi grabbed a fistful of Lucasi's jacket and jerked him about, face to face. "Are you a child? Or is there something else we should know?"

"No," Lucasi said faintly. "No, nadi."

Banichi let him go, roughly. "Do as you wish to do with him, Bren-ji. They are not telling all the truth, they violated basic principles, and he is lying, maybe even to himself. You can take him in, in which case he will probably obey our orders, at this point—or you can dismiss him, in which case he will follow his partner as best he can. At least to her, he has man'chi."

Bren cast a look at that shocked, miserable face—he *knew* Banichi, knew Banichi was both ruthless, and kind-hearted, and this was a very *young* fool, in very deep trouble.

Not behaving rationally. That was what Banichi was telling him. Things didn't add up, not with that lazily moving truck, and not with two young Guild who were close to causing a war with the Marid.

"Nadi?" he asked. "Explain yourself. Explain yourself to me, if you want my help for your sister."

"Everything he is saying is right, nandi. We should have reported, we should have worked with the household, we—"

"Why did you not?" Bren asked. It seemed the central question. "Why did you, together, not do these things?"

The boy looked to be drowning in questions. He looked at Jago, looked at Banichi, looked at him.

"*There* is your question," Jago said harshly. "Banichi has asked it. The paidhi has asked it."

"We are not your enemies!" Lucasi said.

"You wanted to impress your young lord—when it should have been the other way around. Are *you* aijiin?"

Are you crazy? Jago was asking.

It was a damned machimi play. And it was the last thing he wanted. It was the absolute last thing his aishid wanted, he was very sure, two psychologically messed-up young people who were Guild-trained and knew too much.

But one thread did make sense. They hadn't meshed with Cajeiri. They *hadn't* been able to attach. And there might be more than one reason for it. "Understand this," Bren said, "nadi. Your young lord did not grow up on the earth. He learned many different ways up in the heavens. The aiji may have thought that with your excellent skills and your intelligence you might be able to adapt to him—since he may not always give you the signals you expect to have. Are you capable of seeing that? No one warned you. But you were credited for extraordinary qualities, so perhaps his father assumed too much."

Lucasi stared at him, mouth slightly open. And the eyes tracked, locked.

"You cannot see it with *my* perspective," Bren said, "but

surely, nadi, you will have observed that the young lord, despite being the aiji's son, is *not* traditional in his thinking."

Something clicked. One thought so, at least. Lucasi's face looked a peculiar shade.

"Think on it," Bren said.

"Nandi," Lucasi said, "give me the chance. You can. I will *not* fail you."

At doing what? one wondered. Something had just ticked over, perhaps; but he wasn't wired to feel it—he never let himself expect to be, even if he'd just tried to reason down an atevi line of thought.

But in this mass movement of forces, in the fall of Targai, in Geigi's succession to the clan lordship, in the Edi accession to a lordship, and the maneuvering of that truck, a deliberate challenge from the Marid, if the boy was not lying—in all of this, *he* still had an objective. *Barb* was nowhere in the aiji's plans, and not that consequential in Mospheira's, or Shejidan's, or even the Marid's. She was a silly woman. Nobody who'd taken her could communicate with her, and that meant her value was only as a provocation. She was disposable, unless somebody knew what Toby was; and higher and higher up the chain of command, somebody might realize what they had, which would make two governments realize both she *and* Toby had become expendable—give or take the annoyance that would be to the paidhi-aiji.

And the paidhi's not being a warlike office, neither was he on duty, once they had gotten Geigi into Targai, removed Pairuti, and taken *that* stronghold out of Machigi's control. He was dismissed from usefulness, at the moment, and *he* had a promise he had made.

"You will obey my aishid," he said, "on your life, Lucasi, from this point on. Where do you think they were going?"

"The main road. Southeast."

Toward Taisigi territory.

"We had best move," Banichi said, looking Bren's way. "If

you wish to pursue the lady's kidnappers, nandi, best Jago and I go, best we move fast and get light transport from the aiji's forces."

That was sensible. That was the way it classically ought to work. Unlike the situation in which Lucasi had left his young lord, he was in a now-allied house, with two of his aishid left, and surrounded by the aiji's forces, as safe as he would be in Najida.

But Banichi and Jago alone—to take on the Marid, and add themselves to the list of the young fool's mistakes?

"Take some of the aiji's forces with you," he said.

"We cannot, Bren-ji," Banichi said, and the *cannot* was the word meaning *are not of sufficient rank.*

"Then can *I?*" he asked, and Banichi's face betrayed a little reluctance to answer.

"Can I?" he asked again, and Banichi said: "Officially, yes, Bren-ji."

"Find out from their officer how many I can detach."

"You must go with the party," Banichi said, "to have that authority, and that is not advisable, Bren-ji."

"*Not advisable* is spread thickly over this entire situation, Banichi-ji," he said. "We will take the bus, and a good number of the aiji's men, if we can arrange that. Speed is of some use. We do *not* want to enter Taisigi territory."

"Nandi," Banichi said, and turned and went out to the hall. Lucasi bowed deeply and, at Banichi's nod, left with him.

Which left Jago standing there with, by now, Tano and Algini, Jago with a profoundly unhappy look.

"I have promised nand' Toby," Bren said. "Jago-ji, we bring Barb back for *him.* For no other reason."

She seemed to find something ironically amusing in that, God knew what. "Understood, Bren-ji."

In a moment Banichi came back from the hall with one handsign for his partners.

Even Bren could read that one. It said, "Ten. Affirmative."

19

The house was looking different, bare, the way it looked when mani was packing to change residences.

Which was somewhat true. They had all moved to the basement, starting with transporting nand' Toby downstairs. Staff got one of the tall, paneled screens from the sitting room and padded it all about with sheets and pillows, and then used it to carry nand' Toby down the steps, himself gently tied to the screen—Cajeiri had watched the process, dutiful to his promise to nand' Bren, and thought it scary, especially where the stairs turned, but they made it safely. Nand' Toby was not supposed to walk and he was not supposed to be excited, and that process did not violate either, because mani's physician, who supervised, had given nand' Toby a good dose of sedative for the procedure. Cajeiri thought it a very good thing, and he was very glad they had not dropped him.

And next came the job of moving mani downstairs.

And since the physician had promised to stay with nand' Toby for the next hour or so, Cajeiri took Jegari and Antaro and went to help move Great-grandmother.

Mani was not enthusiastic about going. In fact she vowed she was not going until trouble was proven to be on its way, or possibly until after trouble arrived. So all the servants were allowed to do was to get together Great-grandmother's wardrobe and take that down. It was expensive, and bulky, and it all had to be safely hung.

So that went down, boxes handed from servant to servant, because it would have been indecent for mani's garments to be displayed on their way. They would be taken into storage, and they would be unpacked, and readied for wear . . .

Granted mani ever consented to go down the stairs at all, which not even Cenedi could persuade her to do, yet.

"You truly should, mani," Cajeiri said very cautiously.

"Hush!" mani said. And that was that. Cajeiri felt his ear smart even across the room.

So he took himself and Antaro and Jegari out into the hall again to see the stairs clogged with downbound packets of mani's baggage.

Immediately after those, of course, all the historic pieces in all the rooms had to go down—and then all the spare store-rooms were filled, so the servants had to move out all the food, boxes, and jars and sacks of it, from other storerooms and take that up into the kitchen upstairs and the kitchen downstairs, so one aisle of each was filled with supplies clear to the rafters, and canisters were set on the cabinets and the second and third stoves in the main kitchens. It was an impressive lot of food. There certainly seemed no danger of them starving.

Then the most fragile porcelains and the hangings had to go downstairs into all the storage they had just cleared. So did all the handmade draperies, which had to be taken down, and the hand-knotted carpets, which had to be rolled up, exposing the stone and wood flooring that one never saw except around the edges: it was a whole new Najida. There was one manufactured carpet, in the dining hall, which staff said just had to take its chances. But every one of the porcelains had to be individually padded up in pillows—there were a lot of those—and bedded down with the folded hangings. The ancient tea set had to go down, specially: it had a box of lacquered wood.

And then the historic furniture in the sitting room had to go down. Ramaso was really, really clever at telling how to stack it like a puzzle, and with padding between surfaces, so it took up far less space than seemed likely.

Everybody had a cold lunch: Great-grandmother readily agreed that that would do for her; but Cook said he was working on hot soup for supper, along with more cold bread and some pickle: it would be an odd kind of supper, but Cajeiri personally hoped they would all get to eat it in peace and that nand' Bren and nand' Geigi would be back in the morning, and most of all that his father's Guild would sort things out and kick the Marid troublemakers clear back to their own towns. He had seen enough of people shooting up places in his life: he was out of all curiosity how that went. He hoped if people were going to be shot at that his father's men did all the shooting, this time, and that nobody from Great-grandmother's guard got involved, and most of all that if there was going to be more shooting on Najida grounds, they did all the shooting far out beyond the gardens, where nothing that belonged to nand' Bren would get broken.

He wished at the same time that they would find nand' Toby's lady Barb, and that she would not be dead out there somewhere in the fields around the house.

That was the worst thought, and not fortunate at all, so he tried not to think it, even if Great-grandmother called it stupid superstition to believe that thinking about a bad thing could make it happen.

Think about bad things so you *keep* them from happening, mani would say.

Well, he was thinking about quite a few bad things. He had been thinking about them all day, and he was very tired by the time he went back to watching over nand' Toby. His bodyguard was tired, too, though all of them were trying not to show it.

Then the walls shook. There was a deep boom from somewhere outside.

He looked at Jegari and Antaro, who had jumped to their feet.

"What is that?" Toby asked, and tried to sit up. Cajeiri moved to stop him.

"I don't know," he said in ship-speak. "It's all right."

But it wasn't. It was high time for mani to get downstairs, was what.

"Gari-ji, stay with him," he said. And: "Taro, come with me."

They had the bus for transport—thanks to their number. Bren would have preferred something a shade less conspicuous than that ruby red bus with shiny new paint. But they had more than ten of the aiji's men, at the last: his aishid had talked to Hanari, who was the senior of Tabini-aiji's forces on site, and Hanari, who could perhaps have vetoed the whole idea, or wanted to confirm it with Tabini, did no such thing. He assigned ten of his force to go with them *on* that rolling target and they brought aboard communications and a classified lot of other gear.

Sixteen of the aiji's men were staying with Geigi, to augment his small staff, and meanwhile the subclan had sent a representative up to Targai to offer its assistance, since *all* the Guild serving the Maschi had either died in the firefight or vanished toward what border one could guess.

"We have uncovered a sorry mess here, Bren-ji," Geigi said, at the steps of the bus as they were loading. "And one understands the need for haste, and one understands why you have involved yourself, but you are already injured. Take greatest care."

"One hopes to." Bren earnestly did hope to. And he hoped to stay out of any firefight. But one understood the technicalities of why he had to be with the team. With him on the bus, the responsibility was his, and it was not the aiji taking action. It was the paidhi-aiji moving on a personal grievance, which, with his presence in the field of action, did not *require* the formality of a Filing of Intent with the Guild. Filing that paper would have taken hours—and if granted, it would expose his household to a legitimate counter from the Marid. With Barb in the hands of kidnappers, it was still the rule of hot pursuit, and they could even cross a border region without breaking the law. So yes, he understood that part.

He didn't understand what they were going to do once they ran down the kidnappers, which, the more they delayed getting underway, the more likely would not happen on Maschi land. That part was still a little hazy.

But he had a nape of the neck suspicion that the aiji, well aware what was going on, was going to politick hard with the Guild to act on the aiji's personal Filing against Machigi— a campaign that would gather urgent moral force once some Marid agent actually took a shot at the paidhi-aiji. He might have to cross that border on personal privilege. He was taking with him Guild who had a very different reason for crossing that border, and a very different target.

It was so good to be of service.

"You take most extreme care, Geigi-ji. And should this not work out auspiciously—"

"Say no such thing, Bren-ji! But be sure that I am your ally in this and I shall bend every influence I have to secure your hold-ings coastward as well as my own. These rascals have annoyed us long enough!"

Geigi's influence, on earth and in the heavens, was no mean commodity, and Geigi's wit and persuasion and the extent of his connections were nothing at all to disparage. Bren bowed in deep courtesy as the bus engine started up. "My estimable ally. One will not forget this. And keep that waistcoat on, Geigi-ji, at all hours, one begs you! Stay safe!"

He wore his own bulletproof vest. He was so damnably sore and bruised he could hardly make the first atevi-scale step onto the bus, and had to have Geigi push him up from behind. At the next step, he had Jago's help from above, and he got into his seat with the thought that, God, it hurt, and it was going to be a very long and bumpy bus ride. He had a folded silk scarf between his ribs and the vest at the sorest spot. The skin was not broken, and he was relatively sure the ribs were not broken. The general support the vest afforded was welcome enough, but its weight was scaled to atevi strength, it was hot, his head hurt from the fall—he'd hit a chair on his way down, he was relatively sure of it, he was dizzy, and it was a moment after he sat down before he could get his breath just from the climb into the bus.

Banichi and Jago were in the opposing seat. Tano and Algini and their gear were in the pair of seats across the aisle. And that considerable and formidable force, ten of Tabini's finest, was with them.

Not to mention a very quiet young Guildsman sitting midway on the bus, allowed to be with them—but not included in the deliberations. Lucasi no longer had information to give—and he only entertained the hope that they might locate his sister, and Barb-daja, and maybe be in a good enough mood to give him another chance.

Had they had no more force than the paidhi's own to carry on the search, they would have parked the bus still in Sarini province, on reaching that border region, and used their position to try to attract attention—and an approach from Barb's kidnappers, a far, far more delicate operation.

With the aiji's men supporting the operation—they were in a position to make a stronger demand in negotiation: give her back, or we open the doors of this bus and let ten Guild agents into Taisigi territory. The Taisigi at that point might see an advantage in restoring the status quo ante, meaning giving Barb back and getting a mobile Ragi base out of their territory.

It was going to be dicey, if it came to that. But added force, and the aiji's already Filed Intent, offered a real chance of success, both in retrieving Barb, and Lucasi's partner.

The bus rolled into motion, and jolted, and that was just the way the next number of hours were going to go, Bren said to himself. Jago and Banichi spread out a map, discussing it with Tano and Algini, who got up to have a look. Bren couldn't personally see what they were talking about, which apparently involved points of hazard and potential ambush, and the point at which Sarini Province melded into the Marid lands.

At the moment he was content to breathe, and questioned his sanity being here.

Machigi did not have a reputation as a fool. There was that.

Machigi either knew by now or was going to find out very soon what had happened to a Marid operation in Targai.

And what happened next would be up to Tabini *and* Machigi: Machigi's advantage, to conduct a cold war with impunity, was evaporating with every bus-length they advanced toward his district, and Machigi would be up against it—with four other Marid lords watching the outcome and measuring their own chances of making a power grab if Machigi went down.

Atevi politics at its finest behaved in a moderately human way.

He didn't bet this action wouldn't see someone *else* attack Machigi in this little window of opportunity they provided.

One shouldn't bet on that at all.

Mani was not budging. Mani's guard on the roof said that the explosion they had heard had been out on the main road, and they said it involved a truck, far up toward the intersection with the Najida road, and she did not need to go downstairs.

Cenedi was not happy with mani not budging from upstairs.

Cenedi was not at all happy, either, with three young fools being upstairs finding out what was going on. And Cajeiri felt guilty about leaving nand' Toby downstairs just with the doctor, seeing nand' Toby could not talk to the doctor, but it was clear *something* was going on—something that had mani upset and Cenedi furious.

Cenedi had sent men outside and up the road to find out

what was going on, and evidently some of the Edi who were guarding the road had gone out to find out what had happened, because then there was a phone call from the village. Najida was sending the village truck up to the accident, and Cenedi told them drive overland and stay off the road.

Then Cenedi headed for the operations center and shut the door right in their faces, so *that* was unusual.

It was clear no information was coming out of there.

And they had none even when Cenedi stormed out and down the hall to meet the returning truck under the portico. Villagers showed up at the door with injured people from the accident.

Cenedi whirled about. "Escort your lord downstairs," Cenedi said to Antaro and Jegari, with no courtesy at all. "And tell nand' Siegi we need him up here immediately."

"Please," Jegari said, tugging at Cajeiri's sleeve. "Please, nandi."

"Now!" Cenedi said.

It was time to move, and upstairs *did* need nand' Siegi, urgently. Cajeiri headed for the stairs without argument, ahead of Antaro and Jegari, and ran the distance to nand' Toby's room, to pass that word to nand' Siegi: "Nandi, there are injured people. Cenedi asks you come. Quickly. We will be with nand' Toby."

"He should sleep, young gentleman. Keep silence here." Nand' Siegi was on his way out the door, and shut it.

And there they were. Something had blown up on the road, and Guild and non-Guild were hurt. And nand' Bren was out there somewhere, and mani was upset and Cenedi was acting as tense and upset as Cajeiri had ever seen him, not even when bullets were flying.

It was more than a little scary, and it seemed like things were not going at all well. Cajeiri looked about him, somewhat at a loss, and then did take the chair by nand' Toby's bed, and Jegari and Antaro sat down in the other two chairs, and there they stayed in silence for a moment.

Then Cajeiri signed, Guild-sign, "Go upstairs, Taro-ji, and find out."

"Yes," she signed back, and was up and out the door.

Toby stirred, and opened his eyes a bit as the door shut.

"It's all right," Cajeiri said. "Hush, go back to sleep, nandi. Everything is fine."

"Heard an explosion." That was what he thought Toby had said.

"No problem." Cajeiri lied as cheerfully as he could. "All finished. Cenedi took care of it."

"Where's Bren?"

"With Geigi-nandi. All safe. All fine. You sleep."

"Doctor gave me something," Toby said, and his eyes drifted shut again.

Which was evidently what nand' Siegi intended, and probably nand' Siegi had given him something to make that happen. But nand' Siegi was busy upstairs, and there were wounded people and they had no information at all.

It took forever before Antaro came back and opened the door very quietly. She signaled them to come outside to hear, and Cajeiri beckoned Jegari to confirm that he should come, too. So they all three stood outside the door and Jegari shut it very carefully behind him.

"It was some of the aiji's men coming up the Kajiminda road in a truck with some of the local people," Antaro said in a low voice, "and somebody put explosives in the road where anybody could hit it, which is illegal. And there is an Edi camp over in Kajiminda, and Guild in uniform came in with guns and kidnapped a five-year-old boy. Cenedi has called the Guild and asked them to call a Guild Council meeting."

"So can they *do* anything about it?" Cajeiri asked.

"He is asking the Guild to outlaw these Guildsmen."

"File Intent on them?"

"Outlawry is worse than Intent," Antaro said in a voice that all but vibrated with shock. "Much worse."

"If you are outlawed from the Guild, nandi," Jegari said, "the Guild will hunt you down. The illegal Guild used this, in their time in power. They outlawed any Guildsmen that supported your father, during the Troubles. And they would hunt them down and in any shelter, even places they had no business going."

"None of the hunters that got into *Taiben* got out again," Antaro said. "Taibeni took care of them. Our woods are our woods."

"Some of your father's Guild who were outlawed came to us," Jegari said, "and we got them safely to the north, and to the mountains. We young people are not supposed to know that," Jegari added. "But we did know."

"So if they outlaw these people, Guild will go into the Marid to get these people? How is that different than Intent?"

"It is different," Antaro said, "because it is not just *our* Guild against *their* Guild. It will be the whole Guild. *Everybody* against the lord of the Taisigin Marid *and* his Guildsmen."

That was a scary concept. The lord and everybody.

"But what about Lucasi and Veijico?" he asked. "One needs to know where Lucasi and Veijico went! I no longer trust them, but maybe *they* were kidnapped, too! And one needs to know who is out there blowing up trucks, nadiin-ji!" His voice had risen somewhat and he quickly lowered it. "Cenedi will get angry, Taro-ji, if *you* go on asking. So Jegari and I will go up. He will have to start all over with being mad if he catches us. Stay with nand' Toby. If he wakes and asks a question, say this: 'Cajeiri is upstairs asking questions.' "

"Cajeiri is up-stairs. Ask-ing—"

"Questions." That was not an easy word to pronounce. Cajeiri paused on one foot. "Just say 'asking.' He will know."

He left, then, with Jegari hurrying close behind him. It was important to get upstairs and, if they could manage it, into mani's suite, before things changed upstairs. And with Cenedi in a bad frame of mind, and mani upset, things upstairs could change in the blink of an eye.

They reached the top of the stairs. There was a trail of blood right down the hall, and nobody had cleaned it up, though there were servants hurrying the other way. Guards stood at mani's door—but one was Nawari, so he just walked up, said, "Nadi," bowed, and grabbed the latch before Nawari could say a thing.

He got through. Jegari did not.

And mani was in the room with a young Edi villager, clearly doing business, which was not good to walk in on.

He stopped still and bowed, Great-grandmother paying him no attention whatsoever, and after a second Nawari let Jegari on through to stand by him.

"You shall do so, nadi," mani said to the young man, who bowed deeply and took his leave, passing Cajeiri with a bow.

Not a good moment. Great-grandmother picked up a teacup and had a sip of tea, not even looking at him.

So probably the better part of common sense was to quietly inch back out that door and disappear for hours. But the second best thing to do was to stand very, very still until Great-grandmother, quite slowly, had finished that cup of tea and the servant, standing near the fireplace, had poured her another.

Then Great-grandmother lifted her hand and crooked her forefinger. Just that. There was no escape, and there were very many ways to go wrong.

Cajeiri moved. Jegari hesitated a heartbeat, and moved with him. Cajeiri came right in front of Great-grandmother and bowed deeply, without a single notion of what he was going to say, except that he had better not start with a question, which often enough annoyed mani. Mani was clearly not in a mood to be annoyed right now.

He kept his voice low. "You have not yet come down to safety, mani, and we are—" No regal airs with mani. Not now. "One is concerned. There is blood on the hall floor."

Great-grandmother fixed him with a stare he had rarely gotten, not even from his father. But it seemed not quite to focus on him, rather on the general surrounds, and on a host of general problems.

"Barbaric ideas," she said darkly, "this kidnapping, from a region which has long flouted Guild rules. *We* are old-fashioned, Great-grandson. But we are *not* barbaric! We in the East have long viewed the aishidi'tat with suspicion, and to this day the Guild has been scant in the East—but we are *civilized*, all on our own. We have *needed* no Guild to enforce basic civility. We had laws before the Guild arrived, and before we were signatory to the Association! The Marid, however, has a piratical history *long* before humans ever landed on this world and before the Edi ever came to this shore, so they cannot claim they were provoked into bad behavior!"

"What have they done, mani?"

"Done? They have set traps on a public road and like the meanest of cowards have kidnapped an Edi child, a common citizen, from the camp at Kajiminda. Your father's Guildsmen were on the way back from recovering the child when they met an infernal device, and two are dead and relatives of the child are injured. The child, fortunately, was not in that vehicle."

Appalling. Worse than Antaro had said. Barb-daja was kidnapped, an Edi child was kidnapped—it was one thing to kidnap a lord's son, who had protections, and who was political—but one just was not supposed ever to involve commoners, who were immune from that sort of thing, even if there was a Filing. And he had two members of his aishid missing so long that one was obliged to wonder if they were still alive.

He said nothing. Mani said:

"*Our* staff has recovered the child *and* executed justice on these pirates! More, we have identified the pair responsible. They are most certainly employed by a Marid clan whose man'chi is to Machigi, in Tanaja. The Guild is meeting at this hour, for a bill of outlawry."

It was scary. He had heard all of it from Antaro. He imagined the Guild, the loyal Guild, who had been subject to this sort of thing during Murini's administration, was going to hand back the same treatment to the Marid, which had supported Murini. They were out for revenge. And he murmured, because it popped into his head, and he was not good at holding back questions: "Just Machigi, mani, or the whole Marid?"

Mani's hand came down smack! on the chair arm. "There! Just exactly so! Why should you ask that, Great-grandson? Favor us with your opinion!"

"It was stupid. It was stupid for Machigi to do and you said once he was not stupid, mani."

"And?"

He thought fast. "Someone else could have done it to get Machigi in trouble."

"Who then?"

"A rival. Some rival."

"Why?"

"If my father takes out Machigi, they win. So it would either be somebody in the Guild or one of Machigi's neighbors. There is no fortunate third."

"Ha! There is nothing fortunate in this entire situation, except our presence here! And how old are you, Great-grandson?"

Everybody knew how old he was, particularly Great-grandmother, but when Great-grandmother asked, one answered, and answered smartly:

"We are two months short of fortunate nine, mani."

"Ha! I say! Ha! And quite impertinent, to be plural at your age, young gentleman!"

"One deeply apologizes, Great-grandmother."

"But you are correct, Great-grandson! We have not wasted our efforts. *You* see it, you see it quite clearly, as do we! There is, depending on this infelicity of two, an infelicitous duality of possibilities for so stupid a move as this attack." Up went the forefinger. "First, that Machigi himself *did* order this, in which case he is a fool, and should remain in power, since he is on the side of our enemies! But none of my spies have reported that he is ever a fool! Second of this duality—" Up went another finger. "Someone in the Marid is plotting against him, and has orchestrated these kidnappings down very traceable channels precisely to bring Machigi down! We are *meant* to be outraged, we are *meant* to react, and now, by the impending actions of our outraged Edi allies, we are placed in a very difficult position, Great-grandson, which can only delight our enemies! The Edi have just served notice that they will attack the Marid by sea in retaliation. The Gan—the Gan are in the process of being contacted, by what means the Edi have not seen fit to reveal, and are being asked to intervene in a general war against the Taisigi. And *into* this, we inject a decree of outlawry against all the Guildsmen employed by Machigi of the Taisigi. We are highly suspicious of this incident, which would remove the brightest of the Marid lords in favor largely of the two most stupid. We have not lived this long by taking appearances for granted. We are *not* for this declaration of outlawry! Cenedi and I are at extreme odds in this." A deep breath and a calculating look. "And clearly my great-grandson *agrees* with me."

Cajeiri bowed. It was wise to bow, when Great-grandmother had an agenda. "Yes, mani-ma."

"Go tell Cenedi we wish to speak to him. You should find him in operations."

Oh, this was getting dangerous. He had never before been caught between Great-grandmother and Cenedi.

But mani was the one more to worry about. He bowed, he left with Jegari, he went to the door of operations—it was *not* guarded, since it was probably the last room in the house that anybody would want to barge in on—and barged in.

He made it in. One of Cenedi's men leapt up from an adjacent chair and stopped Jegari.

"Cenedi-nadi." A respectful bow. "My great-grandmother will speak to you very urgently."

Jegari did not get time to be let in. Cenedi stood up from

the consoles and came in his direction in grim compliance, and it seemed a good thing just to get out of the way. He followed Cenedi out into the hall and gathered up Jegari on his way.

Back to mani's suite. Immediately. And Nawari opened the door for Cenedi—almost started to shut it, and then did not, as Cajeiri took Jegari right on through with him.

"Come!" mani said, beckoning Cajeiri with a look straight at him and past Cenedi, so he came. Fast but decorously. And it was time to be invisible. He quickly found something interesting about the other wall.

"What have we found out, Nedi-ji?" mani asked Cenedi.

"The Guild will meet," Cenedi said darkly, and folded his arms.

"The Guild will be locked in days of debate during which the situation will grow worse than it is. And what do they know? We are the ones in the midst of this incident. We know the persons involved. We know the likelihood that things are not as they seem. No, do not tell me otherwise! And do not tell me that certain of the Guild in service to certain lords of the aishdi'tat will not take the opportunity to politicize the involvement of Edi in our security arrangements! There will be debate, Nedi-ji. By no means deny that! There will be debate, the debate will scatter off into side issues *including* the Edi, and in the meanwhile we have not only nand' Bren but also Lord Geigi placed in a very difficult situation. If there is a second provocation, it will likely aim at one of them!"

"Then best call them back, aiji-ma."

"Or send the paidhi forward," mani said; and Cenedi seldom looked taken by surprise, but he did, then.

"To do what, aiji-ma?"

"So do you not, Nedi-ji, think Machigi remarkably clumsy, to so flagrantly violate Guild policy with senior-ranked, adminstrative-level Guild and myself here as witnesses? With persons who are as good as labeled Taisigi-connected? We are meant to be outraged. We are meant to have extreme difficulty reining in our irregular allies. Do not oblige them by being outraged!"

"Do you think, aiji-ma, that Machigi has *not* been responsible for the situation in this district?"

"Oh, absolutely he has been responsible, Nedi-ji. But now committed to the hilt, and threatened by our presence, he is vulnerable, and do you not think his maneuvers have alarmed his rivals? This attack was *not* his doing, and one now questions whether prior actions were his doing."

Mani never said Cenedi was wrong. And likely Cenedi was *not* wrong, that was the curious thing. They both were right, and Machigi really was an enemy.

But it was very interesting: there was, mani had taught him, a wisdom in the baji-naji design. It was about flux. And change. One thing could become the other.

Chance—and fortune.

Randomness. And order.

"Look at this," mani had said once, giving him a small brooch with that design on it, black and white. He had sat on the spaceship's deck, at her feet, with the ship on its way to the stars; with this round brooch of black onyx and ivory in his hand, and mani had asked him which was more important, the black or the white. And neither had been greater. "This governs outcomes," mani had told him. "When we say baji-naji, it does not mean 'accident.' It means two powers at work: without flux in the universe, this ship could not move, and we would be like statues, always the same." She had closed his hand on the piece, saying: "Keep it. Remember." And he had. It was in his baggage that he had brought down from the ship. It had gone through the fight to put his father back in Shejidan, and it was safe in his room in the Bujavid, now, in the capital of the whole world.

That moment with Great-grandmother flashed into memory, when she said, "He is vulnerable."

Poised between the black and the white. The tipping point. The scary point.

A person could be really smart, and really clever, but ultimately that person could end up between the black and the white. And he had to make a move.

If somebody was really smart, he understood that.

Cenedi had that look on his face that said he had just this moment understood Great-grandmother. Cajeiri thought *he* just had, and kept very quiet about it.

"When you want to take an enemy in your hand, Great-grandson," mani said slowly and softly, "provide him an exit. And continue to control it. This young man, Machigi, is not a fool, but being young, he has moved too fast, too confidently. He has been high-handed with the other, older lords of the Marid. He has planned everything. He has done everything. These older lords have not been consulted. So they have consulted among themselves, have they not?"

"Yes," Cenedi said thoughtfully, and one could see a spark in Cenedi's eyes. "We are not speaking of a punitive action, then. We cannot divert ourselves to attack some other part of the Marid, Sidi-ji. The Marid Association has *five* aijiin. This act is, whatever its origin, from the Marid."

"Oh, indeed. But we need not attack," Great-grandmother said. "We are thinking of something much more interesting. And something much more challenging to the Marid —baji-naji. Perhaps there should be *one* aiji in the Marid, and we can cease this endless shifting of blame."

A small silence followed. Cenedi gave mani a sidelong look. "If you are thinking what I think you mean, aiji-ma, this is a shift not only in plan, but in policy. In *your grandson the aiji's* policy, as laid down before the hasdrawad and the tashrid."

"Pish. If we fail, he can easily disown us and our entire venture," Great-grandmother said with a dismissive waggle of her fingers, "a matter the Edi should well consider before they take any action to jeopardize our operation or force our hand. But our solution, if we succeed, will *not* cost lives in the aishidi'tat. *If* we succeed, the change in this coast will proceed like a landslide. All things we have set in motion will proceed, and my grandson need do nothing but claim the credit. We are determined, Nedi-ji. Have you a secure contact with the paidhi-aiji?"

Cenedi drew a deep breath and let it go slowly. "Yes, aiji-ma," he said. "We do, that."

"Delay the Guild deliberation. Say that we have a contribution to make and information which must be considered. Let them make a certain amount of fuss so Machigi's bodyguard knows it is under debate. But we shall be late getting essential papers before them. This will work soon or it will not work at all. At very least they will have a more accurate target for their decree of outlawry. At best—they can save themselves the paperwork."

Mani then fixed Cajeiri with a direct and terrible look. "Neither you nor your aishid will have a word to say about this where you can possibly be overheard. Your two remaining bodyguard we consider trustworthy. Beyond this—no one. Not even nand' Toby, should he ask about nand' Bren. *Especially* nand' Toby."

"Yes, mani." Cajeiri gathered a deeper breath. "But—"

"No but, young gentleman! If you wish to know secrets, then consider the lives at stake and keep them closer than your own breath!"

He gave a bow, as deep and as solemn as he could. "Mani. We will not make a mistake."

"Go," mani said then, with a snap of her fingers, and Cajeiri gathered Jegari and left, fast.

Likely, he thought, she had specific things to say to Cenedi that young ears were not meant to hear.

And he wished he knew what was going on, and he wished Great-grandmother would come downstairs where it was safer, but he did not think either was likely to happen soon at all.

20

*T*he aiji-dowager, to the paidhi-aiji, salutations.

The kidnapping of a child and the mining of the Ka-jiminda road with consequent injury to civilians has brought the Assassins' Guild Council into session to debate outlawry for Guild members responsible, for all Guild employed by the responsible clan, and for the clan leadership—for which there is physical evidence. There is a strong possibility that other Guilds, notably the Transportation Guild and the Messengers' Guild, may follow suit.

This is the Guild view. It is our judgement that Machigi would have been a fool to have ordered these acts, and we do not believe Lord Machigi is a fool. It is our belief that someone within the Marid itself, older lords offended by his assumption of power, have moved to focus the wrath of the Guild on Lord Machigi and his guard. Their motive would be to overthrow him, bring war on his section of the Marid, and make the Assassins' Guild and the aiji our grandson the agents of his destruction, with little loss to them.

We alone hold this suspicion as of this hour, and now communicate it to the paidhi-aiji. We consider that if Lord Machigi will consider his own best interests he can be a force for stability in this whole region.

Therefore as the Guild meets to consider outlawry for the persons responsible for two illicit attacks, we direct the paidhi-

aiji to go to Tanaja and work out an understanding between us and Lord Machigi, for the best interests of this district and of the aishidi'tat."

Bren read it twice. A third time. Banichi, who had given it to him, stood in the aisle of the moving bus. Jago sat with a curious look on her face. Tano and Algini, across the aisle, had similar expressions.

It was Banichi's handwriting. Banichi was the one through whom the message had come, in a brief trip to the rear of the bus, where the aiji's men had their communications gear.

"Do *they* know about this?" Bren asked, first, with a shift of his eyes toward the rear, and the aiji's men.

"No," Banichi said. "But we are obliged to inform them unless you decide to put them off the bus. We cannot operate at diverse purposes."

"Jago-ji." Bren handed the note to Jago, who lost no time reading it. She immediately passed it across the aisle to Tano and Algini.

"We cannot afford a disturbance in our ranks this close to our objective," Bren said. "I shall speak to the aiji's men, 'Nichi-ji, on your advisement. I hope I can make them understand the situation." Banichi said nothing. Bren sighed and got up from his seat. "Nadiin-ji, baji-naji."

"Baji-naji, indeed," Banichi muttered, and when Bren left his seat to go back to Tabini's senior officers, Banichi went with him. So did Jago. Lucasi got half out of his seat as Bren passed, his face troubled, but he sank right back again, probably at a cautioning signal from Banichi or Jago.

Bren went all the way to the rear. Damadi, senior of Tabini's twelve, with his partner, rose to their feet to meet them, clearly understanding something momentous was afoot.

"A message has come, nadiin," Bren said, "from the aiji-dowager and from Cenedi at Najida. Some Guild operatives near Najida, traced to the Taisigin Marid, kidnapped a local child, then set a mine in a civilian road. The dowager and Cenedi have appealed to the Guild Council, and a motion of outlawry is afoot in the Guild Council at this moment."

Others rose, a looming wall of dark, aggrieved countenances.

"The dowager and Cenedi have a strong suspicion that this action does *not* in fact emanate from Tanaja nor from Lord Machigi's orders. He is young. He has offended other Marid lords. We suspect he is being set up for an attack by internal Guild forces, which will then mean a power struggle in the Marid, a situation *not* in the aiji's interests. We have an answer as to why that truck we are trying to find has proceeded so deliberately."

There were very, very somber looks at that statement. And he was not done.

"It is not in the aiji's interest to have the Marid end up a headless district, under worse leadership. More, in my judgement, you will not well serve the aiji by informing him of our action. Officially informed, he will have an official involvement, which will invoke a storm of regional interests, none of help to this situation. The aiji-dowager, again without officially informing her grandson, has asked me to go to Tanaja and confront Lord Machigi personally with this theory. In her name, and in mine, we will let him deal with the individuals responsible for this situation and stabilize the Marid. The situation is beyond delicate. What we are doing will not be public knowledge unless it succeeds. Should we fail, Tabini-aiji's administration will not be in the least involved, except to declare that we were lost in a hot-pursuit effort to retrieve my brother's wife, and let him take what action he will take. So this places you, nadiin, in a very delicate position, considering your man'chi, and we are no longer on the mission on which we started. I ask you to disembark the bus and go back to Targai to protect Lord Geigi, or to Najida to protect the dowager and the heir, but not to go back to Shejidan—the aiji himself must not seem to be party to this. My respects to you, nadiin, and I shall order the driver to stop at your request."

He bowed. He started to retreat.

"Nandi," the officer said.

He turned about.

"You will need communications," Damadi said.

"We can manage the equipment, nadi," Banichi said, "if you will do us the courtesy of leaving it."

Damadi said somberly, "One asks that you keep the bus rolling for a space, nandi, nadiin, while we discuss this matter."

Tabini's men were not agreeing to be let off. There was hope, at least, that he would not have to take his bodyguard alone into a situation this dangerous. His stomach, which had sunk entirely when he had read the dowager's order, grew still more upset with the notion there might be support for them—help that might have strings attached. They could not be sending messages back and forth to ask advice, not least because advice could not be given without involving Tabini. But wise heads were together back there.

And one lone problem in their situation stood on one foot behind them, leaning on a seatback, looking at them with anxious eyes.

"Nandi?" Lucasi asked faintly as Bren passed.

One lone problem whose immediate concern had just dropped to the very bottom of the pile, along with every other personal obligation. Along with Barb. Even with Toby. He held a position of trust for millions of people. He didn't have the luxury of thinking of Barb. Or a stray young Guildswoman. Or a very confused young man who wanted a way out.

"We have been diverted, Lucasi-nadi, with extreme regret for the urgency of your situation. We shall pursue our course down this road, but if circumstances have taken your partner in any other direction, we cannot now pursue it. Our orders now come from the aiji-dowager. You may leave the bus and make your own way back to Targai."

"One wishes to stay with you, nandi."

"You have an assignment," Banichi said. "Go to it."

A deep bow. "Nandi, allow me to stay. Allow me to continue."

"The mission has changed," Bren said. "Take Banichi's advice. Go back to Targai. And go ask Lord Geigi if he has a place for you."

"We have lost everything," Lucasi said. "We have nothing. Let me stay, nandi. Let me do whatever duty there is. One asks, one asks, empty-handed."

"This is not a mission for suicides," Banichi said coldly. "That intention has no welcome here. Go do that on your own recognizance."

"One will take orders, nadi! One will do *anything*."

"Then get off the bus and walk back to Targai," Bren said. "Talk to Lord Geigi. I shall count it a personal service. It is very likely Barb-daja was taken by some other clan, and matters have grown complicated." He continued forward to the driver. "Stop here, nadi," he said, before young Lucasi could find out anything or protest further.

"Nandi," Lucasi said, bowed his head then came limping after them down the aisle, holding to the seats and railings.

The bus braked to a stop, the rumble and racket falling to what was, by comparison, a lingering and breathless silence. The door opened, at Banichi's instruction.

"Go," Bren said.

"Nandi." With a bow of his head he ducked down toward the exit, limping, looking very young and pitiable at the moment.

Bren watched him go with painful sadness, but very little regret for the decision—not when the boy's lack of judgement could jeopardize other lives, and the mission, and compromise the aiji's integrity. There was one thing—one helpful thing the boy could do, put Geigi wise to the fact the bus was not coming back, so that Geigi would not be phoning Najida and putting sensitive information onto the phone lines.

Beyond that—

We are going to die, Bren thought, trying out the thought. I am taking Banichi and Jago and Tano and Algini into a situation I don't know how to get us out of. And if we do survive this, that poor kid's look is going to haunt me so long as I live.

He chanced to meet Algini's eye. Algini nodded once, grim confirmation of his dealing. A sweep of his glance left met Banichi—with the same expression.

And in that same interval, while the bus was stopped, Damadi came down the aisle. Alone.

"Nandi," Damadi said with a little bow, "we are with you. Your orders are the aiji's orders."

That many more men and woman were all in the same package. All at extreme risk. All his responsibility.

"My extreme gratitude," he said. "Thank them. Thank them all—for myself and for my bodyguard." If there was a chance of getting out alive if things went wrong—it was in numbers. It was in covering fire.

It meant losing most of these people, if he failed. They would try to keep *him* alive. And it was not a priority he wanted.

He leaned forward to speak to the driver. "Carry on, nadi. Mind any disturbance of the road surface. There was a mine today on Najida road."

"Yes," the driver said. He was himself one of Tabini's men.

Bren straightened up again, caught his balance with the upright rail as the bus resumed its bumpy, headlong speed.

Toward Tanaja. Toward the largest capital of the Marid, a place he had never in his life wanted to see up close.

He sat down, and his bodyguard clustered together over in and around the opposite seats, talking in low voices.

Which left him to consider what he was going to do so as not to die, along with everybody else in his charge.

That meant communicating with Tanaja *before* taking this bright red and black bus full of Tabini's Guildsmen deep into the Marid.

And that meant having something eloquent to say in the very little time Machigi might listen.

He didn't have his computer with him on this trip. It, and all the sensitive information it contained, including reference materials that might have been useful at this point, were back in Najida. That was probably a good thing.

He had, however, a small notebook in his personal baggage. He got up, got that out, and settled down, extending the tray table for a work surface.

He wrote. He outlined. He lined things out. He went to a new sheet, and finally, as Banichi and Jago returned to their seats opposite him . . .

"One is appalled, nadiin-ji," he said, "one is extremely distressed at the situation. One is willing to go, but the risk to my aishid is entirely upsetting to me."

Banichi shrugged. Jago said, "The aiji-dowager has not done this lightly, and the support of the aiji's men lends us a certain moral force, Bren-ji. The sheer number of us and the man'chi involved is considerable. We are gratified by their confidence in us."

"Survival is a high priority in this undertaking," Bren said. "Your own as well as mine—and that is not only an emotional assessment. Your knowledge, your understanding of situations in the heavens, among others, cannot be replaced in the aiji's service."

"Our immediate priority," Banichi said, "is your survival, Bren-ji, and please favor us with the assurance you will *not* take actions contrary to ours. By no means rush to our rescue."

He had done that silly thing, among the very first things he had ever done with them. They had never let him forget it.

"One is far wiser now," he said, "and one offers assurances I shall not." He moved a hand to his chest, which hurt with every breath. "I am wearing the vest, nadiin-ji, and shall wear it in the bath if you ask it."

"You will not need to go that far," Jago said, "if you use

your skill to keep us close to you. Do not let them separate us, Bren-ji, or disarm us. If they attempt that, be certain from that point that they mean nothing good, and harm is imminent, to all of us. At that point, if they move on us, we must take action."

"One understands," he said. He took comfort in their presence and their calm, utterly outrageous confidence. He didn't know where they got it, whether out of being what they were, atevi, and Guild, or out of the moral character he knew they had.

Their devotion, their emotionally driven man'chi, was his. He was absolutely sure of that. There was no division between them.

"I am going to get us out of this alive," he found himself saying. "I need to contact Machigi himself. How can we go about this, nadiin-ji? Should you initiate the contact?"

"That would be advisable under most circumstances," Banichi said. "We can do that, Bren-ji, Guild to Guild. We can attempt to get information in the process."

"I need to know," he said, trying to think through things in order, "if they are aware of the mine on the Kajiminda road and the kidnapping of the child. One assumes they are. I need to know if they are aware that the Guild Council is meeting on a question of outlawry. One assumes they have the means to know it." The Marid Guild had been outcast, though not in legal outlawry, for months, as far as their being accepted in Guild Council . . . those members of the Guild who had been supporters of the Usurper were now, so far as he knew, Machigi's, since Tabini's return to power. That was surely *part* of what was driving Guild deliberations, now. "How close contact can they maintain with the Guild in Shejidan?"

"Likely," Jago added, "the Kadagidi clan Guild that have fled down here will maintain kinship contacts up in the central districts. And one naturally expects them to know any news that has gotten to Separti, where they have informants."

"Find out. And advise them that I have a message for Lord Machigi and wish to speak to him personally."

That should be enough to get the attention of a sane man who had any awareness he was in a trap . . . except, one could not help but think, Machigi was a very young man—in some ways reminiscent of the young man he had just dropped off the bus.

Young, brilliant, so gifted that he had not tolerated many advisers, so confident that he had offended many of his peers —and perhaps now found himself the target of a move both underhanded and well-planned by far older heads: not smarter men, but more experienced. He had never seen a photograph of Machigi. In his mind's eye he kept substituting Lucasi's face in that moment Lucasi had descended from the bus— and that was a mistake. That was a supremely dangerous thing to do.

It gave a faceless opponent an imaginable face, one whose reactions he could imagine.

Imagine. That was the trap. He could lose this mission by a mental lapse like that, but once he had thought it, he had trouble shaking the image. That was precisely the age.

Arrogance. Inexperience. Brilliance. All in one hormone-driven, unattached package. An aiji had no man'chi. He got it from below. And that made him hard to predict.

Machigi would be irate, granted the dowager was right and some other lord of the Marid clans had not only defied him, but actively moved to plunge him into serious difficulty. He would be irate and he would not necessarily know who his enemy was, nor how many of his association might have turned on him.

He would also be, quite likely, embarrassed to be caught without knowledge. He would be in a personal crisis as to how others thought of him, and he would be touchy as hell about exposing that weakness to his enemies and to his own people. The machimi plays, that guide to the atevi psyche, had had that as a theme more than once. Man'chi had turned, not to be directed to him. He was not as potent a leader as he had thought, and now everyone could see it. Others might be talking about him. The servants might become uncertain in their dedication. His spouse, if any, might be reassessing her marriage contract and talking to her kinfolk. It was a potentially explosive situation—both inside Machigi, and inside Machigi's house, once it became known he had been this egregiously double-crossed.

Granted, still, that Ilisidi was correct in her assessment of him.

If she was not, and Machigi really had committed that foolish an act as to order Guild to violate Guild rules, then Guild action would have to take him out.

Unfortunately none of them on this bus would live to see it.

It was going to take a while for Banichi to get through to somebody in Tanaja, quite likely.

And then there might be some little time of back and forth communication between the bodyguards before two lords ever got into dialogue.

So he had time to think. He needed desperately to concentrate, and simply stared at the road ahead, past the seats Banichi and Jago had vacated.

The people he loved most in the world—and this time around, he had to defend *them*. He had to be smart enough first to figure Machigi accurately and then to get a self-interested and arrogant young lord to do a complete turnaround in his objectives, his allegiances, and his—

Well, Machigi's *character* was probably beyond redemption. He would *be* no better than he had ever been. The question was, in self-interest, could he *act* in a way compatible with the interests of the aishidi'tat?

How could he achieve that? Machigi would, assuming he was acting sanely, act in his own best interest. That interest had to become congruent with the interests of the aishidi'tat. And Machigi had to perceive that to be the case.

And the situation *would* have an explosive and embarrassing emotional component: he had first to make Machigi aware of the situation with the Guild, if he was not aware already, and avoid Machigi's indignation coming down on him as the bearer of bad news. He could not seem to despise Machigi in any regard.

But neither could he afford to be intimidated. And it was a good bet Machigi would try to do that.

He thought of the approach he would make.

Getting into Tanaja alive was first on the list.

What did they know about Machigi's character? Without his computer, he had to haul it up from memory, and *arrogant, ostentatious, argumentative,* and *ruthless* were at the top of the list.

Young, brilliant, and *unaccustomed to failure or reversal.*

Ambitious, and already at the top of the Marid power structure.

Challenged from below, really, for the first time.

Humility was going to win no points with this young man. *Brilliant?*

What about *educated?* That was different than brilliant.

An education about the world outside the Marid would be an asset. He couldn't remember data on that. But Machigi, like most Marid-born, had never been outside the Marid. His world experience was somewhat limited. Ergo his education was somewhat limited. He would not have seen things to contradict his own ideas.

Bad trait, that.

One couldn't attempt to intimidate him with education: he wouldn't recognize conflicting data as more valid than his own.

It was a difficult, difficult proposition, this mission.

"Nandi," Tano said suddenly, having been listening to something for a few moments. "Nandi, Banichi has gotten to the lord's bodyguard. He has gotten them to advise their lord you wish to speak to him on a matter of importance."

Get ready, that meant. He straightened his collar, his cuffs, as if Machigi could be aware of that detail; but he was, and it set his thoughts in order.

Points to Banichi, if Banichi could get this man to talk in person. It would be damned inconvenient to have to conduct this argument relayed through his staff . . . a process that could go on for hours and end up with a number of important points taken out of order or lost entirely.

Fingers crossed.

He shut his eyes and waited. Sixty. Fifty-nine. Fifty-eight.

He got to minus twenty, and Tano said: "The lord will be available momentarily." Tano passed him an earpiece and mike, across the aisle.

That was actually amazingly fast. Machigi had pounced on that one. Interesting. Encouraging, even.

Curiosity, maybe. A burning, though predatory, curiosity.

And now there was a very delicate protocol involved. One could not be *waiting* for the other. And one could not be *made* to wait for the other, not without creating serious problems from the start. Algini, with his own headset, was listening, and held up a finger to signal that, by what he heard, the lord was very likely about to take up communication. Two opposed security teams were required actually to cooperate to achieve simultaneity.

He put on the headset. Tano signaled him.

"Nand' Machigi?" Bren asked.

"*Nandi,*" came the answer, a young voice with the distinctive Marid dropping of word endings. "*You are on our border.*"

"It is our hope you will favor us with a meeting, nandi. More than that one should not say in this call. We ask a truce and safe passage to Tanaja, and a personal meeting at the earliest."

A lengthy silence. "*Interesting.*"

"My office is not warlike. Discussion will be, one hopes, of mutual benefit. We ask your active and constant protection on the road to Tanaja, nandi, for very good reason."

A second, shorter silence. Then: *"Come ahead, nand' pai-dhi. You have our assurances."*

That simplified things. One stipulated the road *to* Tanaja. That got a yes.

Getting out again . . . he would have to manage that when the time came.

"One looks forward to our meeting, nandi. Let communication pass now to staff." He handed the equipment back to Tano, and Tano resumed listening. Doubtless Banichi, in the rear of the bus, was handling the specifics.

Bren drew a long breath, thinking of Najida at the moment, his pleasant little villa above a sunny bay. He thought of the dowager and Cajeiri. Of Hanari and Lord Geigi, who would have to pull together a staff and a defense, in a house where Machigi's agents had just been. No little bloodshed there, warfare right on the threshold of the Marid, lives lost . . .

Lives damned well wasted in the long, long determination of ambitious lords to take the West and set up some power to rival the aishidi'tat.

Medieval thinking. Medieval ambitions. Modern ships could power their way around the curve of the coast and see with electronic eyes, could trade, and fish, and prosper on a par with the rest of the aishidi'tat . . . if the Marid ever joined the rest of the world and modernized.

But the seafaring Marid, still locked in the Middle Ages, still spent resources on its fleet, on its old, old ambition for dominance of the southwestern coast. Eastward—eastward on that southern side of the continent, starting from the Marid, there were no harbors, except one sizeable island, which the Marid had: but all along that coast eastward of the Marid was the history of geologic violence—sunken borderlands, swamps, abrupt cliffs, leading toward the forbidding East itself, which was one rocky upland after another. The Marid had long seen *western* expansion, around the curve of the coast, as their natural ambition.

But technology could do so much more for them. Access to space—the ultimate shift in world view that happened among atevi who *could* make that transition—

Giving the Marid more advanced tech, however—that was a scary proposition. In point of fact, the scholarly traditionalists of the north had *nothing* on the grassroots conservatives of the South, when it came to the fishermen, the craftsmen, the tradesmen and armed merchantmen who, point of fact, had not greatly changed their ways or their world view since *before* the first humans had landed on the earth.

What else did he know?

That there was no educational system in the Marid, per se. The whole Marid worked by apprenticeship and family appointment. The classes of the population that needed to read and write, did; the classes and occupations that could get by with the traditional sliding counters and chalk ticks on tablets—did.

Taxes were whatever the aiji's men said you owed.

Justice was whatever the aiji or his representatives or the local magistrates said was just.

It *wasn't* Shejidan. Not by a long shot.

And the Marid as a whole hadn't been interested in having literacy spread about . . . certainly not by the importation of teachers from the north; and there was no way the local educated classes were anxious to teach their skills to the sons and daughters of fishermen . . . any more than most of the sons and daughters of fishermen were inclined to press the issue and leave their elders unsupported while they did it. Especially considering custom would keep them from using that education, and oppose their intrusion into other classes.

A medieval system with a medieval economy that was linked by rail and sea lanes to the far more modern economy of the north. The Marid had always been capable of sustaining itself, if it was cut off. It didn't buy high-level technology. There probably was no television in Tanaja. There was radio. There certainly was armament, some of it fairly technical, imported by one class that *was* technologically educated: there were from time to time fugitives from the northern Guilds, who, rather than face Guild discipline, had offered their services in the South, and lived well. Lately there had been a fair number in that category, fugitives from the return of Tabini-aiji to power. There would be various Guilds in the court of Machigi and his predecessors, and elsewhere across the Marid—Guildsmen, who did the unthinkable, and trained others outside their Guild without sanction of the Guilds in Shejidan. In every period of trouble, there had been the fugitives who had taken formal hire with the various Marid aristocrats. There had been Assassins to make forays against lords of the aishidi'tat.

Or each other.

Always ferment. Always some military action brewing, or threatened, or possible.

It was a long, long history: the Marid exited its district to create mayhem in some district of the aishidi'tat. The aishidi'tat retaliated, occasionally sent in a surgical operation to eliminate a Marid lord, to adjust politics at least in a quieter direction.

Nobody, however, had ever "adjusted" the Marid out of the notion of taking the West Coast.

He couldn't think about failure. He hurt like hell. Breathing hurt if he moved wrong. He could be scared if he let himself, and that was guaranteed failure. He was likely to be tested. He was likely to be threatened. And he was feeling fragile. He had to rid himself of that.

Was Machigi a good lord or a bad one?

A bad one, in the sense of corrupt and self-interested, might actually be easier to negotiate with. A good one, in the sense of looking toward the benefit of his own people, would be harder to compass, in terms of figuring out what his assumptions were and what his concerns were.

A bad man would have a far simpler endgame, one that might be satisfied by personal gain. And quite honestly, nobody had ever wholly discerned Machigi's personal character.

Was Machigi truly as brilliant a young man as rumor said or in some degree a lucky one?

Was he, if brilliant, a tactician or a strategist? Brilliant in near-term results—or in long-range planning?

Was Machigi that rare young man with the nerves for long-term suspense, or would he act precipitately?

Was he traditionalist? Rational Determinist, like Geigi? Or a thorough cynic and pragmatist?

He did wish he could pull down what Shejidan might have.

Banichi and Jago came back to their seats, opposite him.

"Were you possibly able to read the household in that call, nadiin-ji?" he asked.

"One found them well-ordered, and run from the top," Banichi said.

That was a point.

"How much initiative within his staff?" he asked.

"Communication went fairly directly to his aishid, and from his aishid to him."

An admirable thing, correctly sifting out an important communication and speed in their lord knowing it. A lord with his hands on all the buttons, it seemed. Nobody had presumed to stall the communication. Therefore a lack of handlers. That might be in their favor.

He said, somberly, "One apologizes in advance, nadiin-ji, for bringing you into this kind of hazard. And no one could be more essential to any hope of success. I do not expect you infallibly to get me out alive and I know you understand in what sense I mean it. I do expect that if the worst happens, as many of you as possible will get out and report where it counts. Other than that, I give no orders."

"We know our value," Banichi said. "And we cannot give an impression of being willing to tolerate provocations, Bren-ji."

"One trusts absolutely in your judgment," he said. "But take no action that you can avoid. In this, and with greatest apology, if something untoward happens, let me attempt to deal with it first. If I am threatened, I shall take your abstinence as a sign that a reasonably intelligent human *should* be able deal with it."

Banichi actually laughed. So did Jago.

"We are in agreement," Banichi said. And then said soberly: "You will do your best, Bren-ji."

"Yes," he said, with a very hollow feeling in his stomach. "Yes, I shall."

21

Nand' Toby had waked. So Antaro said. And Cajeiri went to his bedside to see, and to sit for a moment. Things upstairs were just . . . scary.

Very scary. And he was going to have to lie as well as he had ever lied in his life.

"Nand' Cajeiri," Toby said to him when he sat down there, spoke very faintly, but then cleared his throat a little and lifted his head.

"Quiet, nandi," Cajeiri said. "Nand' Bren said you stay in bed. Sleep."

"Tired of sleeping," nand' Toby said, but his head sank back to the pillow. "Where's Bren? Has he learned anything?"

Words. Words that never had come up between him and Gene and Artur on the ship. He understood the question. That, at least.

"He went to Targai. He follows Barb-daja. He looks for her, nandi."

"No word from him?"

He shook his head, human fashion. "He's busy."

"Damn, I want out of this bed. I think they gave me something."

"You sleep, you eat, you sleep. Antaro, did the kitchen send anything?"

"One can go get something, nandi."

"Yes," he said, and Antaro slipped out the door and shut it.

"It's been quiet for a while," Toby said. "I heard something blow up."

"Long way." The ship had never had words for long distances inside. Just fore and aft. Deck levels. "Out—" He waved a hand toward the road, generally. "Far."

"Somebody was hurt."

"Nand' Siegi fixed them."

"Good," nand' Toby said. "No word on Barb?"

He shook his head. "No. No word."

"Bren safe?"

"Yes," he said. "Banichi and Jago go with him."

"Good," Toby said. He seemed to be drifting again, then woke up, lifted his head, and looked around him a little. "Where is this?"

"Safe here," Cajeiri said. And pointed up. "Dining room."

"Ah," Toby said, as if that had made sense to him. He lay back, breathing deeply. "You've been here a lot."

He understood all of that. "Nand' Bren said stay with you."

"Thank you," Toby said in Ragi.

He was somebody important, too important to be on errands, there was that. But he was proud when nand' Toby said that.

"Good," he said in ship-speak. "Damn good."

Nand' Toby thought that was funny for some reason. At least nand' Toby grinned a little, which reminded him of nand' Bren. Toby was dark and Bren was gold, but in that expression they looked a lot alike, very quiet, a little shy, and totally lighted up with that grin.

He knew far, far too much of what was going on to be comfortable lying to nand' Toby. He was glad when Antaro came back with a cup of soup and some wafers and gave them something specific to do.

Nand' Toby drank half the soup and ate one wafer, and said he wanted more later. So he was getting better.

There was that.

But talk with nand' Toby was difficult and full of pitfalls, and finally he said, to dodge more questions, that he was going to go upstairs and see if there was any news.

He took his time coming back down. There was nothing more to hear anyway, except that nand' Bren had crossed into Marid territory. He was very relieved nand' Toby had gone back to sleep.

The land sloped generally downward, and the road, as such, was a grassy track, about bus-wide, between low scrub ever-green. Limestone took over again from basalts, old uplift, old violence.

It was not a maintained road . . . but there had been vehicle tracks pressing down the grass and breaking brush in the not too long ago—perhaps traffic that had come from Targai, or to it.

There was no other presence as the sun sank behind the heights. There was a scampering herd of game, and once, rare sight in the west, a flight of wi'itikin from a fissured cliffside. Bren noted that and thought of the dowager, who aggressively protected the creatures in her own province. Ilisidi would ap-prove of that, at least.

The clouds above the western hills turned red with sunset and the driver had turned on the headlamps by the time they came on the sea—a startling vista, stretching from side to side of the horizon: that much red-lit water, and a few small islets, within shadowy arms of a large bay.

Lights sparked the dimming landscape, some near the water, more clustered somewhat inland.

"Tanaja," Bren said, and Banichi and Jago, who had been catching a nap he envied, woke and turned to see.

Most of the bus had been napping . . . the ability of the Guild to catch sleep where it offered was remarkable; and the bus had been silent the last couple of hours, Guildsmen taking the chance to rest now: tonight—

Tonight, none of them could vouch for. Wake us when we come downland, Jago had said; and he just had, faithfully.

Tano went back and waked others. Algini, who had slept only intermittently, did something involving the communications, possibly relaying a message through Targai, possibly just checking, Bren had no idea.

The driver—the third since they had set out this morning—stopped for long enough to trade out, possibly himself to catch a little nap. Bren earnestly wished he could, but napping under such circumstances had never been a skill of his.

He simply sat and watched Banichi and Jago and Tano and Algini consulting together, over at Tano's and Algini's seats; and was aware that Banichi went back to consult Damadi. Otherwise he simply watched those distant lights get closer, and brighter in the declining light.

Then there was a sudden flare of white light ahead, twin headlights. Some vehicle had been waiting for them—a bit of a surprise to him, but not, he would wager, to his aishid, nor to the aiji's men.

The bus came to a slow halt, and opened the door, and two shadowy figures walked into the bus headlights, silhouetted against their own, coming from a truck parked across the road. Those two walked up to the side of the bus.

Banichi ran things now. Banichi instructed the driver to open the door, and one Guildsman mounted the steps and stopped, silently looked toward Bren, and with a sweep of his eyes, scanned back toward the rear of the bus. The aiji's men had all stood up. The tension in the air was considerable. But no hands went to weapons.

Bren stood up slowly, facing the Marid Guildsman, who gave a barely discernible nod of courtesy. Bren returned it, as slightly. Then: "Follow us," the man said, and turned and walked down the steps again, rejoined his partner and returned to the truck.

They hadn't asked anything provocative, such as the paidhi-aiji leaving his protection and coming with them—which they would not have gotten.

They hadn't shown a weapon.

Bren sat down without comment, and Jago sat down opposite him while Banichi instructed the driver to do exactly what the man had asked, and follow the truck. Its headlights lit dry grass, and swept over rock as the truck completed a turn, and then the bus started moving.

Banichi sat down.

"That didn't go too badly," Bren said.

"Trust nothing, Bren-ji," Banichi said. "This is not a place to trust."

"One understands, emphatically, Nichi-ji. But well done."

Banichi shrugged. "Thus far," he said, and that was all.

The dark was full now, with a bright moon in the sky. The lights picked out tall grass, or brush, or occasional pale rock, and the pitch of the road was generally downward toward the distant, moonlit bay. They crossed railroad tracks, and then Bren had an idea they must have arrived very near the city, and he had a notion their position was fairly well on the northern side. He *knew* the maps. He knew the rail routes from years ago, the old theoretical arguments with the Bureau of Transportation. It was a curiously comforting sense of location, as if something had become solid.

A turn in the road brought the city lights much, much closer. He knew absolutely where he was.

And wished himself and everyone on the bus almost anywhere else.

Panic would be very, very easy. But this was not a hazard the Guild could solve, short of turning about and making a run for the border, which was hardly sensible at this point. They were here. They had chosen to be here, on the dowager's order, and there was nothing for it now but for the paidhi, whose job it was, to collect his wits and put himself together.

Calm. The first thing was to make sure the meeting took place.

The next thing was to make sense to someone from a very different region and bearing a centuries-old resistence to every-thing he represented.

It could be done. All of diplomacy was founded on the no-tion that it could be done.

He had talked to the alien kyo. He had made sense of Pra-kuyo an Tep. Could Machigi be that difficult?

Probably. Prakuyo an Tep had owed him a favor, by Prakuyo's lights. It was not exactly the case with Machigi.

Curiosity, however, was an attribute generally of the intelligent—and nobody had ever accused Machigi of being stupid.

Insecurity was another probability: Machigi was young. Inse-curity meant instability. Not set in his ways, at least. But prone to skitter off mentally onto unguessable tracks. His time-scale and expectations, too, would not be that of a mature man.

Arrogance? That went with the office.

Tano and Algini were busy with their seatful of gear. Likely the experts at the rear of the bus, with their own collection of black boxes, were listening to the ambient. Whether they at-tempted to contact their allies at this point, or whether they were only passively gathering information, was a Guild deci-sion, specifically Banichi's, as far as he could tell, Damadi hav-ing ceded command to him—the paidhi-aiji being in charge of the situation. Banichi and Jago both did have recourse to short-range communication, and no reaction came from the truck that was guiding them.

The city was on a level with them, now, and the road be-came a real road, and then an avenue leading inward, but not in a straight line, rather in that sinuous fashion of atevi main streets, with little branches to the side, with clusters of dwell-ings and shops in inward-turned association . . . in that regard, Tanaja was not that foreign. Pedestrians, mostly clustered around restaurants and such, were on the lighted streets—pedestrians who stopped and stared at the anomaly passing them, and cleared a path for them.

The road wended upward slightly, and the avenue became a tightly wound spiral uphill, through gardens and hedges, and this, too, was not that foreign a notion. The citadel of a town was its seat of government, and it was most commonly on a hill—though that hill was most commonly built up and paved over.

This hill was simply gardens, formal gardens, until they reached a lighted building, and a cobblestone drive, and a major doorway.

They were in. They were at the heart of what was not that large a city—Tanaja had a population, one recalled, of about a hundred thousand in itself . . . more of the Transportation and Commerce statistics. Fish. Spices. Game. Roof tiles and limestone. Those were its major exports.

The mind leapt from fact to fact. It was not time to panic. The bus was coming to a stop now, as the truck stopped ahead of them, and more people came toward the bus from the lighted portico.

Banichi got up. So did Jago. "Open the door, nadi," Banichi said, and Bren got up, feeling a little panicked, his collected thoughts scattering. He had no information to process. Just things to absorb, the number of those about the bus that they could see—about twenty, he thought, which probably meant at least that many again that they did not see.

The door opened. Another Guildsman, an older man, came up into the bus and looked at Banichi and Jago, at him, and back over the bus as a whole. It was a scowling, intent face, deliberate, Bren thought, betrayal of hostility, in a culture that avoided display. But no weapon was drawn.

Banichi's face, in profile, was completely serene. So was Jago's.

"The paidhi will come with us," that man said.

Unvarnished, but not impolite, skirting the edge of courtesy. And here it was. Bren moved a step. Banichi and Jago, who were in front of him, moved. And a hand went up.

"Only the paidhi's aishid," the man said, and gave way.

A better requirement than might have been, evidencing a certain willingness to follow the courtesies—or seeking to remove leadership and direction from the rest of the Guildsmen on the bus: *that* was not the case. Damadi was perfectly capable of acting on his own.

Bren descended the bus steps behind Banichi and Jago, and heard Tano and Algini behind him. His bodyguard had their sidearms and their hosts had not objected. That was another courtesy. At this point one took any encouragement one could get.

They reached the cobbled drive, and Machigi's Guildsmen offered them a path up the steps to the lighted portico of the building, and the open doors above.

Golden light, carved doorposts, big double doors: it was at least a formal entrance to the place, not necessarily the main one, but it might be. Banichi and Jago walked ahead of him, just behind the primary two of the local Guild, Tano and Algini behind, with the other half of the local team bringing up the rear. Matched, force for force: a good sign, that. But one didn't take anything for granted. It was, minimally, good behavior in full view of the bus, which now had to be self-contained, a virtual security cell, for many, many hours, at the very best outcome.

And figure that Machigi's forces would be out there arranging themselves around that little kernel of foreign power, to neutralize it fast in any confrontation. If the paidhi-aiji could figure that out, damned sure every Guildsman out there was planning and counterplanning.

They reached the top of the steps. More security stood about the door. The odds were decidedly tilting in favor of the local Guild. But no one moved to interfere with them, and they kept walking, into a hallway smaller than the foyer at Shejidan, to be sure, but certainly ornate, with gilt scrollwork, marble columns, and displayed porcelains of subtle colors—two, astonishingly intricate, columns of sea creatures, flanking another double door on the right.

Fragile. Precious. This was surely not a back entry.

The pale doors between those porcelain towers opened, pushed outward by attendants in brocades and silk. That was their destination, evidently, and their escort led them inside, onto a russet carpet, with a pattern of waves and weeds in muted greens. Precious things were all about them. The furnishings, small groups of chairs, were all inlaid, and a long marble-topped table held a tall arrangement of shell and water-worked stone.

Their escort stopped here. Other Guild entered from a side door and took their places. And still others arrived. Heavy weapons were in evidence.

Bren drew a slow, deep breath and mentally took possession of the room, these people, not least his own escort, calming himself.

A man entered from a side door, a young man in the muted blue and green of Taisigi clan, brocades with the spark of gold thread, ample lace. He matched the description: an athletic young man with a scar on his chin—not an unhandsome young man, with a countenance flawed by a very unpleasant scowl, and carrying an object in his hand, a rather large Guild-issue pistol.

Bren walked toward him, Banichi and Jago one on a side of him, and stopped, then took a step beyond that, and bowed, slightly and politely, the degree for a court official, himself, to a provincial lord. He gave Machigi that, at least, face to face with him.

Machigi did not reciprocate. Bren straightened, and Machigi raised the pistol to aim it point blank at his face.

Well. That was a first.

A gentleman didn't flinch, or change expression. Which left

the rude act just as it was. Rude. And in the possession of the other party.

"Nandi," Bren said moderately. "One appreciates your caution, and your reserve. There are matters underway, however, which my principal does not believe do you justice, and we are not here in hostility."

"Your principal being?"

"The aiji-dowager."

"The aiji-dowager, who has stirred up the Edi pirates and promised them what she has no right to promise?"

"The aiji-dowager, who has heard that the Assassins' Guild council is now meeting on charges that may or may not be justified. I have in my possession a message, an instruction and a question. Did you in fact order the mining of the public north-south road in Najida district, and did you order the kidnapping of a child?"

The gun barrel did not waver. It was no less nor more lethal than the intent in this young man's mind, and he was not stupid, nor cowardly. All the guns round about would not prevent the paidhi-aiji's aishid from taking him out if that gun went off.

"No," Machiji said. "We did not."

"Then I am here to gather information which may change the Guild council debate."

"I have told you all you need know."

"You have not heard, however all you will find of mutual benefit for us to discuss, discreetly, nandi. One gathers that you have confidence in your aishid. I do, in mine. My principal suggests that the attacks near Najida were aimed more at you than at us. She suggests that destabilization of the Marid, while temporarily beneficial to us, would not be beneficial, in the long view, and she is prepared to take the long view."

"Who is your principal?" Second asking of that question.

"So far as I am aware, nandi, *only* the aiji-dowager at this point. The Guild with me, outside, are Tabini-aiji's, but attached to his grandmother in this instance, and under her orders."

"You are fast-moving, paidhi. This morning in Najida. This afternoon in Targai. This evening meddling in the Marid."

"Circumstances have been changing rapidly. It is far from my principal's intent to contribute to instability in this region. If that were her intent, she need only sit back and let appearances carry the debate forward in the Guild."

"Perhaps she intends to tempt me to an incident here and now."

"I am not lightly sacrificed, nandi."

The gun clicked. Dropped to Machigi's side. "You have nerve, paidhi."

Now the pulse rate skipped. One could not afford the least expression. This was not the point to waver, not in the smallest point of decorum—never mind that Machigi was tall, and he was inevitably looking up. "The things I hear of you, nandi, encourage me to believe the same of you. Clearly, with my principal, you have accomplished things in the Marid that have suggested a reconsideration of associations."

"Your principal has no power to negotiate."

"Shejidan has said nothing to prevent her current action. This is, in my own experience of this lifelong association, more than significant."

A moment of silence followed that statement. Machigi's hand lifted. He snapped his fingers. His guard, round about, opened side doors. Bren stood his ground. So did his bodyguard.

"Tea," Machigi said, and with the left hand, without the gun, made an elegant gesture toward a grouping of chairs.

Bren gave a slight nod and went, as directed, to stand by the chairs; his bodyguard moved with him, perfectly in order, as did four of Machigi's. Machigi sat down, he sat down, and servants appeared from the side doors, bearing a beautiful antique tea service, of the regional style.

There was, by courtesy, no discussion of the issues. Which somewhat limited one to the weather.

And necessitated Machigi, as host, defining the topic.

"So how have you found the region, nand' paidhi?"

One had to avoid politics. "One enjoys the sea air, nandi," he said. "And the uplands are quite scenic."

"You are alleged, paidhi-aiji, to have voyaged to very strange places."

"I have, nandi," he said.

"One is naturally curious," Machigi said. "Were there *places* out there?"

"Where we were, nandi, was a place much like the space station."

"A metal place."

"Very much so. Indistinguishable from the ship itself, except in scale."

"And do you take pleasure in such places?"

He thought a moment, over a sip of tea. "Mountaintops, nandi, are similar in some respect: one may be uncomfortable in some regards getting there, but the view from the top is astonishing."

"And what did you see from that vantage, nand' paidhi?"

"Farther worlds, farther suns, nandi, people more different from both of us than we are from each other—but people with whom we have found some understanding."

"What use are they?"

"As much as we are to them—occupying a place in a very large darkness. As Tanaja sits at the edge of a very large sea, with all its benefits. Space does have shores, in a sense, and people do live there."

"The world has had enough foreignness."

"There will be no second Landing. The space station will see to that."

"How?"

"Because outside visitors will be limited to that contact, as much as we find beneficial, and no further, nandi. But we are verging on business, now, one of those matters in which one would very much like to see the Marid have its share."

"Why should you think so? And why should your principal think so?"

"Because the opportunity is that wide. There is no point to hoarding it. If the Marid prospers, it is no grief at all to the world at large. It will *not* disturb the trade of the south coast. The unique items which the Marid produces and in which it trades are *not* duplicated by manufacturing or found in space."

Machigi emptied his teacup and held it up to be refilled. "Another round, nand' paidhi."

That was good. Bren held up his own cup, and they settled back to discussion of more polite nature.

"An extraordinarily beautiful service, nandi," Bren said.

"Three hundred years old," Machigi said, "one of the treasures of the aijinate of Tanaja. The island which produced it was devastated by a sea wave. This service happened to be on a ship which survived, being at sea at the time."

"Extraordinary," Bren said.

"There are a few other items surviving of that isle. But increasingly few. They have suffered somewhat in the centuries since. We have attempted to discover the source of the glaze, but the isle is gone, submerged. We suspect it came from a plant which may now be extinct."

"A loss. A great loss, nandi. The blue is quite deep, quite a remarkable color."

"Greatly valued, to be sure."

"One is honored even to see it."

Machigi made a wry salute with his cup. "And you a human. You are the second human I have ever seen."

Thump went the heart. "The second, nandi."

"There is a woman," Machigi said. "A member of your household, so I understand."

"Barb-daja." *That* took no far leap. But it called into question the dowager's theory, on which they had come here, and the safety of themselves and everyone on that bus. "You have indeed seen her, nandi?"

"Indeed." Machigi said.

"Is she well, nandi?"

Machigi shrugged, and this time set his cup down. "Who is this lady, nand' paidhi?"

"The lady is my brother-of-the-same-parents' wife, to put the situation simply, nandi, a naïve woman of no political connections."

Machigi smiled, and took up the cup for a final sip, then set it down. "Let us get down to business, nand' paidhi."

Bren nodded and did the same, schooling his face to absolute calm. His chest hurt. Breaths hurt, but he kept them regular. He had managed not a tremor in setting his cup down, and diverted his thoughts from Barb and Toby, from Najida and those at risk there, even from his bodyguard standing behind him. And quietly smiled back. "One is very glad to do so, nandi. Shall I give you the dowager's message exactly as it came to me?"

"Do you have it?"

He reached carefully inside his coat pocket . . . the one that did not involve a loaded pistol . . . and handed the folded paper across.

Machigi took it in a scarred hand and read it. He had a young face, lean, hard, that scar on the chin a streak on his dark skin that ran quite far under the chin as well, as if someone had once tried to cut his throat. An interesting wound, that.

Machigi read, folded it in the agile fingers of one hand and handed it back, laying it on the small service table between them.

"The dowager does not have a reputation for such easy trust."

"The dowager, nandi, sees what I see: a situation in which your associated subordinates cannot profit while you exist. You exert an authority they must surely view as dominating theirs, as your interests take precedence over theirs. This is not, in the dowager's view, a bad situation—keeping the Marid from wasteful wars."

"An interesting analysis, paidhi."

"Accurate, I think. It would also be accurate to say that the Marid has long had a quarrel with the aishidi'tat, from its formation, a quarrel regarding the balance of powers in the association. The dowager believes there is a way around this situation with honor."

"Enlighten us."

"One is certain you see it, nandi, but I shall declare it: association of the entire Marid with Ilisidi of Malguri, an association to be, so far as the Marid, under your leadership."

He had actually surprised Machigi, and Machigi let him see it. That was both good and bad.

"A pleasant notion," Machigi said, "but your own man'chi is to Tabini of the Ragi."

"My longtime association is to the aiji-dowager as well, and one might recall, nandi, the aiji's cooperation with his grandmother in providing that force now sitting on the bus, and her providing it to me. What she has done is not done in the dark."

"So, also with his knowledge, she has made a grab for Maschi territory and taken the Edi in as well."

"Neither with his foreknowledge, but with his tolerance, nandi. She has made good on old debts, dating back many decades, even before her grandson's birth, but she has not made any hostile move against Tanaja, nor does she wish to do so, having no territorial interest in doing so. This is one advantage, allow me to suggest, of forming outside associations that do *not* run into the troubled old territory of the central clans. The dowager's lands are distant and, so far as Tanaja is concerned, untrammeled by old debts, except the two obligations on which she has already stood firm. If you should accept her invitation to become her associate, nandi, you may expect similar firmness of alliance, which can cast many old disputes into an entirely different framework of negotiation. Her grandson values her for this quality, and, one may say, respects her alliances."

A lengthy silence, then a drawled: "You have an extraordinary forwardness of address, paidhi-aiji."

"You also have that reputation, nandi, as a man who does not cling blindly to precedent. The dowager values this quality, and suggests it should not be wasted." He saw that look of thought. It was not the time to lose it. "The plain fact is, I *am* here, nandi, meeting with you in confidence, and accurately relaying the dowager's objectives, which are favorable to a negotiation at this point, thus preventing Guild action from destabilizing the Marid. That is the bottom line."

"What is her offer?" Machigi asked bluntly.

"Alliance," Bren said with equal bluntness. "Association. New times, new thinking, horizons not limited to this earth."

"Access," Machigi said, "to the orbiting station."

"That *will* happen, nandi," Bren said. "One has no doubt of it, granted association exists."

"You do not ask further into your own associate's whereabouts or welfare."

"A personal matter. I am here in an official capacity."

"Indeed," Machigi said, leaning back in his chair. "Yet you represent the aiji in Shejidan."

"By courtesy, I represent only his grandmother, who *does* however, hold independent association in the East."

Machigi looked to the side, to one of his bodyguard, and back again, eye to eye and steadily. "*Independence* is an interesting position to hold."

"Propose it, nandi. Independence of the district within the aishidi'tat. One does not say it will be rejected. But," he added sharply, "in order to claim such a position for the Marid, you need an authority equal to the dowager's authority over the East."

"She was challenged as recently as this fall."

"With notable lack of success, nandi. And the East is both hers, and an independent district, with its native rights and prerogatives intact."

Another lengthy silence. "Have you dined, paidhi-aiji?"

"I have not, nandi."

Machigi snapped his fingers. Servants moved into view. "The paidhi-aiji and his aishid will have the guest suite tonight. His company on the bus may be housed in the east wing with whatever equipment they choose to offload."

Crisis. Bren gave a deep nod. "A courtesy much appreciated, nandi, but the bus is self-contained, and my company on the bus is prepared to attend their own needs. One hopes, as negotiations proceed, I shall have other instructions from the aiji-dowager, for their comfort, but for right now, despite your generous gesture, my indications from the dowager suggest my request would not be honored. They are, once we quit the bus, much more under her direct command."

A little steel flicked through that glance. "It is blocking the drive, nand' paidhi. Our suggestion is simple expediency."

"If you request the bus moved somewhat, I am sure we can comply with that very quickly, nandi."

"Let it stay," Machigi said with a wave of his hand. "But where is this trust, nand' paidhi? This offer of association?"

"I have yet to convey your reply to the dowager, nandi. Everything comes from her. When she wishes my company to stand down and leave the bus, it will stand down. But as for myself and my aishid, we are extremely appreciative of the hospitality of your household."

Machigi gave a dark little laugh and stood up. "Follow my servants, and join us in the dining room in an hour. Your aishid may attend your baggage."

"Delighted," Bren said, stood, and bowed in turn. In fact he was delighted—delighted there hadn't been a shootout. Delighted Machigi hadn't pulled that trigger. Delighted Machigi had sounded as intelligent—though also as dangerous—as reports said he was.

And that bit about attending the baggage—no lord in his right mind would have his belongings taken off that bus, put into the hands of servants of a hostile house, and taken into his room. Two of his staff would handle it all the way from the bus to the rooms, while Machigi's staff watched with equal care to be sure that clothes were *all* that came into the house.

The servants gestured the way to the side door. Banichi and Jago went with him, Tano and Algini split themselves off to attend the matter of the baggage, and Bren walked just behind the two servants who led the way—a short distance, he was glad to see, and up only a single flight of stairs. He knew where the front door and the bus were from here, at least.

But that was *not* the knowledge that was going to get them out of this.

The servants opened the doors to a magnificent suite, mostly in sea-green and gold, with pale furniture, and led the way through to a fine bedroom, even with its own bath, an uncommon amenity.

"Very fine, nadiin," he pronounced it.

"Would you care for a fire lit in the sitting-room, nandi?" one asked. "It will grow chill before morning."

"Please do," he said, and looked at Banichi and Jago, just a questioning glance to know their opinion of the arrangements.

Banichi simply nodded. No question every room was bugged to more and less degrees, right down to the bath. He didn't need a word on that score. He simply sat down in a comfortable chair, rested his booted feet carefully on the footstool, and waited, while Banichi and Jago went into that statuelike quiet of their profession, just watching the servants at work.

The fire came to life. And other servants came in, carrying a modest amount of luggage, with Tano and Algini in close attendance.

"Set it in the bedroom, nadiin," Jago said, "with thanks. That will do."

There were bows, very inexpressive faces gave them a last lookover, and the servants retreated out the door.

At which point they would of course be fools to say everything they were thinking.

"How are things outside, nadiin-ji?" he asked Tano and Algini.

"Well enough, nandi," Algini said, and that little formality said he was likewise thinking of bugs. "We have passed word where we are and wished them a quiet night."

"One hopes it will be," Bren said, and cast a look up at Banichi and Jago. "Well done?" he asked in the alien kyo language.

"Yes," Banichi said, and Jago echoed the same.

Tano and Algini had gained a little of the language. They had made earnest efforts at it. And of all means of communication they had, that was the only one no code-cracker could manage.

But one had no desire to frustrate their hosts. It was only a confirmation: he had done what he could, gotten them this far, and God, he wished he could discuss Machigi frankly with his aishid, but their vocabulary in kyo didn't extend that far, nor did it bear on the intricacies of atevi psychology. All he had for comfort was that one yes: they were alive, they were not too likely to be poisoned at dinner—which his aishid would not share—and, disturbingly enough, he had some indication Machigi held some answer to the *other* matter he had come out here to pursue, namely what had happened to Barb.

He couldn't ask. Ethically and in terms of simple common sense, he couldn't make Barb an issue in this.

"One had best dress for the occasion," he said, and got up and went to the bedroom. The packed clothes had been layered with fine silk, which kept them from being too disreputable on being shaken out. The court coat, being heavily figured brocade, had not suffered much. The shirt was a little the worse for its trip in baggage, but with the coat on, the wrinkles would not show; and a fresh ribbon for the queue always improved a gentleman's appearance: those came carefully wound on a paper spool.

Beyond that—the boots could use a dusting. Tano saw to that, and to everyone else's; and ribbons were renewed, Guild leathers dusted with a prepared cloth. They all went from slightly traveled to ready for dinner in a quarter hour, with no conversation to speak of, except a light discussion of the recently dry weather and the quantity of dust, plus the likelihood of rain, since there had been clouds in the west . . . all disappointing material for eavesdroppers, but far from surprising. Guild could convey information by the pressure of fingers on a shoulder, and Bren had no doubt information and instruction was passing that he did not receive. He knew the all-well signal, and got it from Jago as she helped him adjust his shirt-cuffs.

It was even possible that short-range communication was working, in a set of prearranged signals going to and from the bus. It was remarkable if the Taisigi had allowed it. It was certain, if it was going on, that the Taisigi were monitoring it and attempting to decipher it. But evidently the bus was still all right, as far as any of his staff could tell.

"One hopes," Bren said cheerfully, actually hoping it would be reported, "that their cook knows about human sensitivities. One would hate to have negotiations fail with the paidhi-aiji accidentally poisoned."

"This is a worry to us, as well, Bren-ji," Jago said.

"Well, well, I shall have to avoid the sauces and stay to what I can identify," he said. "Wine is safe. I am safe with what I can recognize. Things cooked together in sauce—well, one hopes there are alternatives, or we stay to the bread."

That might send an honest majordomo scurrying to the kitchen to be sure his lord's guest had alternatives—or send him to the references to find out what human sensitivities actually were. He thought worriedly of Barb, somewhere unknown, and *hoped* she was safe and that whoever was feeding her knew humans didn't find a moderate level of alkaloids a pleasant addition to a dish.

"A quarter hour," Banichi said aloud, reminding them all of the time.

His bodyguard would eat and drink either before or after him—after, in this instance, clearly. One could only hope for safety in simple practicality—the fact that things could have blown up before now, and had not. And that there was a bus-load of Guild out there prepared to do damage if things did blow up.

Machigi was not an easy man to read. He had *seemed* to turn receptive. He had showed, if nothing else, curiosity. Keep satisfying it bit by bit, enticing him further and it might be enough . . . but that game ran both directions.

He and his aishid talked about the room, the porcelains, the fine hospitality. And about the magnificent tower-porcelains outside the reception hall, and whether they were all one piece or an assembly of pieces.

They kept the conversation as esoteric and blithely inno-cent as they could manage, not without a certain grim sense of humor. Tano had quite a fund of knowledge regarding the historic methods of firing of large porcelains that easily filled a quarter hour and enlightened the lot of them on the sub-ject, though it probably disappointed any listeners. "My birth-mother's brother-of-the-same-father was a collector," Tano said, "of books on porcelains. I used to entertain myself with the pictures for hour upon hour. One can even venture a guess that those were made in the same tradition as Lord Tatiseigi's lilies."

Victim of more than one disaster, those porcelain lilies.

And Tano went on into detail.

"One hopes these beautiful things will stand untroubled," Bren ventured to say, charitably, and as an advancement of pol-icy. "One can only think, if tourism ever does extend here, they will certainly be greatly admired."

A knock came at the door. They had timed it admirably. Al-gini answered the door and allowed the entry of one of a pair of

Machigi's Guild guards. "Nand' paidhi." A bow. With use of the honorific that acknowledged the paidhi's rank in the aishidi'tat: significant, courteous, and reflecting Lord Machigi's usage, almost certainly—accompanying a gesture toward the door.

"One is honored." Bren acknowledged the courtesy with a nod, and gathered up *only* Banichi and Jago, precisely the arrangement when one guested under uncertain circumstances, and exactly what Machigi ought to expect—two of his aishid staying to protect the room, two to protect him and raise hell in the house if there were any untoward event. They would likewise eat by turns—him first, then Banichi and Jago, then Tano and Algini, who might have to wait quite late for it.

It was what it was: chancy.

But they walked downstairs with their escort, through the elegant hall and on to a brightly lit, quite open dining room.

They walked in, and a waiting servant appeared to indicate a seat, of three, one other place besides Machigi's. An intimate supper, then, with a long table and four servants, besides the obligatory bodyguard. And some third person, of Machigi's choice.

"Bren-ji," Jago whispered urgently, brushing close to him. "*Veijico* has just arrived at the room, under guard."

Veijico. The other of Cajeiri's bodyguard, who'd been tracking the kidnappers.

Oh, give Machigi that: he knew damned well the news would get to him: they were not interfering with short-range communications.

Veijico, whose brother he had personally set off the bus as an insupportable risk on this mission.

Uncharitably, he could not think of a less stable individual to have in the middle of their operations. Or a more unanswerable puzzle to have land in the middle of negotiations.

Where in hell was Barb?

And he could not afford to have his thinking distracted by any personal question.

Machigi showed up in the doorway, with an older man of some presence. Bren gave the correct bow, noting that the standard attendance of two bodyguards per notable provided Machigi and his guest with four, collectively . . . not as if they weren't in the middle of an armed camp and a hostile city to boot.

"My minister of affairs," Machigi said pleasantly. "Lord Gediri."

"Lord Gediri." A second bow, just before they sat down.

And thereafter they had the rules of a formal dinner, which confined conversation to the weather—"One noted a large mass of cloud off the west coast . . . ."—and the surroundings—"We are all quite amazed by those notable porcelains in the outer hall, nandiin. Are they local?"—and the dinner—"One is exceedingly grateful for the special fish offering, nandi. One finds it excellent."

To which: "If we poison our guests we prefer it to be deliberate, nand' paidhi." Machigi and the minister were having sauce with theirs, but the simple, grilled preparation was a pleasant surprise.

There was simple brandied fruit, besides, a safe item. Bread, which was safe if one dodged the pickle. Ilisidi would have taken to that dish in a moment.

It was still best to eat slowly and be alert for effects. But there were none.

Machigi maintained, over all, a pleasant tone to the affair. There was absolutely no mention of business . . . and they came down to the traditional after-dinner brandy, in the adjacent sitting-room, across the hall from the marvelous porcelains . . . still with bodyguards in attendance.

"Thank you, nadi," Bren said to the servant, and saluted Machigi and his minister with a slightly lifted glass. "A very pleasant evening, on very short notice. One is quite grateful for such a kind reception." He had said not a word about a missing Guildswoman delivered to his quarters. Now he did. "Thank you, too, for returning the young woman. Might one ask a further favor?"

Machigi lifted a brow ever so slightly. Perhaps he was expecting a request involving Barb.

"There is a young man," Bren said, "who may be making his way into your district, injured though he is. This is the young woman's partner. If your forces do happen to encounter him, one would be very grateful for his safe return."

"How many people *do* you have wandering Taisigi land at present, nand' paidhi?"

He smiled. "Only those two." And turned sober. "One apologizes for their intrusion. It is embarrassing, under the circumstances."

"Not at the dowager's orders?"

"No, nandi. They have been tracking Barb-daja. Whose whereabouts is a side issue, and *not* in my orders from the dowager."

"Orders which originated *after* you took down the Maschi lord."

"Temporally, yes, nandi. But not stemming from that action. My orders originated after actions at Najida brought down a Guild investigation. Hence her surmise, and her proposal." A nod of respect. "And whether or not she is correct in her assignment of blame elsewhere in the Marid, I have seen enough to suggest she is absolutely correct in her assessment of your worth as an ally, nandi. If some of your subordinates, like mine, have exceeded orders, that is, so far as my judgment, irrelevant to the central point of the matter. You *are* a man of consequence. It would be to her detriment and yours to let fall so *convenient* an alliance."

Machigi looked at his minister, and looked back again, head tilted. "Convenient."

"Convenient, nandi. Your rule over the Marid becomes an asset to all associated powers. And the advantages available in that alliance are far more than any you would cede in the process."

"Allowing Edi piracy to operate unchecked."

"No. That will be another consequence of negotiations now underway. A strong Marid and a strong association on the coast can be better neighbors than that, considering the dowager's potential influence with both. Even the aiji in Shejidan will be behind you in your rights on the shipping lanes, I can state that. Realistically, there may be some resistence to this on both sides. We both know that. But less and less, as both districts become sure of their benefits."

"We are naval powers. We do *not* accept armed ships in our waters."

"The dowager has no interest in the whereabouts of your ships. Your interests in that matter have no possible point of contact. Nor does *she* have a navy. I would be beyond my instructions to recall that there *is* one decent harbor in the East, never more than a fishing village. But it is a broad bay. A far sail, for the Marid. But who knows, for the future?"

Machigi was silent for a moment, then looked briefly at his minister, and back to Bren, saying nothing, but thinking. Clearly thinking.

It was the way atevi association worked. A network of alliances, each dictating the relationship to other networks. Alliance to a power so remote, so generally landlocked, so tied to a neighbor's network—

Could it be of advantage to Machigi?

Would it provoke others in *Machigi's* local associations?

"We have reason to talk," Machigi said, "nand' paidhi. I do not say paidhi-aiji. You *are* speaking for another power at present."

"Yes. In this, I am. I am not in conflict, in doing so. If I am mistaken, I may end up resident at Malguri with the aiji-dowager. But I do not think I am mistaken in this, nandi."

"You have a certain reputation," Machigi said, "as dispassionate. I see it is justified."

Dispassionate. That was an odd assessment. But, he supposed, being immune to certain atevi emotions, or picking them up only in theory, intellectually—he could seem dispassionate, by some standards. Certainly he had no *territorial* history.

"I am fascinated," Machigi said further, "by your accent. Less Padi Valley, more of the classic South."

Southern. It could be analyzed that way . . . recalling that the South had been preeminent in the classic period, and that *that* was the origin of the South's refusal to bow to the Padi Valley-based Ragi as leaders of the aishidi'tat. He bowed in acknowledgment of what was actually a compliment, with the southern conservatives. "My aishid's accent," he said, "is more southern. One is certainly aware of the ancient and honorable traditions of this region."

"I find myself continually amazed that that accent comes out of your mouth. And you do not stumble over kabiu."

"One is gratified by your notice, nandi." Yet another bow.

"We shall speak in the morning, nand' paidhi. Sleep soundly tonight, upon the thought that the dowager is a very wise woman."

Did Machigi mean the dowager was right? That Machigi *was* being challenged?

"Nandi." He rose, and despite the brandy, despite the fact the pain of bruised ribs had settled to a certain level and stayed there—it didn't stay there when he got up. It was with the utmost effort he kept his breathing even and his voice level—he feared his face had gone pale. "One is very grateful for your hospitality."

One of Machigi's guards received Machigi's signal and opened the door. He left, with Banichi and Jago close by him, and the first of Machigi's men, and another, proceeding outward, escorted them to the stairs.

He wasn't sure he could climb those steps. It wasn't poisoning, he was relatively sure of that. It wasn't the brandy. He'd been moderate with that. He set his hand on the bannister and paused at the bottom.

"Your patience, nadiin," he said to the guards in the lead. "One had a minor mishap this morning." Deep breath. He'd at least alerted Banichi and Jago to the likelihood the paidhi-aiji was apt to fall. But if he did—

If he did he could alarm the two in front, who were armed and hair-triggered. "I am feeling quite short of breath, nadiin. Be it understood it was in no wise the fault of the dinner or the brandy. It has just been a very long day. A moment to catch my breath. A bruised rib."

"Nandi." There was a little concern from Machigi's men, who watched from above, and might have no wish to have a problem on their watch. "Please attend him, nadiin."

Jago's hand arrived under his arm. He waited. Took a step upward. He had his wind. He finished the climb with Jago's hand at his elbow, and got a deeper breath.

"Nadiin," he said, "I shall be fine once I have had some sleep. Please be assured so."

"Nandi." A bow as the two reached the apartment door, and knocked on it. It opened in short order, doubtless that Tano and Algini had been communicating.

"Nandi," Jago began to say, "Barb-daja . . ."

"Bren!" The cry came from inside.

He was stunned, walking in on the sight of Barb, in atevi dress, standing there in the sitting room.

He was not prepared for Barb to rush toward him, arms spread.

Barb was not prepared for Tano to whirl about and interpose an arm. It knocked Barb backward to the floor.

Damn, Bren thought. Barb was half-stunned, lying in a puddle of russet voile, hurt, though Algini quickly knelt down to gather her fainting form up from the tiles. She had hit her head. They had scared hell out of Machigi's guards, who had drawn weapons; and Banichi had interposed his body, blocking the door with an arm against the doorframe, so neither of Machigi's men had a target; and Jago was simply holding on to him for safety.

Damn.

"A misunderstanding," he said, for Machigi's men. "She meant no harm. She was frightened."

Guns went back into holsters. Thank God *Banichi* had not drawn. Nor had Jago. Bren found himself shaking in the knees. His breath hurt. Thank God Barb hadn't gotten to his ribs.

"Is the situation safe?" Machigi's men were in the odd position of having to ask Banichi, and Banichi, carefully removing his hand from the woodwork, answered: "Safe, nadiin. She was, as the paidhi notes, moved by man'chi. She is, we hope, uninjured."

"We apologize," Jago said, "for the startlement. You will have known by now, nadiin, that the lady is excitable."

"Nadiin," the other said with a nod, and with a bow: "Nandi."

"We are glad to have recovered her," Bren said with what aplomb he could muster. "Please say so to your lord."

"Nandi." Another bow. Banichi moved inside and carefully shut the door. Barb, meanwhile, was moaning and hiccuping, and Algini was very carefully helping her to her feet.

"One regrets," Tano said.

"You were perfectly justified, Tano-ji," Bren said, thinking of his ribs. "Can we not sit down? Is there tea?" It was automatic when things grew chaotic. And he wanted more than anything to sit down. Soon. And to get the vest off, and see if any ribs were broken.

"There will be tea, Bren-ji," Tano said. "The staff has brought us supper."

"Veijico . . ." he began to ask, but he saw the young woman as he walked in past the ell of the entry: a young woman in Guild uniform, but with a very bedraggled look, stood by a rolling cart that held numerous dishes. "One is glad to see *you*, nadi," he said to her.

"Nandi," Veijico said, and bowed.

"Juniors," Algini commented, settling Barb into a soft chair near the fire, "always get to taste the food first. They are useful for that, at least."

Veijico picked up the plate she had been filling, resumed filling it and said not a thing. Doubtless she had debriefed, in what fashion she could in a place guaranteed to be bugged.

Barb, however, was still somewhat stunned, and crying very quietly into her hands, sitting in a very large chair and mostly swallowed by it.

Bren went over to a facing, smaller chair and sat down, not without a dizzying stab of pain. He *wanted* to be rid of the vest, which was hot, miserable, and damaged in a very sore spot, however much protection it still afforded in other places. He wanted it so much. But one grew a little stiff-mannered in atevi society. One could not just shed clothes in the sitting room. It was stupid, but he endured it. And for what he knew, it was what was holding him up and it would hurt worse when he took it off.

"Toby," Barb said. Just that.

"Toby's going to be all right," he said, and Barb blotted her eyes with the back of her hand and tried to get herself together.

"Cajeiri," she said.

"Was perfectly all right. Had never left the house. Don't mention names of those absent. We're sure there are eavesdroppers and names help them out."

"Where are we?"

Three sensible, urgent questions in a row, after having her brain rattled. He felt a cautiously renewed respect for Barb—who *could* be resourceful, when the chips were really down. He remembered times she had been that. That she'd asked immediately after Toby and Cajeiri—that impressed him a little.

He felt a little ashamed of himself that he hadn't had Barb's fate at all far forward in his mind—only Toby's, and even that far remote from current concerns.

Which, damn it, involved delivering a message and getting people who *were* overwhelmingly important to him out of this place alive. He had an excuse for being cold in manner. He'd been just a little distracted.

"We're in the Marid," he said. "What happened, Barb? And don't name names in telling me."

Tea was late. Veijico was eating and drinking, her assignment, one of moderate hazard, and until Veijico had survived for, oh, probably half an hour, nobody else would risk it. He thought she would. Doubtless Machigi's delivery of, first, Veijico, and then Barb, while he was in conference, was all calculated to rattle him, and maybe calculated to get a dialogue going between Tano, Algini, and Veijico that spies could overhear.

"This is a bad place, isn't it?" Barb asked him.

"We're negotiating," Bren said.

"For me?"

"Honestly, we didn't know you were here. We'd lately figured you'd gone in another direction."

"I don't remember at first. I remember a car. A truck. Something. I remember—a bumpy road."

Every road outside the cities was bumpy. But he said nothing.

"Then there was shooting. She—" Barb half-turned toward Veijico, who had taken her dinner over to the corner; and winced and felt of her head. "God. I don't feel good."

"Repeated cracks to the head are dangerous. The water might be safe," he said in Ragi. "A cup of water, nadiin-ji." And in Mosphei': "Do you need to lie down?"

"I just don't want to move right now." Barb supported her head on her hand, elbow braced against the chair, and she had gone a sickly shade, sweating a little.

"You may be concussed."

"Are we safe here?" Barb asked plaintively.

"Moderately," he said. "Things could be a lot worse. Take deep breaths." He, personally, couldn't take deep breaths, and just wanted to go into that bedroom and lie flat and be waited on. Without the vest. But he wasn't the one who'd taken that crack to the head. "My bodyguard acted on instinct. There were people at the door who didn't know what you were doing. It was a very dangerous moment."

"I wasn't sure. I thought it was them. Your people. I was sure it was. But she—" A little move of the shoulder toward Veijico. "She was here. When I came in. She acted scared of them. So I just wasn't sure."

"You'd been with her?"

"She—she shot the people in the truck. And then other people came in, and we were nearly shot, and guns were going all around us and off the rocks, and she shoved me behind the rocks and then gave up. I think she rescued me from the people who'd carried me here. And then the others moved in—very fast."

Whether Veijico had shot a number of Taisigi clan, or whether she had done for intruders into Taisigi territory was a serious question, one that might bear on Machigi's attitude toward them. And probably Veijico herself wasn't sure. *Somebody* had evidently been fast to react when Veijico had intervened and pulled Barb out of the hands of her kidnappers, and they'd reacted from cover, as if they'd been watching.

That was *not* necessarily the behavior of people who'd been in close communication with the kidnappers in the truck all along.

So very possibly, given Machigi's parting statement that the dowager had been right, the kidnappers were indeed Marid, but *not* Taisigi, and *not* welcome in Taisigi territory, doing what they were doing.

"Good sense that she did surrender," Bren said. "*You* were likely to be negotiated for. She stood a chance of being able to remain near you." He wasn't sure he was going to say that to Veijico, who needed to presume far less than she had, but right now he was grateful to the young woman.

"Tea," Tano said, offering not a tea service for them both, but a cup of tea to Barb. "Please express my deep regrets for the fall, nandi."

Not that Tano couldn't speak human language with fair fluency: he was sensibly admitting less than he could do in the absolute conviction they were spied on.

Bren said, "He expresses regret for your injury."

"That's all right," Barb said, and reached out and patted Tano's arm. "It's all right."

"Nandi." A little bow. A retreat.

As yet Veijico hadn't died of poison. They were close to being able to enjoy their supper. And Barb sipped what was probably safe sugared tea, her hands shaking a little.

"You can just sit by the fire and rest," Bren said, "or you can lie down on the couch." If he were a gentleman in the Mosphei' sense, he'd cede that bed in there to an injured lady. But rank dictated the big couch out in the sitting room was perfectly adequate for a human's comfort, and if he shared that mattress in there with Barb, Jago would not understand the word "expediency."

"Are we going to be able to go home?" Barb asked.

"It's not likely to be tomorrow, maybe not the next day," Bren said, "but we have a good chance of it eventually." He decided to get up. Decided he couldn't: he was locked in place, and the chair arm gave him no leverage. *Hell,* it was going to hurt.

He did it anyway, with an effort, and said, "I think I'm going to go lie down for a while. It's been a very long day. But the food should be safe." This, since Veijico had not demonstrated any discomfort.

"Toby's going to be all right?" Barb asked again.

"I'm pretty sure, yes." He managed a little bow, bone-deep

habit, and nodded to Veijico, who stood by the fireplace, plate in hand, and had just taken another bite. "One is glad to have recovered you safely, nadi."

Caught with her mouth full, Veijico just bowed and looked embarrassed about it. Good, he thought. His staff and Veijico looked to have arrived at some working understanding involving silence and following orders. He simply made his way toward the bedroom, where he could finally lie down and ease his own headache.

Not too bad, he thought, for a day's work.

22

The ribs weren't broken, but one swore they were dented. And one enjoyed the silence of the night—though thinking of a busload of Tabini's people parked in the driveway and enjoying a safe but less fancy dinner of the foodstuffs they had in the bus galley.

Assassination attempts hardly made sense tonight, other opportunities having been let slide. The whereabouts of one lone and unhappy boy still worried him, and one hoped Lucasi didn't shoot anybody and complicate matters.

Or stray over the wrong border, down the wrong road. The Farai lived up to the northeast.

One thought of Najida, and Kajiminda, and Geigi at Targai, and hoped everything was quiet—but doubtless Tabini's forces were keeping a close eye on those.

Which left only Toby, and the hope he was mending without complications. There was long-range radio, but whether or not Banichi had let anybody use it yet was outside the paidhi's ordinary power of decision making—and possibly just a little provocative of their host.

And one wasn't supposed to be worrying about personal issues. It was enough that he had Barb settled down on the sofa out there, and Veijico charged with, Jago reported, keeping her awake, a sensible precaution, considering the knot on her skull. That might go on. Barb could nap through whatever tomorrow brought, considering they weren't likely to be dashing out of Tanaja any time soon.

There was a lot to go over, depending on Machigi's patience.

And it had just become paradoxically important for Tabini's men out there, even if Tabini had Filed on Machigi, to protect Machigi's life and property.

They urgently needed to make a few phone calls, among other things. But the paidhi hadn't much energy left, and he wasn't totally sure he was thinking clearly, not once his head hit the pillow.

Jago came in, a shadowy presence, and sat on the edge of the bed.

He'd opened his eyes. In the light from the door, with atevi night vision, she knew he was awake.

"The situation remains quiet, Bren-ji. When you wish, in the morning, we shall request the Filing on Machigi be terminated without comment. And we shall, from our present position, request a further delay in any Guild deliberations regarding the Marid, pending further information—if you can secure permission for two phone calls. We had rather use the phones and have Lord Machigi completely aware of what we say—lest there be any doubt."

"One is very grateful," he said.

Jago hadn't come to bed. There were some things that might be rumors regarding the paidhi-aiji, but he would not expect her to flaunt their relationship under a foreign roof.

And considering the fact they were surely being monitored—she had said exactly what his bodyguard had officially decided Machigi's men should hear. And she was still awake and in uniform. His bodyguard would sleep by turns, he was relatively certain of that. They probably wouldn't trust the exhausted junior for a solo watch . . . but let her have the night for uninterrupted sleep: likely not.

He shut his own eyes, exhausted.

"Rest, Bren-ji," Jago said.

"I shall be fine in the morning, Jago-ji," he said, and gave his bodyguard no orders, none at all, trusting they knew exactly what they were doing, from now on until morning.

23

Nand' Toby had been restless all night—not asking a great deal, true, but he was awake, and uncomfortable, and Cajeiri, who had bedded down on a pallet on the floor beside Antaro and Jegari, saw him fussing with the blankets.

He really, truly wanted to sleep. They had all been late going to bed, what with the worry about nand' Bren.

But while the servant in attendance—who sat on the chair over in the corner—got up to see to the blankets, it was probably a good idea, Cajeiri thought, for the only one who could talk to nand' Toby to at least find out if he needed anything.

"Bathroom," Toby said, and put a foot over the edge, and got up on his good arm. "I can walk."

"He wants to walk to the accommodation, nadi," Cajeiri said. "Please assist him. By no means allow him to fall."

Jegari and Antaro had waked, too, with worried, weary looks in the dim light.

"He says he can walk," Cajeiri said, "but go with them, Gari-ji. Open doors for them."

"Yes," Jegari said, and immediately got up—he was sleeping in his clothes: they all did, except Cajeiri had hung his coat on a nail by the door, so he could be fit to face Great-grandmother if he had to. The lace on his shirt was all limp, and the shirt was a mess. But he could get another shirt before breakfast.

"What time is it, do you think?" he asked Antaro, and Antaro got up and went out to the hall. One wanted so badly to fold right down into the blankets again and just try not to think about what was going on in the world, which was not good, and which he had been trying *not* to tell nand' Toby.

Who had gotten onto his feet, and was walking, and was going to be asking questions today.

One truly did not want to have to answer when he did.

Maybe it would be a really good idea not to be here when nand' Toby got back. If there was nobody nand' Toby could ask, there were things nand' Toby would not have to find out yet.

He got up, brushed wrinkles out of his trousers, and Antaro came right back in.

"Nandi, Cook is serving breakfast!"

Late. Disastrously late. "Let us go find clean shirts," he said, reaching for his boots. He struggled into them as quickly as he could, while Antaro put on her own. "Mani will expect me."

"Yes," she said, and helped him on with his coat. She was putting on her own as they cleared the door and ducked down the hall toward the stairs, half-running to get up and out of sight.

It was not wholly cowardly, he said to himself. He *wanted* to find out things before he had to worry nand' Toby about them. And he and Antaro scurried out into the upstairs hall—

And came face to face with Great-grandmother and Cenedi, just outside the dining hall.

His hair was a mess. His coat covered a ruined shirt, and only partly hid trousers just as wrinkled.

"Well," Great-grandmother said.

He bowed. Deeply. "Mani, one is in search of clean clothes. One is exceedingly sorry."

"How is nand' Toby this morning?"

"Better. Better, mani-ma." That was a piece of news. "He got out of bed this morning. He walked."

"Nand' Bren will be very glad to know that." Great-grandmother looked pleased in the way she had when she had a secret. Then she said: "The paidhi has engaged Lord Machigi, who is negotiating, apparently in good faith. But you are not to tell nand' Toby where he is. Now go change your clothes, Great-grandson."

"Yes!" Cajeiri said, and bowed deeply and walked away— not toward the room where his clothes were, but back toward the stairs. He kept walking all the way to the servant stairs, and Antaro stayed right behind him.

But once they had gotten onto the stairs and Antaro shut the hall door behind them, he took the steps two at a time, and the two of them ran down the basement hall full tilt, startling two servants with serving trays and a third with an armful of laundry.

"Excuse us," Cajeiri called out, delaying on one foot, then ran on to nand' Toby's room, absolutely brimming over with the best news there could be.

And he could not say a single thing about it.

Except maybe to tell nand' Toby that mani had heard from nand' Bren, and that things were all right.

Or would be. Nand' Bren and Banichi could do *anything*. He had the greatest confidence in it.